T0267370

Acclaim for
ENHANCED

"*Enhanced* thrusts you into an impossible world that somehow feels all too familiar. Peppered with resonating truths about the direction of our society, this fascinating and imaginative story makes you rethink what could be feasible in the not so-distant-future. A must read for fans of young adult literature and science fiction!"

— LORI LANGDON, author of the Disney Happily Never After Series

"*Enhanced* by Candace Kade had me on the edge of my seat from page one. Bursting with rich world building and captivating characters, this evocative sci-fi debut is just the book fans of *Ready Player One* and *The Lunar Chronicles* have been waiting for. From mystery to intrigue and every plot twist in between, Kade's brilliant storytelling is as smart as it is fantastical. I may be a Natural, but everything about this novel *Enhanced* my reading experience. Buckle up—this one will take you for a ride you won't want to miss!"

— SARA ELLA, award-winning author of the Unblemished trilogy, *Coral*, and *The Wonderland Trials*

"Full of action and high stakes, debut author Candace Kade spins an imaginative and futuristic tale of mystery, DNA and danger— don't miss out!"

— NOVA MCBEE, award-winning author of the Calculated series

"A stunning debut filled with action, intrigue and fantastical imagination! Kade's vision immerses the reader in a darkly complex, futuristic world of genetic modifications, disillusionment and fantastical powers. Urban's path to discovery is relatable and loaded with mystery, and the story holds a realism which is sure to resonate with readers!"

— JULIE HALL, *USA Today* bestselling author

"Pulling from her unique upbringing in Asia, Candace Kade brings to life diverse cultural and creative influences to craft a stunning urban sci-fi novel with a pulse-pounding story you won't be able to put down."

— KARA SWANSON, award-winning author of *Dust* and *Shadow*
and co-founder of the Author Conservatory

"A dystopian world unlike any other I've seen. *Enhanced* has it all— high stakes, mysterious threats, college freshman awkwardness, and a plot that accelerates almost as fast as Urban's motorcycle. This book kept me looking over my shoulder while I turned pages faster than I could read."

— NADINE BRANDES, award-winning author of the Out of Time series,
Fawkes, *Romanov*, and *Wishtress*

"*Enhanced* is brimming with action and fascinating technology in a richly developed, near-future world that begs to be explored. The setting perfectly blends with a poignant story of a girl looking for a place to fit in. A great read for all fans of young adult science fiction."

— B.L. DEAN, author of the Shades of Starlight series

"Fans of *The Hunger Games* will appreciate Candace Kade's high-stakes survival games and slick futuristic imaginings. But the true heart of *Enhanced* is its themes about identity, belonging, and finding one's place in the world. I'm excited to see where Kade takes readers next!"

— LINDSAY A. FRANKLIN, Carol award-winning author of *The Story Peddler*

"In her debut young adult novel, Candace Kade builds a futuristic, fictional world like you've never seen, yet it still manages the utmost relevance to our troubled, present reality. An impressive and compelling debut, *Enhanced* boasts a depth of conflict that will wreck your emotions and demand you cheer for Lee Urban on every page."

— TAMARA GIRARDI, author of *Above the Fold* and *Behind the Mask*

"New and innovative. Candace Kade's impressive debut expertly tackles the theme of identity while immersing readers in a futuristic world unlike any other. In this action-packed mystery where the genetically Enhanced are pitted against Naturals, everyone is suspect and no one is safe. Can't wait for what happens next!"

— SANDRA FERNANDEZ RHOADS, award-winning author of
The Colliding Line series

"*Enhanced* is a thrill ride! Author Candace Kade gives us an intriguing premise, complete with an action-packed plot that challenges all of us to consider who we really are. Are we the popularity scores the world gives us, or are we something more? And what will a life of striving for approval cost us? Fans of dystopian and science fiction writing, will appreciate Kade's worldbuilding, and anyone looking for heart in the midst of a wild ride, will enjoy the read."

— SHANNON DITTEMORE, author of *Winter, White and Wicked*
and *Rebel, Brave and Brutal*

"*Enhanced* is unlike anything I've ever read. Candace Kade's debut novel will draw readers into the wonderfully inventive urban sci-fi setting of New Beijing, filled with bot professors, social scores, and genetic enhancements. The story is a fast-paced blend of action, adventure, and mystery that kept me reading chapter after chapter. I loved Urban's story and cannot wait to find out what happens next."

— JILL WILLIAMSON, Christy award-winning author of
By Darkness Hid and *Thirst*

ENHANCED

ENHANCED

THE HYBRID SERIES | BOOK 1

CANDACE KADE

Published by Enclave Publishing, an imprint of Oasis Family Media, LLC

Carol Stream, Illinois, USA.
www.enclavepublishing.com

ISBN: 979-8-88605-034-9 (printed hardcover)
ISBN: 979-8-88605-035-6 (printed softcover)
ISBN: 979-8-88605-037-0 (ebook)

Cover design by Kirk DouPonce, www.DogEaredDesign.com
Typesetting by Jamie Foley, www.JamieFoley.com

Printed in the United States of America.

For mom and dad.
You've lived a great story.

URBAN MARCHED INTO GENE-IQ, CURSING NEW
Beijing's summer heat. She wiped away the sweat beading
on her chin. Her all-black attire, from her heeled boots to her
leather jacket, even the motorcycle helmet in her hands, clashed
with the garish walls of the crowded facility.

Hundreds of stoop-shouldered employees—also in black—
shuffled by her on all sides as she drew near the rows of
Extended Reality Domes. The rows, wider than the Forbidden
Palace, stacked ten stories high and hundreds deep within the
harsh florescent cave. Ice-blue electric light shone out through
frosted glass, silhouetting those inside.

Urban climbed the ladder toward her dome, dexterous as
one of the temple monkeys. She could have chosen the lift but
loathed the stench of so many bodies pressed together.

As she hopped off the ladder onto a walkway, something
rammed into one of her bone-thin shoulders.

"Hey, watch it," Urban snapped.

A towering Super shoved past her but stopped at Urban's
voice. He turned slowly—an Oriental Honey Buzzard sizing up
a particularly scrawny grub.

Urban stretched every centimeter of her one point seven
meters. While she was average height compared to the other

Gene-IQ employees, her head only came to the Super's abdomen. Then again, all Naturals were shrimp-sized compared to Supers.

"I suggest you watch it, *Primordial Soup*," the Super said with a sardonic smile.

A passing employee gasped. Urban's marble-black eyes flashed. She had several retorts at the tip of her tongue but bit them back. She'd gone the whole summer without giving herself away. She wouldn't blow it on her last day. Instead, she kept her head down and feigned submission.

The Super laughed and spun away, his huge feet clanging on the metallic walkway.

Urban wanted to kick something. Stuffing down her anger, she made her way to dome 115424. With a flick of her wrist, she waved her tatt over the scanner. With a chirp, two metal panels slid open, inviting her back to her usual uncomfortable work space.

The ash-gray walls of her cube were like a crematorium. She'd taped up pieces of paper with colorful quotes and sketches to brighten it up. Her high school *gaokao* placement results also hung there—a constant reminder to do better once she started university.

Urban eyed one of her favorite pieces of art, a sketch of a flying crane. The number 60 adorned little cloud puffs under the bird, representing the sosh she needed to be free.

Time for one last ten-hour nightmare. Gene-IQ may have owned all its other employees, but not her. After today, she planned to never come back to the soul-sucking place.

She donned her helmet and slipped on her Extended Reality Dome, or XRD, suit. Cool, soft, smart fabric brushed up against her skin as the external plates conformed to her body. The system scanned her face and booted up. Her internal screen transformed to a live city-penthouse view. Warm terracotta and apricot light reflected off of tall glass windows. A black flag with a golden hammer and sickle billowed in the wind.

The sun's rays warmed Urban's face as the gentle breeze tugged at loose strands of silky black hair. She turned her face toward the light. XR or not, she'd take all the sunshine she could get.

She swapped out her personal ear implants with her company-provided set, and the sweet notes of the *erhu* drifted through her artificial office. While the higher ups wouldn't let her personalize her virtual office, they at least let her select the music.

"Gene-IQ on," she said.

Her view changed to display four avatars waiting in a virtual lobby. Urban used the retina display contact lenses in her eyes to zoom in on them.

One woman had jagged dinosaur spikes that ran down her back and onto her tail. Another had translucent sea-green wings tucked neatly behind her. A man near the back sat rubbing his eyes. He looked ordinary enough, but Urban's system identified him as having modifications in the frontal cortex—enhanced intelligence. Urban hoped he wasn't one of her clients. Smart ones were always trouble.

The last person in the room was more cat than human with fangs, slitted irises, and retractable claws. She also had some sort of skeletal enhancements that enabled her to take hard hits and falls without injury.

Scanning the log of their social scores, or sosh, Urban found them to be 37, 34, 46, and 42 respectively. White-collar workers, but easy enough to handle on most days. *Good.*

With a flick of her wrist, Urban signaled the system to put her into the virtual office. Her screen changed to display a spacious room with a desk, two chairs, and a few tasteful scroll paintings of pagodas hanging on the walls. Urban found herself sitting behind a mahogany table as a door swung open. A voice announced her first client.

It was the woman with the dinosaur spikes. Her avatar ID read: Yu Susan.

"Good morning, Madam Yu. How may I help you today?" Urban used her professional tone, reserved for this job or meeting new people.

"I can't see any of my overlays, and everything is blurry!" Susan slammed her hand on the desk so forcefully, Urban's suit vibrated. "If you don't fix this problem within the next two minutes, I'll blast your sosh so low you won't be able to afford toilet paper!"

Words appeared on her retina display—a script for Urban to read. She already knew it by heart. "I'm very sorry to hear that. Let's see how we can work together to make your experience with Gene-IQ a great one."

A voice only she could hear suggested several possible problems detected with Susan's system. The AI training for this software was fast. Soon, live representatives would be obsolete. Urban wasn't sure if it was just her imagination, but it seemed like the AI-training jobs were slowly disappearing as the artificial intelligence grew smarter.

Urban quickly located the problem. "Looks like you enabled manual mode last night." Urban studied the logs more carefully. "Instead of selecting one of the main enhancement categories to analyze, you selected . . . bacteria?"

"I, well, I was distracted." Susan flushed.

At 0300? Urban had a hunch "intoxicated" might have been a better word, but she kept the thought to herself. "This means, instead of seeing a person's enhancements, you requested to see the genetic makeup of skin bacteria, which is all around us. The request overloaded the system. That's why your overlays aren't functioning."

"Okay."

"This will only take a minute to fix but will require a manual override," Urban explained. "You might experience a temporary bright light. Please close your eyes."

Susan obeyed.

"Gene-IQ disable manual vision. Code 3006."

There was a yell of annoyance as a blinding light flashed.

"Gene-IQ revert to setting 205," Urban said.

Susan opened her eyes and blinked. The timer in the corner of Urban's screen showed one minute and forty-six seconds had passed.

Susan harrumphed as her avatar vanished from the room.

Urban sighed, then created a bug ticket. With their giant backlog of bigger issues to fix, she doubted it would be reviewed any time soon.

A moment later, Urban's rating displayed a satisfaction score from Susan of 4 out of 10.

Urban snorted in disgust. The constant influx of angry customers was only part of the reason she loathed the job. More than that, it was the claustrophobic feeling she had the second she stepped foot into the building. How did so many Naturals do it every day, all year, for their entire lives? Showing up to fix the same routine, easy problems for an entire summer was enough to harden Urban's resolve.

I'd rather die than end up here.

She helped several more ungrateful customers before classical music began playing outside of her dome. Her system sent a message, reminding her to exit her XRD in the next three minutes.

She logged a couple more notes, then scanned her tatt as she exited. The music grew louder by the minute. Employees climbed out of their workspaces all around her. Here, there were no exotic colorings, facial features, and abilities. No one working at the AI factory had parents who could afford enhancements at conception like the Enhanced could.

The music stopped.

Down below, at the very front of the factory, the Super that had bumped into Urban unfolded a flag with great pomp. He tied the flag to a string on the flagpole while another Super stood straight-backed watching. Being the only Enhanced in the building, the Supers towered over everyone else.

An employee next to Urban stared at the Supers with loathing and muttered curses under his breath. Urban watched the Supers with longing, envying their perfectly proportioned muscles. *If only I were Enhanced like them. Getting a sosh of 60 or higher would be easy.*

The black-and-gold flag snaked up the pole.

Only members of the Guard were allowed to conduct flag-raising ceremonies. Since Naturals were no longer strong enough to compete against their genetically enhanced peers, they couldn't enlist. As a result, they had been banned from touching the flag. Flag ceremonies, however, were minor losses compared to other changes that came with the Genetic Revolution.

The Federation's anthem blasted over the speakers. Everyone saluted, their tatts glowing gold as they sang along with the music.

"Rise up, you who refuse to be slaves!" Their voices reverberated off the XR domes in harmony.

"With our flesh and blood, let us build a new Great Wall!
As the Federation faces its greatest peril,
From each one, the urgent call to action comes forth."
Urban's voice joined in the crescendo.
"Braving the enemies' fire! March on!"

Urban sighed. How the times had changed since the anthem had been written.

"Resume work," a robotic voice announced over the intercom. Urban climbed back into the stuffy dome.

As she was nearing the end of her grueling shift, there was only one person left in the lobby. Urban considered taking a quick break before she noticed the sosh of the waiting customer.

Her heart skipped a beat.

95.

The client looked like she was in high school, and the tips of her wavy hair were dyed cabbage green. And yet, she wore a tailored suit and stood in the center of the room as if she owned it.

A quick scan of her enhancements revealed more than all the other customers Urban had seen over the last four months. She had the usual traits of an aristocrat: symmetrical and enhanced facial features, strengthened bones, and a superior immune system with several expensive, but not uncommon, brain enhancements.

After that, there was a long list of improvements Urban had never seen before. Obscure things like Obsidian Residual, which allowed her to change the shape of her pupils, and Retractus Flameous, which converted her hands into flamethrowers.

"*Wakao,*" Urban breathed in Federation Mandarin.

Her heartrate quickened. Her supervisor would be monitoring this interaction. The system recorded any sessions with clients who had a sosh over 60 and would directly ping the manager if they were over 75.

Urban checked the name.

Qing Angel.

Fighting to keep the trembling out of her voice, Urban instructed her system to let Angel in.

"Urban." A voice rang loudly in her ears. "Urban, this is your manager, Troy."

Fine time for the man behind the curtain to show himself. After four months on the job, Urban had started to believe the rumors that he let the bots run the show.

"You're about to deal with a KOL. Do you remember your orientation training?"

"Uh . . . yes, I think so. It's like 'always give Key Opinion Leaders a warm welcome,' right?

"*Wozi* . . ." Her manager swore. "Just don't upset her, okay? She has the power to tank the entire company."

Urban nodded, though she wasn't sure he could see it. She straightened and cleared her throat. "Hello, Ms. Qing. How may I assist you today?"

The client didn't move from her spot near the door. She gave Urban a blatant once-over.

Urban's foot began tapping nervously.

Angel cocked her head to one side as she continued staring. "Why the hurry *Lee Urban*?"

Urban's blood ran cold.

Clients weren't supposed to know their facilitator's true identities.

If Angel had somehow managed to hack the system, then she was more powerful than even her sosh indicated.

Urban remained frozen.

Her manager breathed out a string of curses that jolted her back to attention. He issued commands to people in the background to trace Angel's location and put everything in lockdown mode.

Urban was only half listening. "Ms. Qing. How may I assist you today?"

"I have an important message for you." But before anything more was said, her avatar glitched and then vanished from the room.

URBAN ATTEMPTED TO STEADY HER BREATHING.
"Ms. Qing?"

No response.

Urban waited for Troy's angry voice in her ear again, but he seemed to have disconnected. A moment later, instead of a rating appearing on her screen, an encrypted file popped up.

[For employee 1207930018.]

Impossible. Tendrils of fear curled around Urban's chest. *How does she know my employee number?*

She studied the file, hesitating. Was Angel a malicious hacker? A troll? Everything about the file screamed a phishing attempt. Every other week she'd been forced to endure more obligatory trainings on cybersecurity from Gene-IQ. While the company hadn't had any breaches, the surge in rising data leaks globally was cause enough for caution.

Urban slowly unzipped her XRD suit. *I made it all summer at this job without one incident. Then my last client, on my last day—Qing Angel—hacks into our system to deliver this . . . file?*

Had Angel guessed her secret? What was in that file?

Voice shaking, Urban ordered a search in QuanNao, the all-encompassing VR knowledge center, be conducted on Qing Angel. With a score of 95, it didn't take Urban long to find her.

She was on several of the top trending articles.

Angel was from the Western Federation, and her key words were singing and music. There were check-ins for multiple virtual concerts as well as live ones but all in the Western Federation.

None of this adds up. Why would a famous musician, one from the West, be hacking into Gene-IQ to deliver a message to me?

If this were a phishing attempt, it wasn't a very good one. Urban knew who the culprit was. Since all the sessions were recorded, she even had video evidence.

Heart still beating hard, Urban reexamined the file. Someone smart enough to hack into Gene-IQ would know a manager would be watching their session. If this were an attack, why attract more attention?

Drawing in a deep breath, she opened the file.

A gray box with six spaces popped up in the retina display of her left eye.

<Password needed.>

Urban frowned. She thought for a moment, then entered her birthday.

The box blinked, then another message appeared.

<Incorrect. Three remaining attempts before engaging lock-out protocol.>

At least Angel didn't have access to her birthdate. That Urban knew of, anyway.

Urban bit her lip. What else was six digits long that she would know and Angel had access to? She almost didn't want to guess.

Her PIN? She'd set that up ages ago in case her bio-PIN ever malfunctioned. Urban wasn't even sure if she remembered it.

No, that number had only ever been used once when she set it up. If Angel had access to that and had attempted to steal her identity, Urban would know. Entering it as a second guess, if Angel didn't possess it already, wouldn't be wise. No need to hand Angel her PIN on a lacquered tea tray.

What else was there? Almost everything used biometric screening. Urban couldn't think of any other passwords it could be. Maybe the digits were coordinates? For Gene-IQ?

A quick search in QuanNao pulled up the coordinates for her current location. There were too many numbers to match 6 digits. But maybe with just the first 6 numbers . . .

<Incorrect. Two remaining attempts before engaging lock-out protocol.>

Out of ideas and not wanting to be late for the evening's event, Urban thought best to leave it. She'd finished the job. That's what mattered. She'd never see Angel or her encrypted file again.

Logging out of all her Gene-IQ accounts, she signed her official resignation paperwork, then deleted her notes. She pulled her multicolored sketches off the wall, staring at them a moment.

If it weren't for her desire to be an artist, she wouldn't even be here. No one from the Metropolis so much as set foot in the Outskirts.

No one but her.

Unlike all the other Natural employees barely scraping by, Urban's Enhanced family had more than enough to sustain them. They just refused to share that wealth when it came to her dream.

"You don't have the genetic enhancements to be an Artisan," Father's words still rang in her ears. *"If you keep pursuing this, we'll send you to the AI Factories for the summer to get a taste of what people working without enhancements live like. That will teach you a lesson."*

They hadn't expected her to keep pushing the matter and were shocked to find her gone the next day, interviewing for a role at Gene-IQ. Her parents had spent the summer reeling, covering up for her so that none of their affluential friends found out their daughter was working a low-life job.

Her parents were right about one thing though. Working grueling monotonous hours in the Outskirts had taught her a lesson. Only, it wasn't the lesson they had hoped for.

Instead, it had sharpened her resolve to never take a job she hated again. Rare moments when she had time to sketch and paint were the only thing that had sustained her over the summer.

Urban carefully folded her sketches and tucked them away. With a final sweep of the tiny XRD, she climbed out of the dome.

Instantly, a weight lifted from her shoulders. She smiled for the first time that day, then climbed down the ladder. *I'll do whatever it takes to be an artist,* she promised herself.

She strapped on her black filtration mask, and her retina display flashed a warning as she left the building.

<Entering yellow zone. Exercise CAUTION.>

While New Beijing Metropolis's air was regulated and clean, the Outskirts didn't have that luxury. Since Naturals were too poor to afford enhancements, that meant they couldn't get specialized jobs that paid enough for them to live in the Metropolis. Thus, they were stuck living in the yellow zones wearing masks or else breathing the toxic, polluted air.

Adjusting her mask once more, Urban made her way to an abandoned shack where she'd hidden her motorcycle. Even though she'd installed a complex antitheft device, there was no reason to tempt fate by flashing her wealth around these parts. She'd nearly been mugged her first day in the Outskirts and knew better now.

The leather was hot as she took her seat and strapped on her helmet over her mask. With the gentle whirr of her electric engine, she rejoined the sea of workers sweeping away from the factories. The motorcycle kept the throngs of bodies from crushing her. Even then, the summer heat and the warmth of the crowd emanated around her.

They, too, wore matching filtration masks, which revealed their tired, empty eyes but hid the rest of their faces. Some of them unlocked bikes lined against the street, while others headed for the nearest Bolt line.

Watching them, Urban was reminded why a good sosh score mattered. This was the year she'd be getting hers. Everything from her social life, job opportunities, where she could live, who her friends were, would all hinge on that one number. Most importantly, there wasn't a chance her parents would allow her to be an artist unless she had a high sosh.

I have to get a 60. I have to.

The well-maintained tech facilities faded into buildings with peeling paint and moldy sides that towered overhead. Sagging walkways and tangled powerlines ran between them, blocking out the sunlight. Holographic signs cluttered the remaining real estate. One sign flickered and buzzed, then popped and went dark.

With the little overhead space left, rusty hoverdrones zoomed around delivering packages through dingy alleys and leaning homeless shacks. Dark windows with nothing but shards like jagged teeth smiled crookedly at Urban. The motorcycle crunched over takeout boxes and glass. The alley reeked of urine, but countless pedestrians and bikers seemed oblivious to the stench. Urban was glad for her mask, though she could still catch traces of the smell.

Urban's gaze snagged on a figure sitting in the middle of the road. People flowed around him like a stream, oblivious to his hollow eyes. Beggars weren't uncommon in these parts but what made her do a double take was the fluttering by his side. Two huge wings, once alabaster-white but now a muddied gray, lay next to him.

"Please, some water?"

"Why would we help your kind?" a passerby scoffed. "Get a job. Or are you too lazy like the rest of the Metropolis's *Farmed*?

The man didn't even flinch at the insult. "Please."

Urban's chest tightened. She didn't want to be caught anywhere near the Enhanced man for fear of what the Natural crowds might do to her if she helped. If he were a criminal and someone took a picture of her helping him, it could make her sosh drop. But her heart thumped uncomfortably with the need to do something.

The man's desperate eyes searched the crowd. Sensing her gaze, he looked up, and their eyes locked.

Urban stiffened. Could he sense that she was pretending to be from the Outskirts? That she was really from the Metropolis?

But then he broke eye contact and lowered his head. For the first time, Urban noticed how skinny he was. His tattered clothes hung loosely around his bony frame. He pulled his wings up around himself.

That would be her if she wasn't careful. All it would take is one person finding out her secret. Her sosh would tank, and she'd end up like this homeless beggar. She shuddered.

As she passed, she heard quiet sobs from underneath the feathers.

She closed her eyes, trying to remind herself of why she shouldn't stop. An image of last week's story on the feeds came to mind. It was about a beggar who had robbed and stabbed to death someone who'd stopped to help him. It had been only one District away from here.

But the hunch in the man's back, the look in his eyes . . . She tried to reason with her feelings, but Urban knew she wouldn't be able to ever forgive herself if she kept walking.

Her pulse quickened as she made her decision. A ping to the *Jingcha* for help wouldn't do her any good out here should the beggar prove violent. While the *Jingcha* technically served both the Metropolis and the Outskirts, Urban was convinced they could screen pings from the Outskirts and never even answer them.

The Naturals around her wouldn't help her, either, should things go wrong. She was attempting to help an Enhanced, after all.

She was on her own.

Urban parked her motorcycle, then made her way to a nearby dispenser and scanned her tatt. She selected two bottles of water and a package of dried tofu.

As she made her way back to the beggar, those around her cast furtive glances. Urban hesitated when she reached the man. He was cocooned tight in his wings like a silkworm.

She was afraid touching him might frighten him, so she cleared her throat.

Slowly, one dusty wing lowered, and the man peered over it. His eyes were red rimmed and glazed. He took a moment to register Urban and the extended supplies.

With trembling hands, he took them. He gave a teary nod of gratitude and held her eyes. "Watch out for your social score. Don't end up like me."

Urban went rigid. Did he know her secret? That she would already be facing an uphill battle to maintain a score allowing her into the same social circles as her family?

But his wings furled over him again, and Urban was left with a fleeting thought to link with him to help boost his sosh. She instantly discarded it. Not only would it do nothing since she wasn't eighteen yet, and didn't have her sosh score, but once she did get it, if she was seen to have linked with him, that could hurt her. If he were a criminal and she was associated with him, others might unlink with her, and that would tank her score completely.

She continued on, emotions churning as she zoomed through the Outskirts. As she made a sharp left, Urban's retina flashed a warning.

<Entering orange zone. Exercise CAUTION.>

At least it wasn't a red or purple zone. Red zones were

extremely dangerous. And purple zones were so toxic, they caused instant death. Though Urban had never actually seen one, she'd heard of prisons and hospitals creating purple zones for euthanasia.

She accelerated through the orange zone until she was back in a yellow zone on the Speed Way. Trees slowly began to appear on the roadside, and a brown river snaked its way beside her. The sun dipped out of sight, and soon the only thing lighting the way was the bouncing beam of her headlight and the silvery moon overhead.

To the south a long brick structure stretched along the mountain—the Great Wall. This part wasn't a tourist trap like the restored parts near the Metropolis. It was abandoned and, in certain areas, reduced to little more than a pile of lone rocks. Yet, this wild and rugged part of the Great Wall was even more beautiful to Urban.

She felt a connection to it. Like she, too, was alone and a relic of the past.

A squat structure to her left caught her attention as something metallic flickered in the moonlight. With a mechanical hiss, the MagLev super-speed train pulled out from the stop. It began making its way toward the Metropolis.

Urban grinned. *Perfect. I've been needing more practice.*

She set her retina stopwatch, twisted the throttle toward her, and shifted gears with her foot. A jolt and she was off.

The MagLev crept up on her until they were parallel.

They stayed even for a moment. Neither seemed to move as they flew over the terrain, perfectly synchronized.

Urban crouched lower in her seat, the wind beating against her with tremendous force. At this speed, she was powerful, invincible, and strong. And yet, she was one unsteady movement, one millisecond of lost concentration, away from losing control of her motorcycle.

Slowly, the MagLev pulled ahead.

Urban eased off the throttle, shifted gears, and checked her stopwatch. She'd stayed even with it for forty-three seconds. A new record. *Soon, I'll be able to enter one of the races with this speed. That will for sure boost my sosh.*

She pulled up her final external, client-facing profile of her avatar for Gene-IQ. Her overall rating wasn't bad: 4.4. Not that it mattered anymore. She was about to navigate away from her profile when she noticed something odd. There was an asterisk next to her rating.

What could that mean? What would cause her rating to be pending?

Selecting the asterisk led her to a private chat room only she had access to. After a virtual-bot confirmed her identity, Urban entered. It was dimly lit inside, very uncharacteristic of Gene-IQ's usual, overly bright facilities.

Hovering in the middle of the room spun the encrypted file from Qing Angel.

URBAN SWERVED IN SURPRISE. STEADYING HER grip, she stared at the file. How had it followed her out of her work profile? It shouldn't have been able to do that. She tried to open it.

<Incorrect. One remaining attempt before engaging lock-out protocol.>

Urban was still brainstorming possible answers when the colorful cityscape of the Metropolis came into view. Her retina display sent a warning, and she immediately spotted the source.

A smart light blinked on. Smart lights conserved energy by only activating when they sensed oncoming traffic. They also had the unfortunate ability to clock a vehicle's speed and report anything above the limit.

Urban slammed on her brakes seconds before she reached the light. The last thing she needed was a pending sosh infringement. Mother and Father would be furious.

As soon as she passed the smart light she accelerated again.

Rapidly accelerating and decelerating past smart lights required a manual override, which had been easy for Urban to hack. Now, she could go as fast as she wanted, so long as she paid attention to upcoming lights.

It was one of the few glitches left in the system.

<Entering white zone.>

Her system alerted her to the approach of the Metropolis. White zones had filtered air, clean water, and reduced toxins. They were generally the healthiest environments to live in and comprised the most desirable real estate. Most importantly, they were safe.

She slowed as she approached the barrier that separated the white from the yellow zone. The Zeolite coating was soft and bouncy to her feet as she leaned from side to side to keep her balance.

The coating helped to absorb carbon dioxide emissions, and fresh air instantly filled her mask. Her filtration system clicked off. The sky cleared and giant skyscrapers loomed high. Above the colossal structures, the latest model of delivery drones and small single-person aircraft flew in orderly lines.

Colorful advertisements played on the sides of the buildings. Below them, malls blasted music, and people ladened with giant shopping bags laughed as they strolled leisurely. The scent of jasmine and the sound of K-pop reached her as she passed one of the top designer shops.

Urban wove in and out of the streets full of autonomous cars carrying passengers who were busy eating, relaxing, or engaged in the all-encompassing QuanNao reality world as they rode back home. The traffic was slow tonight, but not for her.

She arrived in thirty minutes flat.

<Now arriving at Evergrande High-Rises. Sosh: 67.>

Still congratulating herself, Urban made her way into a quiet lobby with a bot concierge that ignored her. The switch from human guards to bots had reduced rent rate for those who didn't own their homes. But it had cost the apartment complex a sosh point.

Urban sprang to the public bathroom and threw her backpack onto the sink counter. She stripped out of her Outskirts clothes and tore a brush through tangled knots of matted hair. Pulling out her retina display, she added lubricant to a new pair, then popped them back into her eye. Even after years of practice, it took two times to get them in. Urban huffed in annoyance before switching modes so that her eye color shifted from standard black to an expensive model of deep mossy green.

Rapidly, she applied a thin tube to her lips, which extracted the natural pH levels and left them a rosy red. She slipped on a simple but elegant dress and a diamond necklace. After spritzing herself with perfume, she checked her reflection.

Even wearing the latest luxury brands, and with makeup evening out her skin, she still didn't look exactly Enhanced. Her face wasn't symmetrically beautiful, nor was her skin porcelain smooth, nor her curves perfectly proportioned.

She was too skinny. Her lips weren't plump enough, and her jaw was too defiant. Her large, attentive black eyes were the one feature she was proud of. But even they were the wrong color for the Enhanced. She typically turned them green in the Metropolis.

It was always easier to disguise herself as someone from the Outskirts than as an Enhanced. But she would do whatever it took tonight to keep anyone from suspecting she was actually a Natural by birth. Otherwise, she could end up on the streets like the homeless Flyer. Thinking about the man's dirty, defeated wings made her gut churn.

Taking in a deep breath, she stuffed her smelly Outskirts clothes into the bag, then darted toward the elevator. "One hundred and thirty first floor," she commanded. She scanned her tatt, then the elevator shot upward. Her ears popped twice before it slowed, then stopped.

Exiting the elevator, she made her way down a dark marble hallway. Two funeral-black doors stood rigid at the end.

Before she even had a chance to knock, the doors swung open. Light and music flooded around her. Urban blinked as a servant handed her a warm towelette and bowed deeply.

"Welcome home, Miss Lee."

Urban waved the towelette away. "Are they here?"

"Yes, Miss Lee. Everyone is already in the Great Hall." The attendant hesitated. "The mistress awaits you."

"I know. I know. Take me to her." Urban followed the maid through hallways, flanked by priceless artifacts and collectors' silk paintings featuring ancient temples, bridges, and foreboding mountains.

Such opulence. Her parents were well-known in the city and had paved the way for their three children to follow in their successful footsteps. Being an artist, of course, did not align with those ambitions.

"Art is too risky for a Natural like you and could expose the whole family," Mother had warned. "You need a career where no one will suspect you don't have genetic enhancements. You need to pursue the Giver track."

But Urban didn't want to be a psychologist, coach, or humanitarian worker. Helping the Enhanced live to their best potential when she wasn't even one of them seemed like an impossibility.

She imagined it would be similar to her job in the Outskirts, where she daily pretended to be something she wasn't and did work that drained her. Only with better hours and benefits.

A giant white cat with bright purple spots appeared out of thin air next to her, and Urban smiled.

"Well, hello there." Urban reached down to pet the cat without breaking stride. "Did you miss me Baozi?"

Baozi, the Enhanced house cat, was almost as big as a tiger but gentle and with the manners of a pet. In addition to his exotic coloring, he also could blend in with his surroundings like a chameleon. The entire family had quickly regretted that specific enhancement.

Baozi meowed and kept pace with Urban but then disappeared as she reached the gathering.

The sounds of the Great Hall reached Urban first. Plucked dings and musical vibrations of the zither echoed as guests chattered. Glassware clinked and a fountain trickled.

These were familiar sounds to anyone associated with her parents' fancy banquets, frequently held for business purposes or boosting their sosh. None of their three children were allowed to participate, least of all Urban.

So it seemed strange that this banquet was in honor of her graduation from high school. Naturals weren't exactly forbidden from going to university. No Naturals had wanted to go anyway, after a Natural student had been made an example of over a decade ago.

The student had been brutally murdered by the SAS, or Supers Against Soups, the underground organization started by Supers who killed Naturals that attempted to mix with the Enhanced. It had expanded to include members from other gene pools, but the name had stuck.

Mother had read the story in full gory detail to Urban when she was only seven years old. "This is why you have to be careful," Mother had explained. "There will always be people who look down on you because of your genetics. They don't want you mixing with their own kind."

Urban had cried, but her mother had continued unphased. "It's just the way things are. You can either cry about it or do something. Your best weapon is your sosh. The higher the score, the less suspicious people will be. They'll assume you're one of them. Promise me you'll focus on getting a good sosh."

Her mother had eyed Urban critically, then tipped her chin gently up. "Your second-best weapon is learning to control your emotions. Stop crying."

Now Urban watched with stone-cold eyes as the two Inventors guards flanking the entrance opened the doors. Dread knotted her stomach, but she held her head high.

A gold chandelier dangled from the glass ceiling, and a

full-sized tree, made entirely from jade, stretched from one corner of the room to the other. The windows were lined with priceless petrified wood from the Qing dynasty, and the glittering floors were made of black onyx, mother of pearl, abalone shell, and diamonds.

At the center of the room stood a four-story-high fish tank. Exotic varieties of fish darted in unison, marine plant life swayed peacefully, and a mini golden castle glimmered in artificial sunlight.

Urban despised everything about that gaudy castle and tank. Guests with underwater enhancements—or Aquas—dressed in their finest water XR suits swam through it. They floated under the castle or lounged at a bar with tubes to suck on their drinks. Waterbots resembling metal octopi served the guests seafood hors d'oeuvres with their multiple arms. An Aqua nodded at one of the netted platters of food, and the waiterbot opened it to reveal tofu, which the guest stabbed with a mini prong before it could float away, then shoved it into his mouth.

Usually, the tank was used for Father's work. Once the Federation realized space colonization was impractical due to the ablation cascade, only the elite and military were expanding slowly into safe pockets of space.

The savvy business executives turned to a cheaper final frontier: the ocean. As an Inventor, Father had invested in and helped design one of the first five underwater shopping centers. He'd built this tank to experiment with different concepts. They'd also given Urban's brother Aqua enhancements so he could one day take over the family business.

A guest in the tank waved good-bye to a huddle of Aquas and headed toward a translucent bubble at the edge of the tank. She stepped in and it closed behind her. The water drained away, and a powerful gust of air blow-dried her. Then she stepped out and joined all the non-marine Enhanced guests.

Another movement in the tank caught Urban's eye. An Aqua

wearing bright orange swim attire moved near the bottom of the tank. Urban realized he was sparring with another Aqua, showing off his underwater fight moves. A group of Aqua girls gathered around. They wore flowing dresses that resembled mermaid tails and released bubbles of laughter as they watched. Urban would recognize the flirtatious behavior of her older brother Lucas anywhere.

She would not forget the time Lucas had convinced her to swim with him in that tank. She had been seven. He'd dragged her to the very bottom until all her air ran out. She struggled to get free as terror rendered her mind useless.

As her vision turned black, she clawed wildly at him, but his grip didn't loosen. Urban might have had a chance at a fair fight if she'd arrived at her parents' doorsteps with enhancements—like she was supposed to.

"Give up yet?" Lucas had taunted, his overly perfect face inches from her own.

Though she was convinced her lungs had collapsed, she refused to surrender. She may not have been as strong, but she realized she had two options. One, be crushed by her genetic superiors. Or two, do whatever it took to survive. She chose the latter.

She punched Lucas hard in the groin, and he instantly released her.

Lucas had been grounded for the incident, but that didn't make up for Urban's recurring nightmares. She hadn't gone swimming since. Seeing the tank now, with Lucas inside, caused her to turn away.

Fighting against her genetic superiors had been a daily battle since she'd first been taken from the Outskirts full of Naturals to the Metropolis to live with the Enhanced. Anyone in the Metropolis might guess she had basic enhancements like strengthened bones, increased lung capacity, or a stronger immune system. Despite her asthmatic lungs, which had nearly exposed her on multiple occasions, Urban's family and her boyfriend were the sole individuals who knew the truth. She just hoped she could fool everyone else at university when she left in two days.

Her pulse quickened at the thought.

She scanned the hall for a familiar face. No fewer than a hundred guests, all dressed in their finest, mingled at booths or reclined on plush couches. A mixture of maidbots and Naturals waited on them.

A woman with elegant hair, pulled back into a bun, and a tight smile glided toward her. She held herself regally and walked with the grace of a Flower-Drum Dancer. Her eyes, painted and stunning, were like fire.

"I've brought Urban to you, mistress." The attendant next to Urban bowed and left.

The woman surveyed Urban critically. "You're late."

"Hello, Mother."

The woman's mouth tightened. She leaned closer. "Of all the nights to make a grand entrance, tonight is not the one. You mustn't let anyone know you're not," she lowered her voice to a barely audible whisper, "Enhanced."

Urban wanted to groan in frustration. Pretending to be Enhanced was a normal way of life. If either of her two siblings had been standing there instead, Mother surely wouldn't be treating them like children.

Something stabbed at Urban's waist. She looked down and found it was her mother's progressive silk dress with its layers of blood-red and cream fabric jutting out sharply at the midsection and into Urban's side.

Urban frowned. This was the dress Mother was saving for a special occasion. Urban wondered why she was wearing it now. Her graduation certainly didn't warrant it.

"There's something I need to tell you." Mother stopped abruptly as her gaze flickered over Urban's shoulder. "Someone here might suspect you're not Enhanced." Her voice had an unfamiliar note to it—fear.

Urban's blood ran cold. How could anyone know? It was her family's best-kept secret.

"Why do you think that?"

"We don't know for sure. It could just be a coincidence but . . ." her mother glanced around again, "someone left a note in one of the bathrooms: Soups suck."

Urban swallowed. Only Enhanced who hated Naturals ever referred to them as the unevolved Primordial Soup, or Soup for short.

"I must make sure you're safe," Mother continued. "Stick close to me."

As Urban nodded, she wished for the hundredth time that she truly belonged in the Lee family—that she wasn't just a mistake.

Many years back, when her parents had been caught in a scandal, their soshes had plummeted. They were clever manipulators, however, and willing to do anything to crawl their way back up. They'd leveraged what connections were still able to restore their soshes by helping with charity.

The plan had worked.

What most people didn't know was her sister was that charity. And what Mother and Father hadn't known when they'd signed up for the adoption was that they'd be getting two children—one of whom was a Natural.

04

自外

THE INCEPTOR

"FLORA!" A SHRILL VOICE INTERRUPTED. AN Inceptor marched toward them.

Mother drew herself up.

Inceptors had enhanced brain capabilities that enabled them to detect microfacial movements. Lying to an Inceptor required great skill.

Urban braced herself as she faced the scrutiny of beady brown eyes. There was something cold and knowing in them. She wanted to hide from them, but instead, she feigned boredom and stifled a yawn.

The middle-aged woman's magenta *qipao* was shorter than Urban though appropriate for a banquet. Complementing her traditional look, her black hair was secured in two buns with chopsticks.

"*Zhou* Flora, I've been trying all night to find you." The woman put emphasis on Mother's last name. Like most women in the Asian Federation, Mother had not taken her husband's surname and thus remained a Zhou instead of a Lee.

"You can't hide from me." The woman waggled her fingers at Mother. She had an almost childlike appearance, were it not for her hot-red lipstick and the sapphire-studded glasses that rested at the end of her upturned nose.

"Why hello, Thistle," Mother said graciously. "So glad you found us."

Urban detected only the slightest undercurrent of distaste in her mother's tone. While Thistle flattered mother's dress and commented on the food selections, Urban read stats that scrolled across the corner of her retina display.

Thistle was the owner of an elite gym and had a sosh of 79. Only three points lower than Mother's. She had check-ins at several Flyer obstacles courses and Aqua swim events. There was more info, but Urban stopped reading and returned her attention to the conversation.

Thistle peered over her glasses at them. "Your youngest, I presume?"

"Yes, she is. This is Urban."

The woman gave Urban a once-over, no doubt also looking up Urban's stats with her own retina display. Too bad for Thistle, Urban's sosh wouldn't exist for another couple weeks when she'd turn eighteen.

"And what gene pool will you be joining at university, Urban?" Thistle asked, expressionless. That was one of the maddening parts about Inceptors—they could completely hide their emotions when they chose.

"We haven't revealed our little Urban's enhancements yet," Mother spoke evenly.

"How quaint." Thistle's beady eyes stared at Urban, searching for any weaknesses.

Urban's skin crawled. It was as if the woman was reading her every thought.

"You're too skinny." The woman pinched one of Urban's arms and turned her inquisitive eyes to Mother. "Why would you select such frail genetics?"

This was always the hardest thing to hide, since people in the Eastern Federation held a prejudice toward a body without larger, reinforced bones. Only Naturals or Flyers were so skinny.

"Why don't you know, darling? It's all the rage these days," Mother replied coolly. "Or haven't you attended the latest genetic fashion shows?"

Urban had to hand it to her; Mother was an excellent liar.

Thistle's eyes narrowed. "Hmm . . . very well." With a *harrumph* and another once-over, she raised her glass to someone else in the room and strode over to talk down to them.

Urban sighed in relief, but the night was far from over.

The aroma of Beijing roast duck made Urban's stomach rumble. Glancing over, she looked at the buffet. Beef ribs in black pepper sauce, fried green beans, pumpkin cakes, stuffed pork buns, taro pies, pan-fried veggie rolls, egg custards, beef fritters, coconut pudding, scallops in garlic sauce, and more dishes she didn't even recognize. That was just one of the six tables buried under mountains of food.

Urban wanted to pluck out her favorite foods but knew Mother would insist she make the rounds first.

Mother touched Urban's elbow and leaned in closer to whisper, "We need to get you something you can drink before the toasting starts." She ordered a maidbot over and snatched up a shot glass. Glancing around, she swiftly withdrew a tiny white pill from the folds of her dress and slipped it into the drink. She handed it to Urban as the pill bubbled and dissolved.

"May everyone have a prosperous year!" someone shouted. Urban recognized the voice at once. A man with bushy eyebrows, a crooked grin, and eyes squinted into sunflower seeds surveyed the crowd. Father was in a surprisingly good mood as he raised his glass. "May your children all stay healthy and get into good universities. *Ganbei!*"

Urban's mind flickered. High school had always been violent and dangerous. Even though enhancements weren't allowed to be used at school, no one actually enforced it. Urban had become an expert at keeping her head down, sitting in the back of class, and maintaining a tough demeanor.

Only, at university, it would be students with the best, and even more dangerous, enhancements she'd be facing. She'd heard the universities were stricter at enforcing the rules though. Hopefully in one way at least, it would be easier than high school. She'd have enough to worry about with living on campus and hiding her genetics full time.

The alcohol dehydrogenase pill dissolved in her drink just in time.

All the guests joined in lifting their glasses. "*Ganbei!*" they echoed and drank.

Enhanced genetics meant everyone in the city could drink all night and be only lightly buzzed. Urban, on the other hand, would be red faced and tipsy after just one glass.

Two Flyers, who had been hovering in midair, swooped toward Urban and her mother. They touched down smoothly, not spilling even a drop of their rice wine.

One of the Flyers' sosh was in the low sixties. The other was blocked. He probably had an even lower sosh. Most people with high scores were more than happy to enable public mode and allow people to see their score.

Urban relaxed around them.

One of the Flyers, a man with shiny purple wings that resembled a dragonfly's, tucked his wings neatly behind him. "Flora, I've just read *Sunset of the Shang Dynasty.* Brilliant poems. Absolutely brilliant."

"Why thank you." Mother's tone was modest, but Urban noticed the pride in her eyes.

"Do tell us where you find the inspiration?" a woman chimed in. She wore all black and had dark makeup and gray-and-green wings like a fly's. Her giant shiny eyes stared everywhere at once, reflecting Urban's face in them. "From a foreign land perhaps? Surely not from Beijing."

Mother shifted. While she was originally from Beijing, she'd spent most of her childhood in the Eastern Federation. Why this was a secret, Urban still didn't understand, but she knew better than to say anything. It seemed ironic how her mother had studied abroad, yet she wouldn't even let Urban travel out of the Federation for vacation.

"I get my inspiration from everywhere," Mother went on, her face an impenetrable mask. For an Artisan, Urban thought she had pretty impressive Inceptor-like abilities. "I get some from Beijing, some from places I've seen or read about in QuanNao. Inspiration is lurking behind every corner, I like to say."

"I aspire to be an Artisan someday," Dragonfly said wistfully. "But the odds are against me with so few ever achieving success."

"With practice, you will succeed," Mother encouraged. "With or without Artisan enhancements, you can be successful if you keep at it."

Urban wanted to roll her eyes. She'd had a similar conversation. Only, her parents' reaction had been quite different then.

The two Flyers continued to pepper Mother with compliments and linked with Mother before leaving. Urban watched as Mother's sosh of 82 out of 100 increased a tenth of a decimal.

"Stay here while I find several important guests I'd like you to meet," Mother instructed.

Urban was just starting to relax when she spotted a flash of orange. Inwardly, she groaned.

Her brother strode toward her, his shiny orange-and-white jumpsuit and high-top shoes nearly blinding. He smoothed his perfectly slicked-back hair.

"Whatcha drinking there?" He peered down at her empty glass. "Gin tonic, rice wine, bourbon? Or how about," he lowered his voice, "a virgin drink?"

Urban gave his jumpsuit an exaggerated once-over. "Nice escape from pond prison. Did the mermaids find you a little too fishy for their taste?"

"Quite the contrary," he said with a smirk. "I was being overrun by Aquas wanting to link, so I had to make a getaway. You seem like a pretty good repellant what with your out-of-season dress and all."

Urban folded her arms over her chest. "I don't expect you to know anything about fashion if you can't even recognize PengTai's latest collection."

"PengTai? Really?" Lucas scoffed. "How can you afford that? I thought Mom and Dad only gave allowance to those of us who make good grades."

Urban bristled.

It was true, she had the worst grades in the family. No matter how many tutors and long nights she studied, she'd barely scraped by with a passing score to get into university. She was no Inventor like Lillian, who only missed two questions out of the entire *Gaokao* entrance exam. And she was no Aqua like Lucas, able to achieve extraordinary marine feats and acing the Aqua Academy Exam.

Fortunately, Mother and Father were too concerned about appearances to make Urban pay for clothing on her own. Then again, if it weren't for their obsession of a high social score, Urban wouldn't be here.

"*Ganbei*!" someone shouted, jolting Urban out of her thoughts. "To the health and success of our students."

Everyone raised their glasses. "Cheers!"

Lucas raised his own glass to Urban and winked. "To not getting kicked out of uni your first week," he whispered before he downed his drink. "Or better yet, to getting a sosh that's higher than a street rat's."

"*When* I get a high sosh," Urban retorted. "I won't have bent over backward doing acrobatics in a kiddy pool or linking with every sleezy person I meet. What is yours anyway?" She paid attention to the scrolling stats in her retina display and was surprised to find his sosh had jumped to 73. She pretended to be unimpressed. "That's it? 73?"

"Yeah, right. You'll be lucky to land a 60." He slicked back his hair. "Just know, when you turn eighteen, your sosh can change how people perceive you, but it can't change how you perceive yourself." Before she could respond, he sauntered off toward a group of girls with exotic animal enhancements.

Urban tried to calm her anger as she watched him leave. How did he always know how to get under her skin?

She eyed the buffet, trying to distract herself. Still seeing no sign of Mother, she slinked toward the food. She made it to a set of stairs, but tripped on something, catching her dress on the edge of the staircase.

Urban fell forward.

Suddenly, she was pulled backward and onto her feet again as a figure rolled past her in a blur of white, then came to a standing position. A metallic arm shot out and caught Urban's glass, which was hurtling through the air, before retracting quickly. The figure spun around, extending the cup back to Urban.

"Thanks, Lillian," Urban said, letting out a sigh of relief.

Her older sister's perfectly proportioned and symmetrical face watched her with concern. She wore a simple black pantsuit that only drew more attention to her stunning Enhanced beauty.

Urban wished, not for the first time, that she, too, was Enhanced. She dreamed about it daily, but only conspiracy theorists believed it possible. No one had ever survived the procedure after birth. A Natural surely wouldn't.

"Your newest invention?" Urban motioned to the metallic arm.

"Just a prototype. Along with these." Two mini drones flew out of a hidden compartment in her pantsuit.

"Uh, hate to break it to you, but delivery drones have already been perfected."

Lillian stroked the two bots affectionately. "Not like Peppa and DeDe."

"You named your bots?"

"Of course. Studies show, inventions with names last longer."

Urban just looked at her.

"Watch this." Lillian gently guided the bots into the air, where they vanished from sight. A moment later, several artichoke wontons and a plate from the buffet began flying upward then toward them.

Urban accepted the plate extended to her. "Not bad."

"That's not all they can do," Lillian said proudly. "They can shoot webs, glow in the dark . . ."

The bots dropped the wontons onto the plate. One missed and landed on the floor.

"I'm still working out a few kinks," Lillian admitted. "Dede is a little janky sometimes." She picked up the wonton and guided her bots back out of sight.

Just then Mother returned, carrying two new drinks. "Come." She dragged Urban and now Lillian with her. "There are many guests to meet."

They continued making their way through the guests and *ganbeing* until late into the night. Urban's feet began to cramp from her heels. Exhaustion settled in, making small talk more and more difficult.

Lillian had just left when Father, a female Super, and a man joined them. Father eyed the Super disdainfully behind her back.

The Super towered a full two heads over most the other guests in the room and had an athletic stance. She wore a stylish white XR suit but opted for heels and a top that revealed her bare, chiseled shoulders.

The man, just as tall, wore a matching white suit. With a second glance, Urban realized shoe extensions stabilized him and put him at the same height as the Super.

With tech like that, he's probably an Inventor, Urban surmised. What she would give to own a pair of shoes like that.

Too bad they didn't exist in the mainstream market.

"A toast," Father suddenly shouted. "To our last child getting into university!" He raised his glass.

Everyone followed his example.

"*Ganbei!*"

The guests echoed the phrase, joining him in drinking.

"Ah, you must be Urban," the Inventor boomed a little later. "I hear you're bound for Peking University?"

The couple looked vaguely familiar. Urban's retina display informed her the woman was Sun Stoney, Founder of the Games. The man was none other than Lung Lennox, the head of the board for the Games. Her sosh registered at 90, and his a whopping 96. Now she knew why Mother wore her best dress.

Linking with Lennox or Stoney would boost their soshes big time. One wrong word, one offensive gesture, would eliminate that option.

"Yes, that's right," Urban responded in her most relaxed tone despite the sweat trickling down her back.

"Great school," Lennox remarked. "It's our alma mater. My wife here took the Super Gene Pool Lead while I led the Inventor House. Will you be trying out for the Games?"

Urban hesitated. The answer was a resounding no.

Trying out for the Games would be like waving a giant flag over her head, announcing to the world her Natural status. But she couldn't tell Lennox that. Informing him she wouldn't be trying out might make him think she didn't value the Games. She didn't want him jumping to that conclusion and losing face.

Her parents watched her tensely. Her father in particular looked uncomfortable. Father had always complained about Lennox, convinced the Inventor had more than one main gene-pool enhancement beyond being an Inventor. A ludicrous theory in Urban's mind, since the Asian Federation strictly outlawed more than one. Father's complaints likely stemmed from jealousy more than any real evidence.

Then again, she had always assumed what her father knew about Lennox was from the media. She'd never guessed he actually knew Lennox personally.

Urban realized they were all waiting for her to respond.

"I would be honored to be a Gene Pool Lead," Urban said, thinking quickly but speaking slowly. "Though I'm told it's quite competitive. How did you do it, Stoney? What's the secret?"

Stoney's face brightened, and she proceeded to talk about her days in the Games, sharing her adventures, and imparting tips until even Mother's eyes glazed over.

"Dear, let's leave the Lees alone," Lennox finally interjected. "I think it's time I got you a fresh drink."

"Should you ever want to try out for the Games, let us know," Stoney called over her shoulder. "My husband can put in a good word for you."

Urban smiled back politely as she sighed inwardly with relief. Crisis averted.

As the group dispersed, Urban sank into a plush velvet couch to give her feet a break. Her mind drifted to the encrypted file. What could possibly be in there? What could the code be?

If only she were back in her XRD, maybe she could shift through her old Gene-IQ records and find the answer.

She bolted upright.

That's it!

AS THE LAST OF THE GUESTS LEFT, URBAN entered her XRD number 115424. She held her breath. The file opened and a message popped up in her retina display.

<Lee Urban, stay away from Peking University.>

Urban stared, dumbfounded.

Then another message appeared.

<Deleting this message in 3 . . . 2 . . . 1. This message is no longer available for viewing.>

The file vanished.

Urban wanted to scream in frustration. All that work for a cryptic warning?

And what could she do? She was university bound on Monday. A message from Angel wouldn't stop her. But why would anyone bother going to all the trouble of hacking her identity, attaching a file, and encrypting it?

And how had Angel hacked her? Urban had all the latest security updates and the most expensive software.

As she sat there, Urban was no closer to untangling her thoughts. She finally gave up and retired to her room, instantly falling asleep.

The next day, she was only able to get herself out of bed,

knowing this would be her last chance to meet up with her boyfriend. So, while the rest of the family slept blissfully on, she slipped out of the house and climbed onto her motorcycle. Using her QuanNao account, she installed the latest software update for her bike as she rode.

Her mind drifted back to Qing Angel's warning. Should she tell her parents? What would they do? Would they prevent her from going to university? They'd want to protect her, of course, but she couldn't risk them finding out. Her thoughts raced as fast as her motorcycle as she left the Metropolis.

<Entering yellow zone. Exercise CAUTION.>

Urban ignored the warning as she neared the stacked skyrises of the Outskirts.

She turned onto an empty alley with laundry and sausages hanging outside drying and swaying in the wind. AC units hummed, and XR tech threatened to crowd out the remaining window space.

Her motorcycle shot out of the alley, climbed over a pile of rubble, bumped through the remnants of a dilapidated warehouses, then evened out on a deserted road.

An abandoned structure loomed ahead. The building had once been one of the eight tech training facilities that employed all the Naturals in the Outskirts. It had been shut down after the AI training jobs there had dried up several years ago. Now, broken glass littered the tile floors. The paint on the walls was peeling, and lovers had carved their initials in some of the pillars. At the center of the names was a large $E + U$ with a heart around it. Other walls sported graffiti art and water damage.

Scanning the abandoned structure, Urban spotted a tall figure in a leather jacket leaning against a bike. He removed his black helmet and grinned his usual slow smile, the one that made her cheeks flush with heat.

He was good-looking for a Natural—the curve of his full lips, the twinkle in his eye, his shock of black hair that stood on end and gave him an almost wild look. He was unlike anyone Urban had ever met in the Metropolis. There was something about him that the Enhanced, who'd never had to survive in the Outskirts or breathe a molecule of unfiltered air in their lives, didn't possess.

Urban thought back to when they'd met. It had only been three months ago on her first day in the Outskirts. She'd completed her orientation and onboarding at Gene-IQ and was heading home.

Bodies pressed so tightly up against her, Urban was sure her rib cage would crack. Up ahead, in the sea of bobbing heads, she spotted a refreshingly empty alleyway and squeezed her way into it. Instantly, her retina display shot her a warning.

<Entering orange zone. Exercise CAUTION.>

She'd only ever heard of orange zones or seen them on the flicks she watched. How dangerous were they really?

Urban hesitated. According to her retina maps, if she followed the main road, she'd have to curve around to the Bolt Line. But if she stuck to the alley, it was a straight shot.

She glanced back at the pressing throngs behind her. She didn't like being stuffed between people like *jiaozi* filling.

She studied the dark alleyway more closely. The road was comprised of mismatching concrete blocks and was slick, moldy, and covered in trash. Rats scurried from one corner to another, avoiding large, ominous puddles. The walls were lined with trash bins and rusty barred windows that seemed to close in on her.

Tentatively, she took a step forward into the shaded respite from the sun and people.

Crash!

Urban jumped.

The clattering of glass, banging of metal, and thumping of other debris rang out loudly through the alley. A bot the size of her bed hovered a couple of meters off the ground at the other end of the alley. It had a bin tipped upside down, and a few remaining pieces of trash fell into it.

Urban relaxed and took in a breath, then she walked in deeper. The sounds of the busy street faded.

Something rustled loudly near one of the trash cans. Urban jerked her head in that direction as a man stepped out from the shadows.

"Hello." The voice was gravelly and flat. The hairs on her arm went up.

Urban did the only thing she could think of and sent an emergency ping to the *Jingcha*.

<EMERGENCY-location drop confirmed.>

"Pinging someone?" The man pulled out a serrated knife.

Her stomach twisted. Turning to run, she found the exit blocked by two more figures with arms crossed.

The man behind her laughed, low and guttural. "The *Jingcha* don't answers pings from these parts."

Urban faced him again, cold panic clawing wildly at her chest.

"Don't worry, I won't hurt you. Just extend that pretty little arm of yours and transfer your crypto credits."

But movement caught Urban's eye, and she shrank back as a hooded figure streaked toward them.

In an instant, it disarmed the man and put him in a chokehold. A moment later, the knife rose of its own accord, flying in midair.

The attacker gasped and sputtered as his own knife came within an inch of his neck, then stopped.

One of the remaining attackers shrieked in terror. "He's Enhanced!" They both tripped over themselves in their haste to get away.

The hooded figure remained still a moment after they had fled. Then he loosened his grip on the remaining man in the chokehold.

Red-faced, the man hunched over and coughed and gulped in deep breaths of air, while the hooded figure snatched up the still dangling knife. "It's Li, isn't it?" He spoke quietly, but his voice caried a weight of authority.

The man didn't respond.

"Yes, I thought I recognized you," the figure mused. With a flash of movement, he snatched up Li's arm and swiped his tatt, then he released him.

Li stared. "Did you just—"

"Transfer credits to you? Yes."

Li swiped his tatt to accept the transfer and stared slack jawed.

"That money is to get you through long enough to find a job. No more of this." The hooded figure waved his hands, gesturing at their surroundings. "Don't let me catch you again."

Li said nothing as he took in the words.

"Oh, and by opening my transfer, you've also accepted a bug that will track your whereabouts. Don't try anything."

Li's eyes moved from his tatt to the figure. He looked as if he were about to thank him, but then changed his mind and darted away.

The hooded figure sighed as he watched him leave.

Urban tried to get a better look at her rescuer, but all she could see was a rugged, stubbled jawline and muscular neck. The hood and headset concealed the rest of his face.

The figure turned toward her, and he took a step closer. "You alright?"

Urban nodded. Even though she couldn't see his face, she sensed him studying her.

"So, why's someone from the Metropolis out here?"

"Metropolis?" Urban faltered, suddenly realizing she might be in more trouble than she'd started with.

He pulled his hood back, removed his headset, and stared openly at her. "No one out here has gold irises like yours. Those are the latest retina displays. I thought you were just too poor to buy a headset but seems I drew the wrong conclusion. No one can afford that sort of tech out here." He held up his Razor 2X eye covering. "The best we can do is a three-generation-old headset."

Urban blushed, partially from her stupidity, partially because he was right, and partially because, with his headset off, she saw his face for the first time. "But I thought you were from the Metropolis. The way you made that knife float, that's Inventor tech."

"Who's to say I can't use it?"

"But that's illegal." Urban was aghast. "Only Inventors are permitted to use the tech they create."

"You'll find that things in the Outskirts are not as black and white as they may appear in the Metropolis." He examined the knife he was still holding. Lifting up his hoodie, he tucked it into a bandolier, full of a wide variety of daggers and odd contraptions.

Urban nodded, but mostly to clear the image of the knives and his chiseled bare abs from her mind. "Well, anyway, I better be on my way. Thank you, um . . .?"

"Everest," he finished for her. "Local 'law enforcement' at your service. And you are?"

"Urban."

"Right. Well, Urban, I recommend you stay safe in the Metropolis. But if you do come back," he hesitated a moment, his raven black eyes pulling up to meet hers, "let me know. I wouldn't want you wandering these parts alone."

Needless to say, she did go back. After he rescued her, she knew she could trust him and even took a risk telling Everest about her being a Natural.

"You alright?" Everest jerked her thoughts back to the present. "Is this about uni?"

"I am pretty worried about that," she admitted and relayed her strange encounter with Qing Angel, the encrypted file, and the message Angel had left.

"That is . . . odd. Are you still going?"

"Of course." Urban's words came out more forcefully than she'd intended.

Everest managed a smile, but it thinly veiled his concern. "Just be safe."

A stretched silence filled the air. "Let's ride," Urban finally said. "I don't want to talk about it on my last day."

"You got it." Everest revved his engine and grinned mischievously. "Ready to lose?"

Urban strapped her helmet on. "I never lose."

"Loser buys lunch next time." Tires skidding loudly, Everest's bike leaped forward into the deserted building.

Urban followed with a *whoop*.

Cold, musky air greeted her as she chased Everest down a ramp, weaving between columns and pillars into the underground parking lot. With the solar energy cut long ago, the garage grew dark quickly.

Everest slowed as the blackness increased, but Urban went faster. She flipped on her night vision, and everything lit up in green.

"Try and keep up!" Urban teased as she shot past him.

Zooming through the empty space, she practiced several tight turns and stops in darkness as black as soy sauce. Then she sped toward Everest, and they rode back up into the light.

"You gave up fast," Urban chided.

"I didn't 'give up.' Like a true gentleman, I merely allowed you to go first."

"Is that what happened?" She grinned. "*So* chivalrous." She climbed off her motorcycle and took a sip of water. "Think I can compete soon?"

"Almost." Everest adjusted his helmet and gestured toward the door. "Take it from someone who's won three underground races; there's one last thing you need to know." He led her outside the building to a half-built overpass that looked as if the builders had forgotten to complete it. The sharp ramp leading upward stopped midway, ending in a drop off into empty space.

"Wow, what is that?" Urban stared up in awe.

"That is the final test. Once you land a jump like that, you're ready."

"Up that?" Urban gulped. "You sure?"

"Positive."

"All right then." Urban started toward the overpass. "Let's get this over with."

"Hold on." Everest laughed as he caught her arm and pulled her back. "Do you have a death wish? We're not *starting* with that."

"Oh." Urban felt sheepish.

"Follow me." He led her to a trash heap the size of a smart car. A wooden board rested up against it. "Start with this." He rode toward the trash pile. The board sagged under his weight, and then he was airborne for a few seconds before landing smoothly on the dirt.

Urban copied his example and sped toward the ramp. Right as she hit the board, a wave of doubt flooded her. While not nearly as high as the overpass, the jump was still high enough that if she landed wrong, she could seriously injure herself. Especially if her motorcycle crushed her. In a panic, she tried to slow down and retreat.

Too late.

She soared over the trash heap. Air rushed past her—she was flying. But then she looked down and realized she wasn't going to clear it.

CRUNCH.

A robot's arm snapped underneath, and the motorcycle lurched violently. Tightening her grip, Urban tried to gain control, but the bike skidded, then dropped out from under her. She rolled and landed hard on her side, while her bike tumbled in the opposite direction.

Everest rushed to her side. "You okay?"

She glared down at herself. Her leather XR suit was shredded. The skin on her knees and elbows was bleeding. But otherwise, she was uninjured.

Still, disappointment welled up in her chest. Not again. It seemed like every time she started making progress toward a race, something always happened.

"You were supposed to wait until I taught you how to jump," Everest said as he helped her to her feet.

The fading sun bathed the decrepit structure in violet, pink, and scarlet as they walked back. Everest propped his motorcycle against a wall and motioned Urban to do the same. They leaned up against a cool pillar, Urban resting her head on his shoulder, absorbing his warmth and strength. He smelled of smoke and jasmine. Her skin tingled as he took her hand and brushed his fingers across it.

Urban's eyes twinkled at him. "Looks like you're buying lunch."

"You had night vision! Not fair."

"Then you shouldn't have made the bet," she said smugly.

"I let you win one time, and you get so cocky—"

"*Let* me win?" Urban interrupted. "You lost!"

Everest pushed her playfully to the side, and they laughed.

"Seriously though, great work out there." Everest drew her back to his chest. "When it comes to jumps next time, remember you have to commit to it. Give it a couple more months. The underground races aren't something to rush into. Imagine if we'd gone up the big ramp today and you'd ended up in the hospital . . ."

"My lack of enhancements would have been discovered,"

Urban finished for him. Her face sobered. "I know. But the only way to link with the inner circle in uni is to be known for something—to have a niche. Motorcycle racing is my one shot. Otherwise, I'll never get a high sosh."

"My sosh stinks and I seem to survive."

Everest's score had remained a steady 40. Most everyone in the Outskirts had a sosh hovering around the low forties, and there was no point in trying to increase it. All they could do was keep it from tanking so low they could no longer buy essentials.

"You live in the Outskirts. If you want to live in the Metropolis, you have to have a high sosh. Not to mention, if I had a high sosh, no one would suspect I'm a Natural. I wouldn't have to be on my guard all the time. I could finally just focus on my art." She let out a deep sigh.

Everest squeezed her hand. "Well then, we better keep practicing. Maybe next time, wait for my instructions?"

"I'll try." Urban laughed. "Speaking of practice, how's your music coming? I haven't heard you sing or write anything in a while."

She felt him sigh a little and noticed the black circles under his eyes as he spoke. "Stuck in a rut. I can't seem to find any inspiration for a new song or time to practice. I think I'm just too exhausted."

Urban tried not to shiver. Everest was living her worst fear—being stuck in the Outskirts working long hours, giving his best to an invisible force. Yet on top of his demanding job, he somehow always found time to help those less fortunate than him.

"Maybe if you spend less time helping everyone else and actually spent time on yourself?"

Everest threw her a sharp glance. "If I don't help, there are people who will be taken advantage of."

"But what about you?"

"I'll find time to work on my lyrics and practice," he assured her. "It's my only chance to join you in the Metropolis."

Urban wanted to argue with him, to tell him he was wrong; if he just studied enough or worked hard enough, he could rise above the Outskirts. But deep down she knew he was right.

Everest had made nearly perfect grades in high school before graduating to work at one of the AI tech facilities. After just one summer of working fulltime, he'd risen quickly to the top and had already hit the glass ceiling.

Musicians, writers, and poets were the only ones who escaped the Outskirts. While certain brain enhancements did tend to hone a better ear for music or higher stamina to sit and write, inspiration and the ability to capture life in song or word could be done by anyone—Natural or Enhanced. In fact, most of the notable poets during the Genetic Revolution had been Naturals.

Thus, many of the Naturals in the Outskirts studiously practiced some form of art. That was the ambitious half. The other half . . . she tried not think about her encounter with the attacker in the orange zone alleyway.

"Keep trying," Urban urged. "If anyone can escape the Outskirts, it's you."

Everest nodded but didn't look convinced.

Urban drew circles in the dusty tile floor. "I'll be waiting for you."

The air fell still, and an unspoken weight descended.

Finally, Urban spoke again. "Can you believe uni starts tomorrow?"

Everest smiled at her, but his eyes were serious. "You're brave for going without enhancements. Naturals are . . . not safe there."

"The Outskirts are dangerous too," Urban pointed out.

"That's a different kind of danger. One I'm comfortable with."

Urban eyed Everest's scarred hands. She was sure he was. "Don't worry about me. No one will find out I'm a Natural. I've been doing this my whole life." Her words came out hollow, like she was trying to convince herself too.

"Besides," she added. "No one would ever expect a Natural to attend uni. I'll be hiding in plain sight."

He grinned at her. "Make us Naturals proud, okay?"

"I'll try." She reached back into her motorcycle pouch and pulled out a rolled-up piece of paper. "I made this for you."

Gently, Everest took the paper and unrolled it. It was a painting of two goldfish chasing each other in a circle. "You painted this?"

Urban nodded.

"Wow. It's beautiful. Thank you." His usually fierce dark eyes were tender.

Urban's heart beat faster. Three months of dating, and she already wished she could stay with him forever—just not in the Outskirts.

They remained frozen, staring at each other.

Urban's augmented feed beeped.

A woman with smooth skin and hazel almond-shaped eyes appeared on Urban's retina display. She wore ginormous pearl earrings and cashmere. Her hair was pulled back into an impossibly tight bun.

"Where are you?" Mother's voice was tense. "Come back. It's urgent!"

URBAN STEPPED INTO HER FAMILY'S GAME room and breathed in the smell of oolong tea. The soundproof walls cut out the constant noise of chatter and traffic that usually seeped its way through the walls of the rest of the apartment.

Wooden decorative fans adorned the walls, and a luxuriously pristine white couch wrapped around a marble fountain at the center of the room. Father reclined on the couch, reading, while Lucas teased Baozi nearby. The only sounds were the peaceful bubbling of a fountain and the smack of jade on cedar as Lillian moved pieces in a strategy game.

"Ah, there you are." Mother sat rigidly on the edge of the couch.

"What's going on?" Urban asked.

"It's time for us to go over the rule book," Mother said cheerily then, using her retina display, projected a list onto the wall.

Urban stared at her mother. "I thought you said it was *urgent*?"

"It is. I *assume* you intend to enroll tomorrow like the rest of your peers?" Her eyebrows lifted in question. "In which case, it's of the utmost importance we address this immediately, before I'm out for the rest of the afternoon."

Urban plopped onto the couch and folded her arms across her chest, glaring.

"Now," Mother continued briskly, "I know we've been over this a few times, but I want to ensure you remember it before leaving for uni tomorrow."

A "few times" was an understatement. The rule book was one of Urban's first memories. It was how she'd made it to seventeen without being discovered as a Natural in the Metropolis.

"Rule number one: Don't drink. Ever."

Lucas sipped his own rice wine loudly at this and grinned mischievously at Urban.

"Rule number two: Avoid the Games."

Urban still didn't understand this rule, but she'd argued enough times to know it was a moot point.

"Rule number three: Avoid Inceptors and Givers. Befriend anyone else on campus, just not them. Well, maybe not Inventors, either, if you can help it. They can't read you like an Inceptor, but they're too smart for their own good." Mother gave Lillian a pointed look.

Lillian gave an innocent shrug.

"Rule number four—"

"Tell no one I'm a Natural," Urban interrupted. "Mother, I've been following these rules my whole life."

"University will be different. Father and I won't be there to protect you. Should you be discovered . . ." Her lips tightened. "Just be very cautious."

Urban thought about the beggar again, his vacant eyes haunting her.

A tickling sensation bothered her throat. She coughed once and noticed her family members all glance up in alarm.

Taking a sip of tea, she smiled reassuringly. "Just a little itch."

Everyone relaxed.

Great, on top of all these rules I have my asthma to worry about. She envied the Enhanced with their superior immune systems and genetics that never caught colds or had any sort of lung issues.

"Don't worry," Lillian assured her. "I'll be there, too, just in different classes. You won't be alone."

Urban managed a grateful smile.

Mother smoothed her hair back and continued, "Rule number five: Don't go out late alone. This means you must abide by your university's curfew regulations."

"But Mother," Urban protested. "All the best Key Opinion Leader bashes will go past curfew! How am I supposed to get a high sosh if I'm hiding in my room?" People with high scores always had fans who would be quick to notice and promote their work. All the best jobs in the Metropolis were reserved for those with the highest scores. Some positions she wouldn't even be able to apply without a minimum score of 75.

Mother arched her perfectly penciled eyebrows. "You may go only if it's a KOL event and only if you go with someone else. If SCA alerts me that you have missed curfew for any other reason, you will return home immediately to live with us."

"SCA?" Urban repeated.

"Have fun being babysat again with the Safe Child App." Lucas laughed.

Urban glared at him.

"Yes, SCA," Mother said. "You'll be using it at uni."

Urban's jaw dropped. "That's for little kids. I haven't had it since I was twelve."

"Like I said," Mother repeated firmly, "Father and I won't be there to protect you. This is a precaution we must take to ensure your safety."

"This is ridiculous." Urban ruffled Baozi's hair with displeasure, watching some of the hair fall off and vanish into the wall, wishing she could do the same.

"What's ridiculous is your attitude," Father stated.

Urban stiffened. She recognized that tone.

"You're lucky we're sending you at all. Sometimes, your lack of gratitude for all that we do to protect you is disheartening."

They were approaching dangerous territory, and Urban knew it. Her parents had wanted her to attend a trade school instead of university to keep her safe. The only reason her parents were sending her to university at all was because everyone in their circles attended. In fact, she couldn't think of anyone who didn't have at least a master's degree, and most had their PhDs as well. If she didn't go, it would look suspicious, and the truth might come out.

Urban didn't want to give her parents any reason to change their minds.

At Urban's silence, Father settled back into his chair with a grunt.

"There have been more and more alerts of high-profile students being kidnapped and ransomed," Mother said.

"Did you see the news about the red zone right outside of the city limits?" Lucas said. "It used to be that park we went to as kids, but several mutant animals escaped and are breeding like crazy. Ten people have already died. Can you believe it? Right next to the Guanting Reservoir. That's practically in our backyard!"

"As I was saying," Mother continued, ignoring Lucas, "you will need to be extremely cautious. We will be enrolling you in a few extra activities."

"Activities?" Urban asked suspiciously.

"Self-defense. Maybe some sort of weapons class too."

Urban stared at her mother. "Are you serious?"

Mother locked eyes with Urban. "This is very serious."

"But I won't have time for that," Urban protested. "Especially not with all my homework."

"You'll have to make time. Your priority will be your studies. After that, it's your ability to defend yourself."

"What if I don't go?"

Mother gave Urban her trademark look of disapproval. "You

can start by joining your sister in jiujitsu."

Lillian cheered.

"Why not with me at my underwater gym? We train in jiujitsu too," Lucas piped up with a devious grin. "I know you *love* being underwater."

Urban ignored him. "Not jiujitsu. That primeval martial art is useless."

"Not true," Lillian objected. "If you're attacked and end up on the ground, it's the most practical defense."

Urban sank her head in her hands. "This is a disaster. I haven't wrestled anything since . . ."

"Since that time you attacked Jiaozi after he ate your sushi." Lucas was enjoying Urban's dismay.

Jiaozi, Baozi's mischievous and unruly twin, perked her head up from under the table. She yawned and stretched her flaming-pink striped limbs, then curled back into a ball.

"Jiujitsu is not *wrestling*," Lillian said.

"Regardless," Mother adjusted her bun, "it's time you take up jiujitsu with your sister."

"Lillian is doing it because she's weird and loves that stuff. No offense." Urban cast a glance at Lillian. "But I don't want to spend all my free time rolling around on the ground with sweaty strangers."

"Sorry," Mother said bluntly, and that conversation was over.

Urban ground her molars.

"I also purchased a gym membership on your behalf," Mother continued.

"Why? I already work out like crazy at Qiang Gym so people won't suspect I'm a Natural."

"It's time you work out with the social elite at Infini-Fit. It will give you more chances to link with others and boost your sosh."

Urban blanched. "Don't you need a private invite to even apply for a membership there?"

"Yes." Mother turned to Lillian. "We also got you a membership."

Lillian grinned. "Did my birthday come early? This is amazing!"

Lucas suddenly choked on his tea. "Gah! What is this?" He examined his teacup and sniffed once.

"Really, Father," Lucas scolded, "you should invest in our own tea garden so we don't have to drink garbage like this."

"Even when you average it out over the years, the tea gardens still come out double the price of what we pay for with our current imported selection," Father pointed out. "Outrageous."

Lucas shook his head hopelessly. "You two are the stingiest people I know."

"Why, thank you," Mother said brightly.

Father beamed. "And you'd do well to find a spouse who's smart with their money too."

"But that's after you graduate and get a good job," Mother quickly added.

"Of course," Lucas said innocently. "No dating until then."

Mother nodded. She missed the shared look between the siblings. Most of the kids dated in secret, though very progressive parents allowed for such "nonsense" before their children were firmly established in their careers. Only Lillian knew Urban had a boyfriend.

"One last rule," Mother announced.

They'd already covered them all, what was this?

"It's a new one we've just added." Mother paused and took a sip of tea. "As you know, your first year you will not claim a gene pool but will pursue the general track. For your second year, your Father and I have decided should you be able to get a sosh of 80, we will allow you to join the Artisan gene pool."

An 80? Urban's heart sank. Without joining the Artisan gene pool at uni, there was no way she'd become a serious Artist.

"Looks like you'll be doing acrobatic stunts to boost your sosh after all." Lucas smirked. "I can teach you a few if you'd like."

Urban ignored him as she looked at her mother. "That's impossible. Lucas has already been at school for a year, and his score is only 73. Even Lillian, who's been at school for three years, only has 75. How am I supposed to get there in one year?"

"What's impossible is succeeding in the Artisan gene pool," Father interjected. "Your hand is too unsteady to pass as an Enhanced Artisan. It's too easy to attract unwanted attention. Not to mention, every Natural who makes it out of the Outskirts pursues that path. To beat back suspicion, you need to either pursue another path or maintain a high sosh. If you cannot achieve this, there is no path."

"Maybe you'll finally get a high enough sosh to *belong* in this family," Lucas mumbled under his breath. Their parents seemed not to have heard, but Lillian glared at Lucas.

It was as if Urban had been sucker punched. She'd never belong. Not in the Metropolis, not with her own family. It all centered on the high sosh.

Urban swallowed. "Why does Mother get to be an Artisan?" she blurted.

Mother's face froze.

"Your mother," Father said slowly, "has not migrated from the Outskirts to the Metropolis in the last two decades. She can afford that luxury—unlike you." He leaned back in his chair and closed his eyes.

"What happens if I can't boost my sosh high enough?"

"You mean *when* you don't," Lucas quipped.

Mother swirled the tea leaves in her cup. "In your second year, you'll take the track we've selected for you. You'll join the Giver gene pool."

Urban sat in stunned silence.

Her plan of working hard to maintain grades would be hard enough as a Natural at an Enhanced university. With added fitness and self-defense classes, it would be even more challenging. But her plan of keeping her head down and staying afloat was being flipped upside down. Now, she had to simultaneously be wildly popular, or she'd be stuck as a Giver for the rest of her life.

She bit back several smart retorts. Displaying any more emotion than she already had would only seem to prove her parent's point. *Racing is my only shot at getting my sosh anywhere near 80.*

"I'm sorry." A flash of what looked like concern passed through her mother's eyes, but it was gone just as quickly, and Urban couldn't be sure she'd seen it at all. "Now, as for how to get past the enhancement scanner you'll encounter at registration—" Mother leaned forward and handed Urban a device the size of her thumbnail.

Urban realized it *was* a nail.

"Wear that on top of your real nail. When you go through the scanner, it will override your own lack of enhancements with the ones your father programmed into it. In this case, we've taken a bit of Lucas's. You'll show up as an Aqua with no lethal enhancements."

"Why not Lillian's enhancements?"

"Because your sister also attends PKU, and that would alert the scanner," Mother explained. "With Lucas going to New Shanghai Ocean University, no one will notice. Each University's screening process is completely separate and, due to PPI regulations, cannot be shared."

"Why not Father's then?" Urban pressed. She hated the idea of owing Lucas a favor. By the look on his face, he was just as unhappy about it.

"Because you don't look at all like an Inventor. You don't have the tech or grades for that to be believable," Father said.

Urban turned to her mother. "How about yours then? I could easily pass as an Artisan."

Mother was losing patience. "Just trust us. Lucas is your best bet."

Reluctantly, Urban placed the nail on top of her own. It adhered perfectly with the help of nanotech. The nail looked so real.

"That's all. I'll be off now." Mother stood, then locked eyes with Urban. "Stick to the rules, Urban."

Urban watched her mother's retreating figure, then sighed as she left for her bedroom. She paused in the doorway. This was her last night here. Technically, she'd always have this room to come back to, so long as she didn't mess up too bad at university, but still, she knew things would be different once she left.

She took it all in—the bed by the far wall with an assortment of silk blankets, art supplies, and the furry white rug, now mostly hidden by a pile of clothes. Up against the opposite wall leaned a wooden table covered with calligraphy books and parchment. In the corner next to it a stiff square armchair, the kind traditional tea shops used, stood proudly.

Her eyes flitted over the floor-to-ceiling window overlooking downtown. It was dark outside, and the city was lit up with flashing orbs—each building boasting colors to rival a peacock.

Soon, she'd be leaving all this behind. Tomorrow she'd finally be at uni where her over-controlling parents would be forced to let her live her own life.

She ran her fingers over a wall with photos and her artwork. There were old-school photos from the camera she received on her twelfth birthday. Pictures of Baozi as a kitten, sleeping in her arms. And Lillian having tea with her and laughing, and selfies of them dressed up for the opera. All brought a smile to her lips. Then there was her favorite painting of a goldfish, a *chengyu*, or ancient saying, she'd penned in her practiced calligraphy and a bright-red number 60.

Urban's heart sank at the sight of the number. She went to her art supplies, whipped out a marker and scratched out the beautiful painted numbers. She scrawled over it a crude 80, then threw her pen down and stared at it.

How will I ever get a sosh of 80? It's practically impossible. The alternative was becoming a Giver. But she knew she couldn't sit and listen to people talk all day. It was too much like her job at Gene-IQ where she felt trapped. She couldn't even solve her own problems, much less anyone else's.

She sank onto her bed, her eyes continuing to roam across her room. They stopped on a small, compostable ticket from New Beijing's Art Museum. Everest had taken her there on their first date.

The entrance fee was cheap by Metropolis standards but for someone from the Outskirts, it cost a fortune. Urban had wanted to pay for it, but he'd stubbornly refused. The ticket always made her think of him and his stubbornness. She smiled at the memory but then frowned. *And what about Everest? When will I have time to see him?*

Up until this point, they'd been in similar stages of life. Both working a summer job.

Our lives will start to go different directions.

Suddenly, it was all too much.

She ran out of her room, down the hall, and flung open the door to Lillian's bedroom. She half expected it would be empty, as it had been for the last year since Lillian had been at university.

But Lillian was in the middle of brushing her teeth in the adjacent bathroom. "What's up?" she asked in between toothpaste foam.

She hopped onto Lillian's bed and wiggled under the covers.

"Oh no, you don't," Lillian warned.

Baozi leaped up onto the bed to join her.

"And get your cat off my bed!"

"Aw, come on. It can be a slumber party, just like old times."

Urban could hear Lillian spitting out her toothpaste. "Don't make me use my martial arts on you both." She came and sat on the bed beside Urban. "Aren't you supposed to be getting ready to leave for uni tomorrow?"

Lillian must have read something in Urban's expression because she reached into a drawer, pulled out a dainty box, and handed it to her. "I have a present for you. It's for uni."

Urban opened the box carefully. Inside was a bracelet with a strand of antique jade beads from the Qing dynasty, mixed with holographic metallic beads.

Urban's face brightened as she put it on. "Thanks, sis." She smiled gratefully, then slid off the bed and went to the mirror to study her reflection.

Who do I think I am going to uni? The thought sobered her. The close encounter at work with Qing Angel came to mind and made her frown.

Lillian had begun brushing her hair and saw Urban's face in the mirror. "What's wrong? You don't like the bracelet?"

"It's not that. I'm just worried." Urban twisted the bracelet around her wrist. "Something weird happened yesterday. Someone at work named Qing Angel knew my identity."

Lillian stopped brushing mid stroke. "But that's impossible. Didn't the Union decide ages ago that the AI training jobs should remain anonymous—that your avatar wouldn't be tied to your identity?"

"They did. At the time, their reasoning was people working blue-collar jobs could be treated with equality in the real world without being associated with their hated service avatars." She tensed, just thinking about being known for her 4.4 service rep avatar. Thankfully, apart from this one exception, no one would ever know about her humiliating time as a service rep.

Lillian resumed brushing her hair again. "But that was before enhancements."

"Exactly. So now, with Gene-IQ's software, the identity connection is irrelevant. I mean, one scan of a person with your retina, and you know exactly someone's enhancements."

"The union's privacy law is just one of the many antiquated laws that hasn't kept up with the pace of technological advancements. I get that. But that's why Mom and Dad purchased Gene-IQ's deluxe software." Lillian tapped her temple next to her eye. "So that we could render Gene-IQs scanning abilities void and keep you safe."

"Right. So, if Angel was able to somehow hack the deluxe software to find my identity, that means she also knows I'm a Natural." Urban plunked back onto the bed.

Lillian put her brush down and began patting her face with moisturizer. "But the deluxe software was tested by the Federation's top cybersecurity experts. No one could hack it. It doesn't make sense that someone was able to find out your name." She was silent a moment. "So, are you going to tell Mom and Dad?"

"No thank you, I choose life." Urban made a face. "I mean, they already installed SCA. If they find out about this, they'll probably assign a robo-nanny or security detail to follow me around."

Lillian turned and looked at her. "Let me know if anything happens like that again, okay? And if it gets worse, I think you should tell them. They care about you."

Urban wanted to laugh. Their parents cared about Lillian, because she was a part of their perfect plan, not to mention Enhanced. But Urban? She wasn't even supposed to be here.

URBAN CLIMBED OUT OF THE CAR AS THE DOOR lifted skyward. She pulled out two bursting suitcases from the trunk and, with a purse that kept slipping off her shoulder, made her way onto the curb.

She'd envisioned herself cruising up to campus on her motorcycle, pulling off her helmet, hair blowing in the wind, and striding confidently up to registration. But she decided against that when she realized it would mean another trip to grab all her stuff. Instead, she'd opted for Dad's new smart car, the Wasp G9. She would call for her motorcycle later.

Lillian had wanted to come, but she had the Inventor's fourth year orientation. Urban hadn't bothered asking Lucas. Or Mother and Father. She'd rather go it alone than have them here.

A rush of excitement washed over her. The absence of her hovering mother gave her a renewed sense of freedom.

Urban approached a transparent set of stairs that displayed green grass below. She climbed up toward a silver building with leviathan-sized windows and impossible jutting angles that hung out over the street without any support.

In the corner of her retina display, data about the building scrolled past.

<PKU Academic Building. Sosh: 75. Average number of visitors per year 557,000 . . .>

Urban ignored the stats.

Projected 3D figures clad in red armor guarded the stairs on either side. Urban's eyes widened. She recognized them at once as the Dragon players. Each one was a Gene Pool Lead for the PKU team in the AI Games.

She passed a guy with head lowered, and eyes staring into what felt like Urban's soul. Urban shuddered and turned away from the Inceptor projection.

Then she passed the Super GP lead, who had a tough and fierce beauty about her. She stood in a fight stance and was at least three feet taller than Urban. Her arms crossed over her leather jacket, and her studded combat boots were three times the normal size.

Urban blinked, activating the GP lead's stats. Impressive victories and several clips from a highlights reel played in the corner of Urban's retina display.

Next, an Aqua stood with cascading locks of hair billowing around him as if he were underwater. His charming smile had several students drawing closer to take selfies. A girl squealed when his avatar blew bubbles and winked.

Urban ignored them as she climbed the last few stairs. At the top, a giant 3D banner wrapped around the entrance to the building: "Do you have what it takes to make the Asian Federation's most elite team?"

Inside the building, everything was marble, from the floors to the giant columns that rose to the ceilings far above. Urban wondered if it was designed with Supers in mind. She felt hopelessly small and out of place in it. None of the other students seemed to care though, and Urban focused her attention on them as she got in line.

The girl before her had huge, doll-like eyes, shiny ponytails, and fluffy cat ears poking out from under waves of thick silver hair.

Using her retina display and Gene IQ's software, Urban scanned her enhancements. Gene IQ identified the girl as having Artisan enhancements as well as several smaller ones. Jealousy welled within Urban.

In front of her stood a guy with green scales for skin and beautiful translucent wings that looked like a dragonfly's. When she tried to scan him, she received an error message. He had paid for privacy mode, same as her parents had. Urban wondered what his reasoning was. If she had enhancements, she'd be flaunting them right now, not hiding them.

An uncomfortable tickling sensation in her throat made her stop abruptly. She had the urge to cough but held it in. *Please don't be my asthma flaring up. Please. Not now.*

Her asthma made at least a yearly appearance. Naturally, it always came at the worst times possible.

The itching in her throat became nearly unbearable.

But she couldn't hold it in any longer. Urban let out a squeaky cough, muffling it as much as possible in the crook of her arm.

Relief flooded her lungs as the itch dissipated. *It's not an asthma attack. I'm fine.*

Urban returned her attention to the dragonfly-like boy as he stepped into a see-through tube with reinforced metal cylinders. The doors closed behind him. A machine beeped and then he stepped back out again. A screen above him flashed green for "harmless enhancements."

The next guy in line looked normal enough except for his obsidian eyes with no white in them. He stepped into the scanner. A moment later, he stepped out, and the screen flashed red.

"A general reminder to all students," a robotic voice said pleasantly over the intercom. "Any students with lethal enhancements are not permitted to use those enhancements on campus. Breaking this rule will result in severe disciplinary action. Thank you."

Her virtual welcome packet had stated all students with lethal enhancements were required to declare them so teachers could be notified. Whatever dangerous ones this guy had would be going on a list to each of his professors.

Urban fingered her fake nail and swallowed as she stepped up to the scanner. Sucking in a breath, she climbed in. The door shut behind her with a smooth click.

A moment of silence.

Urban's chest heaved up and down with her rapid breathing.

What if Father's programming goes wrong? What if it doesn't pick up Lucas's enhancements?

Several students in line watched her. What did they see? Was the scanner about to expose her?

Then, with a beep, the screen above her flashed green.

It worked!

Still stunned, she found herself walking out.

Her tatt vibrated as a bot scanned it. "Your student ID is 1009847633. You are now registered at Peking University. Your tatt has been imprinted with a student activation code that will allow you access to all our finest amenities. To complete registration, please log into QuanNao with your new student ID and select your classes."

Elation filled her. She was now officially a part of the class of 2124.

Using her retina display, she logged in with her new student ID as she walked out of the building, impressed by how easy registration was for an unspecified track like hers. Her advisory-bot suggested all the general education courses, so her schedule consisted of AI Foundations, Crypto Currencies, Genetic Engineering, Programming, and one elective. Biopsychology was the only upper-year class she was taking.

None of the classes came as a surprise, since Mother had researched it all ahead of time and insisted her elective be jiujitsu. So, despite her advisory-bot suggesting she take

Genome Editing Technologies as her elective, Urban found herself with Jiujitsu on her schedule.

And an awful schedule it was. She had 0800 classes every morning, and the rest of the classes were spread out just enough to take up all of her Mondays, Wednesdays, and Fridays. Tuesdays and Thursdays were the only days with breaks in between classes. *Why couldn't I have gone to an online university so I could sleep in and attend virtual classes whenever I wanted?*

But Urban knew that virtual degrees, while fairly comparable, wouldn't help her build a network that would give her access to KOLs, and thus, boost her sosh.

Her class schedule set, Urban searched for her dorm. Pulling her levitating suitcases alongside her, she headed toward the south side of campus.

She got the feeling someone was observing her. Discretely, she surveyed her surroundings. The street was wide and devoid of cars but filled with students on hoverboards. The magnetic strips in the road that supported them were only found in certain parts of the city and on campus.

No one seemed to be watching her.

A thunderous roar vibrated through her chest. Urban clamped her hands over her ears as she turned in search of the noise.

A girl with massive wings dive-bombed a skinny guy with peach fuzz and the noise stopped.

"That should teach you to shut up." The girl flew away, leaving the guy splayed on the ground, swearing.

Urban's stomach twisted. *I'll just have to fit in.*

She studied the other students around her. Her retina display showed those nearby had soshs ranging from the low 60s to the mid-80s—pretty high scores for students. Then again, everyone here was either ridiculously smart, fabulously well networked, or wealthy. A few had no sosh at all, either because they weren't eighteen yet, or because they'd opted for privacy mode. Their scores would only become visible to individuals they linked with.

A tingling sensation crept up Urban's spine. Someone *was* watching her. This time, she was sure of it.

Do I look like a Natural? Does someone suspect?

She turned in a circle. Students flew past her on hoverboards or stood talking and laughing, but nothing appeared out of the ordinary.

I'm just overreacting.

She shifted her attention to the buildings she passed, all designed to resemble Ancient China with its sloping brown-tiled roofs and brightly painted, intricate blue-and-green walls beneath. Vividly colored seals and patterned bars surrounded the windows. Each doorway contained a large red door, flanked by pillars.

It reminded Urban of one of her favorite places in New Beijing, the Hutongs. Only the campus was in much better condition, and it was clearly modeled after an ancient emperor's palace rather than a commoner's dwelling.

Pulling up her retina map, she enabled augmented navigation. Virtual 3D arrows pulsed in the street, meshing with her real-time view, and pointing out the fastest path. The timer noted that at her current speed she'd arrive at 0914.

Two and a half minutes later, her retina display flashed an update.

<Now arriving at the Cheng Dormitory for Peking University first-year students. Sosh: 50.>

This was it, her new home. Urban stopped in front of a huge building, black as space and covered in reflective windows. It looked like a giant mountain had climbed up out of the ground in the middle of campus. It had to be at least a hundred stories high, and the odd hole through the center of it for *feng shui* purposes made it look like it had been drilled through.

<Please continue inside for registration.>

Urban switched off the maps view as she headed for the large entryway.

Inside, the air was cool, fresh, and smelled like mint and citrus. Several hovering bots pointed her to screens with lines of students. As she made her way toward the line, she noticed a shadow in her periphery.

Snapping her head toward it, she saw a pristine and shiny bamboo floor. She kept her eyes on the spot but, not seeing anything, finally turned away. Had she imagined it?

A chill settled over her.

After registering for housing, she made her way alone toward the elevators. While she stared at her reflection in the elevator doors, waiting for it to arrive, the hairs on the back of her arm raised.

Something began to materialize behind her, and she gasped.

A masked figure flickered into view in the elevator door reflection.

Urban did a double take. All she could see was his head and part of his torso. The rest of him must have Camo abilities because she couldn't see any of his limbs. The part that alarmed her, though, was the black XR mask he wore that concealed his entire face.

While XR masks were allowed in XRD, the Asian Federation couldn't use facial recognition software to track the individuals while they were worn. Thus, XR masks were illegal outside of the domes.

Urban turned around but saw no one behind her. Glancing back at the reflection in the door revealed it, too, was empty.

The masked figure had vanished.

I'M BEING FOLLOWED. WHY?

Ding!

The elevator arrived, and Urban ran inside. She pressed the 42nd floor, then hit the close button multiple times. With agonizing slowness, the door shut.

Why would anyone follow me? She thought of Angel's warning. *Is it her? Or does she know something I don't?*

Urban slumped against the wall as the elevator shot upward. It wasn't until it dinged again and slowed at her floor, that her heartbeat calmed.

Glancing behind her, Urban quickly made her way toward the west wing.

"4200, 4201," she read out loud as she walked down the tiled hallway. "Aha! 4202."

With a swipe of her tatt, the door slid back. Urban quickly entered and locked the door behind her. She relaxed a little and took in her new surroundings.

The room was clean and smelled of paint. An air purifier in the corner filtered out the remaining fumes.

It was a room no bigger than her one back home but housed four girls instead of one. There was a window at the far side with a love seat in front of it, a sink and a mirror next to the door, one closet, a tiny foldout table, and two bunk beds lining either side of the wall.

Three of the beds had blankets, pillows, and suitcases stored above or below them. The walls next to them were already plastered with Key Opinion Leader posters.

She eyed the only free bed left on the bottom bunk near the door. "Convert to bed," she instructed one of her suitcases. In an instant, it flipped inside out, regurgitating its contents onto her bed. The edges of her blanket, which contained programmed magnets, creeped across the bed where they secured themselves against the metallic bed poles.

She pulled out two of her paintings and a few photos from her suitcase and put them on the wall. Unpacking her art supplies, she placed them carefully next to the window, and an overwhelming urge swept through her.

Checking the time, she took out a weasel-hair brush and began painting the view from her dorm window. As colors slowly took shape on the paper, her heart lifted. This new life of hers was going to be okay. She just had to find a way to be an Artisan.

An hour passed before she completed the painting. She put her brush and paints away and went back to unpacking. She eyed her newly decorated wall. It was missing something. She pulled out the art museum ticket from Everest and hung that up too.

Wondering what he was up to, she was about to video him when two girls barged into the room, talking and laughing. They stopped abruptly upon noticing Urban.

"Well, who's this?" the thinner girl asked. She was tall, with sharp facial features, thick eyeliner, and long dark hair. She wore a trendy metallic dress that clung to her perfectly proportioned body. Urban wondered what enhancements she might have hidden behind her golden eyes. "I'm Li Blossom," she added.

Scanning Blossom with Gene-IQ's software, Urban found the girl's enhancements were on privacy mode. Urban straightened.

"I'm Urban."

"And your surname?" asked the other girl, pushing her way past Blossom. Her enhancements were obvious. The physical ones, anyway.

She had a round face with clear white skin, plump cheeks, enormous eyes, and a soft smile. Urban fought the urge to pinch those cheeks. The girl's facial features were modified to evoke the same emotions from viewers as staring at a puppy or baby panda. The round helpless eyes, the soft nose—all of it a perfect mind trick.

Using Gene-IQ, Urban saw the girl also had a brain enhancement allowing for increased dexterity and fast response times. She wondered why her roommate needed them.

"What's your surname?" the girl repeated impatiently.

Urban would normally be annoyed by the girl's rudeness, but she wasn't. Cute enhancements were the worst.

"Lee. Byronne is my father. And you are?"

The girl ignored the question. "Like the Lee who designed the underwater chain of shopping centers and housing units?"

Urban nodded, still fighting the urge to pinch those cheeks.

Panda girl pursed her lips. "You're so skinny."

"My parents have eclectic taste."

"And I thought my parents were weird," Panda girl said. "I'm Xiao Hazel."

It was time to show Hazel two could play at this game. "Which Xiao?" Urban asked with a yawn, even though her palms were sweating.

"Xiao Yang is my father. He's the industrial engineer who owns Park Way and the luxury hotel chains of XiaoYang, Inc."

"Are you a single child?" Blossom wanted to know, still looking unconvinced that Urban was someone worth their time.

"I wish," Urban replied lightly. "Two siblings. You?"

"Wow! You have two siblings!" Hazel exclaimed. "Your family must own a fortune."

Blossom's head nodded slowly in approval. "I have a brother. Hazel here has a sister. What do you do in your spare time?"

What is this? Twenty questions? But Urban smiled patiently. "I enjoy painting, studying ancient architecture," she thought quickly, "and have recently enrolled in a martial arts course."

"Architecture?" Hazel nearly snorted.

Blossom ignored her friend. "Martial arts, you say?"

"Jiujitsu."

"That's interesting." Blossom cocked her head. "There's a KOL party tonight. We have an extra invite . . . do you want to come with us?"

Excitement shot through Urban's veins. "Sounds fun."

"Here, let's link," Blossom said, extending her wrist toward Urban. "That way we can meet up later."

Urban touched Blossom's wrist with her own and saw their tatts light up in gold.

Hazel linked with Urban too.

Now that they were linked, in the corner of her retina display, Blossom and Hazel's profiles appeared. Urban discretely pulled up her roommates' landings.

Hazel's avatar was an adorable racoon with giant innocent eyes. She had no sosh yet since she was seventeen. Her highest key word was *fashion*.

She was followed by many fashion-industry influencers, along with a few media sources. She'd even published several videos of her own. A quick scan of her check-ins showed her attendance at all the latest fashion events across the globe. There were also several promotions to what seemed to be her own clothing line featuring vintage formfitting *qipao* dresses. There wasn't any info as to her other enhancements on her landing.

Urban expected the same sort of landing for Blossom but was surprised. Blossom looked very much like her real self only older, wiser, and sterner. There were very few photos of her or her avatar, but the few that were displayed were of her holding beakers and wearing goggles. *She must have some sort of brain enhancements.* Her key word was *genomics*—one of the most competitive words to get, since it was always a topic of interest in the Metropolis and among the scientific community.

"Wow, how'd you get a key word like *genomics*?" Urban asked, impressed.

Blossom smiled tightly. "Hard work."

"She's also working on some genetic-engineering research," Hazel gushed. "Once her work is published—"

"My driver is waiting," Blossom cut her off. "We'd better get going."

"*Ai ya* so impatient," Hazel complained. "Your driver is a machine. Don't blame a bot for your lack of patience."

Hazel turned apologetically to Urban. "We've just come here to drop off our shopping bags. But we'll be back." She held up several bags. They were all reusable mesh from *Croix,* the most exclusive athleisure brand in the world. Each purchase probably cost more than an autonomous car.

With their purchases tossed onto their beds, Blossom and Hazel left to do more shopping.

Once they were gone, Urban pulled up her own landing page, wondering what Blossom and Hazel had thought of it. Online, she was a beautiful redhead with bright-blue eyes. It was what she dreamed of looking like. It was nothing like her.

Her top key word was *historical research*, and there were lots of photos of her red-headed avatar posing next to pagodas, decrepit walls, and ancient Asian Federation architecture. Her check-ins included a variety of exclusive opening ceremonies for museums, the reopening of the Terra-Cotta Army, the restoration of the Great Wall, and several other big-name events.

Her own series of vlogs were pretty popular and had been widely shared, some even picked up by a few of the media outlets. Overall, not a bad landing page. Because of it, she was hopeful, come her eighteenth birthday, her sosh would be ranked in the upper 60s.

For now, Urban's stomach growled loudly and refused to be ignored. She changed her retina displays to magenta, making her eyes pop, then pulled her hair into a loose ponytail.

On her way out, she noticed something on the floor. It looked like a badge of some sort.

Urban picked it up, then dropped it as if she'd been burned.

The badge was white with wispy silver letters that spelled *SAS*–Supers Against Soups. Underneath the title, in dark black letters, was the word *member*.

In the story her mother had read to her, the students who had murdered the last Natural at uni had been a part of SAS.

She stared in horror at the badge lying faceup on the ground. Whose badge was it? Was one of her roommates a part of the murderous group?

I'm going to have to be on my guard at all times. Especially when I'm in the dorms.

She considered flushing the awful badge down the toilet but thought better of it. Whoever it belonged to might come looking for it. Better to let them think she hadn't seen it.

Stepping cautiously over it, she made her way to one of the many food courts. Lillian had told her the best one was at the center of a giant underground mall with exclusive access for PKU students. Her retina map led the way.

The center was huge–a labyrinth of restaurants, boutiques, tutoring shops, and XR domes, smelling strongly of cilantro and noodles. Consulting the maps directory, she pulled up all the food options.

There were noodles, pizza, fried jiaozi, traditional Chinese food, burgers, salads, bubble-tea shops . . . basically anything she could possibly want. And for the Enhanced, they could eat all they wanted with no weight gain. Fortunately, Urban had a fast metabolism and didn't have to worry too much about it like some of the other Naturals in the Outskirts.

The place was abuzz with older students, freshly returned from summer break. Urban weaved through them as she followed her retina's augmented navigation. The arrows vanished as she reached a restaurant called Lucky's Dumplings, and she ducked into an entryway with stone dragons guarding it. She served herself fried chicken, steamed buns, and coconut juice before scanning her wrist to pay and grabbing a seat near the corner. From her vantage point, she watched the students.

Several Supers sat at the next table, talking and laughing loudly. Urban found this odd since Supers usually stuck to the north side of town where everything was bigger for them. It was the only part of the city specifically designed with only one enhancement in mind. Though, many of the upper levels of the Metropolis were Flyer friendly as were the underwater facilities—designed with Aquas in mind.

But at school all enhancements coexisted. *No wonder everything is so big.*

The Supers next to her also had wings—a combination Urban had only ever seen in XR. The Asian Federation made having more than one of the major enhancements that granted eligibility to one of the Eight Gene Pools illegal. These students were an exception made by the military.

Urban felt vulnerable sitting by them. One of them could take on *five* Naturals. *What if the "no using enhancement" rules aren't enforced here? What if one of them belongs to SAS? No amount of rolling around on the ground learning "defense" is going to help protect me against someone like that.*

Supers had more than just strength and size going for them. Their resilient bodies could withstand extreme temperatures and take hard hits. They came equipped with night vision, enhanced sense of smell, lightning-fast reflexes, and some microexpression reading.

Basically, all the best enhancements were given to the military. Parents who couldn't afford enhancements got these free if they volunteered their children for thirty years in military service with nothing but room and board paid for. Thus, the military was mostly made up of kids from the Outskirts whose only other option was to be a Natural.

But the Supers next to Urban weren't poorer kids destined to spend their prime years in the military. Standard military enhancements didn't include wings. A quick scan with Gene-IQ showed these Supers had brain enhancements as well. They were bred to be the military strategists and commanders that kept rival federations in check. They could serve of their own free will and get paid handsomely for it.

Urban finished the last of her tasty food and was almost back to the dorms when she got a ping.

[Everest: How are you?]

She wanted to tell him that she was blending in, that so far no one suspected anything. She also wanted to tell him about the hooded figure who had followed her. But she hesitated. What if Angel was still hacking her? What about the SAS member card? Could someone be monitoring her feeds, looking out for Naturals?

She decided it would be best to keep these things to herself until she could see Everest in person. Instead, she sent a generic update.

[Urban: It's beautiful. Roomies seem normal enough. Tonight, I'm going to a party.]

A moment later Everest's face appeared on her retina display in a video message.

[Everest: Hey, that sounds like fun, but ah . . . are you sure a party is a good idea?]

A prick of discomfort crept through her.

[Urban: I have to go to stuff like this to get my sosh up once it's live.]

There, that was believable to anyone potentially hacking her. Even the Enhanced focused on their sosh, and there was nothing suspicious about that. They pinged back and forth until she reached her dorm. Bots were adding the finishing touches to Blossom's and Hazel's makeup as they jammed out to hip-hop.

Hazel noticed Urban. "You're still coming tonight, right? It's going to be so fun!"

"Party starts in the coliseum," Blossom added without turning from the mirror.

Urban blinked. "*The* coliseum? Isn't it closed until tryouts?"

"Not for students. This is like the prelim games." Hazel smacked her lips. "Why do tryouts have to be so far away? I wish I could apply for the team right now. Are you auditioning, Urban?"

"Uh, maybe next year."

"See, Hazel? No one tries out their first year," Blossom admonished. "Usually only fourth years make the team. Anyway, this party's sponsored by the Inceptors, and they get what they want, if you know what I mean."

Urban didn't know what she meant, but she could guess. If the Inceptor House was sponsoring the event, they'd used some heavy influencing skills to get it approved. She thought about her rules from Mother: avoid the Games and avoid Inceptors.

Her heart spasmed at the thought of how dangerous it would be if she encountered more Inceptors. Was it worth the risk?

But if she didn't go, she'd miss out on a prime opportunity to meet top influencers. To avoid being discovered, she had to get a high sosh, and she wasn't going to do that if she passed over the best, and potentially only, invite she got.

Curfew didn't officially kick in until tomorrow, when school officially started. SCA would have no reason to alert Mother. She'd never know.

"Give me your dress for the after-party," Blossom said to her. "It's way too fancy for the Games, and I'll have my driver bring it when he comes to pick us up."

Urban nodded. "Sounds like a plan."

Games, here I come.

09

COLISEUM

MAJESTIC BONE-WHITE PILLARS AND STONE walls rose into the sky. It had originally been designed to be a replica of the Roman Colosseum, but the Federation had outdone the Romans. The PKU Coliseum was twice the size of the original and perfectly restored. Since it was built in the last century, it was also equipped with all the latest tech.

<Now arriving at Peking Coliseum. Sosh: 91.> Urban's retina display informed her.

She had seen it on her vid feed every year as she followed the Games. But, in person, the coliseum seemed even bigger than she'd imagined.

"Stop gawking like first years," Blossom hissed at Urban and Hazel before zigzagging skillfully through the crowd. Urban and Hazel followed close behind, still sneaking furtive glances at the massive structure.

As they approached the huge arched entryway, the crowd began to funnel into narrow lines. Urban's tatt vibrated as she passed the scanner, then she was inside the building.

They found seats and waited for the rest of the spectators to file in. It didn't take long until the lights dimmed. A gust of cool air howled through the room. The crowd applauded in excitement. The disjointed clapping synced into one thunderous rhythm.

With a swirl of mist, a hole in the iron-gray smart floor opened, and a woman on a platform came spiraling upward. Lights of all colors played across the coliseum as the platform rose higher.

"Good evening!" The woman wore a dazzling golden gown, her black hair pinned up by a traditional silver brooch that resembled a delicate butterfly. A matching silver pin glowed with jewels.

"It's her! It's Hong!" Hazel shouted in delight.

Another disapproving glare from Blossom, but Hazel didn't notice.

"Welcome, students of Peking University!"

The stadium went wild.

"Let's have a little fun tonight, shall we? Awaken Samson!"

Amber light bathed the coliseum.

"For you first year students, our homegrown AI, Samson, is designed specifically for the Games," Hong announced. "Few universities can rival Samson or our talented team. The Dragons are currently the Global Games Champions eight years running."

The crowd roared. Some showed their school pride by raising their left arms in salute, tatts glowing red. Urban wondered how they changed their tatt color like that and made a note to ask Lillian later.

Hong waited for the noise to calm down. "Now, what to select? Should we enable training mode?"

There were several *boos* from the audience.

"Or how about entertainment mode?"

The crowd jostled and roared at this.

"What's the difference?" Urban asked.

Hazel shrugged, but Blossom leaned over. "Entertainment mode is what you see on the vid feeds. Samson detects the participants' enhancements and chooses courses, tasks, and obstacles that play to those enhancements. If someone is strong, they'll be tested in strength. If they're smart, they'll be given a challenging puzzle."

"What's training mode then?" Urban shouted over the deafening roar.

"That's only for practice. It's where Samson pits the participants against obstacles that they're weak in. For example, someone with strength will be given a mental problem to solve. And someone smart, a physical challenge. It's how the team actually trains most of the time. It has a lot more people failing and instantly ending the game."

Urban nodded, her eyes glued to the stage. *If only I had been Enhanced, then I could try out for the Games.*

"Today," Hong's voice was declaring, "is a special day. It's the back-to-school party!"

More cheering from the crowd.

"Let's bring out a lead from each gene pool on the team. Starting with . . ." she waited until the crowd grew silent before announcing, "Flyers!"

The cheering resumed, and the sound of wind filled the air as all the Flyers in the stadium, in unison, beat their wings. A man clothed in sky blue traditional *hanfu* robes flew over the crowd to land on the stage.

When the beating of wings subsided, Hong continued, "Next we have Inventors!"

A man with a pompadour haircut and wearing stained silver robes, stood only a few rows down from Urban. Several students shrieked as what appeared to be mini mechanical doll arms lifted him onto the path and carried him to the stage.

Urban noticed the Inventor was the same subtype as her father and sister. She wondered if the team had any of the mental type—the philosophers, researchers, and great thinkers of their time.

"That's not creepy at all," Hong said with a shake of her head. "Moving on before I have nightmares, Camos!"

The platform began to shimmer and change colors. Suddenly, a woman appeared directly beside Hong, who jumped in surprise.

The crowd laughed as the woman clothed in a camouflage-green *qipao* bowed.

Hong looked around the mini raised platform. "How . . . how are you going to get down from—"

Before she could finish, the Camo disappeared.

A few seconds later she reappeared standing next to the Flyer and Inventor on the stage below. The Camos all cheered.

"And I specifically had this platform built to stay out of the way." Hong flashed a smile. "Next up, and I think I'm safe this time, we have Artisans!"

Confetti showered down, and brightly colored streamers fell from the ceiling. Hong looked up in dismay. "That's not on the eco-approved list."

The Artisans in the crowd whipped out all sorts of musical instruments and began playing. A woman cloaked in elegant orange robes danced her way gracefully onto the stage to the beat of the music. Upon reaching her spot next to the others, the music stopped.

"Next we have Aquas!"

A portion of the arena floor turned into a translucent bowl. A waterfall appeared from the roof, pouring down into the arena.

The crowd gasped as a man fell over the waterfall. He dove into the pool, then sank to the base of the bowl, where he stood facing the crowd. The tips of his cobalt-blue robe undulated around him like the arms of a sea creature. Urban watched the Aqua and shivered, reminded of her brother.

The man let out a roar that cracked the giant bowl into a thousand spider webs, which exploded into a million pieces, splashing some of the students.

"And that is one of the many reasons you should never sit in the front," Hong said with a laugh as students scattered to avoid getting wet.

"Next, Givers!"

The crowd fell silent.

"I said, Givers!"

Still nothing.

"I do believe we have a Giver representative for the Games today?" Hong turned around, searching for the missing Giver.

There was a commotion near the middle of the coliseum, and Urban saw someone clothed in silken purple robes making her way toward the front. She stopped at a recycling bin where she dumped a bunch of paper towels. "Sorry, just helping clean up a mess." She hurriedly made her way to the stage, nearly tripping twice before reaching it.

The crowd laughed.

"Adorable." Hong's tone was unamused.

"Amazing how these bumbling absent-minded folk win so many games." She looked up, eyes exaggeratedly wide. "Whoops, was that out loud?"

The crowd laughed again. But it was a well-known fact Givers won nearly half of the Games. Their brains had specifically been enhanced to experience greater empathy, which would allow them to be the best life coaches, mentors, and caretakers. An unintended side effect of this enhancement was that their frontal lobe, which allowed for creative, out-of-the-box thinking, was more developed. This out-of-the-box thinking was the hardest for the AI to predict and thus win against.

"And next we have . . . Supers!"

All the biggest students cheered and pumped their meaty fists in the air. A huge woman in the front row, clad in red, leaped over several rows to arrive on the stage. She landed with an earth-shaking *thump*. The Supers went wild.

"And last but not least, the ones who allowed for all of this to happen—"

The mic cut out.

A man near the front, with shaggy blond hair and wearing white robes, stood. "Inceptors!" he finished for Hong.

The crowd cheered.

The man strode confidently toward the stage.

Hong's mouth moved, but her microphone was still disabled. She fiddled with it, frowning.

"Welcome class of 2124," the Inceptor said to the crowd in a slightly accented voice. "No need to be nervous. This has all been approved by the school board. Relax, Hong, I know you're stressed, but don't let it get to you. What is it? You can tell me. Is it graduating next year? Pressure from your parents? Your boyfriend? Ah . . . so it's your man." The Inceptor nodded knowingly.

Hong's face grew redder by the minute.

"Yes, rumor has it you two have been dating for a while now. Could it be you're having doubts? No, that certainly isn't it. Or could it be . . . No, it is! He's going to propose soon? No need to worry, darling. It won't be tonight."

The crowd hooted.

"By the way, your mic should be working again," the Inceptor said with a smug smile.

Hong covered her face with her hands. "Get out of my head!"

"Darling, I'm just helping you relax. I told you, he won't be popping the question tonight."

"I don't get paid enough for this," Hong muttered. The Inceptor walked haughtily to the other Gene Pool Leads.

Hong plastered on a big smile. "Enough of my personal life! Back to the real reason we're all here. Let the fun begin!"

Everyone jumped to their feet and cheered.

"For tonight's games, we have a team challenge," Hong announced. Several flying bots distributed red armor suits and helmets to each of the eight students. The suits fit snugly over each contestant's silk robe. Then they donned their helmets, which displayed the hammer and sickle emblazoned in gold.

An impressive group. While Urban hadn't watched any of the recent Games, she didn't remember the last team being this formidable. Or maybe they just looked more intimidating in person than on the feeds.

Hong stretched out her arms. "Let the AI Exhibition Game begin!"

THE CROWD CHEERED AS HONG'S PLATFORM spiraled upward into the air far above the transforming arena. Hundreds of metal squares lifted from the flat surface and disappeared, then reappeared at different angles, creating hills and cliffs. Each tile held a piece of the landscape, some had rocks, others grass, shrubbery, or even huge, leafy trees. Still others disappeared entirely, leaving a gap in the platform, which filled quickly with cobalt-blue water. At any given time, the coliseum had hundreds of different arena settings ready to go. It was rumored PKU kept over a thousand bots, which tended to the plant and wildlife necessary for each arena set.

Soon, the arena resembled a wooded forest, with several cliffs, next to a small lake. At the top of a hill, a *hongbao* floated midair. It looked exactly like the red envelopes Urban received every Lunar New Year with money in them. The only difference was this *hongbao* pulsed with light.

"Dragons, what's the plan?" asked the Inventor. His voice amplified over the speaker, and a closeup of his face popped onto Urban's retina display. Urban watched both the tiny figure in the distance of the arena and the closeup in her retina display simultaneously.

"I'll scout the water for clues," the Aqua said, taking off at a sprint toward the deep body of water.

"Everyone else, this way," the Inceptor took charge. The rest walked quickly toward the hill. At the top, the Inceptor reached for the *hongbao*, but an invisible force field stopped him.

"Password needed," a robotic voice intoned. "They look like twin brothers, both sturdy and tall. They work together and go everywhere together. But they only go near solid food and do not care for soup. Who are they?"

The Super sat down. "I hate riddles."

"Hey, guys!" the Aqua yelled from the edge of the pool. "There's another *hongbao* at the bottom of this. I need some help getting it. Flyer, Camo, you free?"

The Flyer and Camo trotted over to him while the rest of the group tried to work out the riddle.

Urban zoomed her augmented feed to the Aqua, Flyer, and Camo section of the arena.

"So, the good news is I can see the *hongbao*," the Aqua was saying.

"And the bad news?" the Flyer asked.

"There's some sort of sea creature guarding it."

The Flyer ruffled his wings. "And you need us . . . why?"

"As bait. And to buy me time."

"Which am I?" inquired the Camo.

"Time." The Aqua turned to the Flyer. "How would you like to be bait?"

"Are you sure whatever is down there will go for something out of the water?"

"Only one way to find out," came the reply.

Hong hovered above the group on a silver platform barely large enough for her feet. "Seems like the riddle still has not been cracked and things are about to get dicey for our contestants," she narrated with a mischievous smile.

Urban found herself leaning in, even though she was mostly

watching on her retina display. It looked just like it always did back home, but she still found it hard to believe she was actually sitting in the coliseum.

A roar sounded from the other side of the arena. A huge saber-toothed tiger padded out of the thick wooded trees. Then another emerged, and another, until they filled the whole forest.

"Well that's a new one," Urban remarked.

"It's not nearly as terrifying as last year's giant boa constrictors." Hazel shuddered.

"Wonder how long it took them to recreate those saber-tooth tigers using their Nucleic Acid Sequences Builder?" Blossom mused. "Genetic engineering of extinct creatures takes years and millions of dollars. I wonder who sponsored the funding."

Urban turned to her. *Maybe I could get her to tell me more about genomics. It might have implications for Naturals. I have to be careful not to ask too many questions though, or she might become suspicions.* "Are you involved with any of the genetic-engineering societies?"

Blossom eyed her a moment. "No." She turned back to the arena, making it apparent she didn't want to continue the conversation.

"Look!" Hazel pointed excitedly. "Someone's in trouble."

One of the saber-toothed tigers locked eyes on the Super, snarled, and bounded toward her. Behind the tiger, several more stepped out from the forest.

"Better hurry your smart brains up," the Super said, stepping away from the group. She picked up a log and held it ready like a baseball bat.

The Super swung her log at the first saber-toothed tiger. The huge creature went hurtling into the thickets, its body bent in two, before rolling to a stop.

Another tiger leaped onto the Super before she kicked it away. Her damage counter dropped a fraction.

At the water's edge, the giant glass wall holding the water

served as both a barrier between the arena and the student body, while also allowing spectators to see inside the lake.

The Flyer hovered low over the water, while the Aqua slinked stealthily into the lake.

"I don't think this is working," the Flyer shouted.

Something caught Urban's eye at the bottom of the pool. It seemed the entire foundation had collapsed. Or was moving . . .

"It's coming!" the Aqua yelled as he resurfaced. "Fly up! Fly up!" The Aqua ducked back underwater and swam down.

The Camo disappeared, blending into her surroundings.

"An excellent diversion, but it might come at the cost of the Flyer," Hong commented over the speakers.

The Flyer started flapping his wings furiously to gain altitude.

What looked like a giant alligator with fins swam upward toward him. The creature broke the surface with jaws snapping, barely missing the Flyer. It fell back into the water with a huge splash that drenched a good quarter of the stadium. But at the bottom of the pool, the Aqua grabbed a hold of the *hongbao*.

"He's got it!" Hong cheered. "But will he get away in time?"

The crowd watched as the creature changed courses. It swam furiously toward the Aqua, who was a blur of cobalt blue shooting upward.

He burst from the surface, and the Flyer snatched him up. The Flyer strained to lift them both into the air and wasn't going to get away fast enough.

The crowd could hear Hong take in a tense breath.

Right then, the Camo reappeared. Half of her anyway, since part of her body was still blended into the water. Her chest had a giant white circle with a smaller black circle inside of it. It resembled a giant eye.

The sea creature whipped its head around to stare at the peculiar sight and stopped.

The giant eye disappeared as the creature snapped its jaw several times in various directions, trying to find the Camo.

Realizing it had been a distraction, the creature returned its climb to the surface but the Flyer and Aqua were already out of reach.

"And they escape!" Hong said excitedly. "A daring and brilliant plan by the Aqua, Flyer, and Camo!"

"So long, ol' pal!" The Aqua waved as the sea creature sank back into the miry depths. A moment later, the drenched Camo joined them on shore.

"Not bad," the Flyer said to her.

She scowled. "I'm never doing that again."

The Aqua laughed as he opened the *hongbao* and pulled out two slips of paper. "Only open the remaining note with an Inventor," he read. He stuffed it into his suit, and they headed toward the others.

A growing pile of injured or stunned saber-toothed tigers surrounded the Super. Despite her victories, she was slowly being overrun. The Flyer instantly took off into the sky and began dive-bombing them and pummeling them with rocks.

Soon other tigers started falling here and there by an invisible force. As one tiger yelped and snarled, the Camo blinked into sight for a moment before blending in with her surroundings again.

The Aqua joined the crew at the top of the hill, where an argument had broken out.

"It seems like no one is able to solve the riddle, and time's running out," Hong informed the crowd.

The contestants stopped arguing and looked up at Hong.

"What does she mean time's running out?" the Artisan asked.

In response, there was a low roar, and a new wave of saber-toothed tigers emerged from the forest.

"Hey, guys," the Super greeted them. "I hope you've cracked the code." She threw down her stick and began to run. "There's too many for me to fight. Run!"

The Giver had her hands out. "Wait! I almost have it!"

"No time. Run!" the Inceptor commanded.

The Giver started, then tripped and fell. The nearest tiger headed toward her soundlessly, powerful muscles rippling with each bound.

"And we have someone down!" Hong shouted.

The Super turned and spotted the Giver. "Save her!" she bellowed. "We need her to answer that riddle!"

The Flyer swooped out of the sky and grabbed the Giver.

As he was taking off, the nearest tiger leaped into the air and bit the Flyer's foot.

"The Flyer must be thanking his lucky stars for his suit," Hong commented as the Flyer let out a yell. "He'd have a broken foot right now otherwise."

The tiger dangled in midair like a giant cat holding onto a chew toy. Slowly, the Flyer and his burden began sinking back to the ground.

With a shout, the Flyer used all his remaining power to launch the Giver into the air, but was immediately dragged down and surrounded by tigers. His damage counter dropped into the red zone as it dipped into the low thirties. It stopped at zero. There was a flash of sky-blue light which scattered the tigers, and then the ground opened and swallowed him.

"And the Flyer is out!" Hong shouted.

Urban let out a pent-up breath. Even though she knew waiting beneath the arena was a squad of Beijing's top physicians and medbots, injuries were still common, and every once in a while, fatal.

The Super caught the Giver and began running. The group of survivors made their way to the other side of the forest, and they frantically climbed up one of the enhanced giant pine trees.

"*Jiayou*! You can do it!" someone in the crowd shouted. It quickly caught on.

Soon the whole coliseum was chanting the encouraging phrase. "*Jiayou*! *Jiayou*!"

Only the Artisan, Inventor, and Aqua were in the tree as the first of the tigers arrived. The Super was still at the base, giving the Inceptor a boost.

Right as the beast entered attacking range, the Aqua roared. An ear-splitting screech filled the stadium. Urban covered her ears in pain.

The Super used the distraction to help both the Inceptor and Giver up.

"Whoever designed an Aqua's genetics should have thought through what their roar would sound like above water," Hong said, lifting her own hands off her ears. "Who cares if it enables them to communicate with sea creatures!"

When the roar ended, the tiger lunged. The Super leaped into the tree and pulled herself out of reach. "Everyone here?" she asked.

"We lost the Flyer and who knows where the Camo went." The Inventor smoothed back his pompadour haircut.

"She'll be fine. Anyone have a plan?"

The entire hill with the *hongbao* was surrounded by prowling tigers.

"Without the Flyer, getting the second *hongbao* just got much more interesting," Hong said.

"Gah, she's annoying." The Camo suddenly appeared on the tree.

The Inceptor almost fell off in surprise. "You're one to talk."

The audience laughed.

"I have the answer to the riddle!" The Giver announced excitedly. "Listen! They go everywhere together and stay away from soup. The answer is chopsticks." No sooner had he said the words than the force field around the floating *hongbao* vanished.

"Great. Now we only have an ambush of saber-tooth tigers to deal with," the Inceptor said sarcastically.

"Let's at least open up the *hongbao*." The Aqua handed it over. "Only to be opened by an Inventor apparently."

The Inventor took the red envelop and unsealed it gingerly. "Tools for your pleasure," he read out loud. He looked back in the envelope but, apparently seeing nothing, shrugged.

Right then, one of the ground tiles retracted, allowing a hoverbot to come flying out. It towed a gift-wrapped box and set it down in the tree before flying away.

The Inventor tore away the wrapping, then gasped. "Tools!" He fingered the long metallic poles, screws, and hammers with admiration.

"Stop drooling and build this . . . this . . . whatever *this* is supposed to be," the Super said. "What exactly is it?"

The Inventor was already hard at work and didn't respond.

Quite some time passed. Normally, it would have been filled with ads, but since this wasn't an official Game, Urban watched the tigers yawn and nap, and then she studied the restless crowds to pass the time.

Finally, the Inventor was done. "And here we have it!"

"Is that what I think it is?" The Giver raised her brow.

"If you're thinking razor-plated stilts, then yes!"

The Super's arms crossed over her chest. "And that's supposed to help us . . . how?"

"Don't you see?" the Aqua said wryly, "now we can beat back a hundred saber-tooth tigers while walking!"

"You're not being very helpful." The Giver tilted her head. "I think this has something to do with the Artisan. Her skills haven't been used yet."

"Neither have the Inceptor's," the Inventor pointed out.

The Giver shook her head. "Think about how all our gifts come together, as a team. These stilts are clearly meant to be used by someone. I don't know about you all, but I don't have the dexterity to stay on those things while surrounded by a pack of tigers. But Artisans are graceful and agile, and if I had to put my money on someone surviving a go on those, I'd put it on our Artisan friend here."

The Artisan raised her brow at this. "So, what's the plan? I dance right over to the *hongbao* on a pair of stilts, pick it up, and then get back on the stilts, all while somehow not being eaten by a bunch of tigers?"

"Close," the Giver replied cheerfully. "We still need several others. This is a team sport." Her eyes flitted over each person on the tree, then stopped at the Camo. "You're up. I think the tigers are programed to guard the hill where the *hongbao* is but not the *hongbao* itself. If our Artisan friend here can kick the *hongbao* off the hill then continue to distract the tigers, can you get the *hongbao*?"

The Camo nodded. "I think so."

"Add the Super and the Aqua into the mix for extra cover, and we'll be set."

"What about me?" Disappointment laced the Inceptor's words.

"Your time will come."

The Artisan fumbled with the stilts. "How do you use these confounded things? Why are there four of them?"

"These two are for your legs," the Inventor explained, "and these are for your arms. You use them to keep balance or you can walk on all fours if it's easier."

She clapped her hands. "Let's get this dance party started." She glanced at the stilts. "This may actually be the craziest thing I've ever done. And that's saying something."

"Go get 'em!" The Giver encouraged the Artisan. The Camo vanished, while the Super and Aqua stood tense and ready.

Several tigers paced quietly, and some had dozed off. At the sound of the Artisan hitting the ground, their ears perked up, and they stared. The Artisan took one wobbly step and then another.

Some of the tigers began standing, several growled.

The Artisan kept walking, each step a little less shaky.

"Don't forget to use your hand poles for balance," the Inventor called out.

With a roar, the first saber-tooth tiger bounded toward the

Artisan. The tiger ran up to her and bit into the pole. The Artisan yelled in panic as she began to fall. Quickly, using her hand poles, she steadied herself and remained upright.

The saber tooth yelped and backed away, a trail of blood forming around its mouth. Then the next tiger approached, and the next. The Artisan swayed dangerously but kept going, even as several more attacked. She tried to steady herself while simultaneously swiping at a few of them with her free pole.

Slowly, she made her way up to the hill, closing in on the *hongbao* when two tigers leaped at once, crashing into her mid-step. The weight was too much and she toppled backward.

With a yell, she extended the pole and knocked the *hongbao* away as she fell. A moment later, she was completely hidden under a mound of ravenous beasts.

The sky flashed orange, and then the Artisan, along with half of the saber-tooth tigers disappeared, swallowed by the retracting tiles.

"Where's the *hongbao*?" the Inceptor asked anxiously.

One of the remaining saber-tooths turned slowly, then began sniffing a trail. Another came alongside it. Heads lowered; their pace quickened as more joined them.

"Uh oh," the Inceptor said as the entire ambush of tigers began charging down the hill.

The Super sighed. "I suppose it's my turn." With a thud, the Super leaped to the ground and charged.

One of the lead tigers pounced.

"Throw the *hongbao*!" the Super shouted.

Out of nowhere, the envelope materialized and flew toward her.

The tiger landed on what looked like thin air. A second later, the Camo appeared flattened beneath the saber-tooth, and the sky flashed green. The Camo disappeared into the earth along with several more tigers as the Super, *hongbao* in hand, sprinted to the trees.

She raced lightning fast, but the tigers were Enhanced and fast learners. This time, some of the pack had remained near the forest edge, cutting off any retreat.

The Aqua roared, but they didn't budge.

"Pass it!" the Inceptor yelled.

The Super leaped in the air and, with all her might, threw the *hongbao*. It sailed straight toward the tree, where the Inceptor caught it.

The crowd cheered wildly.

A moment later the sky flashed red, and the Super was gone.

"And now it's just the four of us," the Giver sighed.

The Inventor shook his head. "Great. All the brains and none of the brawn left."

"Hey!" the Aqua protested. "I'm still here."

"Unless that cliff has a waterfall you can swim up, I don't see how you can help us."

"Yeah, and what are you going to do? Lasso us up there? We don't have any more tools—"

"Shut up." The Inceptor cut them off. He opened the *hongbao*. Instantly, the saber-tooth tigers were swallowed by the flipping of tiles.

The Aqua came down the tree. "What does it say?"

"It says, 'to climb the ladder of success, you must begin at the bottom'."

The four contestants stared up at the looming cliffs.

The Giver blinked. "I'm assuming we have to climb that?"

"Hope you're not afraid of heights."

"Uh . . . actually—"

"You'll be fine." The Inceptor pushed the group toward the cliff.

"Twenty minutes left in the game with only one more *hongbao* to collect," Hong chimed in.

They began climbing with the Aqua in the lead, followed by the Inventor, Giver, and the Inceptor bringing up the rear.

The Giver froze only a few feet off the ground. "This isn't right."

The Aqua snorted. "Don't let your fear of heights stop you."

"No. That's not it," the Giver persisted. "No one climbs the ladder of success out in the open like this. I think we're too exposed." She cocked her head, as if listening. Her eyes widened.

"It's a trap!" She dropped back to the ground, knocking down the Inceptor. The two of them fell in a heap.

BOOM!

An ear-splitting explosion shook the arena. The topmost part of the cliff lit up in brash red and smoky burgundy.

The Aqua and Inventor hurtled through the air and landed hard, suits singed and smoking. There was a flash of cobalt-blue and gray, then the tiles spun and they were no more.

The flames on the side of the cliff vanished with the flipping tiles, leaving a ringing silence in its place.

The Giver picked herself up and helped the Inceptor to his feet. "There has to be another way up. Something more covert."

The Inceptor looked up thoughtfully, then examined a part of the cliff and pressed on one of the stones. It gave way to a set of stairs. "Like this?"

The two of them quickly climbed the staircase until they emerged through a trap door. The Giver plucked the *hongbao* up and read. "You have almost won the race. You pass the person in second place. What place are you in?"

"The participants don't have much time left!" Hong stated. "They must make a decision quickly."

"It's obvious. The answer is first—"

The Inceptor clamped his hands over the Giver's mouth. "Stop!" He looked skyward, eyes narrowing. "It's another trap."

"What do you mean?"

"Hong is trying to get in our heads. To pressure us into making a quick decision. Her tone of voice . . . something was off. Let's slow down and really think this through."

"Thirty-five seconds left," Hong announced.

The Giver chewed her fingernails nervously as the Inceptor closed his eyes to concentrate.

"Fifteen!"

The Inceptor remained silent.

"Ten!"

The Inceptor's eyes flashed open. "It's a trick question. The answer is second place, not first. If you pass the person in second place, you're now in second place."

Realization dawned on the Giver's face.

"Two seconds!" Hong announced.

"Our answer is *second place*," the Inceptor called out.

A moment later, a thunderous clap echoed through the dome, followed by the sound of gears grinding, and then a click.

"Correct," Samson boomed. "Congratulations. The team has won the group challenge."

The crowd cheered, multicolored lights flashed, and music blared. All the participants who weren't hospitalized reappeared on the stage. They bowed and then disappeared again as the crowds started filing out of the coliseum.

"That was amazing." Hazel sighed dreamily. "If only first years were selected more often to compete. I'd love to be in the tryouts."

The thought terrified Urban. After what she had witnessed today, the last thing she wanted was to end up in the arena as a Natural!

THE GIRLS JOSTLED THEIR WAY OUT OF THE coliseum where Blossom's driver was already waiting. She drove a HoneyBee 6F—the latest model of autonomous limos. Inside, it smelled of leather and sickly sweet car freshener. As they settled in, Blossom handed a drab gray dress to Urban.

Urban blinked. "This isn't mine." She'd given Blossom her favorite black dress.

"Ohhhh. Sorry, I think I got the dresses mixed up and brought two of mine instead." Blossom looked from Urban, to herself. "We're close to the same size. Think you could wear it? Going back to the dorms will add an hour to our time."

A wave of anxiety swept over Urban. She had a few personal rules that had helped her blend in with the Enhanced. Avoiding gray clothes was one of them.

While XR suits helped with body regulation, they were designed with Enhanced clients in mind. And of course, Enhanced people could regulate their sweat. Urban had learned the hard way that XR suits couldn't be relied upon to conceal her nerves. Her wardrobe now consisted of mostly black and white.

Just keep your cool, and you'll be fine. There's no other option.

"I'll try." Urban went into a private changing chamber at the back of the limo, where she slipped on the XR gown. It was a nice dress, just a little too loose around the waist and, well, everywhere that counted. Instead of flattering what little curves she had, she looked like a thin, shapeless gray bag. *Great, now my skinniness will be on full display.*

For a second, the thought crossed her mind: *Maybe Blossom switched the dresses on purpose. Nah. It's just an innocent mistake.*

Urban pulled out a huge diamond necklace and earrings from her purse, hoping to spice up her outfit, but they just looked gaudy. She felt like someone from the Outskirts.

She reapplied her PH extractor, turning her lips a deep red, stuffed down her rising fear, then joined Hazel and Blossom. They were getting their nails done by a bot in the front of the limo and gossiping about the Games. Hazel wore a floral dress that came to her neck but had a low-cut back. Blossom's was rather severe looking with pointed shoulders and sharp bunches of fabric down the sleeves. She wore a gold belt and a black choker necklace. Both of them looked stunning, making Urban even more acutely aware of her lack of physical enhancements.

"Wasn't he gorgeous?" Hazel said dreamily. "I really hope I can join the Artisan gene pool." Noticing Urban, she patted the recliner next to her.

Urban took a seat and selected a nail color. A bot began carefully cutting her cuticles as the city streets whipped past them.

"Come on. Inventors are way better," Blossom protested. "Only the best players come from their GP. Who wouldn't want to join?" She turned to Urban. "What about you? What GP are you joining?"

Urban had thought through her answer to this question at length. In the end, she'd decided simplicity was key. "I'm keeping my plans to myself."

"*Ai ya!*" Hazel protested. "Why the one hand behind the back?"

"And you aren't doing the same?" Blossom mused.

"Not with you two!" Hazel said, a hurt expression on her panda-like face.

Blossom examined the progress on her nails. "Some people are cautious for good reason."

"I suppose it doesn't matter anyway, since we can't even apply until we're second years." Hazel sighed.

Urban scrolled through her pings, trying to distract herself from her growing dread. Fitting in while a Natural might be harder than she had thought.

The party was at a private loft downtown. After making a few rounds to build a hit list of people to mingle with, Blossom and Hazel left Urban alone.

With dismay, she realized her alcohol dehydrogenase pills were in her other dress. She tried to find water, or anything non-alcoholic, but found nothing other than hot tea. Holding a teacup at a party would attract more attention than her already lame dress. Urban took a glass of wine and awkwardly held it, feeling hopelessly out of her element.

Stupid lightweight genetics. She wondered if she could go the entire night holding the same drink without anyone noticing. It was so full, though, it would probably spill first. *Why did the Federation have to legalize drinking at sixteen?*

She took a tiny sip and sputtered.

"So, what are you?"

Urban whirled around to find another student with huge muscular wings standing behind her. She checked her retina display but found nothing. His identity was blocked.

She studied the Flyer in front of her. He wore a fine gold-and-white suit with a T-shirt underneath. His mane of black hair was slicked neatly back. His perfect features, paired with a ruggedly sharp jawline, resulted in a striking combination. By the look on his face, he knew it.

Urban realized she'd been staring too long. He grinned as if that matched the typical reaction he got.

"Excuse me?" Urban asked, already annoyed by his expression.

"What are your enhancements? Are you an Inceptor, reading my mind right now?" He gave her a once-over. "Clearly you're not a Super."

Urban raised an eyebrow. "They're a secret."

"Ah, the mysterious category of enhancements I find most intriguing." His voice was just the right amount of charming to be welcoming but not over the top.

Urban smiled tightly.

"Well, in that case, I'm not telling what my enhancements are either." He ruffled his feathers. "I like to keep the ladies guessing."

A laugh accidentally escaped her, and a boyish grin tugged at his lips.

Silence descended, and Urban knew he was waiting for her to take the bait and ask him a question. Part of her was tempted to hand him her drink and leave. Guys like this were all the same. But part of her found his humor disarming. Not to mention, she was tired of standing alone. *I could use some friends. I just hope he doesn't get the wrong idea.*

"So, what brought you here?" she finally asked.

His smile faded slightly. "Same that brought you. The fact my fate is already set since the day my enhancements were selected. Because my parents wanted me to make something of myself, and PKU is the best place to do it. Everyone hopes I'll be a top air-force commander."

"Everyone?"

"Yeah, whatever. Anyhow, I just hope classes are halfway decent."

"Same here," Urban agreed. "I'm signed up for Genetics, and I hear it's one of the hardest ones."

"Which prof?"

"Dr. Huang—"

"I'm in the same class," he said, his boyish grin returning. "Let's link. You never know when I might need to cheat—I mean study with someone." He winked.

Urban ignored his flirtatious gestures. "Ash?" She confirmed as her retina display now showed his landing page and his sosh of 59.

"The one and only."

"There you are!" Hazel cut in. "We've been looking all over for you," she said, pulling Urban away.

"Nice meeting you, Urban," Ash called out as she left.

Hazel glanced back at him. "Wow. I wish he'd link with *me*."

"We're going to be study buddies."

"Study buddies? Is that what they're calling it these days?" Hazel laughed. "Everyone knows Flyers don't study."

Urban was about to protest when Blossom joined them. She extended two fuchsia-purple drinks, but Urban waved hers away. "Still finishing up this one." She held up her barely touched wine, but Blossom snatched the glass and placed it on a passing Natural's tray.

"Not anymore."

Reluctantly, Urban took the new drink. With Blossom's eyes still watching, she sipped it. Liquid burned her lungs, but she faked a smile and managed not to cough.

Seemingly satisfied, Blossom scanned the room. "Meet any interesting individuals yet?"

"I met a Camo who's related to the Duo from Duo Drinks Co. She had a fabulous dress," Hazel piped up.

But Urban wasn't paying attention. She was thinking about her own dress. Sweat dripped down her arms. *Is it showing?*

Before she could escape to the restroom, Urban was swept up in a cycle of introductions and small talk. First, there was the host of the party with a sosh of 81, then some second years all in the mid-60s, and finally, she got lucky enough to be introduced to the Super's Gene Pool Lead, Brooke, who had a whooping sosh of 92. Even though Urban had been avoiding the games for the past few years, she'd seen Brooke on several ads in the Metropolis. She also recognized her as the Dragon player, who earlier that evening, killed several dozen saber-toothed tigers single-handedly.

Brooke had long, silky black hair and thin but striking facial features. Her tough demeanor was more intimidating than her actual size. Unlike most of the other girls who wore elegant gowns, Brooke wore a black pantsuit with chains dangling crisscrossed and arranged haphazardly across her chest and side. Her worn combat boots still had specks of blood on them from the arena.

"Stunning attire, Brooke," Blossom gushed. "Is it antique?"

Brooke gave a polite smile. "It's my mother's, actually. Nearly forty years old, and not a thread of smart fabric in it."

"Incredible."

Brooke waved her hand as if to dismiss the compliment. "So, aside from fashion, what do you two do for fun?"

"Urban does jiujitsu," Blossom offered.

"Really?"

"I just signed up," Urban hurried to clarify.

"I myself am a martial arts fanatic," Brooke said, brightening. "I train in jiujitsu, Krav Maga, and hapkido. I'm always looking for sparring partners. If you ever want to roll with me, just let me know."

Urban tried not to stare at the giant of a woman. Even if Urban had been Enhanced, she'd be crushed in less than two seconds.

"Thank you. What a great offer," Urban said politely, knowing full well she'd never take Brooke up on it.

"Any time. Let's link."

"You can thank me later," Blossom whispered to Urban as Brooke left.

"For what? Volunteering me in a death match? I haven't even started my martial arts classes yet."

"For getting you a chance to link with Wen Brooke. That alone will bump your sosh at least one point once yours goes live. You don't even have to spar with her. Just work out with her once, snap with her, and you'll practically be a KOL."

Training with PKUs strongest women sounded like a terrible idea to Urban, but she kept her thoughts to herself. She didn't want to offend Blossom, or worse, make her wonder why she would never be sparring with Brooke. *I'd rather take my chances with the races.*

Something on Brooke's back caught Urban's eye. Her chains oscillated to her undulating stride. When they swayed just right, they looked like letters . . .

Urban's eyes widened as she took a step back.

There, barely perceptible on Brooke's chains, were the letters *SAS*–Supers Against Soups.

How many SAS members are on campus? What if Brooke finds out I'm a Natural? Will she kill me?

Her heart was still pounding furiously when Hazel shook her. "Hello. Are you even listening? When do you turn eighteen?"

Urban closed her eyes, momentarily blocking out the image of the letters and attempting to focus. "In two weeks."

"And?"

Urban reopened her eyes.

Blossom was watching her suspiciously. "Don't tell me you haven't made plans."

"I haven't really had time—"

"*Tiana!*" Hazel blurted. "What are you thinking?"

"Shouldn't you be planning a big entrance into the sosh world?" Blossom asked. "If you don't have a big bash, your sosh will start low."

"Your birthday is in two weeks, and you haven't even planned anything?" Hazel's jaw dropped. "We have to pull something together immediately!"

Urban had been purposefully avoiding a blowout birthday party because of all the attention it would draw. But they were right. If she expected to get a decent sosh, she had to do something.

"As your roomies, this is a disaster." Hazel moaned. "Each of us should invite all our KOLs. I don't know who'll be able to make it with such short notice. Where will we have it? All the good venues are sure to be booked."

Apparently, planning was underway now. Urban thought for a moment. "What about the Underwater Bar?"

"The original underwater bar?" Hazel asked skeptically. "It would be amazing, of course, but there's no way to get a reservation. I hear you have to book a year in advance."

"My father owns it," Urban said simply. "Let me confirm with him, but I think it will be okay. My siblings host parties there all the time.

Blossom and Hazel stared, then Hazel squealed.

"That would be amazing! I bet all the top KOLs will come if it's there. This is going to be the best birthday ever!"

"That would be a suitable location," Blossom agreed.

Hazel's voice rose with excitement. "We need a DJ, Lung's Peking Duck catered, a sosh curator . . ."

But Urban tuned her out. All she really wanted for her birthday was some time away from crazy parties. She sent Everest a ping.

[Urban: Looks like I'm already getting stuck hosting a fancy bday bash. Do you want to do something earlier in the day?]

[Everest: I was just thinking about that. Something simple? Bubble tea? Or do you want dinner?]

[Urban: Bubble tea sounds amazing.]

[Everest: It's a date.]

Urban returned to the conversation in front of her, feigning interest in Hazel's elaborate birthday plans. Although Urban could use all the help she could get.

"Let's go meet more people." Blossom interrupted Hazel's growing list. "My friend Olive is around here somewhere. She's a Dragon, even though she's only a second year. I'll have to introduce you."

Hazel's attention was immediately diverted. "Is that possible? I thought you said they had to be a third or fourth year to make the team."

"It's ultimately each GP lead's decision. If you've performed well in the tryouts or have a lot of friends in high places, it's possible."

Urban had just decided she should escape to the bathroom to check the status of her dress when Blossom pointed. "There she is."

A girl made her way toward them. The first thing Urban noticed was the girl's incredibly pale skin. She must have had one of the semi-albino enhancements. Everything from her skin, to her hair, to her eyelashes was spotless white. Her eyes were an indistinguishable gray or sky blue. She wore an elegant white dress, covered in pearls and exquisite beading.

With a start, Urban realized her sosh was a whooping 90.

Olive sauntered up to Blossom, drink in hand. "So good of you to join us at PKU."

"We've missed having you over for dinner with your family." Blossom turned to her roommates. "This is Ito Olive, whom I was telling you about."

Olive gave Urban's ill-fitting dress an assessing glance. She didn't even bother hiding her disdain.

Urban tensed. There was also something quick and discerning in that look that made her uncomfortable.

"And you are?" The Inceptor seemed aloof, and everything about her manners and speech was slow, calculated.

"This is Lee Urban from Lee Apps Incorporated, and this is Hazel. Her father is XiaoYang," Blossom explained. "They're my roommates."

Olive nodded politely. "Tell me Hazel, Urban, any plans of joining the Inceptor GP?"

"That would be nice," Hazel gave one of her practiced cute smiles, "but I'm not sure I quite have the genes for it.

I'll probably join the Artisans." Olive seemed not to notice the smile. Urban wondered if Inceptors were immune to its effects.

Olive turned to Urban.

"I haven't revealed my selection yet," she said, barely concealing the tremor in her voice. She could sense Olive attempting to "read her mind." The gray eyes searched Urban's face for microexpressions.

Urban tried to keep as expressionless as possible, even as her heart pounded a hole through her chest. Would Olive be able to see her frantic heartbeat? Could she tell Urban was a Natural? Would Olive know she was lying?

"Hopefully I'll see you in the future. Maybe in the Inceptor GP?"

"Thank you." Urban smiled back, desperately hoping Olive couldn't sense her fear.

Fortunately, the group dispersed, and Urban was approached by two Flyers, who droned on and on about the aerodynamics of their wings and how their genetics had been altered to make them light enough to fly.

Crash!

Urban jumped. Turning, she saw one of the waiters had dropped his tray of drinks. Broken glass littered the floor. A puddle, vibrant with indigo, emerald, and magenta liquids crept across the marble tiles.

"Do you know how much this dress cost?" A girl in a ballroom gown pointed at her crisp white ensemble, which now had a growing red wine stain.

The room fell silent as everyone watched the exchange.

"I'm sorry," the Natural said, attempting to hand her some napkins.

With a snarl, the girl extended retractable claws from her fists. She slapped the napkins away. "You think that will fix my dress?" Her voice rose in pitch. "No. You need to buy me a new one."

The waiter paled.

"You're going to pay one way or another." The girl took a

menacing step toward him.

The waiter glanced down at her claws and stumbled back.

Urban froze.

She knew Natural servants were treated poorly, but the look on the angry girl's face was not reassuring.

The girl took another step closer to the waiter and raised her fists as if to strike. The waiter cowered.

Urban walked toward the girl in the dress right as the girl finally spun away from the Natural, glass crunching under her heels as she left.

The chatter in the room resumed, and the rest of the students turned back to their drinks and to critiquing so-and-so's clothing.

The Natural let out a shaky breath, then stooped to the floor to clean up the mess.

Urban knelt down next to him, and the man looked up, surprised.

Urban nodded at him, reached for a napkin, and began helping.

The man continued staring at her a moment more, then slowly went back to cleaning up.

Urban felt the eyes of the students on her, but continued working until they ran out of napkins.

The Natural stood. "I can get the rest. Thanks." He offered a grateful smile.

Urban smiled back. She looked around then, sensing someone staring, and caught Blossom frowning.

Averting her eyes, Urban made her way to a group in the corner, who seemed deep in conversation. Hopefully, they'd missed the exchange and wouldn't ask her questions.

They'd just completed introductions when Blossom and Olive joined them, but Blossom made no indication that she'd seen Urban helping the Natural.

After introductions were made, one of the students, an Artisan, turned to Urban. "I've had enough standard boring questions tonight. What do you do in your spare time?"

Urban got the impression there was a lot of pressure riding on this question. She took a moment to consider her answer. "I paint." There were several affirmative nods. "I travel and explore a lot. But . . . my favorite thing is to ride my motorcycle. I heard there's a racing club here. I'm hoping to get involved at some point."

"Oh?" Olive had been listening. "I happen to know the club owner."

Urban kept her voice even. "Think you could put in a word for me?"

"I don't know about that. They won't take just *anyone*. The only way in is to pass their initiation race." Olive smoothed out one of the ruffles on her skirt before her eyes went back to Urban. "However, you're in luck. It just so happens their annual inauguration race is in a couple weeks. I might be able to use some of my *guanxi* to get you a spot to compete if you're interested."

If I say yes, my first race will be with all Enhanced racers, which is dangerous.

But her skin tingled with excitement. *Racing is the one thing that could help boost my sosh to 80. I have to take it. It's a couple weeks away. I can practice and get the jump down by then. I think.*

Olive was watching her.

I just wish she wasn't involved. And saying yes will leave me in Olive's debt.

"That would be very gracious of you."

"Done." Olive smirked.

The conversation continued, but Urban was only conscious of every drop of sweat sliding down her arms. Could Olive see it? Almost involuntarily, Urban found herself letting out a breath. Olive's gaze darted back to her, and she narrowed her eyes.

Urban inwardly kicked herself. Mother was right about avoiding Inceptors. They were too observant. She'd become a master at half-truths and deception, but they were masters at uncovering the whole truth, or worse, rearranging it in your mind. *Is that what just happened? Did she just convince me to compete?*

As the conversation came to an end, the group snapped and uploaded their picture. After everyone had linked, Urban noticed the snap had boosted Blossom's sosh a fraction of a point.

"Do you actually know how to race?" Her roommate whispered once the group dispersed.

Urban tried to calm her nerves. "I've been training for it, but I've never actually competed."

"I suggest you prepare quickly," Blossom hissed. "It would be an embarrassment to us all if you accepted Olive's favor and don't make it into the club."

"I'm aware." Urban excused herself and went to the restroom. It was a long trek down a deserted hallway filled with mirrors. She did her best to avoid looking into them. No matter what angle she caught, the mirrors reflected someone who didn't belong.

Alone in a stall, she leaned against the wall, breathing heavily. Her pulse slowed, and her temperature began to return to normal. She let out a deep breath. If she stayed too long, would anyone notice?

A ping from Everest appeared.

[Everest: How's the party?]

The sight of his name brought an image of his piercing black eyes and his teasing grin. Warmth flooded her. She wanted to call him and tell him everything. She could request his XR presence and talk directly to him. XR lines were much harder to hack than pings. Surely, if anyone was monitoring her, they wouldn't be able to overhear their conversation.

She was just about to XR request him when the creaking of a stall door alerted her that she wasn't alone.

Urban remained silent, hoping whoever it was would leave quickly.

But no sound came from the other stall.

Urban checked her retina clock. A minute had passed. She tapped her foot, willing the other person away.

Then a voice whispered from the next stall over, "I'd keep your head down if I were you, Lee Urban."

URBAN'S HEART STOPPED. WHY DID THE VOICE sound familiar? It took her a moment to place it.

It suddenly hit her with the force of a Super's punch. It was the voice of Qing Angel, the one who'd hacked her system on the last day of her internship.

Urban's mind reeled.

She glanced around the stall for something she could defend herself with should Angel attack. There was nothing but a lone roll of toilet paper. Then she remembered the glitch at Gene-IQ. *If I activate the nature vision, and she has Gene-IQ tech, she'll be blinded.*

Urban was sucking in her breath, preparing to disable Angel's tech when the neighboring stall door clanged shut. The click of stiletto heels left the bathroom.

Urban charged out of her stall, but the corridor was silent and empty.

Angel had vanished.

Back in the main room, there was no sign of Angel either. Though, Urban wasn't entirely sure what she was looking for. *She was wearing high heels.* She scanned the crowd. The majority of the women were in stilettoes.

Should I leave the party?

She chewed her lip, weighing her options.

To leave now will attract suspicion from Hazel and Blossom. But staying could mean risking another encounter with Angel— or worse, being exposed.

"Where'd you go?"

Urban turned to find Hazel approaching with a plate piled high with spicy fried potatoes, barbecue lamb, crepes, and other street-food style snacks.

"Restroom. Not feeling so great."

"Like you're sick or something?"

She couldn't have Hazel thinking she was easily ill. She clutched her stomach. "Might have been the street food." She gestured at Hazel's plate. "I should probably go back to the dorms."

Hazel was mid-bite but dropped her food instantly. "Let me order you a ride." Her eyes darted back and forth as she ordered a ride in her retina display, then focused on Urban. "One's arriving in two minutes."

"Thanks." Urban held her stomach and hastily left.

It was strange returning to the tiny dorm room that smelled of Blossom's eucalyptus perfume but was now Urban's home. The little bunk with a few pictures hung on the wall welcomed her back. She was relieved to be there. The day had been long, and she was tired. She crawled into familiar pajamas and pulled her sleep headset down over her eyes and nose. Her mind was still plagued by thoughts of Qing Angel as the cold sleeping gas from her headset began to fill her nostrils. But soon, she forgot everything as her thoughts drifted into dreams.

Urban awoke to her tatt vibrating and bathing the room in a ghostly gold light.

She pulled off her sleep headset and got ready for her first day of classes. Blossom and Hazel were passed out, their sleep headsets still on, learning things at a subconscious level or reaching deeper levels of refreshment while they slept. Their third roommate remained absent.

Urban commanded her bed to make itself and smiled as the covers rearranged themselves into perfect folds.

Her tatt vibrated again. "I know, I know, I'm coming," she said, making her way to the door. A drone hovered before her with a mesh bag in tow. It scanned her tatt before the top unlocked, allowing her to untie the drawstring and retrieve her breakfast. Urban took out the warm congee. The drone dipped slightly, then with a *"Xiexie,"* flew off to make its next delivery.

Urban slurped down the soupy rice as she fumbled in the dark to find her clothes and get ready without waking the roommates. She threw on her most progressive outfit, then blinking, entered the harsh light of the restroom at the end of the hall.

She spun in a circle in front of the mirror, admiring her new clothing. The black XR suit with leggings and reinforced square metallic sections at the joints gave her legs a slender, robotic appearance. Her matching top was black and had two straps crossing in the middle of her ribs, giving her a military look. Amidst the straps were tiny jeweled flowers. It made her feel tough and artistic at the same time—exactly what she was going for. She added a studded bracelet, which doubled as a weapon. Hopefully she wouldn't need it.

She got a ping.

[Everest: Good luck on your first day of classes. You're gonna crush them.]

Urban smiled to herself. She took a quick selfie, then added a filter that made her look like a Kung Fu goddess with hair blowing in the wind and extra layers of makeup and glitter.

[Urban: Thanks!]

With enough nervous adrenaline to keep her awake without her usual latte, she followed her maps to class.

Her first class, Programming, was in a large room with steep sloped seats. She was one of the first to arrive. She took a seat near the back with a view straight down to the podium.

A girl with eggshell and ebony-colored patched skin took a seat next to her. "Hi, I'm Chan Sssslasssh," she said in a vacillating voice. "My brother'ssss on PKU'ssss team asss the Aqua GP Lead. I'll be trying out next year. Who are you?"

Urban noticed the girl's skin had a scaly, snake-like texture to it. "Lee Urban. My father owns the underwater chain of shopping centers and housing units."

The girl flicked her thin, black tongue as she grinned snake-ishly. "Nice to meet you. Let'sssss link."

After linking, Slash's sosh and landing appeared. Since she was a second year, she already had a sosh of 64.

"Oh! I've been following your fassssshion vlogsssss for yearssss now," Slash exclaimed. "I love all the ancient *qipaossss* you've managed to find. Ssssso great to meet you in persssson."

"Thanks!" But before Urban had time to check Slash's landing page, the door at the front of the class opened. A bot walked in, and its name appeared on the smart board: "Dr. Bang." It turned and faced the class, its metallic eyes examining all the students in an instant, recording their attendance.

Dr. Bang was the standard gray-and-black, human-sized version bot available in most households and stores. Its face shield, normally black, was now switched on to display canary yellow eyes and a thin mouth. The slick wires and stylish knobs and gears on the side of its head purred.

Urban grinned inwardly as she noticed the bot's clothing selection. On top of its face shield rested a pair of ridiculous round glasses, around its torso was a collared shirt like a real professor might wear, and XR pants—as if it needed thermal adjusting.

"I thought PKU was supposed to have human instructors," a student with indigo bat wings complained. "Isn't that why they charge so much?"

"That's only for specialized classes—not the gen eds," another student with glowing silver eyes replied.

"Hey! You're in my seat," demanded a student wearing a loose-fitted casual XR vest, sweats, and a beanie—despite the warm weather. His arms were partially covered in black cloth.

Urban recognized it immediately as the latest XR trend. Supposedly it wasn't even on the market yet. How had he gotten it? She looked down at her own suit, no longer content.

The student who looked like a bat leaned back against his seat. "Find a new seat."

"I always sit in the same place in each class," the trendy student with the beanie retorted. "This is my seat."

Bat-wings made a shooing motion with his hands. "Find somewhere else."

"No."

The tension was so thick in the room, you could have heard a grain of rice drop. Urban moved her wrist with the spiked bracelet closer to her face should she need to protect herself.

"Seriously, go get your vitals checked. You sound like you had a hormone overdose or something."

The beanie student stared a moment longer, then slowly walked away. He reached into his pocket, withdrew a pen, and held it clenched in his hand.

Urban frowned. Pens had long ago been rendered obsolete. Why would a student have one? But Bat-wings seemed to know. He suddenly extended his wings, knocking over several thermoses of tea and slapping students in the face. He leaped in the air with a thrust of his wings.

At that moment, the beanie student turned and flung the pen with superstrength, but it passed under Bat-wing's feet harmlessly.

Another student tried to grab the pen out of the air with superhuman reflexes, but he wasn't fast enough. The pen slipped past him and lodged into Slash's neck.

The girl screamed. Though it sounded more like a shrieking hiss. Her scales shimmered and trembled in agony, and she coiled into a ball on the ground. Blood poured out around her.

Urban froze in horror. She had to do something to help Slash, but what?

Both the winged student and the hooded student started crying out in harmonized pain as their tatts glowed amber and their flesh smoked.

"Enough," the probot said calmly, taking command of the situation. "You two will be escorted to re-education, while the rest of us will continue with class."

Two robotic cuffs dislodged from behind panels in the wall. They flew over to the students, attached themselves, then escorted them out of the room. Several medbots arrived as well and carried Slash, now whimpering, out of the room.

Urban was sick. She wished she could help with Slash, but that would cost her an attendance point, and those were tied to her grades.

School was always going to be violent.

"Welcome to Programming." The probot started lecturing as if nothing had happened. "You will find the syllabus in the classroom portal, which I've just granted you all access to. This is not your standard programming course. Much more will be expected of you. I'll be having each of you design one level to an XR game.

"I realized this is probably more advanced than most of you are accustomed to. Do not worry. I will be teaching you everything you need to know. But I warn you, it won't be easy. You'll be pushed to the limit. For those of you used to achieving good grades easily, you might be disappointed."

Urban gulped. *I've never gotten good grades easily in my life. How am I going to survive this class?*

"In fact, to ensure this course is challenging to all, I'll only be giving out one A this semester."

Outraged students booed.

"The student." The probot raised its voice to be heard. It paused, letting the noise die down before beginning again. "The student who can design the hardest level to beat will be awarded an A. Now, onto our first lesson. Programming is a neutral subject. But the power of programming can be used for good or for evil. For instance, the complex learning algorithms I have embedded in my system are used daily to do good. I will impart wisdom upon generations to come. Alas, at my most basic form, I am an imperfect collection of code.

"I'm continuously looking to improve. That's why, per university policy, any student who can stump me or any of the probots, will have period end early for the entire class."

No sooner had it spoken this rule than a burst of questions poured out from students, clamoring to be heard above each other.

The probot put up one metal finger. "Oh, ignorant first years, no one's managed to make me glitch in over five years. Now, so I don't have you all continuously babbling away in my classroom, there's one condition. If you attempt to make me glitch and do not succeed, you will have to write an essay."

The classroom fell silent again.

"As I said, programming can be used for good or evil. You all may have heard of some of the evil examples of hacking that have been in the news; politicians who had their retina memory files wiped, or worse, replaced with fabricated memories. This class is not about ethics. I will leave it up to you to decide right from wrong. I simply will teach you the skills needed to solve the most complex problems. In your advanced classes, you will learn to think critically about the 'why' behind every line of code you write."

The probot went on to give a brief lecture on an article published recently on agile programming in the post-digital age and future implications for society.

"That's all for today's class. Please check your direct connect folder for your assignment, due by next class period. It shouldn't take you more than a couple minutes to complete. You are dismissed."

Urban found herself actually looking forward to this course. *Maybe I can learn something about how Angel hacked my identity,* she thought as she followed her maps to her next class. Soon, she was in the basement of a lab for Genetic Engineering with Dr. Huang, another bot. This one looked exactly the same as the last, only without the eccentric clothing.

She glanced over the classroom, looking for signs of Ash's speckled gray wings, but didn't see him.

"The world of genetics is an amazing one. While I myself may not know what it feels like to procreate, have emotions, make discoveries or other incredible human functions, I've been programmed by some of the world's best on the topic. Trust me, you're in good hands. Welcome to Genetic Engineering."

"If I ever find the person who programmed this probot with lame jokes . . ."

Urban turned and found Ash sliding into the seat behind her.

"That's one tardy for you, Ding Ash."

Ash rolled his eyes but winked at Urban.

Urban turned quickly away.

Dr. Huang began speaking again. "All the course expectations are outlined in the rubric I've sent. Let's get started, shall we?" It clapped its hands excitedly. Whoever had programmed its human like gestures had to be pretty interesting.

"In our history, there have been three pivotal moments: The Industrial Revolution, The Digital Revolution, and The Genetic Revolution."

Urban thought back to her history classes. While they'd always covered the Industrial and Digital Revolutions, information on the Genetic Revolution was scarce at best. When Urban had asked her mother about it, she'd said it was too soon. They were still seeing pieces of the revolution play out today. Mother would know. She'd been a child during the height of it.

"Genetic engineering has changed everything about the world in which we live. It's become a fine art to mix human cells with those of other genetic tissues to advance the human species." The probot began pacing. "But why is it some humans have more enhancements than others? Why not have all of the enhancements at once?"

A student raised his hand. "Money."

"That's what most people assume. It's also incorrect." The bot paused a moment, letting its words sink in. "If money were the issue, why not add to your list of enhancements once you're grown and wealthy?"

Another student raised her hand. "There's a small window of time when an embryo can be enhanced in vitro. You can't get enhancements whenever you want."

The probot kept its glass eyes locked on the student. "But what if you could?"

"Impossible," the student argued.

"Why?"

This time the student remained silent.

The probot continued, "It's not possible because you are particularly vulnerable while in the womb. Once an embryo becomes a fetus, it loses its extreme adaptability. But what if there were a genetic combination allowing for enhancements into adulthood? Money, The Board of Genetic Enhancements, governments; these things all regulate the use of enhancements. They do not control them."

"Where is this crazy bot going with all this?" Ash whispered to Urban.

Urban shrugged, but her eyes stayed glued to the probot and excitement built within her.

"You control your enhancements. That is, your DNA does." The probot paused. "Today, approximately half of the world's population is Enhanced. Most of those enhancements are the standard reinforced bones, better immune systems, etc. Only a select, smaller number of those with enhancements have specialized and rare ones. Every one of you sitting in this room are of that elite number." The bot swiveled its head, surveying each student in the classroom.

"There are many who would like to change that disadvantage. But it's too late for them. They can't go back into the womb to change their DNA. Either you're born naturally, or you're enhanced by scientists while in vitro. You can't be born naturally and still have enhancements."

The probot paused a moment. "But what if there was a way you could? What if a man up until his mid-twenties could change his genetics? How would that affect society? Instead of your fate being determined by your parents before you're even born, you could decide your own destiny."

Urban leaned forward, while the rest of the class shifted uncomfortably.

"Scientists are trying to crack this last code. It's even rumored one scientist has."

A student's hand shot up. "Why haven't we heard about this before?"

The probot ignored the question. "Mankind has one final frontier to crack—the ultimate species. The ability of man to truly evolve—even after birth. This is the final frontier. This is the fourth revolution that will change our world."

Urban's eyebrows furrowed in concentration. She didn't want to miss a single word.

"The history of the Genetic Revolution has its origins back in the early 2000s. Patients were treated with a gene-editing process. Cells in the bone marrow were removed, edited, then reinserted into the body."

"Originally, these experiments were designed to increase the amount of normal hemoglobin in patients with sickle cell anemia. But they discovered that the operation worked more efficiently if done in vitro. And, more importantly, it could also be used to *alter* genes."

"Now, we can change most genes. The next great breakthrough starts with this." The probot projected a VR image at the front of the classroom. "The microneedle patch." A device resembling a black bandage hovered in midair, slowly rotating. The image grew larger, revealing hundreds of tiny needles implanted on its surface. "It's used for transmuting the most advanced changes in genomics."

Urban blinked. She'd seen that patch before. But where? On the news? In a textbook?

She continued staring as the probot went on lecturing. "This may look familiar to some of you who are well-versed in history. Fifty years ago, similar looking patches were the primary method of vaccine distribution." The projection switched to reveal a smaller, translucent patch, also with microneedles. "Now, however, with enhanced genetics, there is little need for vaccines, except of course, for Naturals."

Realization set in. Urban instantly recognized the tiny translucent patches. Her parents had secretly requested the flu patch for her from an Outskirts hospital every fall. She'd place it on her forearm, and it was painless. She'd never gotten the flu and had an appreciation for the tiny patches.

The projection switched back to the larger, black patch. "What you're looking at is not a patch used for routine vaccines. This innovation is being developed to trigger genetic changes later in life. Consider, for a moment, how children grow and develop. For girls, age eighteen is when they've reached their maximum growth potential. Boys usually don't peak until they're twenty-five. Boys have a little more growing up to do than girls it seems."

Several students snickered at this, and the probot paused, a pleased smile lighting up its robotic face. "The point is, while the fetus is in a particularly malleable state after fertilization, humans continue to grow and adapt until adulthood. When you combine in vitro changes with advanced patches, it could one day be possible to insert DNA into the genomes as late as puberty. The patch could activate certain traits so that what previously could only be modified in vitro could now occur much later in life.

"Scientists will one day find a way to make this not only viable but publicly available. It all starts with these microneedle DNA patches. Only three of them have been made—by a leading scientist before he passed away in a tragic explosion. Researchers are still attempting to reverse engineer his work but are missing several key components. Today, only one of the patches has been found. It resides at the Center for Advancement in Asian Genetics, or CAAG, laboratory."

This was the first time she was learning about this larger patch, yet Urban still had the distinct feeling she had seen one just like it in real life before. But how was that possible?

The probot continued to a new topic, and Urban's body tensed with frustration. She wanted it to go back, to keep teaching on the topic.

But the probot droned on about a rare mutation discovered in zebras, and Urban gave up hope. Her mind wandered through all the possibilities of where she might have seen the microneedle patch. As soon as class was out, she wandered down the crowded sidewalk, furiously searching in QuanNao for anything about it.

"Well, that was some crazy talk." Ash interrupted her search.

"Huh?"

Ash looked at her. "Were you paying attention in class? I wonder who programmed the probot. Though, I can't help but wish its bizarre theories were true."

Urban stopped. "Why?"

"Why not? I've been searching QuanNao for anything on

enhancements after birth since that probot brought it up but haven't found much. Just rumors of a scientist who cracked the DNA code. They all looked fake though."

"But do most Enhanc–most people, care about that? I mean, why change our enhancements?"

"Why not? Then I could actually decide for myself what I want to do with my future." Ash glanced at her. "Don't pretend like you don't know what I mean. That's what you want too."

At Urban's startled look he nodded knowingly. "I'm on to you, Lee. Why else would you keep your enhancements a secret? Because you don't want to be boxed in by society telling you what you can and can't do. I get it."

Urban blinked in surprise. How had her refusal to select a gene pool led him to this conclusion? Were others thinking the same thing?

"Anyway, it's all crazy talk," Ash continued. "I haven't seen any scientific evidence supporting any of the claims."

Urban recovered herself. "Then I wonder why the probot would tell us all that."

"To push a political agenda?"

"An agenda to creep out all the first years?"

Ash laughed. It was a charming and warm laugh, reminding Urban of why girls always fell for guys like this. "Who knows. Say, you going to try out for the team?"

"Uh . . ." The change in topics caught Urban by surprise. "I probably don't stand much of a chance as a first year. So no. Are you?"

"Yes! I've got some pretty steep competition in the other Flyers, but think I've got a shot at it. You sure you don't want try out?"

"Quite."

Ash changed the subject. "What've you got going on the rest of the day?"

Urban hesitated. Her plan was to go check out the gym, then get a jump start on studying. It typically took her longer than

Enhanced students to memorize and retain material. But she couldn't tell him that. "I'm going to work out or something."

"That's cool," Ash said with admiration in his voice. "I love working out. Well hey, I'm about to hang with some dudes from my dorm. Wanna join?" He flashed a radiant smile.

Energy crackled between them as he locked eyes with her. Urban's breath caught, but then as she gazed back, Ash's eyes morphed into Everest's fierce black ones. Guilt filled her belly. Her smile tightened. "Sorry. Can't." *I need a way to friendzone him.* "I'm meeting up with my boyfriend."

"Oh." Ash blinked but then regained himself immediately, his confidence and humor not seeming to dip in the slightest. "Next time then."

Infini-Fit was located on the top floor of a skyscraper and had a retractable roof to allow sunlight in when the weather was nice. Today it was closed, the gray sky above visible through the glass.

The gym had an infinity pool with a terrifying view of the fifty-five-floor drop below, an adjustable gravity room, a full-sized turf, a room full of silk ropes for aerial yoga, a wind tunnel, a dark sonar-vision obstacle course room, and a mini fighting ring.

Before she could explore, she was surprised to see Thistle approach. She looked much different than when Urban had met her at the going-away banquet. Instead of a *qipao*, she wore skin-tight breathable pants and a low-cut, florescent top.

"Hello dear," Thistle gushed with way too much enthusiasm. "I heard you joined our gym and wanted to personally give you a tour." Her beady eyes slid over Urban.

Urban wanted to cringe but stood tall and forced a smile at the Inceptor. "How kind of you."

"My pleasure. Anything for my good friend's daughter."

Urban seriously doubted Mother and Thistle were good friends but followed after her anyway.

"Given our state-of-the-art facilities, most of the big-name Gamers train here," Thistle said with pride. She went on to point out the juice bar, coffee lounge, spa, and nap pods. "The gym is open 24/7. Some members practically live here."

They approached a dimly lit room full of giant punching bags hanging from the ceiling. "We pride ourselves in being New Beijing's top-ranked fitness center. If there's anything we can do to make your membership more enjoyable, please don't hesitate to let us know."

Thistle left with an exaggerated smile.

Urban let her shoulders relax. She would have to be careful to train away from Thistle's prying eyes. If she saw just how out of shape Urban was compared to the Enhanced, Thistle might have suspicions.

Urban surveyed her surroundings. Two sweaty men took turns grunting and flipping an autonomous car on the turf. A Flyer, strapped down with weights, flew with all her strength upward in the wind tunnel. A Camo and Super traded blows in the fighting ring before a small cheering crowd. Slender girls with rock-solid abs and wearing all the latest workout fashions sat laughing and sipping smoothies at the juice bar.

Urban fidgeted with her own workout top, wishing she were more fit. She slipped a power-boosting energy pill from her pocket and swallowed it down. With ten more minutes before it kicked in, she headed over to the coffee lounge to wait.

She slid into a booth and noticed a holographic ad swiveling on the tabletop. "Only one month until the Dragon's tryouts begin! Sign-ups now available. Picture yourself in the ARENA." The words were followed by a montage of the past year's most exciting victories. Brooke karate-chopping a bear, someone assembling a primitive aircraft and flying off a cliff, an Aqua wrestling underwater with a giant eel.

Urban turned away, nerves spiking. One time of watching the Games was enough for her to know why Mother wanted her to avoid them. Talk about a death sentence.

After sipping on kale-infused water until her energy boost kicked in, she headed over to the weight racks. Thankfully, due to her daily workouts at her old gym, she lifted the weights easily enough. After completing several reps, she spent some time on a bike, then cooled down on a virtual running machine.

She was feeling good about herself as she finished up with a quick stretch. When she was done, a prickling sensation crept up her spine. Turning, she searched the gym but didn't see anything out of the ordinary.

She tried to shake the sensation as she exited the gym but couldn't help feeling someone was still watching her.

THE FIRST WEEK OF CLASS PASSED IN A BLUR.
Urban's head hurt from all the new things she was learning.
Before she knew it, her first jiujitsu practice arrived.

Urban shuddered as she climbed off her motorcycle into an
empty alley with dark, reflectionless puddles.

Lillian would pick a sketchy place like this to train. While
locking up her bike, a ping from Everest arrived.

[Everest: Wanna grab dinner tonight?]

Urban thought about the mounting homework she had. And
it would be tricky to sneak off somewhere to meet too. But it
had been too long since she'd seen him.

[Urban: Yeah! I'll be coming straight from jiujitsu so I might
be a little smelly.]

[Everest: I'm out. Can't do smelly.]

[Everest: Just kidding.]

[Everest: Like I care. You'd look great even in one of
those gis.]

Another ping showed up.

[Lillian: Are you on your way?? Don't be late your first day
of class.]

Urban checked the time. Class started in six minutes.

She made her way through a tiny door into what looked like the back entrance to someone's house. Urban double-checked she was at the right location before continuing down a flight of stairs into a basement.

Fluorescent lights exposed every crack in the wall and every speck of dirt on the bare concrete floor. It was eerily empty and quiet except for a random pop song playing somewhere in the distance. She entered an all-white hallway with a paper sign with crude characters scribbled on it pointing to the left for the jiujitsu gym. Urban's eyes darted around her surroundings. This seemed like the sort of place people got mugged.

But she relaxed as laughter bubbled from behind a cracked door and voices mingled with the music. She entered a large open room with bright white lights overhead. The floors were made of soft mats, and the walls were lined with punching bags. Urban hopped on one foot, as she pulled her shoes off at the entryway where there was a stack of them. Students dressed in white robes stood, mingling near the center of the room.

One of them, spotting Urban, broke away from the group and trotted over.

"Hey, sis!" Lillian extended a bundle of white to Urban. "Your gi."

"Hurray. I get to join the bathrobe club."

Lillian gave her a little push. "Changing room's back down the hall and to the right."

A few minutes later, Urban stood in front of Lillian again. Her sister helped teach her how to fasten her belt at the front of her gi. Then they joined a line with twenty other students in matching white gis. The instructor paced in front of them. He only seemed a couple years older than her and had blond hair and brown eyes but no obvious enhancements. Somehow, he looked familiar. When he spoke, he had a slight accent, as if he was from somewhere in the Eastern Federation.

"That's Orion," Lillian whispered. "He's the head of the Inceptor's gene pool. Wasn't he amazing in the Exhibition Game?"

Urban realized now why he looked so familiar. "Does Mother know an Inceptor teaches this class?"

"Of course not." Lillian wiggled her eyebrows. "But this is the best school in town. Don't worry, Orion might help give you some instructions, but he keeps his distance. Unfortunately." She gazed wistfully at the instructor. "You'll be fine."

Urban studied the instructor. Would Orion be able to read her thoughts? Find out she was a Natural by her lack of athleticism or her physique?

On the other hand, he was the Inceptor GP Lead. Being in his class alone could potentially help boost her sosh. She glanced at Lillian. If her overly protective sister thought it was safe, it was sure to be fine.

Orion began class with a warm-up, then ordered everyone to sit kneeling.

"Discipline," he began in a low commanding voice, "is the most important thing I can teach. Without discipline, nothing you learn here is of value." He paused a moment. "I'm going to tell you a story, but I warn you, it doesn't have a happy ending.

"A long time ago there was a tribe of warriors. At the age of four, one of the tribal members had captured a horse and broken it in. He grew up to be the best warrior in his band." He then proceeded to tell a long-winded story.

Urban wondered where this was going. Numbness crept up her legs, and she wanted desperately to shift positions, but she noticed everyone else remained perfectly still. She wondered if this was part of a test or had something to do with discipline. So, despite the pins and needles, she remained still.

Orion stopped. "And I'll tell the second half of the story at the end of class."

She couldn't believe it. With annoyance, and pain, Urban joined the class in standing. It was difficult to walk now that she could feel again.

They did another lap around the room before Orion gave a new drill.

"Shrimping, go!"

Urban looked around in bafflement as everyone lined up on one side of the room and started making their way slowly across the floor on their backs and sides.

"What the—"

"Shrimping is one of the key building blocks in jiujitsu," Lillian explained beside her.

"An essential really." It was Orion. Neither of the girls had noticed him approach.

Add stealthy to the list of reasons I shouldn't trust this guy.

"You're new here. I'm Orion." He extended a hand and they shook firmly.

Her breath froze.

His touch was exploratory, like he was reading her life story in the palm of her hands. Would he detect her elevated temperature or pulse? Urban fought the urge to jerk her hand away, knowing that would only attract more attention.

"Urban." She withdrew her hand from his grip.

"A good name," Orion said with an amiable smile. His intense amber eyes studied her.

Urban's heart beat faster.

"This is the sister I've been telling you about," Lillian interjected.

Orion looked at Lillian and Urban relaxed again.

"Right. Let me show you what shrimping is, Urban." Orion led her away from the group and dropped to the floor.

"Shrimping is a form of creating space." Orion motioned Urban to join him on the floor. "You start on your back like this, but then move one shoulder into the mat and you thrust your rear backward and away."

He laughed at the look on Urban's face. "Here, watch this." He gave a quick demonstration. Laying on his back, he pushed from side to side, inching away from her. Urban copied him.

"You got it," Orion coached after a couple of tries. "Good. Keep it up."

He returned to surveying the rest of the class in their warm-up exercises while Urban practiced shrimping in a corner. She felt like a floundering fish, and she was all too conscious of the students' eyes on her.

After a few minutes, Orion motioned Urban over.

He scanned the class, searching for someone. His eyes stopped on a Super. "Craig, come here and pin me down."

A Super with horns on either side of his head came promptly. Urban noticed he had padding surrounding his horns to protect the other students. She tried not to laugh at how ridiculous he looked.

Orion looked at Urban from the floor. "This is one of the worst positions you could be in. It's incredibly dangerous. You need to get out of this fast. Shrimping can create the needed space to escape."

He demonstrated his point by shifting to his side, bracing his hands against Craig's knees, and shooting his backside away from him. He wedged a knee into Craig, locked him into his guard, then swept Craig onto his back. Orion then put the Super into an armbar until he tapped.

Orion made it look easy, but Urban was skeptical. "How does that work if his weight is fully on you?"

"If his full weight were on me," Orion got back on the ground and motioned the Super over again. This time Craig rested all his weight on him.

"You do this." Orion trapped Craig's leg and one of his hands against his chest, bucked upward, and then rolled. While rolling, he scrambled out of the Super's guard and to his side. Orion shot forward, leaning against Craig's chest and trapping one of his arms at an awkward angle.

The Super groaned in discomfort. He tried to fight but then, just as quickly, tapped the padded floor again.

Orion stopped applying pressure. "Even with your lightweight genetics, it can be done."

Urban's face reddened. "My parents thought they'd try skinny genetics," she said casually, hoping to keep him from comparing her to Lillian.

Orion laughed genially. "We all have something unfortunate our parents picked out for our DNA." He stood and helped Craig to his feet. "Anyhow, if something doesn't work, try something else. Jiujitsu is a creative art. It's physical prowess mixed with intelligence. It's a game of moves and countermoves. It's chess but with the human body. Whoever can outthink what their opponent will do next will be the victor."

After practicing some more, Orion gathered the class back together, sitting once again on their knees, to finish his story. "What happened to that brave tribal warrior?" he asked, peering into each one of their eyes.

Urban felt he was seeing into her very soul when his gaze reached her. She knew she should clam up around Inceptors, but Orion was warm and friendly. At least, compared to Olive and other Inceptors she'd met.

"A clever rival band of warriors settled near him. With their guns, they conquered the brave tribal warriors. Eventually the band gave up fighting back. All the warriors of his clan lived harmonious and quiet lives on their tiny pieces of land. And that is the end of the story."

Urban arched a cynical eyebrow.

Orion's sharp eyes caught hers. A slight smile twitched at his mouth as if he knew what she was thinking. "The story is terrible because a brave warrior, one of the most amazing and gifted of his time, stopped fighting. He spent the rest of his life living a peaceful but meaningless life. He was confined to complacency while rival warriors continued their conquest." He paused a moment. "I'd rather die fighting than end up like that."

Urban tried not to wince. She glanced at her sister and saw

she was deep in concentration. In fact, the entire class seemed spellbound by Orion's words.

"What did you think?" Lillian asked later as they left.

"He's either brilliant or crazy," Urban remarked.

"Orion seems a little strange until you start connecting the dots to his stories, theories, and exercises. Then you realize he's a genius."

"All that survival talk . . . I've had enough to last a week."

Lillian picked up on the tone in her sister's voice. "What happened?"

Urban shook her head, not wanting to talk about it.

"That bad?"

"I just had too high of hopes."

Lillian sighed. "Uni isn't perfect. That's for sure. It will get better, you'll see."

"Maybe for you," Urban wanted to say. Instead, she said, "Thanks. See you Wednesday at class?"

"I never miss."

"Why am I not surprised?" Urban muttered as she climbed onto her motorcycle. She realized she had a ping from Everest.

[Everest: Running a little late. Meet at your favorite spot?]

Good. I've been needing some practice. She responded with an animation of her avatar giving a thumbs up.

Urban set her maps to take her the long way on a less-traveled route. She zipped through the city until reaching an underground tunnel with bright lights. Upon entering, she held her breath to see how far she could push her limits.

The last time she'd tried to do this, she'd run out of air seconds before reaching the end of the tunnel. This time, she was determined to get all the way through. *If I'm going to compete soon, I have to be comfortable with faster speeds.*

The lights blurred as she twisted the throttle of her electric bike. Her motorcycle shot forward as she weaved smoothly through autonomous cars.

Urban's vision narrowed as she focused on the road. At this speed, all it would take was a tiny distraction and she could hit a car and wipe out. She didn't want to think about what would become of her if that happened.

Lungs burning, she checked her timer and saw forty-seven seconds had passed.

Halfway.

Ignoring the pain in her chest, she pulled the throttle again so she was flying silently. All her attention focused on maintaining control of her vehicle. The wind beating against her body at this velocity was an invisible barrier, determined to defeat her. She crouched lower to ward it off.

Her entire chest screamed for air. One minute and seven seconds had passed as a bend in the tunnel came into view.

Almost there.

Approaching the corner, she loosened the throttle and waited for the precise right moment.

As she entered the bend, she paused, then smoothly opened the throttle, increasing her speed. Her entire body leaned with the bike so far that her knee nearly touched the road.

Rolling off the throttle, she gradually stood the bike back up as she pulled out of the bend.

Her lungs were on fire.

One minute and ten seconds counted by as the exit to the tunnel appeared.

She gritted her teeth. *I can do this.*

Her limbs tingled. Her lungs were dying stars, caving in on themselves.

Then she was through the tunnel and the sun blinded her. Urban gulped in air hungrily and triumphantly as she checked her timer. She'd made it through the tunnel in one minute and twenty seconds and held her breath the entire time. A new record.

She arrived at the Hutongs, still breathing heavily and only a few minutes late. Her retina display flashed a warning.

<Entering yellow zone. Exercise CAUTION.>

The Hutongs were all classified as yellow zones and had a giant dome over them to preserve the climate and keep its pollution out of the Metropolis. Urban stared through it at the crumbling buildings preserved from dynasties gone by. The familiar sight of smoke from burning coal rose in the air, then stopped abruptly as it hit the dome.

This plot of land was one of the few things remaining of old China. The new melting pot of cultures and tech had cropped up all around, trying to crowd it out, but like a stubborn weed, it refused to be choked away. In this small patch of city, life went on as it always had for the past few centuries.

The trees wilted after a hot summer, their leaves a toasted brown. The one-story houses stood with sloping, tiled gray roofs and cherry red doors. Laundry hung out to dry in the courtyards. On the streets, people walked or rode on bicycles. Pigeons flapped in graceful circles overhead, flying in unison. Urban always wondered how this ancient way of life had survived.

She made her way toward one of the checkpoints through the barrier. She watched a lady with silver skin enter before her. She fumbled for a mask as she, too, crossed the barrier and coughed.

Urban breathed in deeply. The polluted air smelled of roasted corn, firewood, and incense. Only rich city slickers with no exposure to bad atmospheres were intolerant of it. While long exposure was bad for everyone, at least Naturals could breathe in yellow zones without having a coughing fit.

Excitement pulsed through her at the thought of seeing Everest again.

As she made her way through the Hutongs, it was as if all the growing pains the world had been experiencing for the last century had never touched this place. Urban loved the maze of completely impractical and winding narrows streets—each one full of surprises. Here was an old woman with a dog wearing a hand-knitted sweater, a child with split pants, and on the next street, a grandfatherly figure with a missing tooth, selling corn right off a portable furnace on a bike.

It was peaceful in its own way. There were no drone deliveries buzzing by, pings from tatts, or people talking on the streets to unseen callers through their retina displays. There were still sounds, but they were different. Here, people haggled over goods and talked to each other in person. Bike bells rang at pedestrians, and dogs the size of rats yipped at each other.

They were the sort of sounds you never heard in the Metropolis or the Outskirts. Urban had been told they were the sounds of the old Federation.

Here in this patch of land where coal and plastic bags were still used, where social credit was blocked, where the fastest form of transportation was a bike, where the ceilings leaked, the plumbing was awful, it was perpetually too cold or too hot, and the roof tiles didn't match—Urban was at home.

It was like her mismatched DNA belonged here. As if she were meant for a simpler life in the Hutongs. She could let her guard down, be herself. She always felt like she was safer here. The howl of a white temple monkey made her shudder and look to her right.

A looming *paifang* arched over a stone stairway. Behind it rose an overly bright display of hand-painted buildings that reminded Urban of a grinning clown face. A deserted stone courtyard with statues and trees haunted the space between the lurid buildings.

The temple used to be a place to worship the gods or ancestors. As the years went by, and Buddhism declined in popularity, it had morphed into a new purpose.

Now, the temple was a place to house the cremated bodies and the memories of the dead. Urban's grandma's remains were at a similar temple. Lillian and Mother frequented it to access her memories–stored from her tatt. The place creeped Urban out, and she'd only ever set foot in it during the funeral.

Urban walked faster until she passed the temple and entered into a crowded row of souvenir shops. Each store touted traditional colorful papercuts, embroidered silk handkerchiefs, jade rings, tea sets, paintings, beaded necklaces, and hand-painted fans. A hole-in-the-wall restaurant loomed ahead. A giant sign above it read: Auntie Tongtong's Noodles. Urban stepped through plastic flaps, pulled to the side like curtains drawn back, and entered.

No decor adorned the plain white walls, and only simple plastic tables and stools filled the restaurant. Urban took a seat against the back wall with a view of the front door.

"Dear, what can I get you?" A middle-aged woman in a stained white apron smiled down at her. She was skinny, like Urban, and had straight black hair, pulled back into a simple ponytail. When she smiled, she lit up the room.

"Hi, Auntie. How are you?"

"All right for an old woman." She poured Urban a cup of green tea and set it on the rickety table. "You ready to order?

"Two bowls of *chaomian*. One with chicken and one with beef."

Auntie nodded as she tucked her pad and paper into her apron before disappearing back into the kitchen.

The smell of cilantro and beef stew hit her nose as a wave of heat passed over her. The fan beating furiously in the corner couldn't compete against the heat of the cooking fire. The male patrons had their shirts rolled up past their bellies to try and keep cool.

Urban swirled the tea in her cup. She watched as it went round and round with little bits of tea leaves hitting against the sides of the porcelain cup.

It was silent in the restaurant. The only sound was the loud slurping of noodles as the customers bent their heads low to their steaming bowls. A wok scraped against a stove in the kitchen next door, and Urban heard the whoosh of flames.

Auntie had allowed her in the kitchen once. Urban had watched as the cook used open flames and a huge, blackened wok.

Scrape, scrape, toss. Scrape, scrape, toss.

The cook would fling the noodles into the air, and flames would leap around the wok.

Auntie came back out with a platter of noodles and served a patron.

Noodles. Tea. A pair of chopsticks, sitting on a wooden table.

Something about that combination gave her déjà vu.

Then she gasped as she realized what was missing from the picture: the microneedle patch. She knew where she had seen it before. It was next to a pair of chopsticks, tea, and noodles.

At home.

14

THE MICRONEEDLE PATCH

MY PARENTS HAD ONE OF THOSE PATCHES!

It was one of her earliest memories. She'd always assumed the device was some sort of weird bandage. She'd seen it sitting on the table at home, next to a cup of tea and a bowl of noodles and a pair of chopsticks.

It wasn't a Band-Aid but a scientific tool. But why would my parents have one? Were they working for the Center for Advancements in Asian Genetics at one point? If so, why didn't they enhance me? They would have had plenty of opportunity to do so.

"How's my little warrior?"

Urban jumped.

Everest slid into a seat next to her and gave her one of those lazy smiles that made her pulse race. His messy black hair looked as if he'd stuck it in a wind tunnel, and his XR suit had several gashes in it.

Urban eyed him warily. "What happened to you?"

Everest looked down at himself and shifted slightly. "Ah . . . nothing serious. Just a little trouble in the Outskirts."

What was Everest not telling her? There must be more trouble in the Outskirts than he let on. He probably didn't want to worry her.

Her thoughts returned to her discovery. She leaned into him to whisper, "I just realized something."

"Yeah?"

Urban quickly filled him in about the patch and her memory of it. "I have to get to the bottom of this," she concluded. "I have to find out why my parents would have one."

They fell silent as Auntie came by balancing two giant blue-and-white porcelain bowls piled high with steaming noodles

Auntie eyed Urban. "Eat. You're too skinny." Then she left them to their food.

Urban began hungrily slurping down noodles,

Everest waited until Auntie was out of hearing range. "Were you able to find anything about the microneedle patch in QuanNao?"

Urban heaved a deep sigh. "There's not much out there."

"I'll help you look."

Urban brightened. "Really?"

"Of course. If it's important to you, it's important to me." He gazed at her lips, leaning down.

Under the table, their fingers intertwined.

Everest stopped his face inches from her own and pulled back, suddenly remembering where they were. A yearning look was still on his face, but with a wink he dispelled it.

Urban's face had to be the shade of a red paper lantern.

"It's so much fun embarrassing you," he teased.

"Whatever." She brushed him off, then lowered her voice. "We really should be more careful in public."

Everest bent his head so this mouth was directly by her ear, each word a tickling sensation. "Isn't that why we met in the Hutongs?"

"Yes, but students could technically come here. I doubt they will. But it's possible I could see someone I know."

"We'll be discrete," he said, a grin on his face. Everest continued to look at her with soft, smiling eyes.

Noticing his expression, Urban grinned. "Looks like someone missed me."

"And you haven't missed me?"

Guilt shot through her. She'd been too busy with all the newness of uni to spend much time thinking about him. "Aren't you hungry?" she asked instead. "I'm starving after jiujitsu class."

He pulled back in feigned shock. "You actually went? What has the world come to?"

Urban punched him in the shoulder which made Everest laugh.

"Looks like you're on your way to becoming a true warrior."

"*Tiana!*" Urban moaned. "I'm already becoming violent like Lillian."

As they ate, Urban updated him about the Games, her new roommates, her first day of classes, and jiujitsu. By the time she was done, Everest had already finished his food.

"Does anyone suspect?" he asked.

"Remember Angel from my last day at work?"

"That hacker who knew your real identity?"

"Yeah. She . . . was at the bash in person."

"What?" Everest exclaimed.

Urban jabbed him with her chopsticks to quiet down before filling him in.

Lines of worry creased his forehead. "Are you sure you want to stay at uni? Your safety is more important."

"I'm not leaving." Urban balked. "This is my dream. I'm not letting some stupid pop star ruin it for me."

"Promise me you'll be careful?"

"I always am." Urban turned back to her half-finished bowl of noodles. "All the same, I think we should watch what we say in XR, just in case she's still hacking me."

Everest nodded.

"Do you want your bill?" Auntie came back around, and they both extended their tatts.

"Have you eaten, Auntie?" Everest asked respectfully.

Auntie beamed. "Why, yes, I have. Thank you for asking." She tucked her scanner away and gave Urban a warning look. "This one's a keeper. Don't let him get away."

"Yup, he's a great friend," Urban chirped without missing a beat. She purposefully avoided Everest's eyes, knowing he'd probably make her blush again.

When alone again, Everest whispered, "Want to try and meet up on Friday night? Strictly as friends of course," he teased.

Urban smiled. "Let's do it."

He gave her a wink, then was gone.

Urban waited a few minutes before she left too. The second she went through the barrier and re-entered the city, she made her way to the nearest XRD. It was time to get some answers about the patch and her past.

THE REST OF THE NEXT WEEK PASSED BY IN A blur of homework assignments, jiujitsu, practicing on her motorcycle, and researching the microneedle patch. She barely had passing grades in all of her classes, but she'd take that. Jiujitsu was actually starting to be fun, and while she hadn't landed a big jump yet, Urban felt confident in her racing abilities on her motorcycle. The only thing she hadn't made any progress on was the microneedle patch.

The little information she'd found was on the one existing device in CAAG. Nothing more. Though she'd researched it endlessly, she wasn't any nearer to discovering any link to the microneedle patch and her family.

She'd confronted her parents about it, but as she had suspected, they completely denied having ever seen such a device. Even Lillian seemed skeptical of Urban's memories. But Urban knew what she had seen. She remembered the device as clear as day sitting at their house. So why did no one else? Were they all hiding something from her?

All too soon, the weekend was over, and it was another school night.

"The tryouts for the Games start in four weeks," Hazel announced gleefully as the three of them got ready for bed in their dorm room. "I got us exclusive seats in the lounge to join some of the KOLs at our school."

With a crash, the bedroom window flung open.

A figure leaped through and flew across the room.

Hazel screamed.

Blood pumped loudly in Urban's ears. She wondered if she'd be able to use her jiujitsu move to shrimp away if it came to a ground fight. Then, deciding she'd just get squashed like a bug, balled her fists instead.

The figure changed from black to white and started blending in with the wall where she was perched, hands and feet glued to the surface.

Crouched on the wall, the intruder shifted colors and became clearly visible as her head swiveled around like an owl's until it was facing the girls.

Hazel let out another choked shriek.

Urban realized the figure was also a girl. She wore a shape-shifting suit, which changed to resemble jeans, a flannel shirt, and a backward hat, and a mask, which disappeared, revealing her face. Instead of whites around her pupils, her golden irises were surrounded by black, giving her a bird-like appearance.

The girl looked like she was about to say something, then her eyes widened when an alarm started to go off. "Stupid sensors," she muttered. "Knew I shouldn't have used the window."

She leaped like a bird of prey from the wall to the unclaimed top bunk, where she threw back a set of covers, revealing a suitcase. She flung the bag into the closet while she simultaneously dropped from the wall and onto the bed.

As the alarm stopped, Urban realized with shock this was her missing bunkmate.

The new roommate let out a sigh of relief and leaped to the ground, landing soundlessly next to the three girls.

"I'm Coral." She extended her hand in greeting, but Hazel and Blossom were still too stunned to move.

Urban took the girl's hand and shook it firmly. "Lee Urban."

"Nice meeting you, Urban."

Urban tried looking up Coral's sosh but found it blocked, along with her enhancements.

Hazel finally recovered from her shock. "*Ai ya*, what are you wearing? Is that flannel?"

"You must be the roommate who has all the Nature Lite bars." Coral adjusted her backward hat. "Is the cute little panda on a diet?"

Hazel gasped in horror. "I am not on a diet! How dare you insult my genetics—"

"Yeah, yeah," Coral cut her off and turned to Blossom. "Ah, the smart one with science books for a pillow. Are you like a botanist or something?"

Blossom blinked before regaining poise. "What's your surname?"

"None of your business."

Blossom's mouth opened but then shut again firmly.

"Where are you from?" Hazel asked, the remains of a scowl still present on her face.

"The Asian Federation, like you guys."

"You don't sound like it." Blossom's eyes narrowed in suspicion.

Coral sighed. "That's because I grew up in the Western Federation."

Hazel groaned. "A Western Asian mix?"

"I was born here and am a citizen like you. I just spent the years between six and eighteen living in the West."

"Practically a foreigner." Hazel's head sank into her hands. "We'll never get a high sosh with her trailing us."

"Don't worry, I have no intentions of hanging around you two." But she gave Urban a nod before turning and climbing up the wall and into bed.

Hazel shivered. "She reminds me of a rabid owl," she whispered.

Urban was fascinated and wondered how people like that survived in New Beijing. Coral didn't seem to care at all about her sosh or what others thought about her. *What I'd give to have that luxury.*

Coral muttered as she tried to get comfortable. "I forgot how much you all love rock-hard beds."

Blossom and Hazel exchanged glances but followed her example, climbing into their own bunks. Urban did likewise, slipping on her sleep headset. Her thoughts raced—about her new roommate and classes the next day—but the sleep gas filling her nose made her drowsy. She counted to seven before she fell asleep.

The next day, Urban woke up with an odd stiffness. "*Tiana,* is this what jiujitsu does to you?"

On the bunk above, Coral drew the covers over her head. "Some of us are still trying to sleep here."

"Sorry." Urban quickly dressed in silence. Her weather advisory-bot predicted rain, so she wore her warmer, water-resistant XR jumper. Outside the dorms it was a little chilly, and the gray, overcast sky looked like it might start pouring rain at any minute.

Urban followed the masses of groggy-eyed students toward the Zhang Science Hall. Her first class of the day was AI Foundations—a Gen Ed class important enough to be taught by a human professor.

"By next week there's an essay due on the history of Samson and several quiz questions based on your reading assignment," Dr. Xi instructed as she wrapped up class. "Remember, this is all working toward our goal for the end of the semester. I will expect you to have built a chatbot, compared training methodologies to identify the most effective chat-building strategy, and trained an image-recognition model to recognize your favorite sport. Extra credit to the student who can break someone else's chatbot. If your chatbot breaks, I'll be giving you a failed grade on that assignment. Class dismissed."

Urban exited the room, overwhelmed as she headed to Advanced Psychology, where she received more assignments.

Her next class, Crypto Currencies, was even more boring than it had been last week, if that was possible. The probot reprimanded several students for nodding off.

"I still don't get why we even need this class when we all just use our tatts," a voice next to Urban whispered.

Urban glanced over and jumped. While the student mostly resembled a chair, the shimmering backward hat was unmistakable.

"How long have you been there?"

"Long enough for you to notice." Coral leaned back in her seat, becoming fully visible. She was wearing high-top sneakers and a baggy T-shirt. Urban had never seen an XR suit like that.

"Are you in any of my other classes?" Urban whispered.

Coral smirked. "Not that you know of."

After class, Coral turned to Urban. "Want to grab lunch?"

Urban hesitated. Hanging out with Coral wasn't going to earn her any points with Blossom and Hazel. But her new roommate intrigued her. Before she could stop herself, Urban found herself nodding.

"Are you cool with burgers? I've had enough rice already to last me the semester."

They went to a small joint in the underground food courts. Urban's bunkmate slouched in her seat, relaxed.

Urban wondered if Coral was ever stressed. "How's it coming back to the Asian Federation after all these years?"

Coral rolled her eyes. "Bizarre. I swear I'm in some sort of culture shock right now, but no one will believe me. Maybe if I dress more Western, people will believe I'm from the Western Federation."

"You already look pretty Western to me."

Coral flashed a grin, then made a face. "But it's pretty strange coming back. It's like nothing has changed, but at the same time, everything has. I've forgotten a lot of words, and I don't even remember how to use my international tatt. Those are the biggest things. Then there's little things like: Where has my favorite hole-in-the-wall shop gone? Has there always been some giant bubble thing over the Hutongs? Why is everything so dang expensive? How do you say the new words to all the technological advancements invented while I was away? Also, why are all the kids here so scared of their moms?"

Urban giggled. "Because Asian Federation mothers are terrifying. If your parents weren't so westernized, you would understand."

"My mom reminds me of how lucky I am all the time," Coral commented.

"She's right."

"Moms usually are." Coral pulled the pickles out of her burger. "So, what's your plan?"

"My plan?"

"Yeah. Like what's your track? What are you going to do after you graduate?"

"I'm hoping to be an Artisan." She couldn't believe she'd just told the truth. *Hold the cards close to your chest. Get a grip. Trust no one,* she mentally berated herself. "But I'm also interested in the Giver track," she lied.

"I wish I had that flexibility. We all know exactly my job options as a Camo," Coral said. "Your parents must be pretty cool to allow you a choice. That's rare these days to have enhancements for both."

Urban stiffened and quickly changed topics. "So why did you choose to come here? Or did your parents choose?"

"I didn't choose, really. I was placed here."

Urban stopped chewing. "You tested in?"

"Yeah."

"*Wakao*! You must be brilliant!"

"Ah, it's nothing."

"You certainly have the Asian modesty down." Urban laughed.

Coral wagged her finger. "I'm not a total bumbling foreigner."

"That's pretty impressive though. Really. I haven't met anyone else who tested in."

"My younger sister hates me for it." Coral smirked, then took a sip of her drink. "Your parents paid for you, I suppose?"

"Yeah, but my mother came from a poorer family." Urban kicked herself again. Why was she telling Coral all this?

"Oh?"

"It's a long story. Anyway, I didn't get in based on my scores, like you. You're going to have no problems with classes."

"Except my Federation Mandarin is pathetic. It takes me like an hour to read one page of homework. I don't know how I'm going to survive."

So Coral was fairly normal after all. "Maybe we can help each other with Crypto class?" Urban asked hopefully.

"That would be great." Coral nodded emphatically. After a moment of chewing thoughtfully, she turned to Urban. "So, what are your enhancements?"

Urban started. "Me?"

"No, your mom."

Urban stared back in confusion.

Coral rolled her eyes. "No one gets sarcasm here. Yes, you."

"Uh . . . I'm not supposed to say."

Coral eyed Urban. "One of those secretive types huh? All right. I respect that. Now I'm super curious though. And when I'm curious . . ." She disappeared. "I find things out using alternative methods." Coral reappeared and winked.

Urban bit her lip. Did her roommate already know things about her? Who knows where she had been or could go without anyone finding out.

Coral jumped up. "I'm going to be late to class."

Coral headed out, leaving Urban conflicted inside. She wanted to be friends with this odd character, but there were too many risks involved. She sighed and left to go study.

The next day, Urban slept through all her alarms. Coral had to poke her awake to get the noise turned off.

Big black circles resided under her eyes, and her throat was raw. *Oh no, please don't let my asthma be kicking in.*

Frustrated she'd overslept when she had so much studying to do, Urban threw on a dress, snatched up a latte from the hoverdrone outside, then located the closest XRD. As she got off the elevator, a student in the lobby bumped into her.

Scalding coffee burned through her dress. The offending student didn't even apologize as she sauntered away.

Looking down, Urban assessed the damage. Dark brown stains covered the dress, giving it a cow-like pattern. *Of course, I picked today to wear white.* She debated running up to change but didn't want to waste any more study time. Instead, she made her way to the closest XRD.

After logging into the student portal, she saw her first grade result was in for her Programming assignment. She eagerly opened her report.

Sixty-seven.

That score put her in the lowest percentile of the class. And the probot had said this would be an easy assignment.

You couldn't even get a decent grade on an easy assignment, Urban berated herself. *Stupid. At least my parents don't know. I'll just have to pull my grades back up before the end of the semester. I'll do whatever it takes. I won't be in the bottom of the class ever again.*

She logged into the tutoring portal and requested tutors for every class. Unfortunately, other kids must have had the same idea because all the tutoring spots were booked. Urban had to sign up for the waitlist instead.

She got a ping and saw it was a vid message from Mother. She looked like she'd just stepped out of the shower. Her makeup was off, and her hair was soaking.

[Mother: Your scores are completely unacceptable! What are you wasting your time on? Don't make me bring you back home to enforce studying. You know I will. I expect a much better report next time.]

Urban blinked. How was Mother getting her scores? Wasn't SCA supposed to stop sending parents grade reports once she was in college? Then she remembered it was actually once she turned eighteen. Until then, Mother could access all her reports.

What am I going to do? The last thing I need is Mother forcing me to live at home.

Urban ignored her mother's pings and tried to go back to studying, but she was too frustrated to concentrate. Instead, she exited the XRD to clear her head and take a walk.

I try so hard. And for what? I have nothing to show for it. I stay up later than everyone, work way harder, and I still have the worst grades. I wish I had a brain enhancement. Even having just one would give me a better chance in this environment.

But I have to keep trying. I have to do more!

She wanted to talk to someone who would understand her frustration, but Lillian was probably still sleeping, and Everest was already at work.

She checked if anyone had responded to her ping about tutoring. Nothing. She was surprised to see a missed message from Brooke though.

[Brooke: I'm training later today and need a sparring partner. You free?]

Urban reread the message as apprehension snaked up her spine. *I can't train with her! She'd crush me. Not to mention, I don't want to be anywhere near a SAS member. How am I going to get out of this?* She thought for a few seconds before crafting a message and sending it.

[Urban: Sorry, I have several big assignments due and won't

have time today. Thanks for the offer though!]

She had no idea where she was anymore and glanced around. She'd been wandering the campus absently for some time. She paid attention to the words scrolling across the bottom of her retina display.

<Approaching Xi Engineering building. Sosh: 56.>

She'd never seen anything like it. Because it was early, the lobby was empty. Classical music wafted through the air, and the smell of new furniture and flowers greeted her.

She walked across the marble and carpet, toward one of the plush seating enclaves. Displays of wooden animals with feathers and moss growing out of them lined the way.

Urban turned slowly in a circle, taking in the grandeur. At the entrance rose floor-to-ceiling glass. On the opposite wall, bone-white pillars supported a metallic dome like the side of a giant ship. At the base on the floor was a long copper desk with a pot of wilting flowers and a concierge-bot sitting behind it.

Her eye caught on something. What was that behind the desk? At the other end of a hallway stood what looked like a doorway made of pure gold.

She skirted the desk and made her way down the hallway, toward the majestic arched doorway. Urban could make out a tatt scanner at the golden door. *Restricted area? What could be back there?* Her imagination ran wild with possibilities.

Her system flashed a warning.

<Entering purple zone. DANGER!>

Purple? As in the zone that causes instant death? Not possible.

She'd never seen a purple zone when she'd looked at maps of the campus. She scanned her surroundings. Where was the purple zone exactly? Her retina display highlighted the golden door.

It started sliding open.

I'm imagining it.

But the door was definitely opening, and a dark ghostly mist swirled out.

Tendrils of fear shot through her, numbing her mind and rendering her legs useless. The mist inched toward her like skeletal fingers reaching for her throat.

Finally, her legs decided to cooperate, and she turned to run.

She did a double take. The other end of the hallway—from which she'd just entered—was sealed off.

She was trapped.

URBAN FROZE, STARING AT THE DOORS blocking her escape route. Her brain could only process one repeated thought: *How is this possible?*

How did I not notice the doors when I came down the hall?

The temperature in the room dropped. Urban's breath came out in swirls in front of her and then vanished. She wished she could vanish too. She tried pinging the *Jingcha*, anyone, but her messages all bounced back, unable to be delivered.

Think, Urban, think! There has to be a way out.

She commanded herself to remain calm. She searched the area frantically for anything to protect her against whatever was coming from the ominous door.

<Approaching purple zone. USE EXTREME CAUTION.>

Urban tried to ignore the warnings piling up in her retina display and focus. Instead, she found herself wondering what would happen once that mist reached her. Would it burn her flesh? Would she completely disappear into a pile of ash on the floor? Or maybe her body would remain intact, but she'd choke to death.

Stay calm.

She sprinted to the closed doors and rammed herself against them. Pain laced her shoulders. A dull thud echoed in the enclosed space. They weren't budging.

Her heart pounded faster, drowning out the hissing sound of the mist slowly creeping in around her. Ignoring it, she scanned the wall for a tatt swiper. Sure enough, there to the right of the doors she spotted the device. Urban raised her tatt to the wall and felt it vibrate. But her tatt didn't flash gold in acceptance.

Desperate, Urban tried the door anyway. It was still locked.

She tried again. Her tatt vibrated so she knew it had been scanned, but then nothing happened.

Terror clawed at her, sending her nerves skittering until she was forced to lean against the nearest wall.

The door leading to the purple zone was now completely open, and funeral-black mist poured out.

The only way out is if I hack this scanner.

Something cold slid over her arms and she jumped. It was the dark mist. It had reached her.

Urban paused a second, waiting to see if her flesh would dissolve or bubble or otherwise deteriorate. Nothing happened. The mist just felt cold.

Maybe it's only deadly to breathe.

Just before the mist reached her mouth, she inhaled a deep breath of clear air and held it.

I can hold my breath for one minute and twenty seconds. I have to open the door by then.

Back before Lucas hated her guts, he'd enlisted Urban on a few of his prankster missions. One of them had involved disabling a scanner. He'd shown her how, but it had been years ago and Urban had only partially been paying attention.

Now, she focused fervently on trying to remember the steps.

Jamming the scanner required an exploit script. Lucas kept one in his avatar's inventory of items hidden to the public. Since he had allowed Urban to enter into his hidden treasure trove before, she was counting on being able to get in again. If he'd updated his passcode for the room since then, she was in trouble. Not to mention, she'd need access to QuanNao. If whatever interference was blocking her pings for help also blocked access to that . . . Urban tried not to think about what would happen.

Her retina display showed thirty seconds had passed. Her lungs started to burn.

Urban called up Lucas's landing page. *So far so good. Thought it could just be my stored data and not real time.*

Forty-five seconds.

She entered his avatar's landing room.

The door was locked.

No. It can't be.

She tried again. And again.

Locked.

She didn't have access to QuanNao either. She was completely cut off from the world. That meant there was no way for her to hack the scanner. No way to escape.

One minute.

Her lungs screamed for air, but there was nothing she could do. No fresh air left to breathe.

As her counter reached a minute and fifteen seconds, she knew she'd have to take a breath soon.

Suddenly, the door swung open. The mist dissipated into bright sunlight.

Urban stared at it for a second, not comprehending. Then ran toward the door. She collapsed outside, gasping for air.

When she'd caught her breath, she looked up. A security-bot stood over her. Its head swiveled mechanically toward her. "Miss Lee, may I check your vitals? You seem unwell."

"I was attacked! There's a purple zone back there!" Urban turned back to face the room and gasped. The mist was completely gone. The warning on her retina display for the purple zone had also vanished.

"I do not see a purple zone." The security-bot extended

one of its armored metal arms toward her. "May I check your vitals please?"

"It was right there!" Urban shouted at it.

"Do you have an emergency you'd like to report?" the bot asked.

"I just told you!" Frustrated, Urban slowed her speech and clearly enunciated each word. "There is a purple zone back there."

"It seems your logic is currently irrational," the bot said with infuriating calmness. "There is not a purple zone in this vicinity. Why don't you take a seat and relax?"

"Relax? Relax!" Urban was beyond that. "Let me speak to a real person *now*, or I'm going to smash you to so many pieces they won't even take you at a scrap yard!"

"I'm concerned for your mental health," the bot continued soothingly. "I may call in a squad to help if you cannot contain yourself."

Urban realized she was wasting time. "Take me to a human. I have a case to report."

Finally, the bot escorted her to the Security Center. She found herself in a cramped room with an older woman, a Natural by all appearances. She smoked a cigarette and played a game of chess on her desk with a second security-bot.

Urban's system warned her she was entering a yellow zone due to the smoke, but she ignored it. "Sorry to interrupt."

The lady snubbed out her cigarette and waved the smoke away. An air filter clicked on. She slapped the robot to get out of the chair and motioned for Urban to sit.

The smoky air caused an itch at the back of her throat. Urban let out a cough.

The lady scrutinized Urban, her leathery forehead developing a deep row of wrinkles before she leaned back and relaxed. Her eyes glazed for a few moments as she used her retina display to watch Urban's conversation with the security-bot.

Urban's legs bounced as she waited.

A moment later, the lady leaned forward. "Either you've had one too many sleepless nights or you're in some serious trouble."

"Do we have a purple zone on campus?"

The woman stared at Urban. "No."

Urban's legs bounced faster. "But I saw it, I swear! Let me show you my retina vid replay."

"Please do."

Urban live projected onto the wall her retina recording. She found the spot where she was just going into the Xi Engineering building and hit play.

Seeing the golden door to the purple zone again sent a chill down her spine. She coughed several times, and the woman gave her a look. Try as she might, she couldn't stop herself from coughing. *Of course, my lungs are acting up now too.*

When the recording got to the part where her system flashed a warning, there was nothing. Urban kept waiting for the warning, but nothing happened. Her retina replay showed her staring into space for a long time, eventually, turning and running out of the building and collapsing to her knees. She looked like a crazy person.

Urban sat stunned.

There was no purple zone, door trapping her inside, or black mist. It was all gone.

Someone hacked my retina recordings.

Fear squeezed her heart. She remembered hearing about something like this from her Programming class, but wasn't this only supposed to happen to political figures or KOLs? It made no sense to target students.

Why me? Does someone know I'm a Natural? Maybe my parents were right. It's dangerous for me to be here.

"You need more sleep." The security officer wagged a knobby finger at her. "You're not the first one coming in here with tall tales. Too much partying makes people delusional."

Urban decided she had to trust her instincts. She would believe what her eyes had seen, not what her tech told her anymore. Someone had hacked into her retina recordings and edited them with replaced memories. But that was extraordinarily difficult. It would mean overriding just about every security protocol in QuanNao. Who had that kind of power?

Urban stood, beginning to wheeze now. "Thank you," she managed.

The woman looked up in surprise. Urban realized she'd probably never been thanked before. To the PKU students and faculty, she was just another invisible Natural there to serve them.

Urban offered her a smile, then turned and left.

She wasn't sure what to do, where to go, or whom to trust. She finally went back to the parking garage for her motorcycle, looking over her shoulder at every turn. She sent a ping to Lillian before riding toward her parents' house in stunned silence.

Her thoughts raced faster than her motorcycle. *Why would anyone hack my recorded memories?*

There was something that kept tugging at the back of her mind, a piece to the puzzle she had to be missing. She had to keep a close eye on the road to keep from swerving into another vehicle. She was pulling into the garage at her home when she made the connection.

Qing Angel.

That was a person with incredible power and an unusual interest in her personal life. But would Angel really try and kill her? No one could get to that level of fame and be a killer. Could they?

What if she decides to erase more of my recorded memories or replace them with fake ones?

Urban tried to hold back her coughs and wheezes as she entered her apartment. But to no avail. At the sound, two cats came skidding around the corner. Jiaozi sprinted to her side with a loud meow. Baozi was only a few seconds behind. Urban was almost knocked over with the tiger-sized house cats trying to weave in between her legs.

Urban gave them each a quick pat, then darted upstairs to her room with Baozi close behind. Opening the door to her room brought a wave of comfort. It was just the way she'd left it. She breathed deeply of the sweetly scented candles and smell of cat. She looked at her bed. There was a large dent with blue fur on it.

"Baozi!" Urban pointed accusingly at the dent on the bed. "Have you been sleeping there?"

Baozi paid her no attention. The cat ran past her and leaped onto the bed even as Urban watched.

"How dare you," Urban reprimanded. "Down. Now!"

Baozi stared back as if considering whether Urban's threats were to be taken seriously before slowly hopping back off.

Urban started coughing again, and this time the spasms bent her over. When they subsided, she hurriedly turned on a small machine. She waited for it to beep green before sticking in a mouthpiece and inhaling cool mist.

A few minutes of this treatment, and her lungs were adequately soothed. She turned up her favorite playlist, crawled under her warm blanket, and burrowed between the mountain of pillows.

Urban knew she should be studying for her many upcoming tests or figuring out a way to somehow pull her life back together, but she didn't care anymore. She was tired of trying so hard all the time. She was exhausted from having to hide so much. Now, she had serious safety concerns to worry about too. Despite her retina memory being erased, her mind couldn't stop replaying the image of that dark mist creeping toward her.

Should she tell her parents? She needed to be safe. But telling them would surely backfire. They'd barely agreed to allow her to go to uni in the first place. Mother would freak out. She'd probably make her leave uni, and Urban couldn't risk that.

Urban thought about the Natural security guard she'd spoken with. *I have to stay.* She gritted her teeth. *I have to show Naturals what we can do. We may not have superior genetics, but we still have value.*

Her decision to keep the incident from her parents made, she thought about who she could trust.

Everest and Lillian were the only people that came to mind. She quickly sent them both a ping.

She had to plan what to tell her parents, figure out who Qing Angel was, and in the meantime, find a way to protect herself.

She remembered in her Programming course the probot talking about recordings being hacked. Maybe there were resources about how to prevent this from happening.

She logged into her class portal and did a search within her textbook for "memory wipes."

Three results turned up. The first two explained what a memory wipe was. On the third search she found something useful. How to Prevent Your Memories from Being Hacked, the paragraph header read.

Urban skimmed the characters until she got to the part explaining prevention. It started with a program called RET-Anti-Hack, which used asymmetric cryptography. The program provided the digital key, but the private key was the individual's genome. This would ensure only the intended user had access to their messages and stored data.

Each time the retina recorded something, it would encrypt it with a digital key, and then send it offsite as an archive. If anything was changed, a new copy was made, but the old files would still be accessible.

This is exactly what I need.

The directions said to send in a piece of hair or a blood sample to lock the bio-authentication. Urban checked the privacy regulations to be sure there was no way her DNA could be sent anywhere without her authority—and thus her Natural genes be discovered. After an hour of reading the fine print, she was convinced her data would remain anonymous.

She checked the price and winced. It would eat up most of her allowance and summer earnings. No more painting supplies or classes. Not that she had time these days to paint.

Doing some quick math, she came to the conclusion she'd be able to make it through the rest of the semester with what was left of her crypto credits—if she lived off of ramen.

I don't have a choice. She ordered the RET-Anti-Hack, plucked a hair from her head, placed it inside the small interior of a mini drone, and fast-shipped it.

[QuanNao: RET-Anti-Hack will be delivered within four hours. Once the sample is collected, the bio-authentication will become active.]

Urban checked her credits and sighed at how much they'd dropped.

Baozi hopped up onto her bed, avoiding eye contact. Urban gave him a disapproving glare but then relented. The cat curled up next to her, taking up nearly half the bed and resting his giant head on her lap, purring as she stroked him absently. As the adrenaline finally started to wear off, Urban realized how exhausted she was.

I should find Mother before she finds me.

With reluctance, she forced herself out of her room and sent a maid to fetch her mother while she waited in the parlor. She ran her hands through the Peruvian Vucana-wool couch while she waited. A maid brought a pot of steaming green tea and placed it on the imported Italian coffee table.

Urban heard her mother before she saw her. The *slap, slap, slap* of house slippers and then a furious voice. "I cannot believe the low score you received on your first assignment!"

The scent of mother's Bulgarian Rose perfume overpowered the room the second she entered.

Urban braced herself for the lecture. For the next ten minutes Mother berated Urban for her grades and lack of respect for her parents.

Finally, she seemed to have run out of things to say. Urban was about to leave when her mother spoke again. "I just want you safe. To do that, you have to keep up your grades and sosh." Her eyes glittered, and to Urban's surprise, she thought she saw tears, but then Mother spun away.

Urban was too tired to think more on it as she trudged back to her room. She tried to work on her homework assignments. The beginnings of her XR character were finally coming to life. However, her character, an Artisan with spiky red hair, had various odd ticks.

The Artisan refused to walk normally, couldn't grab stuff out of his backpack, and couldn't swim. In fact, the Artisan's entire body disappeared when he went near water. The code was driving Urban mad, but she couldn't figure out how to fix it. The code grew blurry and her bed softer. The last thing she remembered was Baozi purring.

Urban wasn't sure how long she'd been asleep when her door flew open.

"I got your ping." Lillian's face was white. She raced over to the side of the bed and threw her arms around Urban.

Urban leaned up against Lillian for a long moment before they both sat back. She spent the next two hours explaining everything that had happened. By the end, Lillian had grown very quiet.

She gazed past Urban. "This is dangerous," she finally said.

"You're not going to tell Mother and Father?"

Lillian considered it. "No. But we do need additional security for you. Leave it to me. I'll make something up that won't get you in trouble but will get you a guard for protection."

Urban looked at her. "How will you manage that?'

"Don't worry about it. Just leave it to me."

Urban thought a moment. "Okay. Oh! I just ordered a RET-Anti-Hack to help."

"Perfect." Lillian nodded approvingly. "That's just what I was thinking."

"How do you know about that?" Urban asked curiously. "I'd never heard of it before today."

"I know all about the latest tech and trends; I'm an *Inventor*." Before Urban could ask more questions, Lillian rushed on. "Now, you also need some self-defense weapons." She chewed her lip in thought. "I have an idea." Her eyes began darting, searching in QuanNao. "Okay, I speed ordered something for you. It should be here right about when dinner arrives."

"Dinner?"

"I also ordered your favorite street food while I was at it."

Urban sat up in bed. "You ordered fried *jiaozi*?"

Lillian smiled broadly.

"You're the best! I love *jiaozi*."

Jiaozi the cat suddenly appeared on the floor. "Not you." Urban rolled her eyes. "How did I know you were hiding in here?" She darted a glance at her sister. "Remind me why you had to name your cat after my favorite food again?"

Later, Lillian asked in between bites, "How's birthday planning coming?"

"I'm dreading it," Urban moaned. "Thankfully my roommate is helping me." She stopped short. "Oh no! I forgot to ask Father if I could use the Underwater Bar!"

"Let me take care of it, all right?" Lillian put a hand on Urban's shoulder. "All you really need is good food, drinks, a reliable DJ, and a couple of KOLs, and you're set. Do you have those?"

"I think so." Urban looked gratefully at her sister. "At least I heard Hazel talking about them."

"Then you'll be fine." Lillian dipped her *jiaozi* in soy sauce. "Besides, you're not going to have a perfect sosh on the first day. It takes consistent practice to pull it up. Mine was only 58 on my birthday. Everyone has to start somewhere. Don't worry about it."

When Urban's package arrived, Lillian helped Urban install it.

"Oh, cool, you got the latest version of the RET-Anti-Hack. It uses digital-key cryptography to sign all messages. That way, you know it really came from your retina display rather than someone else's. If any memories come from anyone other than you, it will alert the *Jingcha* and you. Pretty awesome, huh?"

Urban shook her head. "Seriously, how do you know so much about this?"

Lilian looked away. "I just . . . really care about safety." She gazed at the ceiling. "That's why I take jiujitsu and work out and—"

"All right, I get it," Urban interrupted as she stared bewilderedly at her sister. Something was suddenly off about Lillian.

"Here, you also need this." Lillian handed Urban another box.

Urban held up what looked like a miniature metal hula-hoop with another, smaller ring inside it. "What is this?"

"It's a stun shield," Lillian said. "It's to keep you safe."

"Never heard of it."

"Watch this." Lillian took the stun shield and activated it. Instantly, it filled with a blue, pulsing laser. "You hold it by this outer ring, and the inner one acts as a defense against any sort of weapon attack. It's a shield." She demonstrated by poking a hanger into it. The hanger popped, sizzled, and bounced back— seared at the edges.

"You can also use it on the offensive." Lillian threw the stun shield, and it bounced onto the ground where it rolled then hit one of Urban's chairs. There was an electrical buzz as blue fingers licked up the legs of the chair. The shield fell over and deactivated to just a metallic hoop again, leaving nothing but the smell of burnt wood.

"Wow." Urban raced over to pick up the shield. "How did you do that?"

"You can activate it so once it's thrown, it administers 70,000 volts to the first object it strikes."

Urban cautiously activated it and took a turn throwing it. The stun shield flew through the air and hit a pillow on the floor. Blue fire shot through the pillow, and it erupted in flames. Jiaozi meowed in terror and leaped off the bed, knocking Lillian over in his mad scramble out of the room.

"Ah! Fire!" Urban frantically snatched a blanket off the bed and smothered the flames. The comforter hissed, and smoke poured out from it, but the flames died out.

When she finally lifted the blanket, only a few charred remains of the pillow were left.

"That was my favorite pillow." Urban stared down at the remains.

Lillian tried to stifle a laugh. "Maybe we should practice on the rooftop."

She picked up one of Urban's paint brushes and some paint. In the quiet gardens of the roof, she drew a target on the side of the wall.

Urban tried throwing the stun shield again. She struck the wall a meter away from the target. The wall turned a burnt black where it had been struck.

Urban cast a worried glance at Lillian. "Think Mother will be mad about the wall?"

Lillian shook her head. "They never come up here. Besides, they're about to have the whole roof repainted. They won't notice."

They spent the next hour practicing activating the defense field and then throwing it at the target.

"Thanks, sis," Urban said with gratitude after hitting the target for the eighth consecutive time. "I think this is good for now."

Watch out, Angel. Two can play at this.

自外

URBAN AWOKE ON HER BIRTHDAY IN A COLD sweat. She'd dreamed no one came to her party. Blossom had berated her for not planning further in advance, and Olive discovered she was a Natural. Two security officers were in the process of escorting her to the Outskirts when she awoke. It was 0530.

In the bathroom, she splashed water on her face to clear her mind. Her system wished her a happy birthday and informed her of all the shops offering discounts or free drinks on her special day. She also got a ping from Lillian.

[Lillian: I was able to get you a Camo bodyguard named Trig. He's waiting outside the dorms for you, but you won't see him. I've instructed him to remain incognito at all times. The last thing we need is to attract more attention. If you open the file I sent, you'll have access to a tracker I've put on him. That way, even though you won't see him, you can know his whereabouts at all times.]

On her way to class later, Urban opened the file and quickly updated her retina maps. Sure enough, there on her map, marked in green, was a triangle about ten meters away, labeled "Trig." Urban glanced in that direction. She saw nothing but a few bushes.

As she walked, she found the triangle moved with her. Trig always remained about ten meters behind. It was strange having someone constantly near, watching her.

Relaxing a little, she sorted through the rest of the birthday pings piling up. She eagerly opened one from Everest.

[Everest: Happy birthday! How does it feel to join me as a mature adult?] There was a video of him dramatically sticking out his tongue and pinching his eyes shut. She laughed, feeling a little bit lighter.

[Urban: About your "maturity". . .]

[Everest: Can't wait to see you this evening!]

[Urban: Same here!]

She wished he could come to the party.

In class, she managed to stay awake and take copious notes. She got her programming assignment back and found, despite his bugs, the XR Artisan she'd created received more than a passing grade. *Happy birthday to me!* Urban thought with pride as she kept staring at her best grade yet: a 92.

In the afternoon, she spent her time in XRD working on assignments. She was stuck on building a level of a game for her Programming class. It wasn't due until the end of the semester, but every time she tried to work on it, she got so frustrated and discouraged she ended up switching to another task. There was no way she would be the one student who managed to build an unbeatable level and secure an A in the class.

Her thoughts kept wandering back to the microneedle DNA patch. She took a quick break to research it in QuanNao. The break stretched into one hour, then two. Before she knew it, the afternoon had passed. She was no closer to learning anything about the device and was now stressed and kicking herself for getting distracted.

All too soon, it was time for the birthday activities, and nervous adrenaline filled her. Urban had heard students many years ago went to university for degrees alone. Grades were all that mattered back then. How she envied those students who didn't have the added burden of a sosh to worry about.

She rushed back to the dorms to get cleaned up for her birthday events. She had forgotten about Trig until he popped up in her maps as a green triangle. Being followed would take some getting used to.

Back in her room, she had a bot fix her hair in curled braids, then put her most expensive dress into her backpack. She was running late by the time she left the dorms.

Despite her speeding, she was surprised Trig somehow managed to keep up. His green dot remained visible close by in her maps. Was he on a motorcycle too?

When she arrived, Everest was already at a private pod in the corner of the shop waiting.

"I'm so sorry. I got here as fast as I could." Urban was still breathing heavily from sprinting up from the garage.

Everest stood. "Don't worry about it." He tucked a stray hair behind her ear. "Happy birthday, Beautiful."

Urban smiled at him as she adjusted her hair band. "It's been a crazy week."

"Let's change that," Everest declared. "I ordered your favorite: iced ginger bubble tea."

"I only have an hour, you know. Then I need to leave for the giant birthday bash my roommates are throwing me."

"We'll make it count." Everest placed his hand softly on the small of her back and guided her toward the pickup counter.

Butterflies erupted in Urban's stomach at his touch, but her gut remained firmly clenched. She wanted to enjoy this moment with him, but she couldn't. Dread for tonight filled her. *In a few hours I'll be getting my sosh. Everything hinges on that score.*

After swiping his tatt, a small window opened, displaying two bubble teas behind it.

"I still can't believe what happened to you with the purple zone," Everest said as they sat down together.

"I feel like I've been thrown into the Games and pitted against all the worst obstacles." Urban sighed. "It's almost impossible keeping up." She told him about her new bodyguard, the RET-Anti-Hack device, the stun shield, and her training regimen.

She was a kite string ready to snap. *Hold it together. Just make it through your birthday bash.*

Everest eyed her with concern. "It's been a rough week for you."

"I'm sorry I'm not fun to be around right now." Urban's shoulders slumped. "I'm just worried about keeping up with my grades, being safe, fitting in—it all just feels impossible. And after tonight, I'll have a sosh to worry about."

"This is really about your sosh, isn't it?"

"A little," Urban admitted.

"I think I have our next date idea."

"You're going to try and help me boost my sosh score?" She raised an eyebrow.

"I'm not totally ignorant about sosh stuff. I just don't care to apply it to my own. But if it matters to you, I'll find a way to boost yours." He grinned at her. "Forget I said anything. It will be a surprise. Here, I want to give you something." He pulled out a moss-green velvet pouch.

Urban opened the bag gingerly, and her eyes widened as she pulled out an elegant silver necklace with a single character dangling from it.

"*Mei,*" she read out loud.

His eyes were soft as he watched her examine the gift. "A reminder you have a boyfriend who thinks you're beautiful."

Urban gave him a quick smile. "Help me put it on?" She lifted her hair and twisted her back to him.

Cold metal slid around her neck. When she faced him again, Everest pierced her with a look she'd never seen before, one that made her breath catch.

"Suits you," he said huskily.

They stared into each other's eyes; Urban's golden ones lost in

Everest's raven black ones.

"Everest, do you—" Urban hesitated and started again. "Do you . . . ever wonder what's going to happen to us? How can someone who's Enhanced be with someone who's not?"

Everest regarded her a moment. "Not really."

Urban stared at him. "But I can't keep hiding you forever."

"Well, the way I see it, we have two options. Either you join me in the Outskirts, or I join you in the Metropolis."

Her heart leaped. "When do you think you can join me here?"

Everest's face hardened, and he poked at the bobas with a straw. "I think it's time we face the hard reality. I'm probably not going to get away from the Outskirts by becoming a famous musician."

Urban gripped his arm tightly. "Don't say that."

"What if I just come to the Metropolis anyway?"

Urban blanched. "What?"

"You seem to manage." Everest pushed his half-finished drink away.

"I—I don't know if you could pass as Enhanced like I can, and I wouldn't want you to have to pretend your whole life." Urban bit her lip, feeling like a fool she'd let that slip. They hadn't talked about their future, even making a reference to anything beyond dating.

But she had considered a future without him, and the possibility was terrible. *I don't want that. I want him by my side.*

Everest seemed not to notice. "Why do I have to pretend? Why can't I just be myself?"

"Not Enhanced?" Urban nearly spilled her drink. "But you would never be accepted."

He folded his arms. "So?"

Urban was at a complete loss as to what to say. The only Naturals who lived in the city were servants or lowly maintenance workers. She didn't want people thinking she was dating a servant. Not to mention, her parents would never allow it. Even her new friends at uni would probably abandon her if they knew. Her sosh would plummet, and then there would be no chance of living in the Metropolis. She could say good-bye to her dream of being an Artisan. She'd have to work fulltime in the tech facilities in the Outskirts, living her worst nightmare.

Everest interrupted her thoughts. "Wouldn't that be better than pretending my whole life?"

"I don't want you to have to pretend," Urban protested. "But I also don't want us to be rejected by society."

Everest leaned back, hurt written on his face. "I didn't realize other people's opinions were so important to you. I'm willing to give up my life in the Outskirts—everything I've ever known—to be with you. I thought you'd be able to bend a little too."

"I am willing to bend. I just thought you'd pretend like me. Or I'd live in the Outskirts."

Everest shook his head. "I won't drag you to the Outskirts. You deserve better. So that leaves me joining your life. But I can't live a lie. I'd rather be myself than live like you."

Urban's mouth fell open, and she set her drink down hard. "So that's what you think my life is? A lie?"

Everest tilted his head and looked at her knowingly.

"You of all people." Urban's voice rose.

"Urban."

A reminder ping to depart for her birthday bash popped up in her retina display.

"I have to go." Urban's jaw was tense and her voice clipped.

Everest reached for her, but she jerked away. She knew if she stayed any longer, all her suppressed fears, anger, and hurt would surface, and she'd start crying. What would Hazel and Blossom say if she showed up to her birthday with tearstained makeup?

"Urban, don't go." Everest's voice was soft as he stared down at his empty hands with hollow eyes.

She couldn't look at him. "I can't be late," she muttered and left. The whole ride to the bash she couldn't escape the haunted expression on Everest's face as they'd parted. He kept pinging her, but she ignored them and tried to force herself to mentally prepare for the party instead. It took all her self-control to keep it together.

She shifted gears and slowed as she left the main road and traveled down a path leading straight into the water. Reinforced glass formed a tunnel around the road as it dipped below the surface. As she entered, Urban was too distracted to hold her breath.

In the day, the surrounding water sparkled, and green light filtered down. Now, it was murky and dark. Little lights lining the road guided her forward as she zipped through the tunnel.

The temperature gradually dropped the further underwater she went. Soon, her XR suit had caught up and kept her warm, but it couldn't ward off the inner chill settling on her chest.

The tunnel ended, opening up into the entryway. After valet parking, she speed walked through a grandiose lobby with images of sea creatures projected onto its walls, and down the escalator to the bottom floors.

A fifty-foot-high, floor-to-ceiling glass wall stood at her right as she arrived. Several glowing jellyfish drifted lazily by. Their florescent blue-and-purple light filtered through the water and cast dancing shadows on the marble floor. All the Reservoir marine life was imported and genetically modified to survive in fresh water.

She breezed past several shops, the entrance to some of the apartments, and finally arrived at the doorway to Deep-Lake Bar. She'd been forced to spend countless evenings down here when her father first opened it.

I hate being this far underwater.

Guests were already milling about, and Urban let out a relieved breath that people were showing up.

"There you are!" Hazel pulled Urban into a private room, smelling overwhelmingly of waterlily perfume.

Urban quickly changed into her best dress, then took a seat in a plush couch in front of a giant gold mirror. A maid in a *qipao* dress poured her jasmine tea while several artists touched up her makeup.

"This is your sosh curator who will be briefing you on tonight's events," Hazel explained, gesturing at a dainty woman with the wings of a butterfly.

"Hello," Butterfly said with a flutter of her wings. "I've persuaded a few KOLs to attend tonight's festivities. I've also invited those within your immediate circle, Olive, Orion, and Brooke. In addition, I've extended invites to a couple of others from Olive's, Blossom's, and Hazel's circles of influence. It looks like possibly five of them are coming. One of them is very important. I think you know who Xinan is."

Urban blinked as she tried to keep up with the conversation, but all she could see was Everest. The hurt look on his face followed her.

Hazel shoved her in the shoulder. "Don't tell me you don't know who that is! The only daughter of ShiFeng's inventor?"

"Right." Urban's voice was empty.

"Olive will make sure you get a photo op with her," Butterfly continued. "There are also several other key individuals present." She listed off those individuals, then explained all the activities planned to help Urban connect with them.

Urban tuned her out. She had argued with Everest before, but this time was different. They'd always avoided the topic of their future until this evening.

If he can't pretend to be Enhanced, how can we be together? If he joined me as a Natural, that would never work. But otherwise, I have to choose to live in the Outskirts or break up.

She fought off a rising tide of tears and tried to think of examples of Naturals and Enhances marrying. Surely someone had made it work before. She finally did think of a few, but they were all famous artists who moved to the Metropolis after becoming KOLs.

There was one other.

Her second cousin had married a Natural. He'd moved to the Outskirts to be with his wife, and Urban hadn't seen him since. He had brought such shame to his family, and his parents never spoke of him. It was as if he'd never existed. *I can't leave everything I've worked for behind. I want to make something of myself in the Metropolis where I have a shot at it.*

But I can't leave Everest. He's the only person who knows the real me and accepts me anyway. And I think I love him.

"What's this?" Butterfly wings interrupted her thoughts. She wrinkled her nose and gestured at the necklace Everest had given Urban.

"Is that even real gold?" Hazel asked skeptically.

Urban wasn't sure what to say.

"That's not going to work for tonight." Butterfly removed the necklace swiftly and dropped it into the trash.

Urban cringed. "Don't throw it away." She fished the necklace out of the trash and slipped it into her purse.

Butterfly sighed in annoyance. "Here, try this instead." She fastened a huge diamond pendant in the shape of a swan around her neck.

"Way better," Hazel admired. "What do you think?"

Urban looked at her reflection in the mirror. A girl with golden eyes, lush eyelashes, and perfect porcelain skin stared back at her. She looked older, bolder, and stunning.

"It's great," Urban finally forced herself to say.

Hazel clapped her hands, pleased with herself. "I know right? Now let's get you out there to meet some KOLs and boost that sosh!"

Urban stared at her reflection.

Everest's right. I'm living a lie.

The thought made her sick.

And there's nothing I can do about it.

URBAN'S BIRTHDAY PASSED IN A HAZE OF selfies, fake drinks, dancing, and linking with strangers. After an agonizingly long night, the countdown finally happened and her sosh, a 51, appeared. Everyone cheered and raged, but Urban blushed and escaped to the changing room. She managed to bump it to 58 by morning, but she knew it would be slow going after.

Her grades took a dip as she spent the next few weeks focusing much of her energy on her score. After her birthday party, her sosh had climbed to the low sixties but had then plateaued. Despite her best efforts, nothing seemed to move it.

The racing event was now only two days away. Urban had been leaning toward bailing, but since her sosh wasn't improving, she was rethinking that option. She knew she had a shot at winning, but she still hadn't had time to practice as much as she would've liked. She gave herself one more day to boost her sosh, and then, if it was still in the low sixties, she told herself she would race. The winner was guaranteed a sosh boost. It was the only way.

Since her birthday, she hadn't heard from Everest. His silence felt like a black hole.

That evening in jiujitsu class, Urban kept thinking about the race and Everest. Thankfully, there were no inspirational stories, just a quick speech about discipline, more shrimping, and some other warm-ups. All of which she barely managed to keep up with. When the warm-up was done, Orion gave them a quick demo on how to do double-leg takedowns.

"Okay, everyone, partner up!"

Lillian motioned Urban over to join her. "I'll go first."

Lillian slid to her knees, her right knee shooting forward and her left leg lagging behind. "How are you liking Infini-Fit?"

Lillian gripped Urban tight around the waist, then pulled her back leg around for leverage.

"Huh? Oh yeah." Infini-Fit was the last thing on her mind, but she couldn't tell Lillian that. If her sister found out about the race, she'd be sure to try and talk her out of it or else would tell their parents. "It was all right."

Lillian bumped Urban to get her off balance, lifted up, then let Urban fall to the ground.

"I just don't dare take any of their classes," Urban explained from the ground. "I don't think I'm in shape enough for that."

Lillian leaned over Urban and dug her elbows into Urban's side. "Why don't you train with me?" she said as she worked a few side-control pressure points until Urban tapped.

Urban stood. "I've seen you at home doing some of your workouts. They're weird and painful looking, and—"

"And they make me strong."

Urban knelt into position next to Lillian. She hesitated, then swapped knees. "Is this the right one?"

"No, it's the other."

Urban quickly switched again, but then stilled. "I know! I could train with Everest. I never get to see him anyway, so it would be perfect."

"Except he can't get into the gym without a membership."

"We could train outside somewhere."

Lillian gave Urban a skeptical look. "If you have time to drive an hour and back to the middle of nowhere to work out, sure."

Urban knew she had a point. "But you're way too fit. I can't keep up. You'll push me too far."

"Are you going to practice, or just keep kneeling there?" Lillian asked.

Urban lifted her right knee, then shot in and hugged Lillian. Urban's knee pressed tightly against Lillian's side.

"Make sure your back leg is stable so you don't fall over," Lillian coached. "Yeah, there you go. Now push."

Urban pushed against Lillian, but nothing happened.

"Keep going, keep going," Lillian said. "You're not going to hurt me."

Urban dropped her shoulder into it, and this time Lillian tumbled over.

"Good, now mount and try and put me in an arm bar."

Urban struggled to remember how to do this, but Lillian gave a quick demo with Urban copying her movements.

"I'll tap when you need to stop," Lillian said as Urban slowly lifted her hand in an arm bar. "There!"

Urban stopped lifting immediately. She pulled Lillian up and they switched positions.

"Anyway," Lillian continued, "you'll get even more fit, I get to do what I love, and we both get sis bonding time."

Urban rolled her eyes. "Sometimes I really feel like I have two brothers."

"So, you're in?" Lillian gripped her tight.

"Fine."

Lillian pushed her to the ground and climbed onto her. "Great! Let's meet at Infini-Fit at 0400. It's when the gym is almost completely dead." After putting Urban in a triangle hold, she stood and gave Urban a hand up.

"I would ask how you know that, but I have a feeling I know the answer."

Lillian clapped her on the back as she left. "See ya later."

On her way out of the gym Urban got a live vid.

[Everest: Hey, *meinu*. Checking in to see how you're doing.]

There was a hesitation–something awkward and foreign in his mannerisms after their last conversation. The trust and ease with which they once spoke was there on the surface, but Urban's stomach twisted underneath.

[Everest: Rough day here in the Outskirts. There were some thieves trying to break into our building. Me and a few friends taught them a lesson. Just the usual.]

He paused for a second, and Urban noticed his bedroom behind him. What looked like giant pillows but were actually sonic vibration basses took up most of the space. The walls were covered in posters of his favorite bands, Wu Pine, ARMY, New Order, and his all-time favorite, the TingBings.

Only one wall wasn't plastered in posters. Instead, it had a lone painting of two goldfish. It was the painting she'd given him. Warmth trickled through her every time she saw it hanging there.

[Everest: Anyhow, let me know how you're doing.]

Urban live vid requested him back as she climbed on her bike. "Hey there. Glad you're okay." She smiled and he smiled back, but it felt forced. They chatted about school and work for a few minutes, talking about everything except their recent argument.

"So, what are you up to tonight?" Everest asked, his voice oddly cheery. He gave an uncertain smile, and Urban wished he weren't so far away so she could lean up against his chest and feel his arms around her. It always seemed easier to dispel awkwardness and hard conversations in person.

She was careful to avoid bringing back up their argument from the other night. *I don't have the strength to deal with that right now.* The upcoming race also loomed at the back of her mind, but she knew bringing that up would probably cause another fight. She'd tell him later.

"I'm on my way home from jiujitsu."

"Nice. How was your birthday?"

Urban hesitated. "All right. My score is 62 now so that's an improvement from 51, but I need it to be much higher much faster." *It hasn't changed. That means tomorrow I'm racing.* A flash of panic overtook her.

"I know why you're doing this, but please be careful." He studied her face for a minute. "So why only all right?"

Just like Everest to pick up on small things. She sometimes wondered if his medical genomics records were wrong and he had Inceptor enhancements after all.

She pulled her eyes off the road for a split second to glance at her display. He was looking at her with tender concern, giving her butterflies.

Urban turned her noise-cancellation setting on as she weaved through traffic. No one on the street would be able to hear anything from outside of her motorcycle helmet.

"Sometimes I don't think I can keep up, whether it's school or a workout class. On top of that, I'm trying to schmooze with all these popular kids, and it's just, it's just—"

"Not you," he finished for her.

She paused a moment, his statement taking her by surprise. "Well, it is. But yeah, it's not. But it also sort of is because I have to, but then—ugh!" She let out a frustrated sigh.

"Hey, it's okay."

Urban inhaled sharply. Her throat constricted, and she forced herself to concentrate on the road. "I should go."

"All right," he said reluctantly. "But only if you promise to see me soon." He winked.

Urban slammed on the brakes to avoid running a red light. "Sure. Just let me know when."

"All right. Night." Everest smiled, then cut the connection.

Her anxiety heightened. *How are we going to work? He's*

never here. He can't relate to most of my new life. He's not willing to fake it to join me here.

She thought about the alternative, and her chest constricted.

I'm not leaving him. There were so few guys like him left in the world. She couldn't think of anyone else who was tough but gentle, artistic and kind, street smart but also book smart. Someone she could trust with her Natural secret. Someone who completely understood her and around whom she didn't have to pretend. Everest accepted her as she was. *I'll never find another like him.*

Back in the dorms, her room was empty—the roommates were still out, partying most likely. Urban stayed up studying until she had a headache and her vision turned foggy.

Crawling into bed, she wiggled under the covers and cranked her sleep headset to high sleep mode. She counted back from ten as the cold sleeping mist filled her nostrils. She made it to six before she fell asleep.

Urban woke up the next day acutely aware it was the day of the initiation race.

Since Lillian didn't know, Urban would have to figure out a way to lose Trig on her own. Over the last couple of weeks, Urban had been experimenting with invisible Trig's following capabilities and was impressed.

She couldn't lose him on her motorcycle, nor could she escape him by going into crowded spaces—the bodyguard was impossible to shake. Which was fine, except for on a night like tonight when she didn't want her plans getting back to Lillian, or worse, her parents.

There only seemed to be one way to ditch Trig. After Urban had charged her motorcycle, she programmed it to be air dropped to her destination. Then she made her way to the nearest underground ZipLine. The sky overhead was a swamp of gray. A chilly breeze swept dried leaves toward her, and Urban zipped up her leather jacket.

She noticed Trig's familiar green triangle in her maps as she waited for the next ZipLine to arrive. She stepped in once its doors opened and saw Trig following in the compartment next door. Urban's pulse quickened as she waited until the doors started beeping and then leaped off right before they shut.

With smug satisfaction, she watched as the ZipLine sped away, taking Trig with it. Then she turned, got on a different one bound for the Outskirts, and found her motorcycle. From there, it was an easy drive.

Urban arrived at the location for the underground race and double-checked she had the right address. Sure enough, her augmented map said *NingShan*, which was two hours out of the Metropolis. Apart from the dried, overgrown grass blowing in the wind, everything was deadly silent.

She stopped in the middle of the highway to study her surroundings. There wasn't a single person in sight, despite the high-rises surrounding her on all sides. Several of them still had scaffolding and cranes, as if the builders were only on a lunch break and might return at any moment.

Urban had heard of these ghost cities. They were hastily raised in the early 2000s to support the growing influx of people migrating from the countryside to the city. There'd been too many of them built, and several of the cities hadn't been able to sustain all the people and had been abandoned. Most of these cities had been repurposed into AI training factories or corporate offices.

She continued on again, following her augmented map and weaving her way through wide streets and skyscrapers.

Urban pulled up to a drab skyscraper towering above the others. Her map showed her the location for the start of the race was at the top. Inside, several flares illuminated an impressively large but empty lobby. Footprints and tire tracks made a clear path through the dust-covered tile floors to the escalator.

As she neared the roof, the sound of the bass thumping and

people talking reached her even before the ding of the elevator.

The doors opened, revealing to her right, the New Beijing skyline, lit up in a brilliant patchwork of color. To her left, the bare BaiHua Mountains rose up like haunting burial mounds.

Urban followed the sound until she rounded a corner and spotted the people. Surprised filled her as she recognized one of them.

"Coral? What are you doing here?"

Coral leaned back on a slick black-and-green hovercycle. "Same as you. I'm here to boost my sosh by winning the race."

This struck Urban as strange. Now that she thought about it, she realized she'd never seen Coral's sosh. Since her roommate refused to link with anyone and her setting was on privacy mode, her sosh was anonymous in the real world. *It must be really bad if she's here tonight too. I hope she's not a good racer.*

Her spine tingled. Looking up, she spotted Olive in the crowd. The pasty girl gave her a cold nod. *The last thing I need is her getting in my head.*

She also noticed another familiar face. Lillian.

Had Trig followed her after all and then notified Lillian? Urban checked her maps, but there was no sign of Trig.

"What are you doing here?" Urban hissed as Lillian pushed her way through to her.

"I could ask you the same," Lillian whispered.

"How did you find me here?"

"I got worried when you didn't answer my pings. I hacked mom's SCA and traced you here."

"You hacked SCA? This can't be happening," Urban muttered under her breath.

"Please tell me you're just here to watch." Lillian grabbed her arm. "These races aren't safe."

Urban checked her fuel gage. "Thanks, Mom, but I think I can take it from here."

"Don't do this." Lillian's voice turned pleading.

"Listen," Urban huffed, "just 'cause you get carsick doesn't mean I shouldn't race."

"That's not why I'm here, and you know it." Lillian crossed her arms over her chest. "I'm not leaving without you."

Urban glanced both ways, then walked her motorcycle off to the side of the crowd. She turned to Lillian and pulled up her visor. "Listen, I don't have a choice." She lowered her voice. "My sosh isn't getting any better, and the winner gets a boost."

"Have you considered what happens if you lose? It's an extreme game of truth or dare, and—"

"I wouldn't take truth. And whatever the dare is, I would suck it up and endure."

Despite being out of earshot, Lillian lowered her voice more. "What if it's a dare only an Enhanced person could survive?"

Urban looked away. "That's not going to happen. Besides, I won't lose. I'm better than you think. It's the one thing I'm good at."

"Racers to the start line!" a voice boomed.

Urban pulled her helmet back down with a snap and left. She noticed in her maps the familiar green triangle had reappeared. *And he's back.* Inwardly, she groaned. Then another thought cheered her. *Let's see if you can keep up in a race, Trig.*

"Looks like we have a decent lineup tonight." A barrel-chested Super surveyed the contestants as they pulled up to the line. He checked his retina display. "Newbie Lee Urban joins us. Welcome, rider!"

Urban frowned. Wasn't Coral a newbie too?

The Super turned toward several crisp, collared-shirt observers in the crowd. "A big thank you to our sponsors for this event. Give it up for the Inventors."

Everyone cheered and clapped. The Inventors gave curt head nods toward the middle rider on an extremely long behemoth of a metal machine.

The announcer followed their gaze. "The standing champion

is still none other than the Inventor B-string player Xin Trina!"

There was a smattering of applause mixed with grumbling.

"For tonight's race, the winner is the first one to cross the finish line at the top of that building." The announcer pointed at the skyscraper next to them. "The loser is the last person to cross. The fastest route is marked for you, but feel free to blaze your own trail. Now for the rules." He laughed. "What rules? Now, who's ready for some street fighting? I mean racing?"

An Artisan turned up the music on his bike. As it shook with each beat of the music, Urban realized where the music was coming from—his wheels. He sat atop a motorcycle attached to wheels that were actually giant bass-thumping speakers. Urban gaped.

A guy with a goatee, tattoos, and what looked like an old-school Harley, flipped a switch. Instantly, spikes popped out of his motorcycle, nearly popping the tires on the bike next to his. He flashed a devilish grin.

The Inventor next to him lay down on her long motorcycle. Her crisp, formal attire looked completely out of place on the metal machine. She tilted barrels on the sides of her motorcycle skyward and fired an electric shock.

Lillian was right. There wasn't room for mistakes.

Without any enhancements to protect her or give her an advantage, she could die.

Goosebumps rippled across her arms. Panic threatened to overwhelm her, but she bit her tongue and distracted herself by double-checking that her helmet was on tight.

Blood pumped loudly in her ears.

"Ready?" the Super boomed.

Engines revved.

19

自 外

ENHANCED RACING

URBAN'S VISION NARROWED, BLURRING OUT the crowd. She focused on the parking lot with the pulsing blue augmented arrows marking the course.

"One, two, three, GO!"

Urban pulled hard on the accelerator.

Her motorcycle was specifically designed for quick bursts of speed to get around Smart lights. She went from zero to max torque and power, instantly leaping ahead of the others.

The Inventor caught up to her as she sped down the ramp to the floor below and reached the first bend.

Urban kept her speed until the last second, then slammed on the brakes and skidded across the pavement as she rounded the bend.

Beside her, the Inventor quickly pulled ahead miraculously.

Urban glanced over and saw the Inventor had launched a hook to grip the opposite wall and then whipped her bike around the corner with lightning speed.

A moment later, they came to the next bend. Again, the Inventor sped ahead with the use of her metallic hook.

Another racer began pulling up close behind her too—a Flyer.

At the next corner, the Flyer extended his wings. They worked like a parachute, instantly slowing his momentum.

Then with incredible speed, he flipped his motorcycle in a new direction and accelerated past her.

Urban ground her teeth.

She heard another racer close behind, but she made it the rest of the way down while managing to stay ahead.

At the bottom, the arrows continued through a brightly lit garage. The Flyer and Inventor were nowhere in sight, but the other racers weren't far behind.

Out of her peripheral vision, Urban saw Coral creeping up on her. Urban swerved to the right, blocking her from passing.

Coral slammed on her brakes, then skidded left.

Urban moved left, cutting her off.

"Get out of my way!" Coral yelled.

Urban laughed. It sounded strange in her helmet.

Coral tried another angle, but Urban cut her off.

Suddenly Coral, along with her whole motorcycle, disappeared.

"What?" Urban said in shock. Then realizing what had happened, she groaned. "Stupid Camos." She swerved right then left, trying to block Coral wherever she was. She heard the screeching of wheels behind her, but then all was silent.

Coral was gone.

Checking her augmented map, Urban saw the red square representing Coral pulling ahead of her. There were only two racers behind her now. But she noticed with satisfaction that Trig's green triangle was a long way off.

The garage ended and a building closed around her. At least, that's what she thought it was. Her field of vision was narrowed to the marble path illuminated by her headlight. Everything else plunged into darkness. Urban switched on her night vision and easily weaved in between giant pillars, around debris, and through puddles.

What is this place?

On her left, the road seemed to drop away into nothingness. Urban angled closer toward it and made out tracks. Up ahead she spotted a decrepit train cart.

So this is what a train station looks like.

Before she had more time to take in the wonders of the historical site, she heard a strange clanging noise next to her.

Glancing down, she glimpsed what looked like a metallic anchor being pulled away.

Clang!

This time, the sound came from the other side of her motorcycle.

She turned and glimpsed the guy with the tattoos. He reeled in the anchor before aiming it back at her.

"Not today." She swerved out of the way and behind a pillar, skidding so hard she almost wiped out. She heard the metallic ring of the anchor as it hit the marble surface where she'd just been.

Suddenly ear-splitting music vibrated through her body. She clawed at her helmet to try and plug her ears.

She checked her mirror. The Artisan on his bass-pumping motorcycle tried to pass her.

Stupid enhancements.

His wheels trembled with each drop of the beat. He cranked the sound up higher until Urban was sick. The tattooed rider was also having difficulty. He swerved and almost hit a pillar.

The tattoo rider fired his anchor at the Artisan's motorcycle, but there were no spokes on his musical wheels, and the anchor bounced off harmlessly.

Urban's head screamed in pain. "Find another route," she ordered her augmented map.

A moment later two options appeared. One would take three minutes longer than her current route. The other was—

She blinked. *How can that be?*

It was two minutes faster than the track set for the racers.

She zoomed in. It seemed to be weaving through some tight spaces and went through an orange zone. She hesitated for a split seconding before deciding. *I'll be fine on my motorcycle.*

The music was so loud she wanted to throw up. Desperate to

get away, she followed her augmented maps and swerved toward the platform's edge. Taking in a deep breath, she launched herself over the edge and onto the tracks.

She landed hard but steadied herself and kept going, bumping over each track as if she'd grabbed a jack hammer. The tracks sloped upward until finally she was out of the train station and back into cool polluted air. She watched carefully as the tracks began to deteriorate into pebbles and overgrown weeds.

Following her maps, she veered off the tracks and onto a narrow road. The abandoned buildings turned into rubble. She almost spun out twice on loose bits of gravel and debris.

Gritting her teeth, she kept her speed, refusing to slow, and weaved in and out of the narrow, ghostly streets. Even with her filtration mask on high mode, the dust she kicked up caused her to start sneezing.

After blinking to clear her watery eyes, she slipped around another corner and found the path completely blocked by rubble.

"I don't have time for this." She slid to a halt and pulled up maps. If she backtracked, she would definitely lose. Maybe there was a way over the pile. She studied the rubble, then hopped down from her motorcycle.

She walked her bike up to it. It was slow going, but she made it all the way to the top before slipping and sliding down the other side. She climbed back on and sped the rest of the way through the orange zone. Once she exited the last street, she checked her augmented map.

"Yes!" Urban pumped her fist in the air. "First place!"

She followed the map toward the finish line and noticed the Inventor creeping up behind her again.

Urban sped around a corner into another abandoned garage. The ramp slanted upward this time.

"Not this again," she moaned as she began speeding round the bend.

The Inventor started to pass her. With a dip of her head and a salute, she rounded a corner and pulled back into the lead, leaving Urban fuming.

The Flyer wasn't far behind. By the time Urban reached the top, both had passed her. She checked her map and saw Coral had fallen to last place, and now the Artisan was the next racer behind Urban. She wondered what had happened to Coral.

At least I'm not last.

At the top, her map showed she was close to the finish line. There was a ramp at the edge of the roof that looked like it led to a large jump between several buildings before landing on the finishing building.

Her body froze. *I'm sure there's a safety net or something below.* She tried to console herself. But she knew there wasn't. *You can do this. Just get lots of momentum. You have to do this. There's no other choice.*

Her bike calculated the speed she'd need to be at to make the jump, then began automatically accelerating along with her beating heart.

Urban flew across the deserted roof and up the ramp.

As she got closer, a message flashed across her augmented display.

<Child Safety App accessed.>

"Whaa—" Urban realized with horror it had to be her mother accessing her system. *Not now.*

Her motorcycle was linked to her account. If her motorcycle went into lockout mode, it would stop accelerating, and she wouldn't make the jump. She pushed harder on the speed and hit the base of the ramp.

As she was halfway up, a red warning light flashed.

<Child Safety App going into lockout mode. In Three . . .>

Urban's heart turned to ice.

<Two . . .>

She considered bailing but was too far along the ramp. She remembered what had happened when she'd gotten cold feet the last time she'd tried a jump. Everest's words came back to her: *"You have to commit to the jump. That's the key."*

<One . . .>

She neared the end of the ramp.

<Lockout mode activated. Please contact your system administrator for access.>

Urban's overlays went dark.

Her motorcycle stopped accelerating. Nothing but her momentum hurled her over the edge.

As she rose in the air, it was as if time slowed.

She saw the waiting crowds. The Inventor and Flyer were already at the finish line. Lillian stared up at her. The thought that this was probably her doing crossed Urban's mind. Why else would they be locking her out of her system right now?

Then Urban looked down, and her stomach tightened. She had to be at least thirty stories in the air. As she drew nearer the other building and dropped, she sensed someone staring at her.

At the building across from her, a figure stood in one of the balconies—a masked Flyer.

As Urban approached the other side, she realized she'd fallen even further. Too far.

She tried to do another reboot of her system but was still locked out. Not that it would do any good.

All was silent and dark except the air whistling through her helmet as she plummeted to the ground below.

URBAN'S MOTORCYCLE DROPPED OUT FROM beneath her as she fell one floor, then two, then she lost count.

How much of the landing would she feel? Hopefully she'd die instantly.

I don't want to die.

She would never get a chance to do so many things. Her life had been too short. *Why is life so unfair?*

Suddenly, something hit her side hard, knocking the wind out of her. She rocketed toward a window, bracing herself for the impact.

With a *crack* and then a *crash*, glass shattered, exploding dozens of glistening shards around her. But Urban felt no pain as she tumbled onto a concrete floor. As she rolled to a stop, something solid pressed up against her chest. With her system offline, her night vision was out, and she couldn't see in the blackness engulfing her.

Someone let go of her waist and feathers brushed across her skin.

A flare sparked to life and bathed the darkness in red light.

Urban gasped. A masked Flyer stood cloaked in shadows, staring at her.

She was in too much shock to say anything as the Flyer picked glass out of his wings.

He inclined his head. "You should be more careful." His voice was grim and higher pitched than she would have expected for his size.

Without another word, he leaped out the nearest window and vanished.

Urban stared after him in stunned silence until the flare began to sizzle and pop, and she realized she'd better leave before it went out and she was plunged back into darkness. Wiggling her toes and fingers, she found them all to be in working order and breathed a sigh of relief. Shakily, she pushed herself into a standing position.

The flare popped again, and this time, went out.

In the darkness, Urban groped her way for an exit. She bumped into something smooth. After finding the handle, she let herself out.

In the hallway, cold, musty air and cobwebs greeted her. In the distance, she heard a commotion.

She tried to remember which building she'd crashed into. She was pretty sure it was the same one she was supposed to land on. She found the elevator and pressed the top floor. As she drew nearer to the roof, the upheaval grew louder.

With a *ding*, the elevator opened to total mayhem.

The Artisan's motorcycle was still pumping bass and vibrating the roof. Barely audible above it were screams, angry yelling, and crying. People ran about in total confusion, others stood in huddled corners silently talking.

"Where *is* she?" the announcer yelled at some Flyers. "She can't just disappear into thin air. If her motorcycle is down there, she has to be too."

One of the students noticed her. His eyes widened. "There she is!"

Several people looked where he was pointing. The music

stopped. Everyone turned and ran toward Urban. One person outran all the others.

Lillian didn't loosen her grip for some time. When she finally did, she had tears streaking down her face. She said nothing, just kept squeezing Urban's hand as if to assure herself her sister really was alive.

"I thought I'd failed," she whispered numbly.

What on earth does that mean? Before Urban could ask, Coral was beside her. "You alright?"

Urban nodded weakly.

"What happened?" someone asked.

"Yeah! Where did you go?"

A million questions followed.

"Let's get you home." Lillian didn't seem angry at all. Urban wasn't sure what she had expected upon returning, but an "I told you so" wouldn't have been a surprise.

"Wait a second!" a voice boomed. "We still haven't announced the race results." The announcer stared at her.

Urban faced the announcer as the crowd fell silent.

"And the loser is . . . Lee Urban!"

Urban stood dumbstruck.

"Ridiculous," Lillian snapped.

"This is street racing." The announcer shrugged. "Bike or no bike, she came in last. That makes her the loser."

Lillian pushed her way to the announcer and stood centimeters from him, stretching every bit of her one-point-seven meters. Even then, she only came to the Super's chest.

"She almost *died*." Lillian's voice was ice, her eyes hard as obsidian. It was a tone Urban hadn't ever heard her sister use before.

Even the Super seemed taken aback by her intensity but quickly recovered. "It's the rules."

"Rules are made to be broken," Lillian argued, glancing around for support. "Isn't that what street racing is all about?"

A couple whoops and a stray clap from the crowd.

"Listen, if she wasn't planning on taking the risk, she shouldn't have raced," the Super retorted. "Tell you what, I'll let her delay fulfilling her truth-or-dare, seeing as she's had a rough night." There were several *boo*s at this. "That's the best I can offer."

Lillian's face drained white.

"Truth or dare? Choose!" the announcer bellowed.

"Choose! Choose! Choose!" the crowd chanted.

The Super held up his hand for silence. "What will it be?

Urban swallowed. "Dare."

"I was hoping you'd pick that." An abominable grin crossed the Super's face. "Your dare will take place at a time and place of our choosing. For now, you are free to go."

Not knowing was worse. "When will I be notified?"

"You won't." Came the smug reply.

"But then how will I know where to go or what to do?"

The Super laughed. "Oh, you'll know."

The group began to disperse. Urban was one of the first to leave. She didn't want to stick around and see Olive's gloating eyes or face Lillian's "told-you-so's" or endure Coral's questions.

But before she could escape, Lillian cornered her. "What happened out there?"

"You tell me," Urban hissed.

Lillian's brow furrowed.

"Don't pretend you didn't rat me out to our parents." Urban attempted to move by her, but Lillian blocked her.

"What are you talking about? I didn't tell anyone except Trig."

"Then who accessed SCA and locked me out as I was going up that ramp?"

"Is that what happened?" Lillian gasped. "Mom told me the last time she accessed SCA was yesterday."

I've been hacked. Again.

Urban started off, and this time Lillian let her pass.

How do I keep getting hacked? It's like someone has my root password or something. But that's impossible.

Her mind was still whirring as she reached ground level and found her motorcycle, or what remained of it. Her heart sank. There wasn't so much as a stray part worth salvaging.

Her most prized possession was strewn in pieces across the overgrown street. A knot twisted in her stomach as she picked up a fragment of it. *This could have been me.*

She sank down onto the deteriorating sidewalk in a hidden alley to avoid everyone while she waited for a rental to be air dropped. She checked the price of the rental and sighed. *I'm definitely not going to make it through the end of the semester with enough crypto points now.*

She filtered through her list of friends, checking off anyone whom she could ask to borrow from. But the thought of it brought her so much shame. The only people she felt she could even ask were Everest and Lillian. But Everest barely had enough for himself and his own family. And Lillian . . . *I can't exactly ask her after what just happened.*

It grew still and silent as the last of the crowd went their way.

So much for racing. So much for staying out of trouble. Mother and Father are going to kill me if they find out I totaled my motorcycle.

Once on her rental, she sped out of the ghost city, the familiar green triangle followed close behind. Frustration overwhelmed her. *I can't even escape my own bodyguard. I can't get freedom in any part of my life. If I had a high sosh, I wouldn't have had to risk my life at all.*

At the thought, she checked her sosh and saw her near death and disappearance had helped her pull it up to 65. Not bad, except she was out of crypto and wasn't planning on risking her life again.

Maybe working out with Brooke isn't such a bad idea after all.

THE NEXT DAY, CLASSES PASSED QUICKLY, AND Urban spent the remainder of the day in XDR, working on her homework assignments. She went to her favorite virtual library to plug away at her AI Foundations chatbot. After an hour, she switched to her genetic engineering assignment.

In most of her classes she maintained a steady C. In AI foundations, her grade had dropped slightly, despite her best efforts. She was hanging on by a thread. Only in Biopsychology did she have a high B. She frequently logged into the grades portal just to stare at her B with pride. *I have to pull my other grades up, too, or mother will start stripping my freedom away.*

Everest location requested her, and she realized it was already time for their virtual date. Where had the day gone?

Urban approved the request, and Everest materialized instantly. His avatar looked almost identical to his appearance in reality. While most Naturals had enhancements in QuanNao, Everest didn't. That was just like him, transparent about everything and always making the best of what life handed him. Urban's avatar fingered her bright-red hair as he approached.

He wrapped Urban in his strong embrace. It was safe and peaceful there, and a warmth trickled through her core. He smelled like jasmine and something else Urban couldn't quite place—something tantalizingly dangerous.

"Hey, what are you doing for Mooncake Festival?" Everest asked as they pulled apart.

Urban's gut tightened. She was relieved he was acting normal after their last few conversations, but she also knew he was going to be angry if she told him about the race. Their relationship was already precarious these days with the unspoken question of their uncertain future looming ahead. Should she bring it up?

"That's a great question," Urban responded. "Mother's trying to get the family together, but I don't think Lucas can make it, and Lillian might be a no-show too. She'll probably just cancel." She eyed him. "Why?"

Everest stuffed his hands in his pocket. "Want to celebrate with my family?"

Urban blinked. "I thought your parents didn't know about us."

"They didn't."

Urban inhaled a couple of deep breaths before enabling private mode so none of the other avatars could hear their conversation.

"You told your parents about us?"

Everest's expression remained neutral.

"I thought we agreed to keep this a secret!"

"I can't keep lying to them. They're constantly trying to set me up with other girls."

Urban's heart plunged. "Why?"

Everest's foot tapped nervously. He shrugged. "My parents are the only ones I know eager to have their son dating."

"You're Chong Everest! You mean to tell me you can keep thugs in check but not your own parents?"

Everest ran a hand through his thick hair. "If you think I'm stubborn, you should meet my parents. It's getting out of control. I had a girl show up at work the other day—whom my parents sent."

"Don't you think you should have talked to *me* about this?" Urban gripped his arm. "What have you told them about me?"

Everest put a hand over hers. "Relax. I didn't tell them anything about you except what you're like. I didn't give them your name. The last thing I want is them creeping on your avatar. They're actually happy I'm dating. It gives them hope of achieving their lifelong dream of getting a grandchild." He gave a wry grin, then grew serious. "But they do want to meet you in person."

"This is a disaster! What happens when they find out I'm a Lee? Or worse," she lowered her voice. "I live in the Metropolis?"

"Urban." He held her gaze. "They don't care about those sorts of things."

Urban exhaled. "I don't know. It sounds risky. What if your mom reaches out to mine or posts something on QuanNao?"

Everest laughed. "My parents are terrible with tech. They barely know how to check their sosh. I doubt they could figure out how to find and then message your mom even if they wanted. All they want is to eat mooncakes and enjoy time with us. The way I see it, the only real risk is your parents finding out via SCA." He wiggled his eyebrows. "But I think I have a way of getting around that."

"I don't know . . ."

"Come on. Why not? You can't spend Mooncake Festival alone."

The idea of spending one of her favorite holidays alone in her dorm bothered her more than she cared to admit. But the way he always talked about his parents made her jealous. What would it be like to have parents who were proud of you? To belong? Maybe she still had a shot at that. She doubted anyone from uni would be in the Outskirts anyway. So long as SCA wasn't an issue, it seemed like a low enough risk.

Urban relented. "All right, I'll come."

Everest's face lit up. "The office is halfway between PKU and my house. Let's meet there Thursday night. I'll show you how to disable SCA there."

It dawned on Urban she had a new problem. "What type of

mooncake do your parents prefer? Do they like the ice cream versions or are they more traditional? Do they like the tart ones? Is there a certain brand they like? I have no idea what to bring."

"Relax." Everest calmed her again. "They'll like anything you bring."

Typical Everest response.

Urban hesitated, wanting to tell Everest all about the race. As her coach, he was the one person she always talked with about racing. It was odd not letting him know about it—and that she would have placed third, too, if she hadn't been hacked.

Thinking back to that moment, the horror of dropping off the ramp returned. If it weren't for the masked figure, she would be dead right now. Everest would be furious with her if she told him.

"You okay?" Everest asked.

"Just thinking." Urban forced a smile. "See you Thursday!"

"Can't wait, *meinu.*"

"Great!" Urban dissolved the bubble and with it, Everest.

Guilt welled up in her for keeping the race from him, but it was for the best. She'd tell him later when she wasn't so stressed and their relationship was more stable.

Sighing, she checked the time and realized over an hour had passed. Concerned she'd lost so much time, she put on some music, then began working on researching chatbots in earnest. She stayed until late in the night. When she found she had reread the same paragraph five times in a row, she finally headed to bed.

The next day, Urban regretted having agreed to such an early morning meeting with her biopsych group.

Orion was already there. He wore a stylish XR suit that resembled wool and accentuated his muscular chest and biceps. Urban quickly looked away and went through the buffet line. She selected hot soy milk, fried *youtiao*, and a boiled egg, then remembered her fast-dwindling crypto points.

Cheeks burning, she quickly put everything back and grabbed a large bowl of rice porridge. That was her best bet at quenching her hunger for the lowest price.

"Hey, Orion." She set her tray down next to him.

Her instructor looked up from his breakfast and gave her a stunning smile. "Hello! You look familiar."

"I'm in your jiujitsu class."

His face lit up. "Ah! Urban, right? I knew you looked familiar. How are you liking it?"

"So far it's been great."

His eyes held such intensity Urban quickly focused all her attention on her porridge.

"It's all a mind game," Orion tapped his head. "That's why I love it."

Urban wondered if Inceptors had a natural predisposition to this martial art given their ability to outthink others. She also wondered if he could sense her discomfort.

"Hey there. Is this the biopsych class group?" A Super approached, balancing a tray buried in steamed *mantou*, pickled vegetables, and sweet-potato pancakes. He had spiky black hair and red eyes that gleamed mischievously.

"You must be Sun Clay." Orion gestured at an open seat. "Let's start with introductions, shall we? I'm Orion. I'm a fourth year, and I'm in the Inceptor gene pool so this is a required class for me." He looked to Urban.

"I'm Urban Lee, and I'm a first year. I'm taking this class because it's one of my requirements for the general track."

Clay momentarily paused from shoving *mantou* down his throat. "Clay. Third year. My advisor AI messed up, and I missed the prereq class I was supposed to take. This was the only substitute. I couldn't care less about biopsych. I just need a passing grade."

Urban glanced at Orion, and they shared a concerned look.

Clay continued cramming food into his mouth. Urban found herself wondering if Supers always ate that much and if so, how they could afford to live.

"All right then," Orion said after a moment. "Let's focus on the assignment we have due for next week. I don't think it should take long."

They spent the next thirty minutes pulling sources and forming a point of view on the psychology of persuasion. Orion took the lead, and Urban and Clay supported him in fact-finding for each of his theories. The time passed quickly, and soon the three of them were heading to class.

As they entered the classroom, Clay ditched them to sit in the back corner, but Orion followed Urban. "Mind if I sit with you?"

Urban nodded as they took their seats.

For the first time, Urban found it difficult to concentrate in her favorite class. Her attention kept getting pulled back to the Inceptor beside her. Being in his group project might boost her sosh. He seemed genuine too. She actually found she wanted to be his friend, and not just for appearances.

Finally, some things are starting to look up for me. Keep hanging out with Orion and just get a picture with him, and that's sure to help my sosh one or two points. Combined with Brooke, I'm already looking at around 66 or 67.

The trouble was afterward. Urban knew no other KOLs except Olive, and she had the feeling Olive wasn't the type to give sosh-boosting selfies out at random. Especially now that Urban had lost the race. With each jump in her sosh, getting to the next, higher number, would be harder.

"See you in jiujitsu tomorrow?" Orion asked once class was out.

"Tomorrow?" Urban blanked. "Me and my—" She recovered quickly. "I mean tomorrow, I'm going to celebrate Mooncake Festival. Is class still happening?"

"Oh right. Mooncake Festival. I forgot. No, class is cancelled. I'm kind of a space case." He motioned at his head, but the sharpness in his eyes was anything but starry. "See you next week then?"

"Wouldn't miss it! Jiujitsu that is, not class. I'll be at class regardless. Nothing special there. Your class is what I wouldn't miss. Jiujitsu class, I mean." She was prattling.

"Cool. See you then."

Urban watched Orion walking away, grateful he couldn't see her burning cheeks. *What is wrong with me?*

She shook her head. *I have a boyfriend.*

But Orion didn't know. Hardly anyone one did.

22

URBAN STARED AT THE SQUASHED MOONCAKES hanging from her motorcycle handlebars. She shouldn't have taken that turn so tight. She blamed it on her nerves. That, and her rental motorcycle still felt foreign to her.

Those mooncakes cost me seven meals. They better be worth it. With each purchase, she got closer to having to ask her parents for more crypto points. Then she'd have to explain about the purple zone. She was already on thin ice. That conversation might just tip the scales, convincing her parents to make her come home.

Her calculations showed if she ate cheap meals, she could buy three more days' worth of food. Then she'd have to tell either her parents or ask Lillian for more points.

Everest was leaning against a wall, waiting. His eyebrows went up at her approach. "New motorcycle?"

Urban was about to tell him it was a rental but then realized that would probably require a long explanation resulting in a confession. "Uh, yes."

"Nice."

Fortunately, Everest didn't press her on it. Instead, he winked. "Ready to trip up SCA?"

"I was ready the moment my parents installed it."

Everest extended his hand. "Give me your retina displays."

Urban blanched. "What?"

"That's how your parents won't know where we're going. The GPS tracking device is connected to your retina display. Take it off and send it home via a drone delivery. No one will be the wiser."

"But—but—I need them to see."

"You can see just fine," Everest assured her. "Besides, I think you can survive one evening without them."

Urban hesitated, then popped out her contacts and handed them reluctantly over.

Everest stuck them in a delivery drone's small mesh bag. "I've programed this drone to only take main routes and fly at the speed of traffic so it won't alert SCA to suspicious activity. Give me your thumb."

Everest pressed her thumb against the sealed mesh enclosure. "Now, the only way to open it is with biometric authentication. And that's it. It will be waiting for you when you get to the dorms."

"But I still have to get all the way home without it?" Urban was aghast.

Everest brushed her concern away. "You'll be fine."

Urban felt naked without her retina display there to answer questions or point out the path as she followed Everest to the underground Bolt Line.

She hadn't used the Bolt for transportation in ages. She'd only ever used it once before switching to her motorcycle. The scent of sickly sweet smoke, mold, and trash seeped through her mask. Naturals jostled her on all sides. Everyone seemed eager to get back to family and celebrate the holiday. Many of them carried colorful boxes containing mooncakes.

They passed through a security detector, then crammed into a massive line. Soon they were stepping into a tiny, two-seater pod.

Everest selected the address. His tatt vibrated, confirming the payment, and an air-filtration unit clicked on. Then their pod accelerated away from the station.

Urban removed her mask. "Think your parents will like these mooncakes?"

"Like I said, anything you bring them will make them happy. They're not picky."

"Sounds like someone else I know," Urban remarked with a slight smile.

"You say it like it's a bad thing." Everest's eyes twinkled. "Not bad. Just . . . difficult sometimes." Her smile grew.

The conversation dwindled, and Urban's nerves intensified as they got closer to the destination.

Everest intertwined his fingers with hers. "They're going to love you."

Urban nodded and tried to steady her breathing.

They got off at *Chaoyangmen* with a flood of other Naturals. They fastened their masks back on, then left the station, the stench of sewage hitting them instantly. Despite a cool autumn breeze, the bodies pressed up against them on all sides caused Urban's XR suit to work overtime to keep her cool. She checked to see if Trig was following her but then remembered she didn't have her retina display.

She wished she could switch on her shaded retina filter. Stacked apartment buildings glowed in the fading sunlight, blinding her. The patterns, colors, and architecture looked like a mismatched stack of toy blocks.

This doesn't look structurally sound at all. Father would have a heart attack if he could see the blueprints for this. Despite the queasy feeling in her stomach from their apparent instability, Urban felt safer here than she did in the Metropolis. Hiding the fact she was from the Metropolis while in the Outskirts was definitely easier than hiding she was a Natural in the Metropolis. With Everest at her side, surviving in the Outskirts was like playing on easy mode. Too bad she hated it here.

A hard shove from a passerby pulled Urban's attention back to the streets. A quickness accompanied the residents' steps as did the excitement in their voices. Everest led her down a narrow alleyway with wires and power cords tangled and drooping. She guessed it to be an orange zone, though without her retina display she wasn't sure. Even the darkened street didn't seem dangerous for a change.

Urban had never sensed the Outskirts so full of hope before. *Why can't it always be this way? Would it be different if Naturals had access to enhancements?*

Everest stopped in front of a tiny entryway. The gate was so small she would have missed it on her own. It had a dusty pin code set in a skyrise of blue, brown, and silver apartments. Everest waited as the additional facial-recognition software scanned him, and the door opened.

"Wow, still has a pin?"

Everest gave a rueful nod. "Should give you an idea of how old these apartments are."

Not comforting, Urban thought, but she didn't voice her concerns for fear of coming off as pretentious or as a wimpy Metropolis dweller. *If Everest lives here, it must somehow be safe.*

Inside, a tight, dimly lit hallway led to two sets of elevators. A rat scurried away. There was a distinct smell of rotting trash as they climbed into the cramped elevator for the 105th floor.

Before she had a chance to second guess the whole trip, they were ducking under a low doorway and into an apartment. The cheerily bright interior smelled of steamed rice and stir-fry. The space was narrow and yet somehow, fuller than her mansion back in the Metropolis.

"Hello, dear!" a lady who looked like she could be in her late thirties greeted Urban. A man with black hair, graying at his temples, smiled and stepped forward.

Everest removed his mask. "Urban, meet my mom and dad,

Mr. Chong and Mrs. Guo."

"*Shushu hao.*" Urban addressed the older man in the traditional greeting and then turned to his wife. "*Ayi hao.*"

"Have you eaten?" Everest's mother asked.

"Not yet. I brought you a little something. It isn't much." Urban extended her gift of mooncakes to them, desperately hoping they wouldn't notice the smashed ones.

"You shouldn't have!" His mother took them and handed them to a maidbot. "We are grateful for your kindness. Now, come, come."

She ushered them both into a living/dining room where the maidbot set the mooncakes down. In the tiny room sat a loveseat, coffee table, two small cushions, several decorative braided knots, and a paneled XVR setup on the opposite side.

Delicious-smelling dishes covered the coffee table. A porcelain bowl full of tofu and bok choy soup sat still steaming. Platters of thinly sliced fried potatoes, steamed beef balls, egg custard buns, and more stir-fry dishes than Urban could count, made her stomach rumble. The smell of it was heavenly. It seemed like it had been ages since she'd had a real meal and not just rice.

"Did you make all this yourself?" Urban stared in wonder.

"Of course. With a little help from Everest." His mother took a seat and motioned Urban and Everest toward the loveseat. "Can you handle spice?"

Urban smiled. "Oh, yes."

"Good! Then you can also try this dish." She gestured at some bell peppers and beef swimming in red oil. "It's a little spicy."

"It all looks delicious," Urban said, watching as Mrs. Guo heaped food into her bowl.

Mr. Chong began eating, and the rest followed.

"You must also try this honey-glazed pork," Mrs. Guo insisted.

"Don't worry about me, Auntie," Urban protested. "I can serve myself."

Mrs. Guo clucked her tongue. "Nonsense. You're our guest."

"It's a rare occasion when our son brings home such a beautiful girl," Mr. Chong said, gesturing at her with his chopsticks. "You're the first one."

"Dad!" Everest exclaimed. His father ignored him.

"So, Urban, tell us about yourself," Mr. Chong said.

"Yes!" Mrs. Guo piped up. "What do your parents do? How many siblings do you have? What part of town do you live in?"

They were all innocent, normal questions. Ones she was used to. But Urban wasn't sure how to answer this time. When the Enhanced ask her, she'd have to prove her worth by listing off all the most impressive connections and accolades about her family line.

Now, she didn't want to impress. In fact, she didn't want to make Everest's family lose face. Even for them to know she came from the Metropolis . . . they would be mortified.

"Urban has a ton of hobbies," Everest said coming to her rescue. "Don't you?"

Urban picked up on his cue and began talking about her love for painting, exploring, photography, and architecture.

"She's quite the adventurer," Everest said proudly.

"Sounds like you two are a good match. My Everest has had an insatiable appetite for adventure ever since he was a little boy," Mrs. Guo said as she refilled Urban's bowl with stir-fried corn and pine nuts. "He used to love all buttons and gadgets. When he was five, he became obsessed with our maidbot, Flower. He'd follow her around the house and repeat whatever she said. That's when we realized if we switched her to other languages, he'd pick it up pretty quick.

She set Urban's bowl down. "One day, he decided he wanted to feed Flower. But of course, Flower isn't programmed to take orders from a child, so she wouldn't obey his commands to 'open her mouth' or 'eat this rice.' He became so frustrated, he tried to force feed her. Nearly broke the thing."

"Poor Flower was missing an eye and had a stutter for a year after that," Mr. Chong added, laughing.

Everest shook his head. "Might I add, I also fixed her several years later?"

"Only after your Federation English had become a stuttering mess of 'help–help–help' and 'I've lost my eye! I've lost my eye!' And–"

"Dad!" Everest interrupted.

But they all laughed, and the conversation drifted until Mr. Chong turned to Everest.

"Did you hear about the latest enhancement scandal?"

Everest frowned. "No. What now?"

"They found someone with four primary gene-pool enhancements."

"What? But that's impossible–"

"There will be no talk of enhancements today," Mrs. Guo interrupted firmly. "Not on a celebratory day." Her face changed. "Confounded enhancements, always ruining everything."

For the first time in her life, Urban found herself relieved to not be Enhanced. What an odd feeling it was–not having to hide anything.

"Don't be so quick to judge," Mr. Chong chided. "Not all Enhanced people are bad."

"Maybe not, but the rich always are. If it weren't for them, our dear Everest would have made it into uni and not be stuck working here."

Urban nearly choked on her tea. What if Mrs. Guo found out *she* was rich?

Everest bristled. "Ma, it's not the fault of the rich either. Now let's forget about all that and enjoy the holiday like you said."

"Of course." Mrs. Guo was about to heap more food on Urban's bowl. "You need to eat more. You're too skinny!"

"May I use your restroom?" Urban asked quickly.

"Of course, dear." Mrs. Guo showed her the way and flipped on the light, illuminating a tiny toilet with a shower overhead.

Urban closed the door and leaned up against the wall. She shut her eyes and listened to the steady hum of the bathroom's air vent. *I'll never fit in anywhere. Not in the Metropolis. Not in the Outskirts. Not even with my boyfriend's family.*

She rinsed her face as she tried to drown out Mrs. Guo's additional comments about the rich. *I'm always hiding who I really am.*

As she returned to the room, Everest watched her with concern.

"Shall we go to the roof to view the moon?" Mr. Chong suggested.

Mrs. Gou began to bustle about. "Yes, let's find a spot before everyone has the same idea."

They rode the elevator to the top of the building, where a dark staircase led to the roof.

Several families already sat in plastic chairs, sampling mooncakes.

"Sorry, I don't have any chairs," Mrs. Guo apologized. She spread out several layers of old paper on the ground next to the wall, and they sat down on them.

Urban's hand found Everest's. "This is great." She looked up at the bright, perfectly round moon.

Everest tightened his fingers around hers.

As they opened up the mooncake box and began eating, Urban finally relaxed. They joked about embarrassing stories from Everest's past, talked about their favorite mooncake flavors, and Everest and Urban tried to one-up each other's *terrible job* stories from their different AI training positions.

All too soon, she found herself bidding them good-bye.

"So nice meeting you, dear." Mrs. Guo's eyes were tender as she cupped Urban's hands in hers. "Please come back."

"I will, Auntie."

On the way home, the Bolt was almost entirely empty. Their pod arrived immediately but smelled foul. One of the seats had a suspicious liquid on it.

Urban was still evaluating the seat when Everest finished selecting their address. "Here." He sat down on the one dry seat and motioned for her to sit on his lap. "The safer bet."

Urban sat, and he wrapped his arms around her waist, caressing her neck with his finger. "You're amazing. You know that, right?" he whispered in her ear.

Urban wriggled around to face him. She tried to wipe the silly grin from her face but couldn't. "You know these things are monitored right?"

"And? I'm sure they've seen worse."

She leaned her forehead against his, gazing into his raven-black eyes.

"Do you think your parents liked me?"

"They loved you."

Urban sobered. "But they don't know my family history."

"Neither do you."

She paused at this. He was right, but she refused to think about it now and snuggled against him.

How am I so lucky? But then she remembered the conversation at dinner. *What would happen if his parents knew I came from the Metropolis? Would they tell him we had to break up? Or maybe they would insist I join him in the Outskirts.*

She wasn't sure which was worse, losing Everest or working endless hours at one of the dead-end AI training facilities.

As they rode in silence, she thought back to her race again. She knew she should tell him but didn't want to ruin such a perfect night. *I'll tell him next time.*

Her thoughts slowed as the pod stopped.

"So soon?" Everest said softly.

"We could just ride the Bolt all night." Urban was only half kidding.

"Didn't you say you have a big homework assignment due?"

"Yes, but I'm sure I can finish it later."

Everest shook his head at her. "Right. Come on, let's get you to the dorms."

When she didn't budge, he sighed. "All right, we'll do this the hard way." He swooped her up in his strong arms and carried her all the way up to the street before setting her down laughing.

They walked the rest of the way through the deserted streets with his arm around her waist and her head leaned against his shoulder, staring at the moon above them.

She wanted to freeze this moment of happiness, to stay by his side forever. But she wanted to be with him in the Metropolis—not here.

Climbing onto the motorcycle, Urban hesitated. Her eyes flickered up to Everest. The intensity of his gaze made butterflies beat against her insides wildly. He stepped nearer, closing the gap between them.

His charcoal eyes went deep into her very soul. With Everest, she was seen, heard, and understood. There was nowhere else she was safer. Every fiber of her being was focused on him and the warm tingling sensation running up her spine where his hand rest on the small of her back.

His soft lips pressed up against hers, and the world faded away.

All that existed was the two of them.

Suddenly, Everest jerked away. "Sorry."

Urban gasped for breath. "Wh—wh—what is it?" Her cheeks flushed bright red.

"Emergency ping," he said. "I have to go."

"Oh."

"So sorry," Everest said again, then gave a charming grin. "See you soon?"

Urban batted her eyelashes at him. "If you're lucky."

Everest blew her another kiss, then left.

As she made her way back to the Metropolis, Urban felt her world split in two. And with it, a deep chasm formed in her chest.

How long can I straddle two worlds?

URBAN WOKE THE NEXT DAY UNABLE TO
breathe. She bolted up in bed, gulping down air. Each breath
was labored and painful.

Not this. Not today.

Dread layered her gut in thick, sticky syrup. She knew
this feeling.

The last time she'd experienced this had been a year ago,
when she'd been forced to go to a private hospital to get steroid
shots. She had a test in forty minutes. She didn't have time to
drive to a private hospital, and going to a public one was a sure
way to get her medical genomics records in a database that
would feed directly to her school.

Instead, she took what medication she had, ordered a hot
tea, and crammed for her test. Hoping for the best, she headed
to Crypto Currencies.

In class, the probot turned on the XR test-room setting, and
Urban logged on. Her red-headed avatar sat at a lone chair in
the same classroom. The probot and the classroom were still
visible, but all of the other students had vanished. There were
now several sheets of paper and a pencil sitting on her desk.
Urban switched on classical music before turning to the test.

She was on question ten out of fifty when the coughing

started. She took a quick swig of her lukewarm lemon tea to try to calm her lungs and her rising panic.

"Are you okay?" someone whispered.

Urban blinked out of XR mode in her retina display and to dual vision. Coral leaned closer, concern etched on her face. "You alright?"

Urban clenched her hands under her desk. *Remain calm. Don't let her see how you're feeling.* "Yes. Fine. Drink went down the wrong way."

She coughed again before switching back to XR mode. With enhanced immune systems, none of these students had ever had so much as a sniffle in their lives. Unless they'd been to the Outskirts, or choked on food or drink, they'd probably never experienced a cough.

Her lungs grew itchier and more irritated by the minute. Fear gnawed at her.

Focus on the test. It's the fastest way out.

Cough.

She wrote down her answer to question twenty-three.

Cough. Wheeze.

She read the next question and answered it.

Cough. Cough. Wheeze.

The now-cold tea wasn't helping.

She tried to concentrate.

It was getting more difficult to focus. She was hyperventilating.

Cough. Cough.

What would happen if she went to the hospital and her medical genomics charts were shared with PKU? *But I can't breathe. I'm going to have to go to the nearest public hospital. How long will it take to get to the garage, ride my motorcycle to the closest ER, then get a steroid shot?*

Calculating the time made her breath come in quick shallow gasps. Urban wanted to leave, but she forced herself to remain still. She tried to call her motorcycle to have it air dropped near the classroom but found her system was in lockdown mode. She forgot testing periods meant no communication with the outside world.

Cough. Cough. Cough. Wheeze.

She was on question forty when the coughing got out of hand.

Switching back to dual mode, she bit her lip. The students who hadn't opted for noise cancelation were casting sideways looks at her.

She answered question forty-five.

Cough. Wheeze. Cough. Cough. She was struggling to breathe.

The classroom tilted and swayed. What was this? Dizziness? That was usually the last sign before she passed out.

I have to go. Now.

Ding!

Her retina display confirmed her test submission.

Urban's lungs burned too much for her to care about not having completed it. Several students stared as she bolted out.

Once outside, she called for her motorcycle to be air dropped, then wheezing and coughing, she stumbled toward it.

Her chest was tight with pain as she rode.

As she arrived at the hospital, she hopped a curb and left her bike leaned up against a wall. Tripping into the ER, she made it to all the way to the friendly receptionist-bot before her strength vanished.

She collapsed. The corners of her vision turned black.

When she awoke, her throat was worn and raspy, but her chest cool. She could breathe normally again. Florescent lights blinded her, and a medbot pricked her arm, then left.

Where am I?

With a start, she realized someone was holding her hand. Her gaze followed the arm. A familiar head leaned on top of the mattress, fast asleep.

"Lillian?"

Her sister jerked upright. She had dark circles under her

eyes, and her hair was a tangled white-blond mess. She was momentarily disoriented before giving Urban a sleepy smile. "You're awake."

Urban reached out and touched her arm. "You didn't have to come."

"Don't be ridiculous. You'd do the same for me if this were one of my migraines."

Despite being Enhanced, Lillian would occasionally have bad migraines. After years of quietly seeking out medical help, their parents had finally given up on finding a cure. Fortunately for Lillian, the migraines usually only happened once a year and were easy enough to hide, so as not to attract any more attention to the Lee household.

"What happened?" Urban glanced at her surroundings in confusion. The last thing she remembered was arriving at the hospital.

"You passed out. Fortunately, Trig brought you here immediately."

Urban blinked. "Oh." Scanning her augmented maps, she saw Trig's faithful presence out in the lobby. "You should give that guy a raise."

There was a loud purr, and then something jumped on top of the table.

"Baozi!" Urban leaned forward and hugged the giant cat. "Is he allowed in here?"

"Course not." Lillian winked.

"The things you get away with."

"Anything for my little sis." Lillian turned serious. "How are you feeling?"

"Fine. Now." Urban hesitated, suddenly embarrassed. "Lillian, I'm sorry for the way I treated you at the race. I just really need a high sosh. Or . . . you know."

Lillian studied her sister. "What is it?"

Urban hesitated, then told her about where all her crypto

points had gone.

"Of course, I'll help you," Lillian told her after listening, then glanced at Urban. "How have you even made it this long with so few points?"

"I've been eating a lot of rice," Urban confessed.

Lillian eyed her with concern. "Just ask next time."

"Hopefully there is no next time."

"Agreed." Lillian turned to the wall and gestured to Urban's projected vitals. "I've already booted out the healthcare bots and tweaked all your data so no one will know you-know-what."

The things my family has to do to hide my genetics . . .

Urban sat up with a jolt.

Maybe the reason her family denied having ever seen the microneedle patch was because they were telling the truth. Was it possible her memory wasn't from her world in the Metropolis? Was it possibly from before she'd been adopted—when she was still in the Outskirts?

Urban thought back to her adoption. She was three when she arrived at the orphanage. She had an image of a dark corridor in the orphanage and Lillian standing in front of her to protect her from something. But that was her only memory before coming to the Metropolis. Surely there should be more from that age. She was pretty sure her subconscious blocked the rest.

Urban concentrated hard to bring back the image she'd had of a patch sitting next to a bowl of soup and chopsticks. The bowl was porcelain, white-and-blue but cheap-looking, and the chopsticks were the wooden kind found at hole-in-the-wall restaurants, not the lacquered black ones at her house.

She realized the memory was not from her home in the Metropolis, but from her birth parents, whoever they were, in their house. Her birth parents had somehow had the microneedle patch. But then why hadn't they enhanced her? Why had Lillian been enhanced? And why didn't Lillian remember it?

"A 'thank you' would suffice," Lillian was saying. "I mean, it was pretty easy for me, cause I'm a brilliant Inventor and all, but I did just hack several personal data sets and break through two security protocols to do it."

A headache crept across Urban's temples as questions flooded in. Dry paper sheets crinkled under her as she leaned back against the bed.

"Do you remember anything about our birth parents?" Urban asked suddenly.

Lillian frowned. "What?"

"Our birth parents? What were they like? Do you have any memories from before the orphanage?"

Lillian looked at her in bewilderment. "What does this have to do with getting you out of the hospital?"

"Nothing. I just need to know."

Lillian continued to look at Urban, then she answered slowly, "I was four. Not really. Why?"

Disappointment filled Urban. How was it possible Lillian couldn't remember anything, but she could?

Maybe she'd imagined the memory. Was it possible she had somehow retained a memory from when she was three years old, before arriving at the orphanage?

"Urban?" Lillian's voice cut into her thoughts. "What's going on?"

Urban debated telling her sister, but she wanted to have more proof about her theory first. Lillian was already looking at her like she'd grown two sets of wings. If she told her sister now, Lillian might tell their parents or insist she stay longer in the hospital. "Nothing. Just curious."

Lillian eyed her a moment longer, then changed the subject. "By the way, I also hacked the bio printer to release an extra steroid to take with you."

Urban's eyes darted to a 3D printer whirring away in a corner where it was creating a shot and loaded vial. "I swear, if all Inventors are as clever as you, society is doomed."

Lillian grinned as she handed the finished product to her.

Urban examined the vial, then looked up. "How did you know I was here?"

Lillian's eyes darted to Urban's wrist. "Mom and Dad got a couple pings from SCA showing you violated some traffic regulations. Then they got a notification saying you'd checked into the ER and were being administered treatment. Since I was the closest, they pinged me, and I came straight over."

Lillian seemed stiff and uncomfortable. Urban had seen her talk that way before when she was lying to their parents.

"And?" Urban probed.

"And what?" Lillian looked confused.

"And what else aren't you telling me?"

Lillian avoided Urban's eyes. "What do you mean?"

"You know what I mean." Urban watched her toes curl and uncurl at the edge of the blanket.

Lillian began picking imaginary specks of dirt out of Baozi's fur. "I have no idea what you're talking about," she said.

Urban let out an exasperated sigh. "Fine. So, are Mother and Father mad?"

"Not mad. Just concerned." Lillian hesitated. "I think they're wondering if they made the right decision letting you go to uni."

Urban bolted up in bed again. "They can't make me go home."

Lillian pushed her gently back down. "They're not. I think they're concerned about how you'll hide this"—she motioned at the ER room—"from the other students if you don't get better."

Urban had been wondering that exact thing. "I'll find a way. I'm sure none of the students today will remember. They were all too focused on the test. Mostly."

"And what if you need emergency transport again?"

"I can bring my nebulizer to the dorms. That always helps calm my lungs down."

"But how often do you have the dorm room to yourself?

You can't use it in front of your roommates without attracting suspicion. What if you need it in the middle of the night? That's when it's usually bad, right?"

"Sometimes," Urban admitted. "I might be able to go out to the garage and hook it up to my motorcycle."

"And how are you going to get out of the dorms?"

"Learn a few tricks of the trade from Coral."

Lillian cocked her head. "Who's that?"

"One of my roommates." Urban fingered her jade-beaded bracelet. "She has a way of tripping the curfew."

"Hmmm . . . if you say so. Here, drink this. It will help your immune system." Lillian handed her a wolfberry tea. "Are you ready for me to take you back to the dorms, or do you want to stay here a while longer?"

Urban pet Baozi and watched the cat rub her head against her hand. "I think I'm ready to go."

Back in the dorm, there was a delivery of street food and a teddy bear from Everest. Urban's heart warmed at the sight of it.

She took a picture of the gift and sent it to Everest.

[Urban: What's this?]

[Everest: I was going to send you flowers but realized that might tip people off to your dating status. Lillian told me what happened. How are you feeling?]

[Urban: I'm fine now. Thank you. I've named the teddy Crackle.]

She took a video of her cuddling with her teddy bear.

[Everest: Tell Crackle to back off. That's my woman!]

Urban smiled to herself. It was strange how just a few words from Everest could calm her down. How did he always know the right thing to say and do?

Between pinging Everest, sleeping, and sipping wolfberry tea, the weekend passed by quickly. But Urban grew more stressed as she fell further behind in her schoolwork.

Monday was the Annual Games preparation holiday, and

Urban spent it resting and attempting to get caught up on homework. Normally, it was one of her favorite holidays, and she binge-watched all the activities.

But today, she only allowed herself short breaks to watch the feeds of exotic animals purchased and being brought into the arena, or the new robotic advancements that would be incorporated into the Games. It was rumored there was even a half-robotic, half-flesh dragon being created.

By the time Tuesday rolled around, she had regained her strength but was tight with worry about her looming assignments.

IT WAS DARK AND STILL WHEN A BLARING WAIL awoke Urban early on Tuesday morning.

"Already?" She moaned as she crawled out from under her warm covers. Shivering, she sent Lillian a quick ping.

[Urban: On my way. See you soon for torture.]

[Lillian: You're coming! Dreams really do come true!]

On her ride there, she decided to search in QuanNao for anything about her birth parents. It had been years since her last search. When she'd first found out she was adopted, she'd scoured XR daily for anything on her birth parents. Were they out there somewhere? Did they love her? Why had they given her up for adoption?

But she'd never found anything. Eventually, she'd stopped looking.

Now, she remembered the hopelessness of the quest. Her adoptive parents wouldn't tell her which orphanage she'd come from, but she guessed it was one of the three based in New Beijing. She looked like the Naturals who lived in those parts.

By the time she'd arrived at Infini-Fit, she wasn't really surprised at being no closer to learning anything regarding the microneedle patch or her birth parents.

Despite the energetic music blaring overhead, the gym was

deserted at this hour. Urban searched for Thistle anyway, but with relief, realized she wasn't there.

After scanning in, Urban headed over to the enclosed turf, noticing her bodyguard Trig still followed her, even into the gym. After her ER incident, his presence was reassuring. Urban had a mental picture of him doing an invisible workout with her and almost laughed.

"There she is!" Lillian jogged over.

"Where's the nearest coffee machine?" Urban yawned. "It's way too early for you to be this perky."

Lillian grinned and rubbed her hands. "You'll be awake soon enough. Come on, let's jog around the track to warm up."

Urban debated taking an energy pill but decided against it. With the gym deserted, it was a rare opportunity to practice without one.

After jogging, they did a series of warm ups.

"That's enough. Cooldown time."

Urban looked up in surprise. "We're done?"

"I don't want to push you too much. Now it's time for a little more practice with this." Lillian pulled out the stun shield and handed it to her sister.

Urban glanced around and lowered her voice. "Is that a good idea?"

"It's fine. The military Supers and Flyers all practice here with their weapons." Lillian led her to another part of the gym where a variety of lanes with targets awaited them. This early in the morning, they were all empty.

Lillian picked a lane with a human-shaped dummy and adjusted it so the target was only ten meters away.

They practiced until eventually Lillian left to train with her own weapons. Urban watched as Lillian entered an enclosed space with metallic balls shooting at her from all angles. She blocked with different-sized force fields. Then she went over to a dummy and began her own target practice with a metal arrow that shot from her arm, lodged into the target, then retracted so the dummy was dragged toward her.

Having decimated the dummy, Lillian moved to a zero-gravity obstacle course. She experimented with different gages on her weapon, using the propulsion to rocket her through hoops, over hurdles, and under low-hanging walls.

She even tried several underwater exercises but ended up sputtering on the surface and adjusting several of her malfunctioned inventions.

Urban continued to observe her sister out of the corner of her eye. Lillian was not someone to be messed with. Sometimes, Urban wondered why Lillian was on the Inventor path and not some military track instead.

Thirty minutes later, Lillian left to shower. Urban sent Everest a live vid.

[Urban: So, you'll never guess what I did today.]

She switched the focus from her face to her retina display and looked around the gym, taking in her surroundings.

[Urban: I'm at the gym working out. At five in the morning. Can you believe it? Also, let me know if you're free today. I miss you.]

She watched the video replay, then sent it. This early in the morning and covered in sweat she looked terrible. "As good as it gets."

Urban debated going back to sleep but decided to cram for an upcoming quiz instead. After showering, she found a deserted restaurant, perfect for eating breakfast and working on assignments.

When the gym began buzzing with early-morning workouts, Urban took it as her cue to leave. As she passed the target lanes a thick, metallic smell filled her nose, and she stopped abruptly. Something about the scent was familiar.

Turning, she noticed one of the obstacle courses with targets had a Super running through it. She had unnaturally long and powerful legs, but that wasn't what caught Urban's eye. The Super aimed a weapon at her target and fired.

Urban admired the sleek Magtouch M600—the latest in weapon advancements. She'd seen its release announced in the news feeds but never had she expected to see one in person.

She watched in fascination as the Super hid behind a corner and detached what looked like the barrel of the gun so it bent around the corner at a 90-degree angle. Then, from behind the wall, she took aim and blasted the target on the other side.

She snapped the barrel back so it was straight again and sprinted toward a small body of water. Diving in, the Super sank to the bottom of the pool, aimed at another target, and blasted it from underwater.

Urban turned away, still sniffing the air. Why did the scent of this smoke trigger something? Why did she have the distinct impression she'd smelled it before?

An image flashed in her mind.

Everest.

He smelled like this.

That was impossible. Only military personnel were authorized to use the Magtouch M600. The penalty for illegally owning one was a lifetime sentence. They couldn't even be found on the black market.

Everest wasn't in the military, so there was no way he owned one. She had to be imagining it. That smoky smell following him had to be from the Outskirts. There were always fires out there.

Urban shook her head to clear her thoughts and headed to class.

In Genetic Engineering, the probot wore a ridiculous suit and tie and strutted about proudly as it gave its lecture. Urban found herself wondering how many outfits the probot owned and who paid for them. Did it actually earn a salary? Go shopping?

Before she realized it, class was out, and she'd learned

nothing. She inwardly berated herself.

In her next class, she took notes as soon as it started. Twenty minutes in, Ash sat next to her.

"That's one tardy for you Ding Ash," the probot announced.

"Okay, I deserved that one," Ash conceded.

"Next time, arriving after fifteen minutes will count as an absence."

Ash waved dismissively, then leaned in close to Urban. "How would you like to get out of class early?" he whispered.

Urban looked up, startled. "How?"

"You know the rule about if a probot glitches or gives a wrong answer, class is cancelled?"

"Yeah, but no one is ever successful. They've had decades of rebellious students attempting to ruin them. I think they've learned pretty fast."

"None of those 'rebellious' students were as smart as I am."

Urban rolled her eyes. "Says the Flyer."

"Hey! That doesn't mean I don't have brains."

"Your point?"

Ash grinned. "If I can get us out of class, will you hang out with me for the rest of the class period?"

Urban hesitated. What did he mean "hang out"? If this was like a fake date or something she wasn't interested. But Ash knew she had a boyfriend. He wasn't hitting on her. Was he?

She decided it didn't matter because there was no way he was getting them out of class. And if by some stroke of luck he did manage, she could use the break. Her brain had been dragging all day. "Sure."

Ash grinned mischievously. "Watch and learn from the master."

He raised his hands. "Dr. Bang, I have a question."

The probot stopped its lecture. "Ding Ash. What is your question?"

"What is the solution to the equation for 78 divided by 4?"

Dr. Bang froze, and Urban thought Ash had actually done it, when it spoke again, "That would be 119.5."

"No, you're wrong," Ash corrected. He projected a link displaying the correct answer in QuanNao. "It's 19.5."

Dr. Bang froze again. "That's not possible," it finally said.

"You're wrong!" Ash declared gleefully.

The probot began shaking its head, walking forward, then backward, agitated. Its head jerked to Ash. "You are right. I seem to be in error. Class is cancelled for the day, per school policy."

The class cheered.

Ash took a bow before extending his arm to Urban. "And you doubted me."

Urban reluctantly took his arm as they walked out of the building together. "What did you do?"

Ash grinned. "At the end of the day, probots are just advanced algorithms. They can't take into account context. When they hear 'what is the solution to the equation for' and then a number, they think the 'for' in that sentence is the number four and is a part of the sequence. Thus, their calculation is off. That's why in elementary school we're taught to be precise and say things like 'what's my code sequence for the number . . .' Using slang throws them off."

"Interesting," Urban mused. "So, where to?"

"I was gonna suggest we do some boxing together."

Urban stilled.

Ash gave her a cursory glance. "But I don't think you brought your workout clothes."

Urban breathed easier.

"So, if we're going to play hooky and not work out, the next best thing would be . . . well, I'll just show you. Are you afraid of heights?"

"No." Urban eyed him suspiciously. "Why?"

"Great, cause it's going to take a little . . . maneuvering to get there."

He unfolded his sleek speckled wings and motioned for her to come closer. "The easiest way to do this is for you to stand on my boots and grab my waist."

Urban's eyes widened. "But that's illegal. There are weight limitations. You can't just fly with me."

"I just tripped up our probot. You don't think I can navigate around a few other dumb rules?" He laughed at her expression. "Come on, it's perfectly safe."

What looked like a clear force field formed around them.

"What's that?" Urban asked.

"Invisi-field."

Urban eyed it skeptically. "Those only work in XR, not in real life."

"Not this one." A roguish smile stretched across his face.

"We'll be invisible?"

"Not exactly. It's a prerecorded image of me flying that will be projected over us. No one will be the wiser. And I've been practicing in the wind tunnels with extra weight so that's not an issue."

"I thought you'd put on a couple pounds."

Ash rolled his eyes. "You know what I mean." He poked her. "So? Coming?"

Urban wanted nothing more than a break from the tedious classes and homework assignments. Not to mention, she'd always wondered what it would feel like to fly. Now she would actually get to experience it.

"All right," Urban relented with a shake of her head. "Just don't kill me."

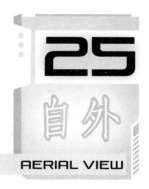

URBAN STEPPED CAREFULLY ONTO ASH'S GIANT boots and grabbed hold of his firm torso. His arms wrapped around her and tightened.

Ash beat his powerful wings, and they shot into the sky.

"Wow, you're surprisingly light," Ash commented. "In flight school they teach us only Naturals, Flyers, and a couple other obscure enhancements are this lightweight. All the other Enhanced have denser bones. Maybe you have some Flyer in you yet."

Urban remained stiff and quiet, hoping the conversation would veer elsewhere.

When Ash stopped talking, she glanced down. Her stomach dropped. They were past the drone flying zone and weaving in between skyscrapers along with other Flyers. She gripped him tighter.

"Better than class, huh?" Ash asked.

"This is insane!"

"Yeah, you're so light, it's never been this easy. I bet I could even do some tricks." He began gaining altitude quickly.

"Don't you dare!"

Ash paid no attention as he swooped down, spinning in circles. He did a few more aerial loops before evening out again.

"I'm going to kill you," Urban gritted out, her eyes shut tight.

Ash chuckled. "Says the girl who's not a Flyer and hundreds of feet above the ground. Yeah . . . I don't think so."

His flying slowed and they landed. "You can open your eyes now."

As he set her down, she took in her surroundings. They were on top of one of the tallest skyscrapers, taking a seat on what looked like a pagoda rooftop. There were no Flyers this high, but down below, there was a steady stream of them, and then drones, and then on the ground level, smart cars and people walking. There were buildings as far as she could see and, in the distance, rugged brown mountains.

Her vision swam. She scooted away from the ledge.

Ash dangled his legs, carefree. "Don't worry. You're not going to fall."

I'm not going to be a scaredy cat around one of my few friends. Determined to prove herself, Urban forced herself to the edge where she hung her legs over the ledge. *Great. Ash is my only ticket down.*

Ash gazed out over the city. "This is my favorite spot to think."

"Flyers think?" Urban couldn't resist the jab.

"Ha. Ha. This one does a lot actually." He let out a sigh. "Too much."

Urban wasn't sure whether to say anything or not.

Ash straightened, tucking his wings. But something about his wistful, sad gaze made Urban curious.

"What do you think about when you're up here?"

Ash paused. "My career choice. Or rather, my parents'. If they made the right one. Like seriously, wings? Do you ever wonder what your parents were thinking when they designed your genetics?"

"What are you talking about? I would kill for wings."

"Flying is amazing, but you get used to it after a while, and it just becomes a part of life. I'd much rather be an Inventor, using my intellect to make an impact in the world or even a Giver. There are only a few career paths for a Flyer." He detached what looked like a thick black stick from the back of his XR suit. Urban had never noticed it before.

"This is a polearm. Every military Flyer's weapon of choice. It works well for crane-bot, the martial art that incorporates flying." He switched it on, and the tip blazed blue. "I'm only an orange belt, but I'm hoping after five more years of training to become a Master."

"Why a Master?"

"Cause, you get this amazing weapon." Ash projected a pulsing stick with two sharp, wing-shaped lasers at the tip. "Way cooler than mine and easier to fight with. The crane-bot founders only give them to people who've perfected the art though." With that, Ash switched off the projection.

"So, why aren't you interested in one of the Flyer paths? Crane-bot sounds pretty great."

"True, but it's just not me."

"Ash," Urban said slowly, "why are you telling me this?"

He placed the polearm carefully back on his suit before responding. "I get the sense you're not content to live out the enhancement track your parents picked for you either. You even keep your gene pool a secret from everyone. That's pretty rare these days. I guess it makes me comfortable talking to you about it. Most people just laugh me off."

"Oh. Thanks, I guess."

"Take it as a compliment." Ash grinned. "So, what about you?"

Urban stiffened. "If you're hoping to get me to reveal my enhancements . . ."

"Dang, so close," Ash said playfully. He turned serious again. "But really, I think about this all the time. What I'd give to be an Inventor."

What I'd give to be anything. Urban thought ruefully.

"Sorry, didn't mean to put a damper on the conversation." Ash seemed to sense the mood shift. "You asked what I think about, and I'm an open book."

How opposite we are. Urban thought. *I need a friend like this.*

"Anyhow, if you know of any Inventors, let me know. I'm super into smart chicks."

Relief flooded her. Ash wasn't hitting on her. "I'll keep my eyes peeled." She winked.

"Say, you're not one, are you? I swear, if you've been holding out on me . . ."

Urban threw up her arms, laughing. "I'm not an Inventor, I promise."

Ash eyed her suspiciously a moment more. "If you say so."

"Actually, my roommate and sister are both Inventors."

Ash brightened. "Be my wingwoman? Please? I might even let you cheat off me in class if you do."

Urban snorted. "Yeah right. Although . . ." She peered down at the long drop below. "I'll cut you a deal. Get me back to the dorms without any tricks, and I'll introduce you to them."

"Brilliant!"

They continued talking about their genetics class, martial arts, and all the worst and best bashes they'd been to in the last year. The sun set, and the city lights flickered on—a brilliant rainbow of flashing lights.

An alarm beeped in Urban's retina display. "Oh shoot!" She jumped to her feet. "We have to go! I forgot I have jiujitsu class."

She was one of the last ones to arrive at the gym. The rest of the class was already seated on the floor. She took a place near the front next to Lillian.

Orion gave her a slight nod, then began the lesson. "Lately, I've noticed a few of you rushing through the motions. When you practice a move, take your time. Jiujitsu is like trying a new food. You don't scarf it down. You take a small bite and chew it slowly. Maybe you like it, maybe you don't."

He paused and eyed them all. "Or take another example. It's like pursuing a woman. You give her flowers, tell her she's beautiful, take her to dinner, then you hold her hand, next you kiss her, then you ask her to be your girlfriend, then eventually, marry her. It's a slow process. Kiss her right away, and you'll get slapped. Ask her out too soon, and she'll say no. Jiujitsu is no different. Take your time."

There were a few chuckles and titters. They began their warm-up and then watched as Orion demonstrated their newest defensive move with Craig.

"Partner up," Orion ordered when the demo was done.

Another girl teamed up with Lillian, leaving Urban to scramble for a partner. She glanced around the room and found most everyone had already found someone. Craig, the Super, was the only one left. He clumped toward her.

This is going to be so awkward.

Craig also looked uncomfortable. "I'll go first," he suggested, lying on the floor and motioning for Urban to sit on top of him. He executed the move flawlessly, then turned to her. "Your turn."

Urban dropped to the mat with dread.

Craig tried to be gentle but being gentle for a Super was like asking a grizzly bear to afternoon tea.

As soon as he was in place, Urban wanted to tap out. She gasped for breath. Her ribs were surely snapping under his weight.

Taking several deep breaths, she tried to calm herself. An Enhanced student with reinforced bones would probably be fine in this situation. She had to be too.

She focused all her energy on trying to free herself. Her attempt was clumsy and weak. The Super shifted under her efforts but otherwise didn't move.

She tried again. Craig moved a little more but not enough. The stench of his sweat dripping down on her was nauseating.

Urban tried a third time, giving it everything she had and growling through gritted teeth. The Super almost moved but still no luck.

Urban wanted to cry from the pain and her inability to do anything about it. She was reminded of the time Lucas dragged her to the bottom of the pool and almost drowned her. Only, she couldn't exactly hit Craig in the groin to free herself this time.

Orion came over and pulled Craig up, and fresh air immediately filled her lungs again.

"Watch." Orion motioned to Craig and demonstrated the countermove slowly with him. "It's not about brute force, but leverage. Try with me."

Orion was significantly lighter than Craig, and Urban realized it was because he was putting the majority of his weight on his hands and knees instead of crushing her chest.

His face was inches from her own, and she noticed the texture of his stubble. Her nerves spiked with him so close. The scent of him filled her.

Urban shook herself. Why was she noticing these details rather than remembering the move she was supposed to be executing?

She tried the defense and this time managed to flip Orion. It was clumsy, but she still counted it a win.

"See?" Orion said with a wide grin, and she found herself smiling back. "Much better." They practiced several more times before she returned to Craig. Then it was back to having her lungs crushed and hyperventilating. Only this time, she was able to flip Craig.

By the end of class, her back and chest were sore, but she smiled with pride.

"Are you okay?" Lillian whispered.

Urban rubbed her ribs. "I survived."

"Next time let's make sure we partner up."

The next morning, Urban surveyed the damage. Her ribs were

definitely bruised. Pulling on her XR suit was a painful ordeal.

She was curious if Orion would join her in biopsych class. Sure enough, a few minutes later, Orion sat next to her.

"Hey, hey. How you feeling?"

"A little sore," Urban admitted.

"Sorry about that. I keep telling Craig to partner with someone his own size." He gave her a smile that made the blood rush to her face. Fortunately, Dr. Botteria began class, and Urban turned away quickly.

What is wrong with me? Get it together! You have a boyfriend.

She let out a frustrated sigh. Orion gave her a concerned look.

Right. And he's an Inceptor.

Urban tried hard to focus on Dr. Botteria's lecture but found it difficult with Orion so near. His profile was visible out of the corner of her eye. Next time, she would be sure to sit somewhere else.

"Let's meet soon to work on our group project," Orion called out as he left.

Urban nodded without turning.

In Crypto Currencies, it was a relief to sit next to Coral. Her roommate was wearing a backward hat and high-top hover shoes, though why she needed an extra boost when she jumped, Urban wasn't sure. Then again, it was Coral. Who knew what sort of trouble she'd be getting into.

"What happened last class?" Coral whispered.

"Uh, what do you mean?" Urban stiffened. "I just choked on my water."

"Yeah, and *gullible* is written on the ceiling." Coral gave her a look. "You were like dying."

Urban twisted the hem of her XR suit. "My body's just weird like that. Sometimes I choke really bad."

Thankfully, the probot chose that moment to start class, and Coral stopped asking questions.

After class, Coral walked out with Urban. "Hey, I'm going to grab a quick lunch and work on our homework assignment. Want to join me?"

Urban wondered if Coral would ask any more questions, but she seemed to be past that.

"How about DingDing's Dim Sum?" Urban suggested. She knew the students with a high sosh all despised the place and wouldn't venture near it. She also happened to love dim sum, and the place was a great study spot.

Coral agreed, and they soon found themselves in a bamboo booth with robots pushing trays full of assorted food past them. Urban's mouth watered at the sight of snow-pea sprouts with shrimp dumplings, custard-roll sponge cakes, chicken and roast pork bundles, turnip cakes, deep-fried crab balls, red-bean balls, and eggplant stuffed with vegetables.

Urban snagged some chicken feet off one of the trays.

Coral watched Urban stick the foot in her mouth to chew around the bone and made a face.

"Get used to it. You're in the Asian Federation."

Coral grimaced. "Thanks for reminding me."

As Coral plucked a sesame-seed ball off a tray, Urban noticed a tattoo. "What's that?"

"What?"

"Your tattoo." Urban pointed.

Coral looked down. "Oh." She rolled up her sleeve.

"*Weiji?*" Urban read. "Crisis?"

"Seems strange, I know, but I like how the character is made up of the two parts, *wei*, meaning dangerous, and *ji*, meaning opportunity. For every crisis, there is both danger and opportunity. It reminds me to keep a positive outlook."

"That's cool." Surprisingly.

But Coral just nodded and turned back to the homework. "Okay, so what does question number seven mean? Do you get it? I don't recognize this word, and I keep getting a weird translation from my retina auto translator."

Urban took a look. "You're right. When translated it does come out weird." Urban spent the next three hours helping Coral understand the questions and a few of the other terms in their textbook. In return, Coral helped Urban with some of the equations she couldn't crack.

"You know, we make a good team," Coral commented as they left.

As the dorms came into view, Urban looked up. "Say, how hard is it to get around the curfew system?"

Coral stopped walking. "Don't tell me you found yourself a boy that fast."

"What?" Urban was confused. "No." But then she thought better of it. This was the perfect excuse. "Well, actually . . ."

"Who is it?"

"Just . . . someone."

"Aw, you're no fun."

"The curfew hack?" Urban pressed.

Coral eyed her. "It's supposed to be a Camo-exclusive trick. But you did just help me with my homework." She paused. "All right, I'll tell you. All you need is a halocaster and something weighing roughly the same as you. The weight trips the bed monitor, and the halocaster needs to be programmed to display your retina so the retina scanner will be shut off. And that's all."

At Urban's confused look, Coral added, "It's super easy. I'll show you."

"Thanks. And, Coral, please don't tell anyone about my boyfriend. My parents would kill me if they found out."

"So, he's your boyfriend already?"

Urban bit her tongue. She hadn't meant for that to slip out.

"Don't worry," her roommate assured her. "Your secret's safe with me."

That night, while Hazel and Blossom were out, Coral showed Urban how to trick the curfew system. She also gave her a carabiner and some other gadgets to help her rappel out the window.

"And no one's going to spot me just climbing down the side of the building? Is this even safe?" Urban glanced down at the forty-two-floor drop.

"You'll be fine. I'm never spotted because I blend in with the wall. So that could be problematic for you. Just wear your XR mask so the cameras can't trace your identity, and you should be good. If you give me a heads up, I can probably shut off the surveillance for a couple minutes."

"I knew I kept you around for a reason."

Coral grinned.

SATURDAY ROLLED AROUND, AND URBAN'S body tingled with excitement and dread. Today, she was meeting up with Everest. Today, she had to tell him about the race. She finally felt confident their relationship could handle the stress of that conversation.

No more secrets.

After a hurried breakfast, she threw on some makeup and the necklace Everest had given her before slipping out of the dorm.

As she drove, she thought back to the last time they'd been together. Had it really only been last weekend? Mooncake Festival felt like forever ago. If only he didn't live so far away, then maybe they could see each other more than once a week.

An hour later, Urban slowed her motorcycle and pulled off the Speed Way and down a winding road lined with gnarled trees. The road was abandoned and uneven, and she bumped down it until she spotted what she was looking for. Up ahead leaned a decrepit bus stop with faded advertisements, collapsing sides, and a partially caved-in roof. Only the bench remained intact.

Everest was already there and leaped to his feet upon her arrival. He drew her head to his chest, and Urban recognized the familiar scent of jasmine and smoke. The smoke wasn't saccharine and putrid like the Outskirts. It was acrid and sharp, like the Magtouch M600.

That's not possible. Everest works at the AI factories. She thought about his dealings with crime in the Outskirts. *I've seen his weapons. He doesn't own a highly illegal gun. Where would he even get one?*

Urban was still pondering this when she realized how long and tight Everest was holding her.

She tried to relax in his warm, strong embrace, but his heart was beating too quickly. Something was wrong. Urban's pulse quickened.

When he released her, they sat down.

"Urban, we need to talk."

Urban blinked. "Is everything okay?" Had he found out about the race? Surely not. How could he?

"I've been doing a lot of thinking about . . . us." Everest was avoiding eye contact.

Urban's breath hitched. Something was definitely wrong.

"I haven't had time to work on my lyrics since last summer." Everest ran a hand through his hair. "I'm not going to suddenly become a famous songwriter or be able to join you in the Metropolis."

Urban tensed.

"Even if I were willing to live a lie in the Metropolis, I don't think it would be possible. My sosh is too low."

No. No. No! Urban wanted to stop him. To scream. Instead, she found she was paralyzed, watching a death sentence unfolding in slow motion in a purple zone.

"I don't think we could get it high enough. And it would be obvious I'm a Natural."

He cupped her quivering chin gently in his hands. "Urban, I can't and won't let you throw away your life for me. You have to stay in the Metropolis and—"

"Stop," Urban blurted.

"Urban," Everest pressed on, "it's time to accept that I won't be a part of that dream in the Metropolis." He paused and took a deep breath. "We need to break up."

Urban's back went rigid. "No," it came out a croaked whisper, "we can make it work! There's all kinds of tech that could help us. Your sosh might not be perfect, but I'm sure I could talk Mother into giving me more money to buy them. I could—"

"Urban—"

"If we try harder, eventually we can figure this out! There's always a way." Urban was trembling now. "There's always a way!" she insisted again.

"I hate this as much as you do," Everest's voice cracked. "I would do anything to be with you." He tucked a strand of hair behind her ear and looked at her with a firm resolve. "Anything *except* suck you down to the Outskirts."

Tears poured down Urban's face. "But there's always a way." She didn't sound convincing, even to herself.

Everest said nothing but pulled Urban close to him.

They sat unmoving as the sun crept slowly across the hazy sky. Time seemed to stop and yet fast forward, all at once. The pain in Urban's chest was agony. The only thing that consoled her was Everest's warmth as he held her. She knew soon, that, too, would be stripped from her.

Her heart cracked.

Moisture landed on top of her head. Was he crying too? She'd never seen Everest cry before. She looked up at him. His eyes were red-rimmed. Their gazes locked and she willed him to stay, pleading with her eyes.

Once he left, there would be no one who understood. Only Everest knew her for who she was and loved and accepted her.

A million unsaid words traveled between them in silence. He squeezed her tight—a blanket of comfort wrapped around her.

"I'm going to go." He gently extracted himself from her. Cold air rushed between them, and the world became hostile again.

Her brain couldn't seem to grasp what was happening. Numbness crept into her chest.

"Good-bye, my one-of-a-kind *meinu*," Everest said gently. He touched her cheek and walked away.

She stared after him, unwilling to believe the truth.

As his familiar leather jacket and black helmet disappeared slowly into the horizon, the chasm in her chest grew wider.

Then, everything shattered.

Urban hunched over as an exploding star swallowed up her heart, then imploded upon itself. Her whole body caved in—destroyed.

She fell to the ground, and a cloud of dust curled around her. *No. No. No!*

She tried to forget the past hour. It had to be a dream.

But the longer she lay there, the more certain it became. Sobs wracked her body. Dust filled her nostrils. Leaves blew past her, uncaring, and hurrying to some unimportant destination where they would decompose. A lone bird chirped overhead. How did the world keep spinning and functioning as it always had when Urban's own world crumbled?

With difficulty, her eyes opened again. Her fingers traced the dust and picked at pebbles. Strange how her whole life she'd walked upon the dirt but never taken the time to notice it up close. Her attention was completely focused on it now. Thinking about anything else was too painful.

She wasn't sure how much time had passed when it grew dark. The pebbles cut into her skin, and the dust made her sneeze.

Picking herself up slowly, she brushed bits of rock off. They left indentions on her body, and she wondered idly how long the marks would last.

With great effort, she managed to drag herself to her bike. Hopeless thoughts ricocheted in her mind as she drove back to the dorms in shocked silence.

Thankfully, her roommates were all out when she got back. Urban sent Lillian and Coral a ping. She wasn't sure why she included Coral. Maybe because, apart from Lillian, Coral and Ash were the only people who had known about her relationship.

Coral immediately responded.

[Coral: Where are you? I want to come give you a hug. Also, where does your bf live? I'll hunt him down and make him regret breaking my roommate's heart. He's no match for me!]

Oddly, this response brought a sliver of comfort to Urban, even if the offer to beat up Everest was ridiculous.

Stepping into the bath, she flipped on XRD mode and let the ice-cold water wash over her. When she opened her eyes, she was under a waterfall in the sunny tropics. Warm sunlight touched her skin, and the raging waterfall beat down on her back.

She turned in a circle, noticing the radiant green foliage and the clear pool of water in which she was standing. A rainbow of colors shimmered in the mist hovering over the water.

Urban leaned against a mossy rock and sank down into a turquoise pool. The waterfall continued to beat against her, harsh, uncaring, relentless.

She wasn't sure how long she'd been there when her augmented feed beeped. It was Lillian. She hesitated, then clothed her avatar in a swimsuit before approving Lillian's request. A moment later, her sister's avatar appeared in augmented reality.

Lillian looked like a cyborg warrior with metal legs and arms and extra attack items like homemade shields and spears. The only resemblance she had to her physical self was her identical white-blond hair and big brown eyes.

Lillian looked around in confusion at her location. She shuddered as her XR suit gave her body the illusion of being drenched in cold water. Her avatar's cropped hair flattened and clung to her chin, dripping wet. She scanned the surroundings until she found Urban slumped to the side. She sloshed quickly through the pool to her sister.

"Sis." Lillian's voice was tender as she sank into the water next to Urban. She rested a hand gently on Urban's shoulder, but without her XR suit, Urban couldn't feel it. There was nothing but ice water to console her. Her teeth began to chatter.

Urban flipped to dual vision so she could see the tropical paradise overlaying her bathtub. She cranked the water up to hot, then returned back to the lush jungle.

"What happened?"

Urban told her sister everything, and when she was finished, Lillian let out a long breath. "I'm so sorry."

"I just can't believe . . . he left me." A tear slipped down Urban's cheek. "I tried to persuade him we could be together . . . it didn't work."

They sat in silence, save the roar of the waterfall.

A beeping noise made Urban flinch.

"Sorry." Lillian swiped her tatt, silencing the noise. "That's my alarm. I have a mandatory Inventor House meeting I have to get to." She studied Urban with a furrowed brow.

"I'll be fine," Urban assured her. "Go."

"Are you sure?"

Urban nodded wearily.

"Ping me if you need anything," she said, then vanished.

Urban checked the time. It was 1800, but she wasn't hungry. Instead, she dried off from the shower, dressed, and had a motorcycle air dropped outside.

The cafés, dim sums, and stir-fry shops lining the street poured out light and laughter as she cruised down the main strip. Inside, groups of friends talked, laughed more, and shared food.

A pang of loneliness hit Urban as she watched through the window.

Tires skidded as she swerved off the main road and toward the Hutongs. She needed to get away from all the bright lights and happy people. After parking, she passed the barrier from clean air to pollution, and made her way through the quiet streets of the Hutongs.

She passed Auntie Tongtong's noodle shop and memories flooded back. The last time she'd been there was with Everest. Souvenir paper cuts hung for sale in the shop windows. Urban's heart felt like a knife was carving her instead of the paper.

She blinked hard and looked up at the sky to try and stop the tears. Pigeons circled overhead. Around and around they went, going nowhere.

Watching, she breathed deep until her heartrate slowed.

As she entered the market, the smell of rotting vegetables and fish assaulted her nose. Around a corner, she nearly ran over a couple leaning against a pub door.

"Sorry," Urban mumbled. She tried to clear the image of them kissing from her mind, but it was too late. Sorrow engulfed her.

It felt strange—this sudden shift. Going from having a person who was always there for her to total emptiness. The world was somehow colder.

Why couldn't we work? Urban's vision blurred with tears. *I lost the only person who truly knew me.*

A reminder to get ready for the Games interrupted her thoughts. She contemplated bailing. *But luxury seats are hard to get, and there are sure to be many KOLs there. I can't let my sosh tank too.* Swiping at her eyes, she took a huge breath and found her way back to her motorcycle.

Once back at the dorm, she changed quickly into her favorite black dress. It was tailored to fit her perfectly, and she paired it with white high heels made of recycled technology. Around her neck and covering her chest, she tied a black leather strap in a series of knots that gave her a modern look. A bot worked on her hair as she stared at her reflection.

Vacant, red eyes stared back. She realized she was still wearing the necklace Everest had given her. *Mei*, the character read, mocking.

Urban swallowed hard, then took off the necklace and dropped it into the trash. Tears filled her eyes again, but she blinked them back. She snatched up her electric concealer and zapped up all the red spots around her eyes. Too bad it didn't also remove puffiness. Opening her lips, she applied a thin tube, which naturally brought up the pH levels. A few seconds later, her lips glowed a dark, glossy pink.

Grunting at her appearance in the mirror, she set off.

The luxury seats were actually a large room, spacious enough to hold over a hundred guests. Urban had known it would be a fancy affair when Hazel gave her the dress code, but even then, she hadn't quite been expecting this. The guests all wore cocktail gowns or lavish black suits and held wine glasses. They congregated near the smart glass, watching as the announcer walked onto stage.

This time, Hong's shining hair was let down and looked like a river made of gold, streaming across her back. "Good afternoon and welcome to the first round of the 23rd annual Dragon tryouts!"

The crowd went wild. Urban strode toward the window, happy for an excuse to be anti-social. She skirted roughly past drinks, hors d'oeuvres, and polite chitchat. All she wanted was to be alone, to slump into a corner and never speak again.

"This year we will be accepting two new recruits to join our elite team. Tonight, we have ten contenders, nominated from their respective gene pools, to participate."

Urban turned away from Hong and listlessly eyed her surroundings. Marble statues and priceless paintings of ancient emperors and empresses glowered down at her. Soft classical music drifted through the room but couldn't drown out the wild roar of the crowds below nor her spinning thoughts.

"Samson has a few surprises for our contenders this evening," Hong continued, and Urban's attention returned. "But first, let's make sure we have the right setting selected. Samson, enable entertainment mode."

"Entertainment mode enabled," a deep voice amplified through the coliseum.

The crowd cheered.

"Now, let's meet tonight's brave contenders."

Several holes formed in the stage, but only nine people rose through the platform. There were two Supers and a Flyer. Urban couldn't tell which gene pools the rest were from.

"First up is Han Rocky!" The Flyer bowed and the crowd cheered. "After that, we have Li Blossom."

Urban started. *Blossom? My roommate?* The jumbotron zoomed in on the contestant, showing a slender woman with slick black hair, dark eyeliner, and sharp facial features. *That's Blossom all right. What's she doing out there? I didn't know first years could try out.*

After Hong announced the other contenders, they were all taken beneath the arena. The box guests grew bored waiting and moved away from the windows and toward a bar. They scanned their tatts and ordered fancy drinks. Urban checked her crypto wallet. She had enough to buy a few virgin drinks, but she should probably save it for food or dire emergency situations. *I'm going to have to ask Mother for more points eventually,* she thought with dismay.

Urban stared down at her feet, swallowing. She had to socialize. *I hate this.* But she knew no matter how she felt, she would always be trapped in this deadly social game.

The grandiose lounge was tastefully decorated with rich carpets, cozy armchairs, and dazzling chandeliers. The mirrors on the ceiling reflected huddles of laughing students. By the smiles and candid nature, Urban guessed everyone here knew each other. She scanned the room for Hazel. *Maybe she'll know more about Blossom.* But she didn't see her.

Great. I hate breaking into tight-knit circles like this. She straightened her shoulders and walked across the soft, red carpet, approaching a group that looked a little less like an impenetrable fortress than the rest.

The talking stopped awkwardly as the person speaking, a pasty girl with stringy blond hair and deep hollows behind her eyes, stared. Her skeletal face was stunning and somehow beautiful in a terrifying way. Urban wondered what enhancement she had.

"Sorry to interrupt. I'm Urban," she said, waving her hand at the group and giving an overly confident smile.

The blond eyed her a moment. "Anyway . . ." With a deep voice that seemed unfitting for such a thin girl, she continued a story about how half of her friends hadn't made it into the same classes as her this year so she was all alone in two of her classes.

Urban tried to stay focused on the conversation. *Why is this so hard tonight? My family's honor is on the line. If I don't keep this up, I'll be shunned from society. I'll never get to be an Artisan.*

But the thought of pretending again made her heart sink. How many times had she been something she wasn't?

The first contender in the tryouts started, and the group dissipated. Urban rushed to see if it was Blossom.

In the arena, the stage dropped away, revealing some sort of suction at the bottom. A Flyer flapped furiously to keep from being pulled down into it. Two huge moving objects emerged from the hole.

The crowd gasped as they realized what the objects were—enlarged pterodactyl. One of them raced toward the Flyer with a high-pitched screech. It knocked the Flyer against the force field wall separating the arena from the students, and his damage counter dropped. Trapped against the force field and the pterodactyl, the Flyer tried to escape, but his damage counter went into the red zone, then zeroed out.

"Contestant finished." Samson's voice boomed.

There was another short break. Urban scanned the room, trying to find someone who looked approachable. Where was Hazel?

"Hey, Urban. Long time no sssssee." A girl with black-and-white skin, like snake scales, made her way over. "We met in Programming, remember?"

How could Urban forget? The memory of Slash writhing in pain on the floor with a pen lodged in her neck still haunted her. "How are you feeling? I haven't seen you since our first day of class."

Slash smiled and flicked her black tongue. "Yesssss. That was an unpleassssant few hourssss. I'm fine, but I ended up dropping the classssss. That'sssss why you haven't sssssseen me. I'm ssssso glad I bumped into you again."

"Same here." Urban was glad to talk to someone she already knew. It felt like the pressure to impress was already removed. "Do you know anyone here?"

"A few people in the Inventor Houssssse invited me. I'm hoping to join them next year. What houssse are you eyeing?"

"I haven't selected one yet," Urban confessed.

Slash's brow wrinkled. "Very interesssssssting. Hm . . . I'm actually going up to the Inventor'sss exclussssssive sssssuite. Would you like to join me and meet a few of them? I believe the Houssssse lead will be here tonight to obssserve the tryoutssss."

Having someone help with the introductions was always the best way to go. Besides, she needed something to take her mind off of Everest. "I'd like that."

"Excellent." The curve of Slash's lips reminded Urban of a snake's. "Follow me." They approached a set of elevators.

Urban hesitated. She noticed her bodyguard in the corner of her maps, ten meters off, per usual. But he couldn't follow on elevators without being conspicuous. But stepping on the elevator would mean leaving Trig behind, and Urban was starting to appreciate his constant presence.

He'll find me as soon as I get to the suite. Besides, nothing can happen to me in the coliseum. There are people everywhere.

Urban followed Slash onto the elevator and watched her swipe her tatt before pressing one of the top floors.

The elevator shot up.

"You're going to love the view," Slash said.

The elevator doors opened, revealing a smaller, but just as luxurious, lounge with several dozen Inventor House representatives. In their midst was Lillian.

Urban's relief evaporated when she noticed Lillian staring wide-eyed at her. She tried waving at her sister, but Lillian remained frozen.

Her spine tingled. Something was out of place.

A flash of yellow eyes caught her attention, and she realized Coral was also present, watching her with a grim expression. An Inventor studied her through a mirror at the bar and Urban caught the eye of another off the reflection of a glass table. She realized everyone in the room was watching her.

Why?

Slash led Urban to a large window overlooking the tryouts. An Inventor stood aloof and alone, observing their approach. His identity and sosh were blocked, but he looked familiar. By his fashionable suit, and the way everyone gave him a wide berth, Urban quickly pieced together where she'd seen him— the Exhibition Games. He was the Inventor House lead.

Slash left Urban with him.

"Ah, you must be Urban." The Inventor was the same height as Urban, but his pompadour haircut gave him a few extra centimeters. A shiver ran down Urban's spine. Something was definitely not right. There was something intentional about all this. Lillian was nervously chewing her lip.

"I don't believe we've met before. I'm Hou Hawk." The Inventor extended his hand, and Urban caught sight of a strange-looking watch as she shook it.

She wasn't sure what was expected of her. The rules to this social game didn't follow any pattern with which she was familiar. After several seconds of silence, she opted for directness.

"Is there a reason why I am here?"

Hawk smiled broadly at this and looked Urban in the eye. "Because you chose this, did you not?"

There was something about the way he said this that gave Urban pause. An unspoken, added layer of meaning seemed to weigh each word down. She waited for him to explain.

The Inventor polished his black-and-gold watch meticulously.

Back in the arena, it looked like a scene from a dinosaur flick. A Super threw tree trunks at a T-rex while trying to solve a complex algorithm. A moment later, a herd of raptors overtook him. His damage counter plummeted until he zeroed out.

"Contestant finished!"

Several people booed as the contestant disappeared underground and the arena reset.

Hawk's wide and easy stance shifted slightly, and he looked back at Urban again. "You chose to participate in my motorcycle race did you not?"

Urban opened her mouth, then closed it again. So, this was about the race? Was he shaming her because she'd lost? Was this Olive's doing?

Hawk watched the arena as the eighth contestant rose out of a platform to compete.

Familiar long black hair caught Urban's attention. It was Blossom. She was about to compete. *I wonder what trials she'll have? Does she stand a chance at winning?*

"You chose this, my dear." Hawk's voice intruded in her thoughts. Urban forced herself to turn away from the arena to face him.

Hawk placed a hand on her shoulder.

Alarm bells went off in Urban's head. Instinctively, she pulled away, but Hawk's grip tightened.

With a sudden flick of his watch, a needle protruded from a hidden compartment and stabbed her. There was a prick of pain, and he released her. Everyone in the lounge focused only on her.

Urban turned to run. Her brain was sluggish and foggy. Her feet felt like they had delivery drones pushing them in the opposite direction.

I have to get away.

A cool numbing sensation tickled her hands and feet.

She noticed Lillian staring in horror. She reached for a chair to steady herself, then dropped to the floor.

The last thing she remembered was lying down on soft carpet.

Then, everything went dark.

URBAN AWOKE IN PITCH BLACKNESS. IT WAS cold and smelled of moldy air. She reached for her blanket but couldn't find it. Coral had to stop turning the temperature down so much or she was going to freeze. A gentle hum in the background made her want to go back to sleep.

"Urban, are you alright?"

The voice carried urgency, and Urban realized it was Coral's voice. Odd. Why would she be asking a question like that? Something at the back of her mind attempted to surface. It was some sort of bad dream. Something crazy that made her nerves spike.

"Urban." This was Lillian's voice, full of static.

What is she doing in here?

"You need to get up *now*." Lilian was using her low and serious voice, reserved for emergencies. It still sounded like she was speaking through some sort of microphone.

Blinking, Urban searched for her sister but couldn't see her. Her blanket was gone, too, and she lay on something hard and cold. Her hands brushed up against smooth glass. With a jolt of alarm, she sat up and groped in the darkness. She was surrounded by a glass cage.

"We have two minutes and counting." Coral again, this time

sounding frustrated.

Urban curled into a ball.

"Urban, do you remember what happened?" Lillian asked gently. Her voice sounded odd, and Urban realized it was because it was coming from her earpiece.

"You've been passed out for the last thirty minutes," Lillian told her. "This is all part of your dare with the Inventors. Remember?"

Inventors.

The word rang a bell. Like the Inventor's House. This all had something to do with her bad dream didn't it? It involved following Slash up to the Inventor's lounge and meeting Hawk and . . .

And then it all came back.

"Where am I?" she croaked, her mouth dry.

"One minute, twenty-seconds," Coral said.

"Coral has been very helpful and hacked your feed so we can communicate with you," Lillian said. "Do you remember we're in the middle of tryouts for the Dragons?"

Urban's head was foggy again. What on earth did Coral and the Games have to do with her current predicament?

"One minute," Coral cut in.

Lights flooded the room. After blinking away the sudden brightness, Urban found she was in a large capsule encased with mirrors. She was wearing a strange flexible but armored suit and a helmet with a hammer and sickle on it. How had she ended up wearing that? Why did the suit look so familiar?

"You're about to be the next contender," Lillian stated, fear in her voice.

Urban squinted in confusion. Then her eyes widened, and her heart leaped into her throat. *No. It can't be.*

As if to confirm Lillian's words, the roar of the crowd, though muffled, vibrated the mirror. Her adrenaline kicked into overdrive.

"The Inventors nominated you as their GP representative. That's the price you have to pay for losing the race."

Urban could hardly think. "But—but I'm not an Inventor."

"Doesn't matter," Coral cut in. "They can nominate whoever they want."

"Coral?" Urban peered up at the ceiling as if in search of her roommate. "Does she—does she *know*?"

There was a moment of hesitation before Lillian replied, "She figured out you are a Natural and approached me to help. Now, we don't have much time," Lillian continued, her rushed voice strained. "You and I both know what this could do to your genetic disposition. Coral is attempting to override Samson. She is excellent at breaking into things and getting around rules, like you said."

Urban was too stunned to speak.

"All the other contestants have been on Entertainment Mode, playing to their strengths. They go out on stage and Samson throws challenges at them based on their genetic enhancements. Obviously, that won't work for you. But we think we've found a way to keep your genetics a secret."

"Twenty seconds," Coral interrupted.

"Since you don't have any genetic enhancements, enabling training mode should spit out a bunch of challenges for you. Our hope is, it will be just the same as any other contestant, and no one will be the wiser that we switched modes."

"Meaning?"

"Just go out there. You'll be fine."

"Ten seconds."

Urban tried to smooth out her ponytail, then realized how silly that was. "You're sure you can manage that?"

"Working on it," Coral said. "I'm also going to hack the database and alter the code so no one knows we changed modes. But I can do that while you're in the arena."

Had anyone ever hacked Samson before? What if their theory

was wrong? What if she went out there and nothing happened?

Everyone would know I'm a Natural. Her skin crawled at the thought. *My family would be destroyed. I'd be banished to the Outskirts, and now I don't even have Everest out there.*

With a mechanical hiss, the ground started moving Urban upward. The ceiling above her slid back silently. The thunderous roar of the crowd poured in, reverberating off the cylinder walls and rattling her teeth.

"*Jiayou*, sis." At Lillian's words, the connection cut off with a click.

As Urban spiraled upward into the coliseum, the first thing she noticed was the bright lights. After already being temporarily blinded, she could barely make out the crowds beyond. There were so many of them. Their deafening roar filled her ears and shook her to the bone.

The second thing she noticed was the smell. She'd never been this close to the arena and the scent of freshly cut grass actually helped to calm her. Inhaling deeply, she tried to focus on the grass and not the fact she was the next contender in the Games.

What if I'm exposed? Fear pounded wildly in her chest. She inhaled several more breaths of air.

The crowd cheered as Urban stepped off the platform and onto the crisscrossed patchwork of metallic tiles making up the arena.

"Ladies and gentleman," Hong's voice rang out loudly from above, "we have our tenth and final contender for the night, Lee Urban!"

Overhead, the projector displayed a close up of Urban to the stands. She appeared even skinnier on screen. Wide-eyed and with disheveled hair, she looked as if she'd just rolled out of bed.

"Let's pull up our newest contender, shall we?" Stats appeared on the projection listing Urban's age, weight, classes, birthday, avatar, and landing page. Hong scrolled through her data. "Interesting." She clicked her tongue. "Nothing about her enhancements to be found. The secretive type, hmm? Well, we'll find out your secret soon enough dear. Samson, do your work!"

"Initializing enhancements," the deep rumbling voice said.

The coliseum fell silent.

Please, please, please let this work.

Hundreds of spectators watched with anticipation. Were Brooke, Orion, Hawk, and Olive out there? She bet Hazel was probably having a heart attack right now. Blossom and Ash were probably completely baffled as to how she'd ended up down here. Were they live streaming this? Urban's heart stilled. What about Mother and Father?

Samson remained silent.

Usually, he's selected a challenge by now. What if he does nothing? Do I just stand here?

The crowd began growing restless.

"It's not every day we have a candidate who stumps Samson," Hong declared. "I wonder what her enhancements could be?"

Urban shifted from foot to foot.

The ground trembled. Or was it just her imagination?

She caught a waft of something. It smelled like . . . wet animal?

Something roared in the distance.

Urban's feet grew unsteady beneath her as the ground trembled again. And again. The tremors increased in frequency and force until the entire platform swayed. Urban fell to her knees, her protective suit preventing her from any scrapes.

The crowd gasped as the stage transformed. The tile beneath Urban remained firm, but the rest flipped over, revealing a newborn playing field. Three different ecosystems began to take shape: polar ice caps with white bears roaming its surface, a desert grassland with wildebeest grazing, a tangled forest with timber wolves stalking below the branches, all separated by frothing water with dark shadows moving beneath the surface.

Urban climbed a hill on the grassland to better survey the landscape.

If I were a Flyer, I'd easily avoid most of these animals. If I were an Inventor, I'd create some kind of shelter. If I were a Camo, I could hide. Urban went through each gene pool, knowing exactly how'd they respond. *But what is a Natural supposed to do?*

Boom!

The peaceful ecosystem shattered.

Urban stood stunned, trying to make sese of what had just happened. Everything erupted into a frenzy. The wildebeest ground their hooves and stampeded. Five puzzles with five golden keys popped up around Urban, floating in midair. Part of the stage fell away as a giant robotic machine climbed out and began shooting at the hill. Urban dove to the ground as lasers whizzed over her shoulder.

She tried to remind herself it was just a robot. But it was a robot programmed to kill.

The smell of smoke filled the air.

The animals all faced her like she was one meal dropped into a cage of starving creatures. Urban scrambled up the hill to get away.

Then the stage transformed again. The lighting dimmed, and the air turned frigid. A snowstorm whipped her hair wildly, and the wildebeest slipped, struggling to climb toward her.

Boom!

A grenade exploded into the base of the hill.

Urban's ears rang.

Shock numbed her. This was not normal. No contestant had ever faced this many obstacles. Coral must have broken Samson.

Through burning eyes, she watched chunks of dirt and grass rain down around her through black smoke. The huge robot prepared to fire again.

Urban quickly slid down the other side of the hill out of the line of fire. Just in time.

Boom!

Before she could catch her breath, the stage groaned again. A giant obstacle course dropped from the ceiling and dangled midair. Monkey bars, hoops, swings, rope ladders, all of it a circus acrobat's dream. But then, instead of a cushion beneath, flames erupted. *An obstacle course set over fire. Perfect.*

"Test me if you can," Samson said. "Test me to impress your fans. Test me, for I lifted the ban. Test me . . . test me . . . test me . . . test me . . ." Samson glitched. "Lifted the ban . . . the ban . . . the ban." Urban's image flashed onto the projector, then her landing page, then an image of the arena, then a ton of images flashed at once, so that nothing was recognizable.

The coliseum began to shake again, this time with the force of an earthquake. Pandemonium broke loose.

The wildebeests began running in frantic circles and leaping wildly. Hundreds of bats poured through an open panel, filling the air so thickly, Urban could hardly see. Snakes popped out from every surface and slithered in her direction.

She shuddered. Real animals possessed a more deadly threat since they couldn't be programmed to stop attacking like the robots could.

Everything went dark.

Urban's heart crashed in her chest, almost drowning out the cacophony surrounding her.

Then the lights in the stadium flashed back on, revealing pterodactyls swooping through the sky.

Darkness again.

The lights came back on in blood red. Urban watched as more timber wolves poured out of an exit in one of the tiles.

A piercing screech, amplified a hundred times, blasted through the air. At the sound, goosebumps crept across Urban's flesh.

One of the ice peaks began shaking, grew red, then exploded.

Lava spewed upward and then sizzled as it bubbled across the snowy tundra section of the arena. Urban's lungs burned from the acrid air, and her heart spasmed. Coughing, she found a dial on her suit that increased the air filtration and punched it hard. A second later, less smoky, but not entirely pure air, eased her lungs.

On the opposite side of the arena, an enormous wrecking ball with giant spikes—each the size of a tiger—dropped from the ceiling. It swept across the sky from one end of the arena to the other straight at her. Urban dove out of the way. Wind howled over her as the wrecking ball swept past.

Deadly gases escaped from holes and floated toward her.

A spaceship crashed fifty meters away, exploding. Flames and chunks of metal launched into the air. One landed next to Urban.

Fire shot up her side, and her damage counter dropped fifteen points.

"Ah!" Urban beat at the flames with her hand. She tried to snuff it out. But it was like one of those trick birthday candles Lucas always used that kept coming back on.

Finally, the flame dissipated as her protective suite absorbed the fire and cooled her body. Urban rubbed her shin.

A strange sound, like that of a lion's roar mixed with a high-pitched bat's shriek, erupted, and Urban spotted a freakishly large serpentine creature flapping onyx wings.

That can't be real.

She watched as the enormous creature took to the air, scaley wings nearly blowing Urban away as they pushed upward. Her eyes bulged.

Definitely real. Must be some mix of robotics and skin grafts. I doubt it's actually a live dragon. Despite what her brain told her, she was filled with dread.

"Get it away!" Hong shrieked over the speakers. Urban looked out at the coliseum and saw she wasn't the only one with problems. Hong was swatting at a persistent bat, and several students jumped out of their seats and were running.

Samson was designed to keep all its challenges contained within the staged area. *Something definitely must have happened when Coral hacked it.*

Half the crowd was covered in snow, and the other half coughed from smoke. Several shrieks near the front pinpointed where some of the snakes had escaped.

"What's going on?!" Hong had finally gotten rid of the bat and was now peering anxiously down from her platform high above the arena. "Samson, stop!"

But Samson had no intention of stopping.

Instead, a lump of snow emerged from one of the tiles. It grew taller until it finally stood over ten meters high. As it took a shaky step, Urban realized it was some sort of large robotic creature—like a snowman, only with obsidian beady eyes and razor-sharp endless rows of teeth. Urban knew, if she made it out alive, she'd have nightmares of the thing for months. She shivered.

"Enough! Shut Samson down *now,*" Hong commanded. She seemed to be listening to someone in her retina display before barking: "Yes. Whatever it takes. Samson has lost his mind."

She paused a moment before speaking again. "What do you mean that will endanger her?"

Hong's face drained of color. "Her protective suit will shut down with it?" She hesitated, casting a furtive look at Urban. "The entire stadium is at risk. We have to do it."

Urban, hearing Hong's words, assessed her surroundings. Thick smoke, mixed with snowfall, clouded her vision. The air stank of melting metal and burning rubber. Her shin was still warm from where her suit had caught fire.

Several snakes slithered toward her. A pack of timber wolves picked up her scent and now circled the hill she stood on. A pterodactyl swooped down and would have taken off her head if she hadn't dropped to the ground. Which was just as well because the giant death machine was firing another round of explosives at the hill.

Boom! Boom! Boom!

Urban pressed her body tighter to the icy ground, feeling its coolness through her suit. Then, dusting the snow off, she stood.

"Lee Urban," Hong said over the speakers. "Get to high ground. Your suit's going to be deactivated."

Urban looked around. *I am at high ground. There's nowhere for me to go.*

A moment later, everything went dark again. Her suit loosened around her; its hard exoskeleton turned soft. Fear shot up her spine like razored chopsticks.

I'm on my own.

With a flash of florescent light, the coliseum came back into sight. The giant robot froze mid-step. The volcano ceased puking fire. The air warmed and it stopped snowing, though smoke still lingered in the air.

Coughing, Urban watched as giant glass walls began rising up around the stage to contain the frenzied animals. As it rose, several animals leaped over the barrier and began wreaking havoc in the stands.

A low growl redirected Urban's attention.

A giant timber wolf stalked toward her with its head lowered, teeth bared, and hackles raised.

Urban looked about wildly for something to help defend herself. A rock, stick, anything she could use to keep the timber wolves at bay.

Frozen grass swayed stiffly around her. The hill was barren.

Out of the corner of her eye she noticed movement: the wrecking ball. It had slowed down but still swung from one end of the stage to the other. A thought struck her. *Those spikes look just the right size. My gloves still have good grip, even if not activated. Yes, I think it might work.*

She looked back at the timber wolf, now joined by two others. Urban stumbled backward.

Sensing her weakness, one of the timber wolves inched closer. The others started closing in.

Urban glanced back at the wrecking ball. It was halfway across the stage but approaching quickly. She had to get to it.

She crouched, readying herself as the ball swung closer, every muscle in her body tense.

Screaming with the effort, she leaped and caught hold of one of the dulled spikes. The timber wolves raced at her and launched into the air, snapping at her feet as Urban was swept from the hill and to safety. She felt dizzy with relief.

Heat crept up her legs. Peering down, she realized she was nearing the fire obstacle course. Since Samson had been shut down, the entire tennis-sized course was ablaze.

Urban's vision swam at both the distance to the ground below and the fire. *This isn't a game anymore.*

With shaky arms, Urban hauled herself up onto one of the higher spikes so that she could stand. The wind whistled through her hair as she swung across the arena, surveying the damage.

If an entire zoo were to be released in the middle of a war zone, this was what Urban imagined it would be like. Dung and the metallic scent of blood filled the air. The arena was a melted slush of blackened snow and embers covered in animal prints. The timber wolves cornered a lone mammoth, the wildebeests stampeded toward the snow monster, and the polar bears were trying to avoid the snapping jaws of the sea creatures as their patches of ice melted under them.

The barrier around the stage groaned as it rose higher. Another set of enforced metal bars descended from the ceiling. Until the two met in the middle, bats and pterodactyls flew freely between the arena and the crowds.

Outside of the barrier, Camos worked together to capture unsuspecting animals. Aquas stood guard around helpless groups of students, roaring at any animals that came too close, while Supers tried to corner the timber wolves and other larger creatures.

A deafening screech reminded Urban she still wasn't safe. Rushing wind fluttered her hair as the dragon swooped by, breathing fire on the ground below and causing the timber wolves to abandon the mammoth and leap to safety.

Why didn't it shut down with the other robots? It's not a real animal. Is it?

The dragon's wings tilted, and it turned slowly. Its obsidian eyes blazed in the flickering flames. As it moved, its head adjusted, and the beady eyes focused on the swinging wrecking ball. They locked on Urban.

Urban climbed to the other side of the ball away from the dragon. She had just reached the other side when flames shot out around her on all sides. The air grew thick and hot. Acrid smoke and burning rebar stung her nostrils.

I have to get out of this death trap. Urban hurriedly scanned her surroundings but could see no way of getting over the quickly closing barrier.

Looking down, she realized the ball had stopped swinging and was now hanging over the portion of the arena with the murky lake. Her body went rigid at the sight of the water.

One of the polar bears fell off its ice patch and into it. A frenzied feast broke out from the circling sea creatures.

Urban felt faint.

The dragon sliced the air with its sharp wings and turned back toward her.

"Uh oh . . ." Urban climbed to the other side of the ball, but the metal surface was still crackling and red hot from where the dragon had just breathed. With a yelp, Urban quickly retreated back to the other side. Her hand was burned, and one of her boots was melting from the heat. *There must be a way out of this. Think.*

Below her, the sea creatures had finished with the polar bear and had sunk back under the water, lurking for their next prey.

Urban let out a ragged breath, trying desperately to control her rapid breathing. *Calm down. Now is not the time for a panic attack.*

Breath in.

Breath out.

Several breaths later, an idea began to form. It was completely crazy. But it was something.

She looked down at the water again and became light-headed.

"I can do this. I can do this."

Her breathing came fast and short as she stared unblinking at the ominously placid water.

A roar jolted her back. Urban grit her teeth, then began stripping off her suit. *I really hope I'm wearing something underneath this.*

To her relief, she found herself clothed in a layer of black spandex. Balling up her heavy suit, she chucked it as far as she could away from her. *Please let my suit distract them.* She silently whispered.

After a moment's hesitation, she took in a deep breath, then jumped.

As she fell, a mad thrashing of fins, teeth, and claws broke the surface where her suit landed. Her jacket was ripped to pieces.

Nearing the water, she kept her body straight and plugged her nose.

A moment later, the icy water punched her in the face. The shock of the frigid water made her let out an underwater scream.

Fear rendered her limbs useless.

She began to sink.

Visions of Lucas drowning her at the bottom of their house pool filled her mind.

Then the image of the polar bear being devoured hit her. There were worse things than drowning.

She kicked furiously, clawing her way back up.

Breaking the surface, she whipped her head around until spotting what she was looking for. She swam erratically toward the iceberg.

Behind her, she heard the sounds of splashing and kicked harder. She inhaled water and coughed. Her lungs were itchy and burned, but she continued swimming blindly.

Her hands bumped into something cold and hard. She stopped. Opening her eyes again, she pulled herself up onto the ice shelf as fast as she could, rolling onto it.

Behind her, the depths frothed with snapping jaws. Water splashed up onto her panting chest. Urban quickly rolled into a seated position.

The nearest part of the land was too far to swim to with all the sea creatures. Even with another diversion, she wouldn't make it halfway before she'd be devoured.

Beyond the land, the glass panels sealing her in were almost shut. Soon, it would be just her and the wild animals stuck inside.

The ice shelf lurched, and Urban lurched with it. Ignoring the cold, she pressed her hands up against the ice block, peering below. A huge, alligator-like creature disappeared into the depths, then came back to the surface, smacking its head against the ice.

Crack!

A hairline fracture appeared in the ice.

Urban's eyes widened in horror.

Crack!

The fracture grew, spanning almost the entire ice shelf. *There must be a way out. The barrier is almost shut, and I'm trapped on a quickly breaking iceshelf in nothing more than spandex.*

I should have never raced. I should have never tried to impress Olive at that first party.

Why did I care so much about my sosh? If I hadn't been

obsessed with it, I'd be sitting safely in the stands right now instead of here. Maybe Everest and I would even be together.

Her vision blurred.

Everest was right. I shouldn't have risked my life for my stupid sosh. Living in the Outskirts is better than dying.

Urban hugged her knees to her chest. Her body shuddered involuntarily.

I'll never know where I came from, who my real parents are, or why they didn't enhance me.

Tears began slipping down her cheeks. She tried to stop them, conscious of the cameras, but the projector above was still flickering in and out.

No one will care, either, because hardly anyone accepts me for what I really am.

I don't accept me.

The truth hit Urban harder than the next crack from below. She realized in that moment it didn't matter if all of PKU watching didn't really know her. The person whose acceptance for her limitations she was trying to get, in vain, was her own.

Her chest tightened as the tears poured down. *And now, I'm going to die without that chance.*

Crack!

The iceshelf split apart.

自 外

URBAN SCRAMBLED BACKWARD AND AWAY from the cracks spidering across the iceshelf.

Woosh. Woosh. Woosh.

The sound of beating wings jerked her gaze upward.

Urban's mouth fell open. "Ash? What are you doing here?"

Ash landed on the ice next to her. His normally slicked back hair was disheveled. "Oh, you know, just scouting out a good study spot for midterms."

Urban stared.

"Rescuing you, dummy. Now hurry and climb on!"

Urban scampered onto Ash's feet as his arms wrapped tightly around her. His body tensed as they leaped into the air and began flying.

Snap!

Beneath them, the ice shelf disintegrated into a hundred tiny pieces. Jaws gnashed up through the gap where they had been standing. Goosebumps spread across her arms.

"Remember those aerial tricks we did?" Ash yelled above the commotion.

"The ones that nearly killed me?" Urban tightened her grip on him.

"Consider those practice."

"What do you mean?"

A thundering roar drowned out Urban's voice.

Ash flew faster. "One ton of artificially inseminated flesh coming our way!"

Behind them the dragon's eyes gleamed as it stared fixedly and flew with determination.

"Faster!" Urban cried.

Ash grunted and his wings beat quicker.

As they reached the edge of the arena, the space between the two closing barriers narrowed to a thin gap.

"Hold on!" Ash dove toward the space. At the last second, he tucked in his wings, and they shot through.

The barrier smashed shut behind them. A moment later it glowed red as the dragon spewed flames against it.

Ash peered down at the chaos below as they flew out of the coliseum. "Sure am glad I skipped studying tonight for this."

Cool air greeted them on the other side of the arena where students were flooding out.

"Promise me you'll try and be safer?" Ash asked as he landed gently on the lawn in front of her dorm.

"I'll do my best," Urban said earnestly. "And, Ash—thanks."

"What are wingmen for?" He winked, then took off into the night sky.

Urban considered going back to the dorms but knew she'd be bombarded by her roommates and others as well. She wasn't ready for that yet. She sent a quick ping to Lillian, letting her know she was okay, then climbed wearily into an XRD pod and promptly fell asleep.

She wasn't sure how much time had passed when she awoke. When she got out of the pod it looked like midday, and her retina display flashed 1302. Groggily, Urban made her way back to the dorm.

Blossom and Hazel were already awake and had the news projected on the wall. They leaped up at Urban's arrival.

"Urban!" Hazel ran to her. Blossom even gave Urban a welcoming smile. "Are you okay?"

Urban nodded. "Yes."

"Can you believe it?" Hazel squealed. "The one time I wasn't at the Games I miss all the excitement!"

Urban turned to Blossom, suddenly reminded she hadn't had a chance to watch her performance. "I saw you also tried out, but I didn't get to watch. How'd you do?"

"Not as good as you." Blossom eyed Urban lazily. "That was no ordinary feat you accomplished out there."

"Yes! What enhancements do you have that allowed you to do that?" Hazel demanded.

"Uh . . ." Urban realized she hadn't thought up what to say.

"We've been watching the news. They're saying you knocked the trials out of the sky," Hazel went on excitedly. "Nothing like what you did has ever been seen before. Your sosh already jumped crazy high."

Blossom watched her curiously. "How were you able to do that? You must have a pretty rare combo of enhancements to break Samson."

"You can tell us," pleaded Hazel. "We won't tell anyone about your special enhancements."

"Sorry, but I like to keep them private." Urban smiled sympathetically.

"Why do you have to be so mysterious with us?" With a sigh of resignation, Hazel motioned to the wall projection. "Come watch."

She unpaused the broadcast, and a gorgeous woman with thick black hair and horns protruding from her head, continued speaking.

Urban's brain raced. What had happened back in the arena? Lillian and Coral had switched Samson to training mode. So why had it crashed?

Samson's never tested someone like me. Because I don't have

any enhancements, and Coral hacked it, it must have detected so
many areas to challenge, it just spit out everything possible and
glitched in the process.

She suppressed a sigh. *Now everyone thinks I have some sort*
of incredibly rare enhancements that broke Samson. I'll have a
million people trying to figure out what my enhancements are.

She thought back to her genetic-engineering class, where
Ash had managed to trip up the probot. *Something isn't adding*
up. I shouldn't have broken Samson. Even in training mode, it
shouldn't have acted like that. Samson has had years of experience.
It shouldn't have gone crazy like that. Surely, they would have
programmed it to handle a Natural.

Unable to come up with any answers, she turned her attention
to the broadcast.

"Miraculously, only a few students sustained injuries. Beijing
authorities are still tracking down a variety of escaped animals,
including three timber wolves, a mammoth, several hundred
snakes, two pterodactyls, and the abominable snowman." The
announcer stopped at this, her face reddening as she checked
that she'd read the last "animal" correctly.

"Yes. Well, if you happen to notice any of these creatures,
please stay away and report to the authorities immediately. In the
meantime, PKU president Dr. Gong has announced all classes for
the rest of the day are cancelled while authorities remove animals
from campus. Until then, students are advised to stay indoors.
As for the upcoming Games, looks like they'll be postponed until
PKU can import more animals and fix–"

Hazel cut the live stream. "This is *awesome*! You broke
Samson and shut down the whole school."

Blossom pulled up a real-time sosh tracker of PKU's KOLs.
"You're the top-trending PKUer right now. Wait. Actually, you're
the top trender in all of *Beijing*."

Urban leaned back against the couch, stunned.

"Have you not checked out your sosh recently?" Hazel twirled one of her blond ringlets. "It's at 87."

Urban's mouth fell open. "What?"

"You're going to help me boost my sosh, right?" Hazel asked hopefully.

Ping! For a second, Urban hoped it was from Everest, but then her heart sank as she remembered their talk. Had they really broken up? Was it really only yesterday? She swallowed hard.

[Orion: Are you safe? What happened?]

Urban's eyes welled up. She'd give her sosh of 87 just to have Everest back. She wanted to ping him now. To tell him about everything she'd just been through. Instead, there was no one she could genuinely trust. No one except Lillian, and Urban was already dreading that conversation.

She was alone.

Urban blinked back her tears and sent Orion a quick response.

[Urban: I'm fine. Thanks for checking.]

She scrolled through her other pings and was amazed to see she had hundreds. Anyone and everyone she was linked with seemed to want the inside scoop or to check in on her. There were pings from Brooke, Olive, her classmates, and others. Even Lucas had sent her a note with a screenshot of her looking terrified in the arena, which he had turned into a ridiculous meme. Urban deleted that message. There were also several invites from KOLs to hang out. She stared.

"What is it?" Blossom asked, noticing Urban's wide eyes.

"I got a ping from the school's president."

"Dr. Gong?"

"Let us see," Hazel demanded.

Urban projected her pings on the dorm wall. "It looks like some sort of invite . . ."

They read the message together, and the room went silent.

Blossom was incredulous.

"You're invited to PKU's exclusive Key Opinion Leader Celebration!" Hazel began jumping up and down on her bed.

"Only the very top KOLs will be there. You will say yes, won't you? This is sooooo exciting! And you'll bring us as your two plus ones, right?"

Another ping came in. [Orion: Can I bring you anything to eat?]

"Orion is pinging you? Slipped into your private messages, huh?" Urban had never seen Blossom so excited before.

"Are you two talking? He's such a *shuai ge*. What I'd give to have the Inceptors gene-pool head pinging me," Hazel sighed.

Urban flinched. The thought of dating anyone other than Everest stung. *I'm not ready to move on.*

Blossom had plopped down, and her cardigan opened slightly. Something inside caught Urban's eye. It was a badge of sorts, sewn onto her clothes. Urban tried to make out the words, then gasped.

SAS member.

It was the badge she'd found on the floor in their dorm room the first day. Blossom was a SAS member. Did she know what Urban was? What would she do if she found out?

Blossom caught sight of Urban staring and frowned. She looked as if she were about to say something when a pounding on the door interrupted them.

Without waiting to be let in, Lillian burst through, rushing straight to Urban.

"You're safe." Her face was ashen. "Last I saw, you were getting whisked away, and I couldn't find you. There's something wrong with your SCA, and we couldn't track you, and I wasn't sure where you were, and all of us were freaking out, and I thought—" Urban had never seen Lillian so rattled.

Urban put a hand on her sister's arm. "It's okay, Lillian. I just got back."

Lillian looked like she was about to cry but then held it in.

"Is this your sister?" Blossom gave Lillian a cursory glance.

"Yes." Urban drew Lillian closer. "Meet my roommates, Blossom and Hazel."

Lillian nodded politely but her eyes kept darting to Urban.

Hazel projected a screenshot she had taken of the invite from Dr. Gong to the KOL Celebration. "Look what Urban just got invited to!"

"You took a screenshot?" Urban was dismayed. "Don't show anyone."

"Why not? You're a top KOL now. You should be proud," Hazel said, unphased.

Lillian had stiffened. "Let's go. Mother and Father are at home and want to talk to you."

Hazel turned on her cutest pout face. "Do promise us you'll take us with you to the KOL Celebration?"

"I don't think she'll be going," Lillian cut in. "Come on, Urban, let's go."

Lillian didn't say anything more as she led them to the Wasp G9.

Once they were in the car, Urban looked at her sister. "Go ahead and say it."

"Say what?"

"I told you so and you never should have signed up for that race, or something else equally big-sister-like and annoying."

Lillian gave a short laugh. "I mean, I wasn't going to say it but . . ." Seeing Urban's expression she stopped short. "Listen, let's just forget about that. What I wanted to ask you was how you ended up in the Inventor luxury suite? At our mandatory Inventor House meeting, Hawk announced our house would be taking a new approach to the Games. Then, during the tryouts, he told us our next contestant would be walking through the doors . . ."

"And it was me," Urban finished ruefully.

"I nearly had a heart attack."

Urban let out a deep breath. "That explains a lot. Though I don't know why the Inventor's would waste one of their house representative spots on me."

"I found out later Hawk lost a bet to Orion. The loser had to accept the loser of the race you competed in as one of their two candidates for the tryouts. Filling one of their two spots with a dud contestant would really hurt them. Or so they thought. After your performance, I'm sure Orion is kicking himself for not having you represent his own GP."

Urban rubbed her temples.

"In the meantime, do you have a plan for what you're going to tell our parents that won't get you grounded for the rest of your first year? I'm sure they've already seen the feeds."

"Working on it." Urban chewed her nail. She wondered if Everest had watched her experience in the arena as well. What was he thinking? Should she ping him to let him know she was okay?

She quickly rejected the idea. He'd broken up with her. If he was worried about her, let him reach out.

When they arrived home, the maids informed them the family was in the tearoom.

Lillian led the way past the silk paintings and down ornate halls. "I forgot to give you this." She dropped something into Urban's palm.

"The bracelet you gave me." Urban looked up with confusion. "Where did you find it?" She tried to remember when she had lost it.

"Dr. Gong has been messaging Mother and Father about you. He wanted to make sure they weren't upset or going to give the school a bad name. He visited them actually. Apparently, you lost your bracelet in the arena."

"It's amazing I got it back." Urban fastened it on her wrist. "I'm going to call this my lucky bracelet."

Lillian smiled, then quickened their pace.

Outside, on the roof, gray, overcast skies and cool air swept over them as they entered the garden. Bonsai lined the square slabs of stone leading the way over black pebbles.

At the other end of the garden stood a large circular door made of intricate wooden patterns. At its base on a straw mat lay four sets of shoes.

Urban gulped. The whole family was here, but who was the fourth person?

As they drew closer, a portion of the wooden door automatically opened, allowing the girls to enter.

The tearoom only had one true wall, the one they had just entered through. The other three were all smart glass, which could be lifted at any time. Currently, they were all down, keeping in the room's warmth but displaying the lush garden beyond their transparent walls.

The room was simple and had bamboo matting and one low dark wooden table at the center. Mother, Father, and Lucas sat on the floor around it with steaming cups, tea pots, and jars of tea before them.

On the other side of the table, a man sat with his back turned to Urban. Mother and Father sat rigidly, staring at him. Even Lucas's eyes kept shifting to the man and then back down again.

"Ah, the hero returns." The man turned to face the doorway.

Urban recognized the head of the board for the Games at once.

"Urban." Mrs. Zhou's voice was hollow. "Lennox has graciously paid us a visit."

URBAN STOOD BEFORE THE CELEBRITY WHO had built Samson, nerves spiking. This couldn't be a good sign. Had he discovered her secret? Was he here to expose her and her family?

Mustering as much confidence as she could, she smiled. "What an honor to meet again, Lung, Sir."

Lennox waved his hands as if swatting away her formality. "We're all friends here. Join us." He gestured to the table, turning Urban into a stranger in her own house.

As she and Lillian sat on the matted floor, a maid served them both tea. The room fell into a tense silence, the only sound the pouring of the hot liquid into porcelain cups.

Lennox took a sip, then set his cup down. "Urban, your performance in the Games was quite spectacular. No one has ever survived without their protective suit, let alone faced all of the most challenging obstacles at once."

Urban stiffened, but Lennox seemed not to notice. "I have taken a special interest in it. Since my original design for Samson, the algorithms have evolved. Part of my role on the board is to supervise Samson's evolution. There's something that's been troubling me, however." He looked down at his nearly empty cup and motioned a maid to refill it.

Mother bristled at the implied lack of hospitality.

When his tea was replenished, Lennox continued, "Nothing in the original programming accounts for what happened in the arena. I've gone back and analyzed all of the data to try and identify if there was a modification somewhere in the programming that could explain it. My team and I are at a complete loss. So, I thought I'd pay you a visit."

He looked straight into Urban's eyes. "What enhancements do you have?"

Urban was jolted by his unexpected directness. Mrs. Zhou's teacup tilted, threatening to spill. Everyone's eyes were on Urban. Her mouth felt as if someone had stuffed it with sticky rice. Her mind whirled with possible explanations.

Was now the time to announce her fake gene pool and enhancements? Did her parents want her to tell him she was in the Giver gene pool? But if she said that, she'd be stuck.

Or she could declare herself an Artisan. Then mother and father couldn't go back on their promise to allow her to pursue that path. But Lennox might see through it. Afterall, countless Givers and Artisans had competed before and never had Samson wreaked such havoc.

She could feign innocence, but would he believe it? That could give her parents a chance to step in and offer an explanation if they had one prepared.

"I understand your family has been keeping your enhancements a secret, and for good reason." Lennox interrupted her thoughts. "And I would, of course, keep your enhancements private. I am only trying to understand how to improve Samson for the future."

His eyes searched her as if he could determine her enhancements merely by looking. Urban chanced a glance at her parents. There were no answers on their expressionless faces.

Swirling her tea in uncomfortable silence, Urban frantically wracked her brain for anything in her AI classes that could help her. All she needed was an explanation just believable enough that Lennox would buy it.

Her class with Ash came back to her. She could picture the time he had tripped up the probot and they'd spent the rest of the day flying. An idea began to form in her head.

Urban looked up at Lennox. "I don't have any revolutionary enhancements," she said truthfully. "I do have something Samson has never seen before. That's why the AI wasn't sure how to respond. If I step into the arena again, its faulty response won't happen now that the model has evolved. You don't have to worry about shutting the school down again."

"The school shutting down isn't my primary concern. While I'm sure Dr. Gong would love to avoid a repetition of that event, I found the whole escape quite entertaining." Lennox winked as if sharing a private joke. He continued, "My interests lie with dissecting what happened so that I can improve the models. The PKU team is one of the best, and Samson gives us the home-court advantage, since it's the most evolved AI. If there are ways to ensure more victories in the future by further improving Samson, I am most interested."

Urban tried to keep her face impassive. The ploy wasn't working, but she had to try one more time. Otherwise, her last option wasn't a pleasant one.

"And I, of course, would love to assist," Urban assured him. "However, I, too, am at a loss for what could have caused the meltdown. My best guess is the odd combination of my enhancements is an unlikely one that Samson hadn't predicted, and somehow it triggered a glitch. No algorithm is perfect. Machines are always evolving. I doubt we'll see a glitch like that again in Samson." She took a sip of tea and tried to keep her hands from shaking.

"I heard about your little bet." Lennox leaned back. "I know you're not an Inventor."

"Oh?" Urban blinked in surprise.

Lennox waved a hand dismissively. "But I'm not interested in any of that. What I am here for is knowledge. I'd like to know what you really are so that I can improve the algorithms."

"I'm sorry, that's private." Urban's voice was taut. It looked like going on the offensive was her only option now.

Lennox's eyes narrowed. "So you won't help me?"

"I would love to." Urban mustered the most realistic, relaxed smile she could manage. "I will provide you with my medical genomics record once you provide me with yours."

That sucked the air out of the room.

All it would take was Lennox calling her bluff, and they'd all be ruined. If he revealed his genetic enhancements to her, Urban would be forced to reveal she was a Natural.

Lennox's demeanor changed. His obsidian eyes turned cold, and his jaw ticked.

Urban lifted her chin and stared defiantly at him. Could he hear the frantic pounding of her heart? *Please don't call my bluff.* She forced herself to keep a steady gaze.

"I see." Lennox's voice was brittle now, all pretenses of warmth gone. "If you value your privacy above the better good of the PKU team," he stood abruptly, "then I have nothing more to discuss."

Mother rose quickly to her feet. "Lennox, might we interest you in staying for supper?"

"I am quite short on time, Flora." Lennox cut off her feeble attempts to salvage the situation.

Without so much as a parting word, the door slid shut with a *bang*, and Lennox was gone.

"Well done, sis." Lucas snorted. "You managed to rile one of the most powerful men in the Asian Federation."

"What was I supposed to do? Tell—"

"No!" Mother interrupted. "Of course you couldn't tell him about your enhancements. You must keep those private."

Urban's eyes widened. "What do you mean tell him about my *enhancements*?"

Her father let out an unnaturally high-pitched chuckle. "Why just that. Lennox is of course an honorable man, but these sorts of secrets enviably end up leaked to the public."

What was happening? What was this misstatement about Urban having enhancements? She regarded her parents' rigid posture. Lucas and Lillian had relaxed the instant Lennox had left, but her parents hadn't.

Lucas was looking at them with suspicion. "What on earth are you two talking abou—"

Mother uttered a little cry and checked the time. "We must save this for later. We're late for an important engagement."

Urban got up slowly and found herself wrapped in her mother's arms and her Bulgarian perfume.

Mother's lips pressed lightly against Urban's ears. "We're being watched," she whispered. "Be careful. Meet us at *Ayi's* Famous Duck restaurant tomorrow. We'll explain."

As Mother released Urban from her embrace, Lucas stepped up to her. "Mom, are you alright?"

"We're just so proud of our daughter." Her eyes glimmered, and her voice was husky. "A KOL!" The shift in her demeanor was startling. Urban found herself wondering how many times her mother had faked her emotions in the past and she had never even realized it.

Lillian had just sat, quietly observing. Once their parents left, she gave Urban a confused shrug before taking her leave. Urban wanted to tell her what Mother had whispered, but there was no way to do so discretely.

Was it just this room being watched? The whole house? Was it video and audio? Something else?

Urban resigned herself to wait until later. Tomorrow morning, before class, she'd get up early and leave the house to talk with Lillian.

Urban retreated to her room, the warring thoughts and emotions threatening to overwhelm her.

Who's watching us? Have I put my family in danger? Why does Mother want to meet at the hotel? Is it safer there?

Her thoughts drifted to Lennox's visit. *Have I made a new enemy? Will he continue to badger me with questions about my enhancements? How am I going to keep hiding I'm a Natural now that everyone is watching me?*

She collapsed onto her bed, exhausted. Her eyes flitted over the walls full of artwork, and eventually her spirits lifted.

On the bright side, I can be an Artisan now. I'm the Inventor House lead for the Games. I'm a KOL. I can be anything I want.

And yet, she felt empty inside.

Instead of giving her the freedom and fulfillment she'd been craving, she was more trapped than ever.

I thought boosting my sosh would fix everything. So why do I feel so broken?

Thoughts of Everest came, but she forced them away. She had enough on her mind. As she curled her knees to her chest, the pounding of her heart lulled her to sleep.

When she woke an hour later, it all came crashing down around her. She tried to go back to sleep to escape the pain, but she wasn't tired enough. To distract herself, she logged into QuanNao and found she had 2,763 new pings. It was like all the birthday pings she ever got . . . combined. All the trending articles were still about her.

[*The Girl Whose Enhancements Broke PKU's AI*]

[*Breaking Samson: One Contestant's Strategy to Get Accepted onto the Dragons*]

[*How Today's Tryouts at PKU Involved the Entire School*]

[*PKU's New Hero: The Girl Who Broke Samson and Sacrificed Herself to Save the School*]

She felt a sense of pride before she remembered what would happen if anyone found out the truth. Shame welled up in her. She was nothing but a fraud.

With a sigh, she opened the last article and watched a vid clip.

"While it's still unclear how or why the contestant decided to try out, everyone was pleasantly surprised to see something refreshingly new." The satirical vid showed pandemonium in the coliseum as animals escaped.

Her system flashed a warning.

<Warning: Reaching maximum storage capacity. Consider archiving old messages.>

Urban commanded her AI assistant to prioritize messages to people she interacted with regularly or who had a high sosh. Three hundred messages remained, and she waded through them slowly.

What was this? A message from Croix the luxury athleisure brand?

Urban scanned the ping.

[Dear Miss Lee—as you probably are aware, our brand represents the rebels and the brave. After your tremendous display in the tryouts, we at the Croix company think you could be a good fit as our next top representative.]

Urban was momentarily stunned. Was this actually happening? Quickly, she turned back to the message and skimmed it.

[We'd like to set up a meeting to explore if a partnership would be a good fit for both parties. Should you be interested, send us your agent's contact, and we'll work directly through him or her. Thanks for your time and consideration. We look forward to hearing back from you.]

Urban imagined herself featured in some of the top Game ads, repping Croix fashion. Her, a top brand representative? It was all so unreal.

Would they rescind their offer if they found out she wasn't a professional KOL and didn't even have an agent? Where did one even find one?

What would happen if people found out that her lack of enhancements actually broke Samson. She'd seen a KOL caught having an affair whose sosh had fallen so low he couldn't even use public transportation. Would that happen to her?

She squeezed her eyes shut.

Everest appeared in her vision. It was as if a Super had rammed into her chest, jarring her. She tried to distract herself with more messages, but there was no escape. Everest's hollow eyes bore into her everywhere her mind went.

Memories of Everest crowded—unwanted and unstoppable. His words haunted her: *"I'd rather be myself than live like you—"*

Grief wracked her body violently. *He's right. I have everything I worked so hard for—a high sosh and a chance to be an Artisan—but it's not enough.*

She looked around her room and got up. She picked up a goat-hair paintbrush, ink, ink stone, and a sheet of rice paper. Instantly, some of the tension melted away. When was the last time she'd painted? She stared out at the city skyline, deep in thought.

At first, the brush was foreign in her hand. But then, slowly, the familiar rhythm came back to her as she drew a thick black line—the character for one. *It's just me. I'm alone.*

Urban thought back to her childhood and constantly having to hide. She'd always been alone. Pretending to be something she wasn't.

I'm nothing but a fake. I'll never be enough. No one except my family and Everest knows the real me. Everest left, and my family doesn't really care about me, except maybe Lillian. Lucas hates my guts. Father and Mother probably wish I'd never shown up on their doorstep.

I'll never be accepted.

The revelation came with a cracking in her soul.

"I'll never be accepted," she repeated the words as her hand slowed to a stop on the paper. Black ink spread, creating a blot she couldn't erase.

I'll never be accepted because I'll never be known. If I were actually known, I'd be rejected as a Natural.

Her strokes turned hard and thick as she added more around the one thick line.

Dread curled in her stomach at the thought of taking a hard look at herself. What would she find?

Urban painted faster now, rounded curves and sharp lines. The only alternative was continuing to leave her current thoughts unchecked.

It was time to confront this, to confront herself.

Setting her brush down, she pulled up several recordings of her childhood. The augmented vids played over her immediate surroundings. A too-thin eight-year-old with muscular legs and chopstick-thin arms sat alone at a desk. Her black pigtails were tied into decorative homemade hair bands. Her miniature XR suit had fake rhinestones covering one sleeve and paint on another.

The vid cut short as the teacher headed toward her. She'd gotten in trouble for not adhering to the school uniform that day. She'd been different from the start.

Urban rewound the vid recording back and froze it. Her decorative suit glowed from the gems, her braided ribbon hair bands shone, beautiful and one of a kind.

Urban selected another memory, this time her at the *gaokao* placement exam. She was in a room full of students with glazed eyes as they took the test virtually. Only three students had opted for paper exams. Two of them had disabilities, the third was her.

Teenage Urban sat with hair straightened and the tips bleached white. Her XR suit blended in with those around her now, but she wore electric shoes (before her teacher had found out about it) and her old-school pen was the kind that allowed the choice of several different colored inks with each click. The girl looked terrified, and Urban realized this was her first panic attack.

But then the girl did something strange, she hunched over her exam and began doodling on the back page. Her breathing slowed, and her eyes lost their wild look. Slowly, a beautiful self-portrait emerged, smiling, giving her the courage to go on.

The girl flipped the exam back over and started answering questions as fast as she could.

Urban switched out of her memories and surveyed her room. Her artwork, her collection of photos, even the way her furniture was artfully placed, brought joy and beauty. She had always been able to create hope in a world of chaos and pain—despite being a Natural.

She turned back to the paper, and her strokes became finer and intricate.

"*My one of a kind* meinu," Everest had called her. One of a kind.

Urban stepped back from the calligraphy painting. The characters *jue wu jin you* stared back at her. "One of a kind," she whispered, not even realizing she had been painting the ancient *chengyu*.

The characters formed a picture, a self-portrait.

Some of the lines in the characters were messy, others strong, but all of them uniquely hers. They weren't like the perfectly square characters that appeared in XR. These handwritten ones were flawed but beautiful.

Just like me.

The thought came out of nowhere and left a lightness in her chest.

She may not be an Enhanced, but that didn't matter.

Her sosh didn't matter. What other people thought of her didn't matter.

All that mattered was that she was unique for a reason. That she was herself.

30

RETRACTUS FLAMEOUS

THE NEXT MORNING, URBAN WOKE, SORE AND on the cold, tiled floor.

She startled as she realized the time. There was no chance to tell Lillian. They'd have to catch up after class.

Throwing on some clothes, she pulled her hair into a messy bun and checked the mirror. She had botched her eyeliner, and she also had weird wrinkles on her face from sleeping on the floor.

"*Ai ya,*" she said at her reflection.

She threw open the curtains to give her more light to fix her makeup.

Brilliant rays of saturated plum, vibrant orange, and rich cinnamon lit up the cityscape. Blinking back the sudden brightness, she lingered, staring at its beauty. Something was different today.

A lightness filled her chest when she saw the ink stains on her fingers, and a smile crept across her face.

"*Jue wu jin you,*" she whispered. "Unique."

It all came back to her.

She stood there a moment longer, enjoying the beauty and filling her lungs with big, slow breaths of air.

Then her retina display beeped, and she was jolted back

to reality. She quickly touched up her makeup, then darted to class.

She was relieved to find the way there peacefully empty. For once, she was grateful her first class was so early. A faithful green triangle trailed her. She'd almost forgotten about Trig. His presence brought her a wave of comfort. *I'm never ditching him again.*

In AI Foundations, Urban would have given anything for Coral's enhancements to blend into her surroundings. Students around her kept taking selfies with her in the background. They shot her sideways glances and whispered. She felt like a KOL. She *was* a KOL. That would take some time getting used to.

But the students weren't the only ones to take an interest in her. Halfway through the lecture, Dr. Xi called her out. "Lee Urban, are you present today?"

Urban nervously stood, trying to recall the appropriate response.

"Urban here is a perfect example of how artificial intelligence can only go so far. At some point, even the most advanced AI, such as Samson, will be overcome."

Dr. Xi leaned forward, using her desk to steady herself in her excitement. "Tell us, how did you do it Urban? What enhancements do you have that could confuse the most sophisticated Gaming AI?"

The class collectively turned to her.

"Uh," Urban faltered. "I'm going to keep my enhancements private for now."

"Come, come. There's nothing to be ashamed of."

Urban shifted uncomfortably.

Dr. Xi was gripping her desk so hard her knuckles turned white. "I realize some people consider enhancements a private matter. Really though, it's something to be celebrated." She paused a moment, as if hoping Urban would reconsider. When Urban remained silent, she reluctantly began her lecture.

Urban sat down, relieved.

Her mind replayed the events of the past few days, over and over. It all seemed like a weird dream.

She looked at Dr. Xi, droning on from the front of the room, and shook herself. She was definitely sitting in class right now and not asleep.

She kept sorting through her messages. There were a couple of random pings from her new fan club, more invites, and several ridiculous screenshots from Lucas, which she ignored.

Nothing from Everest.

Her gut was crushed, run over by a hoverboard.

She'd thought maybe he would have messaged her. After all, she'd almost died.

But, of course, he hadn't. He'd already moved on—like she should.

She wanted something to give her hope for them again. But there was no hope. They really were done. *Get over it,* she berated herself.

"I'll be reading off the highest three and lowest three scores in the class."

Urban's attention jerked back to the present as Dr. Xi spoke.

"This has your latest test factored in. Last place in the class we have Li Apple, Ye Tu, and Gua Chenchen."

Urban let out a breath. She wasn't last in the class.

"And in first place," the professor continued. "We have Qing Angel, Sun Trace, and Wong Fawn. Well done to all of you."

Qing Angel? Urban's blood ran cold. She'd completely forgotten about Angel. *She's in my class? What is she doing here? Which student is she?*

Urban tried to remember what Angel had looked like in XR. All she could remember were her enhancements. The only physically noticeable enhancement was retractus flameous, which had allowed her hands to convert into flamethrowers.

Her eyes swept the classroom, searching for anyone who

might have that. Most the student's hands were under the desks or hidden from sight. With a class this big, how was she ever going to find out who Angel was? She couldn't exactly go up to each student and examine their hands.

Urban considered just asking the teacher who Angel was but thought better of it. Angel was a KOL. Most KOLs had agreements with anyone who had access to both their online and physical identities in order to keep their privacy. Dr. Xi would be legally bound to keep Angel's identity secret.

But it came to Urban that maybe she could use her fame to her advantage. She could voluntarily take pictures with the students and use it as an opportunity to catch a glimpse of their hands while she was at it.

She discarded the idea quickly. Angel wouldn't be lining up to take a selfie.

Then another idea struck her. It would still require using her newfound influence but with her teacher instead.

Urban waited until all the other students cleared out before approaching her professor. "Dr. Xi, may I speak with you in private?"

"Why of course." The teacher hastily ushered Urban to her office.

On two of the walls, projections displayed logs updated in real time. Ancient calligraphy covered the other two. Urban's footsteps crunched with each step as she entered. Dried sunflower seeds littered the floor.

Xi took a seat behind her giant wooden desk and pushed a bowl toward Urban. "Snack?"

Urban politely took a handful of seeds and began shelling them. Not because she was hungry, but because she thought the gesture might help.

Dr. Xi smiled approvingly and popped a sunflower seed into her mouth.

"I'm working on a research project," Urban began. "I'm

trying to test a hypothesis of mine about certain . . . genetic enhancements and class rank." She paused, collecting her nerve, then plunged forward. "I'm wondering if I may have the class roster containing the list of lethal enhancements."

Dr. Xi's hand momentarily hovered over the bowl. She regained herself and began cracking sunflower seeds again. "That's highly confidential information."

"I don't need access to the whole list. I'm really just trying to find out if there's any sort of reverse correlation with top performers in class and dangerous enhancements. I'd only need the top three."

"I'm afraid that wouldn't be prudent."

"You know," Urban said slowly. "I haven't told anyone about how I cracked Samson. The press has been hounding me, along with friends, roommates—everyone."

Dr. Xi leaned forward in her seat.

"It's confidential information. But I might be willing to give you a clue as to how I did it if you shared something confidential in exchange."

Dr. Xi was torn, her eyes darting from Urban to her sunflower seed stash and then back again. She bit her lip and regarded Urban carefully. "I suppose it would be all right for me to share three students' information. It's not the actual list after all."

"Oh, thank you!" Urban held out her wrist.

"I'm removing the rest of the students." Dr. Xi's eyes darted about feverishly as she carefully modified the data. She nodded to Urban, and they bumped wrists. Urban's tatt vibrated, and a file popped into her private feed labeled Advanced AI Class: List of Lethal Enhancements.

"Now." Dr. Xi nearly grasped Urban's arms in excitement, but stopped herself. "Tell me. How did you do it?"

"The clue I'll give you is a simple one: how is Samson trained?"

Dr. Xi's eyes narrowed in concentration.

"Think about it." Urban stood. "I've got to get to my next

class. Thank you again."

"Yes, yes," Dr. Xi said absently as she gazed off into space, thinking.

As soon as she was out of Dr. Xi's office, Urban opened the file. Sure enough, there it was, Qing Angel and a laundry list of lethal enhancements, including her flamethrowing hands. Urban quickly scanned the file until she found Angel's school ID. Then she copied the ID into the school's public database.

A student's face appeared, and Urban gasped.

Staring back at her was none other than her roommate, Qing Coral.

URBAN'S HEAD WAS STILL SPINNING WHEN SHE walked to Biopsychology. She'd never realized who Coral was because she'd never seen her digital avatar. She would have recognized that blue-haired avatar immediately. That was why Coral had never linked with her. That was also why Coral didn't care to play the sosh game.

Trig's familiar presence in her maps was her only comfort as she retraced all of her conversations with Coral. Her stomach knotted.

Coral knew she was a Natural, her class schedule, where she lived, she even knew Urban had a secret boyfriend. *Had* being the key word there.

She thought back to the motorcycle race and being locked out of SCA. Urban remembered that terrible moment when her motorcycle dropped out from under her. Originally, she'd thought it was her parents who'd locked her out of SCA. *But it had to be Coral, right? Who else could hack me like that?*

Coral lives with me and knows I'm not Enhanced. So why didn't she kill me in my sleep or something? Why wait for the motorcycle race? And how did she race and hack me at the same time? Did she run a script she wrote ahead of time? But how would she have known I would be there?

She went through her other interactions with Coral—Angel. They had all been warnings. Coral had multiple opportunities to kill her if she wanted. *Maybe there's someone else who wants me dead. But why? And if not Angel, then who?*

As Urban took her seat in the next class, several students discreetly took selfies with her, but she ignored them. Only Dr. Botteria seemed to mind as she doled out punishments on any students she caught.

It makes sense why Coral's not from the Asian Federation now. Everyone here knows all the top KOLs, but few people know of some of the Western ones. I've been rooming with one of the West's KOLs this whole time and didn't even know.

But why would she help me with my homework, teach me how to trip the curfew? Was it all just a trick to get me to trust her? And I thought she was trustworthy.

A hand on Urban's shoulder made her jerk.

"Sorry, didn't mean to scare you," Orion said quickly. "How you holding up?"

For a panicked second, she thought Orion had read her mind and knew about Angel. Then she realized he was talking about being a Key Opinion Leader.

A student leaning behind her crashed to the floor after leaning too far in her seat to get the optimal selfie. Urban let out an exasperated sigh. "That"—she pointed at the student sheepishly picking herself up—"pretty much has been my life since the Games."

Orion smirked.

"Five marks, Miss Fei." Dr. Botteria glowered at the blushing girl. She drew herself up and addressed the class. "If I see one more student taking a photo, I will deduct twenty marks from *everyone.*"

The class quieted down at that.

Orion waited until Dr. Botteria resumed her lecture. "You okay?"

"I'm fine." How to even begin to answer the question. *Everyone thinks I have some incredible enhancements. The thing that makes me a KOL is fake. My roommate has been trying to kill me all semester. Yeah, I'm fine.*

She swallowed hard.

"You sure you're alright?" There was a look of deep concern in Orion's vivid blue eyes.

Urban avoided his gaze. "I'm fine," she repeated and turned her attention back to the front of the classroom, hoping Orion would do the same.

She could sense him staring at her a moment longer, then he focused on the teacher.

When class ended, students filed out around her, taking longer than usual as they tried to get pictures with her. Urban brushed past them and was about to send Lillian a ping when she remembered her mother's warning. Were her pings being monitored? She took a few extra seconds to craft a discrete message just in case.

[Urban: I have big news. It's about my friend Angel. Let's meet at *Ayi's* Famous Duck restaurant.]

No sooner had she sent it than another ping arrived. But it wasn't Lillian. Her heart skipped a beat.

[Coral: Are we still on for our usual study sesh?]

Oh no. She'd forgotten she told Coral they'd study after class. She thought fast as she wrote a response.

[Urban: So sorry. I have an interview. Some news source wants my take on the tryout disaster. Being famous is a pain!] She sent a GIF of a Flyer hiding his face with his wings. She reread the message, satisfied Coral wouldn't be suspicious.

[Lillian: Just got out of class. Will be there ASAP. You mean this place right?] Lillian shared the location for a roasted-duck spot in the Outskirts.

Urban was about to respond when another ping arrived.

[Coral: Let's meet at *Ayi's* Famous Duck.]

Urban's blood ran cold. *Coral's hacking my pings! But pinging me now is like admitting she's reading my pings. Why would she do to that?*

Urban pinged Lillian back.

[Urban: Actually, how about that section of the Great Wall we used to visit as kids?]

A second ping appeared.

[Coral: Or we could meet at the Great Wall? I'm very *serious* about this study sesh. Wouldn't want to *blow* our exam.]

Stupid. Coral will just follow me out to the Great Wall now. I have to think of another place she can't find.

Urban reread Coral's ping. *There's something odd. It almost feels like there's a double meaning behind her words. But what?*

Try as she might, Urban couldn't crack Coral's hidden message. If there was one at all.

I have to get help.

Urban thought for a moment, then sent another message to Lillian. [Urban: Actually, how about we meet at Lucas's favorite restaurant.]

[Lillian: Got it. I'll let the rest of the family know to meet us there.]

Urban reread her ping, satisfied her sister would know that meant their dad's Underwater Bar but Coral wouldn't.

Still, she would have to find a safer way to get to there—a way Coral couldn't possibly track her on. Even with her motorcycle, she could potentially be followed.

Then she had an idea.

Ash instantly answered her augmented vid request. Urban saw a confused but pleased look on his face. "Miss me?"

"Oh, uh . . . sure." Urban hesitated. "Can I ask a favor of you?"

"You still owe me for saving your life."

Urban bit her lip.

All traces of joking vanished from Ash's face. "You look nearly as bad as when I last picked you up in the Games. What's going on?"

"I'm sort of in trouble. Any chance you could come to the science building and give me a lift?"

"On my way." The vid cut out.

As she waited, Urban thought back to Coral's warning. Why was Coral hacking into her messages and warning her? Nothing was making sense.

She was still thinking about Coral when the beating of wings pulled her from her thoughts.

"What's up?" Ash studied her.

"Can't explain now. I need to get to the pier by the Guanting Reservoir—without anyone knowing."

"I'm your guy." He flashed a radiant smile. "All aboard."

Ash flicked the projection over them. "And now we're invisible." His arms went around her waist, holding her securely as they launched into the air.

There was a sense of security high up in the sky. Coral—Angel, couldn't sneak up on Urban with her Camo abilities now.

No one could.

But then, in her maps, Urban noticed Trig still tailing them. How was he keeping up? Lillian hadn't been kidding when she'd said she'd find the best man for the job. This guy was something else. But, if he could still track them, could Coral?

Urban contemplated this possibility as they flew over the Summer Palace and the city dissolved behind them.

Ash coughed as the air thickened with smog. "If I'd known our excursion would involve a trip out of the Metropolis I would have brought my filtration system."

They reached the Outskirts but flew until the Guanting Reservoir and the giant arching bridge over it came into sight. Wispy, leafless trees lined the road leading to the mossy green water. Few vehicles, hoverdrones, or hover cars traveled this far from the Metropolis. A dusty nut-brown road snaked through the forest, with only a few toy-sized cars on them. The sky was completely empty, except for one other Flyer.

Urban cocked her head as she watched the approaching Flyer. Something seemed strange about him. Then she realized what it was. "Is that a Super Flyer?"

Ash looked in the direction she was pointing. "*Tiana*! It is!"

"I've seen that same tech on my sister. I thought only Inventor's used it."

"Two gene-pool enhancements is super rare but three . . . is impossible. Unless he's from the Western Federation."

The Flyer was close enough for Urban to get a good look at him now. She'd never seen someone so big flying. And his wings—freakishly large and blood red—were scaled like a serpent's. It reminded her of the horrible image of the dragon from the arena. Each wing thrust sent a torrent of wind toward them as he approached.

The Flyer glided left, directly in front of them, then pulled up so that he blocked their path.

Ash had to veer quickly to avoid running into him.

They both stood facing each other, wings beating hard to keep them upright.

Can he see us? Urban wondered. *Surely not. With the halocaster, he should see nothing but sky.*

And yet, the Flyer seemed to be staring right at them. Sweat trickled down Urban's neck as she waited for him to move on.

Instead, the Super pointed a device at them, and a jet of red flew from it.

Pop!

The holographic image concealing Urban and Ash immediately disappeared. They were fully visible.

"That's what I thought," the Super said in a rasping and rather satisfied voice. He gave them a once-over that made Urban shudder.

"Definitely Inventor tech," Urban whispered.

"You don't know me." The Super bobbed up and down with each beat of his powerful wings. "But the girl you're carrying belongs to me. Please hand her over, and we'll both be on our way."

Ash's body tensed against Urban. "Do you know this creep?"
Urban shook her head.

"My friend says she doesn't know you, so I suggest you flutter your pretty little wings out of here."

The Super snorted but didn't move.

"So long," Ash tossed out and started to swoop away. Though Ash spoke with casual confidence, his heart hammered quickly against her body.

"How I've missed the chase." The Super grinned sardonically, then shimmered and disappeared.

Urban gasped as Ash swiftly ascended. "He's a Camo too!"

"Impossible," Ash growled, and his grip on her tightened. "Hold on while I lose this joker." He tucked his wings and dove straight down.

Urban's stomach lurched. This was much worse than the aerial trick.

She wasn't sure how long they were free falling before Ash pulled up abruptly under the bridge. Heat emanated from it, the thunder of cars echoed loudly above them, and the wind brushed her hair against her face.

Ash scanned his surroundings before flying back up toward the other side of the bridge. A strange whistling sound filled the air. A moment later, a body slammed into them hard.

Urban couldn't breathe. It felt as if her lungs had been crushed by a dragon. She let go of Ash in pain, but his arms remained wrapped around her.

Sputtering, Ash rose higher into the sky. At the top of the bridge, he dropped swiftly, then began weaving skillfully between the suspensions.

The pillar next to them exploded, and they dove out of the way just in time.

Urban's heartbeat vibrated her chest. *We're going to die.*

They hovered low above the water and zigzagged in unpredictable patterns. Water sprayed up in glittering green plumes on all sides, pelting them with icy droplets.

Ash pulled up sharply, then twisted and looped through pillars and poles.

A particularly close explosion singed part of Urban's boot. Her body tensed. *We have to find a way to escape.*

Ash's movements were slowing. He narrowly missed colliding into a wall. Sweat dampened his chest, and his breath came in gasps, but still, he held her tight.

"He's too big, and you have added weight," Urban yelled as they dove again.

"The sky is blue, and there's water below us," he wheezed in between gulps of air. "What other generalizations would you like to point out?"

"My point is, this won't work. We need to go on the offensive. Use your Flyer weapon."

Ash looked down at her. "That requires my hands."

"Then use your hands."

"But how—"

Urban interrupted him. "I'll still be holding on to you. I'll be fine."

Ash looked as if he were about to object, but a particularly close blast had him drop suddenly. Urban thought they might spin out of control.

"Fine," Ash shouted above the whistling of air as they fell. "When I pull up—hold on."

They flew upward again until they were far above the bridge. Ash released his grip on Urban and whipped out his polearm. With a burst of electric energy, the stick flashed ice blue.

There was a warm tremor in the air. Ash turned and sliced his weapon through the sky.

There was a sizzle and a growl of anger.

"Got 'em!"

A bloodied flesh wound appeared where the polearm had struck.

"Now we'll be able to see him coming," Urban said excitedly.

"That will do you little good," a raspy voice said from behind.

They spun around. A stick, pulsing red with two sharp, wing-shaped objects, hovered in midair.

"A laser hand ax," Ash breathed. "How dare you steal that from a Master of Crane-bot."

There was a brittle laugh. "What makes you so sure I stole it?"

Ash gritted his teeth. He hovered in midair with his weapon extended.

Gravity tried to pull her away, but Urban's arms dug into his waist, and she pressed her head tight against his chest.

The crimson hand ax flew through the air toward them. Ash blocked it just in time. The blow vibrated through his body, and Urban barely managed to keep her grip.

Then they were diving, twirling, jabbing, and blocking in a flurry of red and blue sparks, ten kilometers above the bridge.

Each strike of the Super reverberated through Urban's skull. He was putting his larger body mass into each swing.

Ash snarled, barely managing to hold against the attacks. His movements grew sluggish.

Urban desperately wished she could do something to help rather than weigh him down. She looked at the placid green Reservoir below and gripped Ash in a death vice.

No one would survive a fall this far. Even if there was water below.

Ash parried a blow meant to decapitate him. He was too tired to jab back even though his attacker's exposed shoulder was wide open.

With a sudden burst of energy, the hand ax came flashing back around. The weapon caught the hilt of Ash's polearm, then slipped over it and sliced his hand.

With a screech of pain, Ash spun to get away.

Urban's grip loosened.

A boot landed hard on Ash's shoulder, barely missing Urban,

and sending him reeling backward, wrenching him from her grip. Suddenly she was falling.

"No! Urban!" Ash yelled. He dove toward her, but something invisible struck him hard in the jaw. The hand ax slashed toward him again, and he dodged just in time.

The last Urban saw of Ash and the attacker was a flash of red as she plummeted toward the bridge.

32

自爱

TRIG

THE SOUND OF WIND ROARED PAST URBAN AS she fell. It smacked her in the face, making it difficult to breathe. Her heart pounded wildly at the approaching cars and bridge below. In her peripheral she saw a Flyer, but it wasn't Ash. She twisted her head and saw Ash and the Super still fighting above.

At that moment, strong arms grabbed her and jerked her upward.

Urban looked up and found herself staring into the masked face of a Flyer.

The same Flyer who saved her at the motorcycle race and followed her the first day on campus.

"You have to help Ash!" she screamed at him. She craned her neck to try and spot Ash. "Ash!"

"As your protector, I must get you to safety first," the masked Flyer replied calmly. His voice had a foreign accent.

"What?" Urban faltered. "My protector?"

"I'm Trig."

Details that had baffled her started clicking into place. Not only was her bodyguard a Camo but also a Flyer. That's why he was nearly impossible to shake off. He must be from the Western Federation, where having two enhancements wasn't that uncommon. That's why he had an accent.

Urban turned her attention back to the skies. Was Ash okay? She spotted him in the distance with flashes of red and blue surrounding him. "Ash!" she screamed. She tugged at her rescuer. "We have to help him!"

"I have to get you to safety."

"No! Go back," Urban insisted.

But Trig only continued his descent.

Frustration bubbled up in Urban. Why wasn't he listening? She was tempted to fight Trig but knew that would probably end poorly. If she won, she'd only succeed in plummeting to her death.

Her gazed returned to the two tiny figures fighting far in the sky. Ash had sacrificed so much for her. How could she just leave him?

Trig hauled her back to the side of the Reservoir she and Ash had just flown over. A navy car idled on the side of the road.

A door opened, and Lillian waved from within the vehicle. "Get in!"

Trig touched down gracefully onto the pier, and they both sprinted to the car. No sooner was the door closed behind them than the car skidded away onto the bridge.

"I'm so glad Trig got to you." Lillian's face was ashen. "I saw that Super up there and then you were falling and . . ." Lillian's voice trailed off.

Urban wanted to ask Lillian about how she'd found Trig for hire, then remembered something. Trig had been there her first day of class. But that was before Lillian had hired him. So why had he been there?

Urban hesitated, questions burning, but decided Ash was the current priority. "We have to help my friend Ash! He risked his life for me and is still battling that psycho."

"There's not much we can do," Lillian said apologetically. "But I think your friend can take care of himself. The attacker isn't targeting him, after all."

Urban wasn't so sure, but she knew that tone. Lillian wouldn't budge. Not to mention, since her sister was the one who had called the vehicle, she had access over it and could override any of Urban's commands to stop the car or try and get out.

In the silence, Trig retracted his mask. Urban took in his features for the first time. He was impeccably dressed and looked like he belonged at a fashion show, not invisibly trailing people.

"Surprised?" Trig asked as if reading her thoughts. "I'm from the African Federation. It's a lottery system there, and I was the lucky winner of two main gene-pool enhancements."

Urban had a million questions but decided to focus on the most pressing issue at hand. "Do you guys know who's following me? The guy has Camo, Super, *and* Flyer abilities and maybe even Inventor enhancements. That's four! I thought that was genetically impossible."

Trig patted his voluptuous hair smooth. "Apparently not."

Lillian grimly dislodged her daggers and spun them deftly in her hands.

"Roll down the windows," Lillian commanded the car.

But the windows remained closed.

Lillian frowned. "I said roll down the windows."

Still nothing. Lillian glanced around the interior of the car. "Anyone have a bag in case I need to throw up?"

Urban was about to respond when a rumbling *boom* shook the car.

The car trembled so violently Trig hit his head on the ceiling.

Urban tumbled to the floor. She peered out the window and let out a choked scream. "The bridge. It's—it's gone!" How was it possible that the road in front of them simply disappeared into water? Horror filled her. Had their attacker blown up the bridge to try and drown them?

"Stop the car," Lillian ordered.

Nothing happened.

"There's something wrong with the car." Lillian's eyes feverishly darted about in QuanNao. "I don't have access."

Urban yanked at the door handle. "It's locked!"

"Whoever is attacking us must have your SCA PIN," Lillian grimaced and clutched her stomach. "That's how he hacked you before, in the motorcycle race. It also means he has control of our car right now."

"But how?" Urban asked, horrified.

"We're almost to the end of the bridge," Trig said, the first trace of concern in his voice. "We need to get out *now*."

"I'm trying to do a manual override," Lillian said tensely.

Urban watched as their car zoomed toward the gaping hole in the bridge. "Hurry!"

"It's not working." Lillian punched the car door in frustration.

"We're not going to make it." Trig's voice was tight.

Urban's throat went dry. Water. Trapped underwater. Anything but this. Images of her breath running out as Lucas dragged her to the bottom of their pool swirled in her head.

"Plan B it is," Lillian continued grimly. "Strap in, guys."

Urban's face was ashen. "We'll drown."

"Do it," her sister ordered.

Urban obliged.

With a lurch, the car sailed off the pavement. Time seemed to slow as they plummeted toward the dark green liquid mass.

"Hug your knees," Lillian commanded.

As they neared the water's surface, a blue orb popped up around the three of them as Lillian released a force field.

Then they slammed into the water. The impact knocked the wind out of Urban, momentarily stunning her.

The car began sinking. With it went Urban's last shred of hope.

Dots clouded her vision as growing amounts of water lapped against them. The pulsing blue force field kept a bubble of air protectively encompassing the three of them even as they slipped further into the icy depths.

"What now?" Urban asked, voice quavering as she tried desperately to rein in her panic.

"We wait," Lillian said simply. "I've run a few different calculations. We have forty-three minutes before we run out of air." She gave Urban a knowing look. "That's only if we breath normally."

Urban closed her eyes in an effort to stop hyperventilating. *It's fine. We have enough air. It's fine.*

"So, we wait for our attacker to assume we're dead?" Trig remarked.

Lillian nodded. "I should be able to get us out of the car by then."

With a bump, the car settled at the bottom of the Reservoir.

Trig stretched and leaned back. He kicked his feet up on the seat in front of him and stared at the fish swimming past his window.

Urban tried to focus on her breathing and not the fact they were deep underwater. Trapped. *We're going to make it out alive. I can breathe,* she consoled herself. *But why is someone trying to kill me? Are they gone now?*

As if in answer, something thumped against the car, throwing Urban off balance. "What was that?" She looked out the window.

"Interesting. He's also an Aqua," Trig observed.

"*Five* enhancements?" Urban could hardly believe it. "That's basically a human weapon."

Lillian's eyes darkened. "Yes. It is"

Sure enough, while they couldn't see anyone, bubbles and water currents streaked past them in the wake of the Super as he swam away. If Ash hadn't beat the Super, that could only mean . . .

No.

Urban refused to allow that possibility in. Ash was okay. He had to be.

The Aqua slapped a device onto the trunk of the car. It began rapidly beeping.

"Cover your head!" Lillian ordered.

Boom!

Everything flashed red, then went dark.

When Urban's ears stopped ringing and her eyes adjusted to the darkness, she noticed the blue force field still held but had shrunk.

"All right, new plan." Lillian unbuckled her seatbelt. "Get to the surface as fast as possible. Underwater is our attacker's home turf."

"So is the ground," Urban pointed out as she wriggled away from her seatbelt. "And the air."

"We have to take the fight to land where we at least stand a chance," Lillian said.

Another explosion detonated, throwing Urban forward onto the floor. The force field flickered but held firm, though it decreased in size again.

Outside of the protective blue force field bubble, Urban saw the car breaking into several pieces. The roof fell away, along with one of the doors.

"*Tiana*," Lillian exclaimed. "Looks like he has an underwater NBI."

"A what?" Urban balked.

"An NBI. Neutral-beam injector." Lillian switched several settings on her metal arrow. "Never mind. Just hold on to me."

Urban eyed the device. "What are you doing?"

"Blasting us out of here."

"Will that work?" Urban grabbed on tight to her sister.

"I've been working on this underwater upgrade for a while, but it's just a prototype," Lillian confessed.

Trig wrapped his long arms around Urban and Lillian, encompassing them with his wings.

"Hurry, I think he's coming back," Urban urged.

Lillian dialed the setting to high, then fired the weapon down at the ground. The force of it propelled them in the opposite direction, upward.

They were halfway to the surface when an invisible body hit them so hard Urban's teeth rattled. The force field shrunk so it barely encased the tips of Trig's wings.

Their momentum no longer carried them. They slowed to a stop in the middle of the Reservoir—twenty feet from the surface.

Lillian looked up. "Looks like my prototype needs a bit more work." She checked several settings. "And my force field can't take many more hits."

Another body slam sent them spinning in circles.

"What if Trig pulls us out?" Urban offered, desperate to find a way. "Could you shoot your arrow thing up to him, and he could fly us out of here?"

"Nothing like a good experiment to find out." Lillian unstrapped her goggles from her suit and handed them to Trig. "Take these."

The invisible attacker battered into them again. The force field was now so small, it was hard to breathe.

Urban squeezed her eyes shut to keep from panicking. Each breath came labored. She wasn't sure if it was the oncoming panic or an actual lack of oxygen. She could only hope it wasn't her asthma.

"We have enough energy for just one shot, so don't miss it," Lillian warned. "Now go!"

Trig launched himself out of the force field and swam upward. Lillian waited one second, then two. Movement in the water alerted them to their attacker's presence, heading toward Trig.

"Close your eyes," Lillian instructed Urban.

A bright light filled the water, and the Aqua roared.

When Urban opened her eyes, Trig was gone. Relief filled her. Hopefully that meant Trig had made it safely to the surface. But it also meant Lillian and Urban were alone in the water with their attacker.

With the last propulsion of her weapon, Lillian launched

her arrow skyward, and it disappeared out of the water and into the air.

Nothing happened. Then they started sinking.

Panic clawed at Urban. They were so close to the surface and yet so far away.

Urban gripped the chain alongside Lillian. She needed something to hold on to. The chain tightened.

"He got it!" Lillian declared in triumph.

With the chain pulling them, they shot quickly to the surface and broke through to fresh air. They glided on top of the water as Trig dragged them toward shore. Lillian released her now-miniature force field, and they all collapsed on the cold, muddy beach, gasping for breath.

"Where did he go?" Trig panted.

"Don't know." Lillian sat up and looked around. "I ordered a car be dropped and requested a protector-bot. They won't be here for another fifteen minutes though. In the meantime, Trig, scout the perimeter. I'll protect Urban. Let's meet at the road."

Lillian spoke with more authority than Urban had ever heard from her. Trig launched himself into the air and shimmered out of sight.

Lillian threw up her one remaining force field, then they made their way toward the road.

The city and its accompanying sounds were long gone. The bridge and the main road were far away, and they were in a sparse forest, silent except for the wind howling through the dead trees. They stuck to an overgrown trail as they headed up a hill.

They were entering through a small clearing when Urban felt it—the whoosh of air. It seemed so out of place in the quiet, it took Urban a second to place it.

"Incoming!" Trig warned from somewhere above.

There was a sizzling sound as if something were being charged or booted up, and then, a scarlet streak of electricity shot out toward them from the sky. With a loud pop, Lillian's force field disappeared.

"Stupid NBIs," Lillian muttered.

The sisters sprinted toward tree cover. Lillian pushed Urban behind her and scanned the sky. Her laser daggers pulsed blue at the ready.

Urban detached her stun shield and activated it. How she was supposed to use it on an invisible attacker, she wasn't sure, but she had to try.

The overcast clouds were no help either. Urban glanced up, hoping to spot a break of sunshine. *All we need is his shadow.* But the gray clouds were thick and heavy, and Urban knew they couldn't wait around in such a vulnerable position.

A swishing noise grew nearer.

One second, Lillian was standing in front of Urban, the next, she was hurtled into a tree several meters off.

"Lillian!" Urban screamed, watching her sister slump to the ground.

Lillian moaned. Swaying from the impact, she slowly got back to her feet.

Urban scanned her surroundings.

Thud.

The force of the Super landing nearby caused the earth to tremble. She felt the vibration of each giant step coming toward her.

She still couldn't see anything when thick hands grabbed her from the front. He put her in a choke hold. Something hit her stun shield, deactivating it.

Urban's body froze in terror. She was now defenseless—just like always. *I have to do something.*

Clunk.

One of Lillian's metallic arrows struck the attacker, the force of it knocking the wind out of Urban and jolting her out of her panic. Her attacker must be wearing heavy armor, because he merely grunted at the arrow lodged in his protective exoskeleton.

Lillian pulled on her chain, attempting to reel the attacker in. Instead, she was jerked off her feet. The attacker pulled her toward him with one hand, while keeping a firm grip on Urban with the other.

Urban seized the opportunity and twisted to escape, but it felt like a block of cement was sitting on her.

She wracked her brain for a jiujitsu escape technique, but all those scenarios on the ground hadn't prepared her for a choke from behind. She tried throwing her elbows at his head.

The attacker tightened his grip, which imprisoned her.

Lillian was also having difficulty. The Super continued reeling her in like a fish as she struggled wildly. A tide of dirt accumulated before her feet as she forced her heels into the ground. When she was only a meter away, the attacker turned and swung his hand ax at her.

Lillian quickly rolled out of the way just in time.

The attacker leaped into the air, squeezing Urban all the more. As they got further away from the safety of ground, she felt sick with dread.

"Save Urban!" Trig yelled as he slammed into the attacker.

The impact set Urban's teeth on edge but caused the attacker to let go. The force of it also dissolved both Flyers' Camo abilities, so they were clearly visible as they plummeted.

Urban fell with them but out of reach.

"Peppa, Dede, do your thing!" Lillian released her two hoverdrones, and they flew toward Urban.

Everything was a blur of motion.

Right as the bots reached her, ropes shot out of them like webbing from a spider. They wrapped around her like snakes constricting their prey. The wind whistled through her ears as she fell. Netting sliced her skin, and she stopped falling abruptly.

To her surprise, she found she was dangling from a net in a tree.

"Maybe her hoverdrones are a little bit more advanced than most," Urban muttered to herself as she examined the ropes holding her upside down. From her vantage point, she watched as Trig and the Super crash to the ground. As the dust settled, the Super vanished.

All was silent.

"Trig!" Lillian screamed and sprinted toward him.

Trig tried to sit up but collapsed.

A tickling sensation crept up her throat. A wave of dread washed over her. With every barrage on her lungs, her asthma would flare up again. She recalled the extra steroid shot Lillian had given her. Where was it? Her pocket?

Lillian was almost to Trig's side when she was intercepted by an invisible force. She landed hard on her back.

Something launched itself on top of her, leaving indents where its weight pressed against her stomach. Lillian grappled with the invisible attacker, executing a flawless jiujitsu flip. But with her attacker mostly invisible, she wasn't able to protect herself from the uppercut that caught her in the jaw.

I have to get out of here and help her. Urban frantically surveyed the trap she was in. The drop down was about ten meters, and the netting had no obvious release mechanism. Then she realized she was still holding her deactivated stun shield.

If she activated the shield now, with her arm wedged between the netting and her side, she'd slice herself open. Coughing again, she began wriggling to move her arm out from under her.

Lillian's face turned red as the Super strangled her.

Come on, come on. I have to help protect Lillian!

Triumphantly, she finally freed her hand.

Lillian lifted her arm at the attacker. A spray of metal pellets shot his shoulder. Blood dripped from the faintly visible wound.

With lighting speed, he picked her up by her other arm, and threw her against a tree trunk. Lillian's limp body slid down into a crumbled heap.

"No!" Urban screamed hoarsely.

She activated her stun shield and fried the ropes holding her captive. With a thud, she landed hard on her side.

Wheezing slightly, Urban could see part of the attacker's torso as he turned and approached her. But her focus was on Lillian. Why wasn't she getting up?

One of the Super's eyes narrowed, and he suddenly dropped to the ground. A laser polearm whizzed over his head.

"I'm pretty sure you've used up at least two of your nine lives," she heard a familiar voice say, and Ash swooped down from the sky.

"Ash!" Urban cried out as relief filled her. It was oblivious he had taken a beating. His left arm was bleeding, and his suit was burned in multiple places.

She was about to speak more, but it was hard to draw enough breath. Wheezing, she remembered the extra steroid shot and reached into the folds of her XR suit.

Empty.

Where could her extra shot have gone? She put it in her XR pocket every day. Did it fall out while she was flying? Or maybe when she was in the net? She searched the ground in panic, but there were no signs of it. *We have to escape before I can't breathe at all.*

She looked up to see Ash diving out of the way as the Super thrust his hand ax at him.

Ash's speckled wings beat hard as he rose with the Super in close pursuit. "Get to the safety of the road!"

"I'm not leaving my sister!" Urban gathered enough breath to yell.

Ash suddenly tucked his wings and twirled about so that he faced his attacker. He sliced the air with his polearm before continuing his spin and dropping out of reach.

The slice struck the Super in a weak point in his armor. A shrill scream of pain erupted, and the Super crashed to the ground.

Urban reached Lillian's side and tried to listen for breathing but was interrupted by her own coughing. She anxiously felt for a pulse while keeping tabs on Ash out of the corner of her eye.

The Super became visible again, lifting himself shakily. Ash dove at him.

Dodging at the last second, the Super barely missed the polearm but was hit hard by Ash's knee and thrown into a tree.

Urban found a faint pulse and let out a shaky breath. Carefully, and with great effort, she picked her sister up and began half dragging, half carrying her toward the road. The effort of it taxed her breathing, and she strained for air.

Meanwhile, Ash pierced the Super's wing to the trunk. Crimson scaled wings thrashed, and blood streamed from the wound.

Ash punched the Super in the face.

But the Super somehow slipped away, and Ash's next punch hit the trunk instead.

With a gasp, Urban realized the Super had left his wing behind, still lodged in the tree. He shimmered and again became transparent, except for the blood dripping from his chest and his bruised and swollen eyes.

Urban ignored her limbs screaming with exhaustion. The effort of toting Lillian continued to cause her chest to constrict. She was light-headed from the lack of air. *I have to get Lillian to the road. Surely the car will be there by now.*

"Stupid lizard enhancements," Ash swore as he tried to dislodge his polearm from the fluttering wing stuck in the tree.

A dart flew through the air and hit Ash in the back. With a flash of brilliant light, spider webs of electricity spread across his broad shoulders.

Ash fell to the ground, writhing in pain.

Not Ash too!

He went still.

"No!" Urban screamed, but with that she began coughing

violently, and her vision swam. When she could look up again, she saw the Super coming toward her. With most of his body still transparent, it looked like a lone eyeball and torso floating her way. His glowing amber eye had a scar running through it that made her shudder.

He approached her with the hand ax spinning and confidence in his movements.

She was on her own.

URBAN'S FATIGUED LIMBS SCREAMED IN PAIN. She set Lillian gently down and activated her stun shield and faced the attacker.

"Leave us alone," she wheezed. Her voiced sounded weaker than the declaration she felt rising up inside her. The bodies of Ash, her sister, and her protector lay at the edge of her fading vision. Were they alive? She forced herself to take slow, deep breaths.

The Super roared, shaking the ground. Urban clamped her hands over her head and fell to the earth. Her ears rang painfully, her breath came in ragged gasps. *I don't have much longer before my asthma completely takes over.*

When the roar ceased, she stood as quickly as she dared, determined to finish this. Her mouth was like sandpaper.

The Super glared and sprinted toward her, but Urban stood her ground. She threw her stun shield at him with all her strength.

Her training paid off. Her aim was perfect, but the Super deflected it easily. Urban saw reinforced metal protecting his thick, muscled body where the shield struck him.

That was my one shot.

Her body seized with deep coughing. The sudden lack of air

caused a maelstrom of terror to rage within her. It was as if she was breathing through a tiny straw. Each breath, trying to suck in more but failing.

Helplessness creeped in as the Super drew closer. *I can't win against him, and I can't get enough air.*

The Super pulled out a pulsing indigo blade and sliced effortlessly through a tree branch in his way. With a sickening feeling, Urban recognized it as Lillian's blade. Anger bubbled inside her and with it, sudden determination.

As he closed in, she wracked her brain. She couldn't outrun him. She didn't have a weapon. If Lillian couldn't defeat him with her martial arts, there was no way Urban's limited jiujitsu exposure would help. She was too small. Too weak. Too slow.

Just like I always am against the Enhanced.

No.

Don't give up. There has to a be a way.

The attacker was almost close enough to shove the blade up her rib cage. Or would he slice one of her main arteries and let her bleed to death?

Urban scanned her surroundings. There was nothing but dead trees. Ash and Lillian still lay motionless. A sinister puddle of blood surrounded Trig.

The Super was even bigger up close. Urban didn't reach his chest. He also had all the latest tech. She was pretty sure the NBI gun was illegal.

Something out of the corner of her retina display caught her eye. It was a pulsing force field around a red zone.

What is that doing here? Then Urban remembered. *It's where the mutant animals escaped to.*

The animals were wanderers. Homeless. Hunted. Not allowed to live in a society where their DNA didn't match the plan others had for them.

Like me.

Her attacker lashed out with his knife.

Urban dodged.

Just like those animals, my DNA is one of a kind.

An idea came to her as she turned to face him again.

Gene-IQ might not have fixed the glitch yet . . .

Urban locked eyes with the Super. "Gene-IQ disable manual vision. Code 3006!"

The Super screeched and clawed at his eyes, trying to shield them from a light only visible in his retina display. He dropped the knife.

Urban kicked the weapon away and slammed into the Super. He stumbled backward and lost his balance. Both of them tumbled down the hill. They rolled to a stop next to the red zone.

Urban's retina display screamed warnings, but she ignored them. She scanned the Super, now visible again, until she saw what she was looking for.

He scrambled up, still blinking from the light, but Urban was already on him, snatching the NBI gun from his hip.

The weapon felt foreign in her hands. Shaking, she lifted it, then aimed at the force field pulsing around the red zone. Inhaling, she pulled the trigger.

Nothing happened.

Urban examined the gun. Had she pulled the trigger correctly? Was there a safety mechanism? *Please don't let this thing be tatt activated.*

She clicked a lever down, then tried again, even as the Super launched himself at her.

This time, a brilliant flash of light shot from the weapon and struck the force field. Electricity crackled through the air. With a *pop*, a portion of the force field went down.

Urban kicked the Super square in the chest, sending him reeling again. He collapsed on the ground just inside the red zone.

The Super picked himself back up, swaying. Urban wasn't sure if he could see her, but she kept the gun trained rigidly on him.

There was a distant animalistic screech that caused the hairs on the back of Urban's arm to stand on end.

Realizing where he was, the Super stumbled forward, trying to escape the deadly zone.

"Stay back," Urban commanded.

The Super ignored her warning.

Urban fired a beam, aiming for the patch of dirt in front of him. Her aim was off, and she blasted the tip of his reinforced boots.

The Super jumped back in surprise. He shook his head as if trying to see.

Another screech erupted—this one closer.

Then there was a different sound, a powering up of electricity. The force field blazed back to life, trapping the Super inside.

Urban lowered the weapon, watching the Super stumble away into the darkening evening. The gun's metal was cold, and she dropped it.

Urban's vision grayed.

Can't breathe.

Falling to her knees, she sank to the sharp, stiff grass.

All she could see was a fallen leaf in front of her. Consuming pain crushed her lungs, and she gasped desperately for air.

She became vaguely aware of foreign metallic boots stepping onto the leaf. Something sharp pricked her thigh.

The boots retreated as Urban's vision faded black.

She wasn't sure how much time passed when she regained consciousness. Her lungs burned, but she could breathe.

She sat up and looked around. The forest was empty and silent.

Trying to rise, Urban almost passed out. She leaned against a tree before hobbling toward the road.

A brand-new Wasp G9 sat idling by the side of the Speed Way. The back door stood ajar, and two people sat inside. A protector-bot emerged from the trees and headed toward her.

"Lee Urban, you have received a steroid shot to help with

your asthma. May I run more diagnostics to treat your other injuries?"

But Urban ignored the bot and went toward the vehicle.

"I will return to treat you later, Lee Urban," the bot said, then disappeared back into the forest.

Urban's shoulders sagged with relief when she saw it was Lillian and Trig inside. She scrambled into the car.

"Urban," Lillian croaked, managing a weak smile.

"I'm so glad you're safe." Urban blinked back tears.

A moan made her turn.

Trig was in a fitful sleep. He had a tourniquet on one of his arms and was no longer bleeding. "Is he alright?"

Lillian nodded. "Yes, but he's lost a lot of blood."

"What about Ash?" Urban's brow furrowed in concern.

Lillian shrugged weakly.

Urban looked around in search of him.

There, at the tree line, the med-bot carried what looked like a giant fallen sparrow. Ash's speckled wings were crusted in blood and dragging in the dirt.

Urban jumped out of the car.

"Will he live?" Urban gripped the bot so tightly its metal edges left dents in her fingers.

The bot continued on and set Ash down in the car. "He is unconscious from an electric shock. His recovery will be 100 percent."

Urban exhaled a pent-up breath.

Trig stirred, and his eyes cracked open. He blinked a few times before focusing on Lillian.

"How you feeling?" she asked gently.

Trig licked dry lips. "Not bad now that I'm drugged up."

In addition to his tourniquet, an IV dangled from his arm. The protector-bot really had outdone itself.

As if on cue, the bot flipped open a cavity of its arm and withdrew a tinged vial. "Please move aside while I administer this to Ding Ash."

The bot tipped Ash's head backward against the car seat, then poured the liquid into his mouth.

Ash coughed and bolted upright. His eyes opened wide. He stared at his surroundings and blinked in confusion. When his gaze landed on Urban, he seemed to register something. "I can always count on you to spice up my day." He grinned. "So . . . what happened?"

Urban opened her mouth but stopped as two red-and-black SUVs, each with a golden hammer and sickle emblazoned on the doors, pulled up beside them. "Now the *Jingcha* decide to arrive."

Several heavily armed bots and one Super stepped out of the vehicles.

"We received several distress pings." The Super took them in with sharp, observant eyes. "Everything alright?"

Ash rolled his eyes. "Just dandy."

Urban ignored Ash and went on to explain what had happened.

When she was done, the Super spoke, "You say the assailant left behind a wing?"

Urban pointed. "Over there."

"Good." The Super nodded. "We'll collect some samples. It will take some time for the results to be processed. But don't worry, we'll track him down. In the meantime, I suggest you all get some rest."

"Thanks," Urban said.

They piled back into the car and traveled down a road, which disappeared into a glass tunnel beneath the water. The car didn't slow as it approached the tunnel. The next instant, they were underwater, zipping along on dry road underneath the glass passageway.

Urban shivered at the sight of the water above them but was grateful this time the water was behind a foot of reinforced smart-glass.

The temperature dropped the further they went, and the car began warming their seats and pumping heated air. Swaying reeds stretched through the murky, blue water like gnarled fingers.

<Arriving at the Lee Aquatic Center. Sosh: 77.> Urban's retina display informed her as they approached.

While a valet-bot parked their car, the group stumbled into the hotel and toward the Underwater Bar.

With Ash and Trig leaning heavily on Urban and Lillian, it was slow going. Urban realized how ridiculous they must appear. With all the dried blood, shredded clothes, bruises, and injuries, they looked like the military Supers returning from a particularly tough training session.

It was still early for the dinner crowd, but at least a dozen Enhanced already waited in the lobby. They wore elegant silks and jewels the size of small teacups and had their hair neatly styled. Several of them stopped talking to stare at the approaching group.

Urban kept walking. The last time she had been here, she was wearing her best dress for her birthday. That felt like years ago.

Several Natural attendants started toward the group, along with two Super security guards. *Oh no. Please don't let them kick us out.*

The guards and attendants stopped abruptly as Urban got a ping.

<Identity confirmation from Lee's Underwater Hotel & Bar. Welcome, Lee Urban!>

She breathed a sigh of relief. Her parents must have sent orders to expect them.

The attendants and guards went back to their stations, though they cast sideways glances at the ragtag crew passing by.

After what felt like three dynasties had passed, they reached the yawning entrance of the bar.

A hostess nodded stoically, then led them through a glass tunnel, surrounded by more water. Looking up, Urban saw the entire Reservoir above them. Gold, peach, and lilac rays of sunlight undulated through the emerald water.

The hostess stopped at an elegant metallic doorway, then gestured them in. "Your guests have arrived," she announced, then left.

The salty and bitter smell of seaweed and oolong tea greeted them as they entered the room. Mother, Father, and Lucas sat alone at a giant full-sized conference table. Behind them was a wall of windows. The fading rays of the sun danced on the floor in rippling waves. Colorful schools of fish and a hammerhead shark swam lazily around them.

"Finally." Lucas drummed his fingers on the table. "Now that Urban's here, can we get some answers as to why we're all sitting here like tuna in a can?"

Mother and Father sat at the conference table. Father scowled, taking in their ragged appearance. "What happened?"

"We were attacked," Urban said bluntly.

The color drained from Mother's face. Lucas stopped his tapping.

"What?" Father's jaw tightened.

Urban quickly explained.

When she finished, Mother leaned forward. "This is more serious than we thought." She stopped talking and stared at Ash as if just remembering he was there. "I'm very sorry, but this is a *private* meeting."

"Ash is a good friend of mine." Urban motioned at his injuries. "He just risked his life for me."

Mother hesitated, then motioned for them all to sit. "You could use more friends like him." Her tough demeanor melted away into exhaustion. Dark circles lined her eyes. Her normally immaculate hair had several strands escaping from her bun.

There were already three cups of cold green tea set out when Trig, Lillian, and Urban sat. Mother quickly rose and poured another and set it before Ash.

"How is it possible we were attacked by someone with more than two enhancements?" Urban asked. "I thought that was illegal. Don't the Federations have rules against that?"

"Technically, that's what the Nonproliferation Treaty for Deadly Enhancements is designed to do," Father agreed. "But in every society there will be always people who find ways to circumvent the regulations. The more important question, I believe, is why was he after you?"

Urban fingered her teacup. "That's what I was hoping you could tell me."

Mother sighed. "Our house is currently being watched. I'm sure these events are linked. That's why we're here anyway. It's much harder to overhear conversations through water, and we believe the hotel hasn't been bugged. Yet."

"What do you mean 'watched'?" Lillian inquired.

"Lennox's visit wasn't just to interrogate Urban," Father said. "He planted several bugs in our house."

Lillian's eyes widened.

"So, remove the tech and be done with it." Lucas chugged his tea. "I don't see why this is a big deal."

Urban couldn't believe he could be so callous. Then again, he had tried to drown her.

"It's not that simple." Father shot him a glare. "We've found other bugs too—not just the ones Lennox planted. It seems our house has been under watch for some time.

Urban thought back to the start of the semester and how her mother had run through all of the rules with her. If anyone had been listening at the time, they would know Urban was a Natural. "How long has the house been bugged?"

"We don't know. But we think it had to be after you'd left for uni. Otherwise . . ."

Otherwise, we'd all be in serious trouble right now. Then again, maybe that explained everything. But why would someone go to all the trouble of attacking her? If they knew she was a Natural, they'd just publicly expose her and be done with it. Wouldn't they?

"We're in the process of removing the bugs," Father informed them. "We're monitoring everyone who comes in and out of the house to see if they plant any new ones."

"But we still don't even know who *they* are," Lucas pointed out.

Father's face darkened. "Supers Against Soups."

Urban's mouth fell open. "SAS? But why?"

Father let out a deep sigh, as if resigning himself to something. "You know how we were caught in a scandal years ago that dropped our sosh and nearly destroyed us?"

Urban, Lillian, and even Lucas nodded. Trig and Ash watched them all, listening intently.

"There was no scandal." Father's voice was toneless. "We found ourselves on the blacklist of SAS. A fake scandal was devised and publicized by their members to destroy us."

Urban was stunned. "Why?"

"Your Father and I used to be involved in something SAS disapproved of." Mother took up the tale. "There is scientific research being conducted around enhancing individuals after birth. The Center for Advancement in Asian Genetics, or CAAG, was leading the way in discoveries on this frontier." She poured herself more tea before continuing, "There were great advancements being made until SAS got involved. SAS members prefer to have a genetic advantage over Naturals. They want to keep it that way. They destroyed the labs and killed everyone involved."

"The explosion," Urban breathed. She remembered the eccentric genetic-engineering probot talking about it. "It wasn't an accident. SAS was behind it?"

Mother nodded solemnly. "But not everyone wanted the research to stop. A group of people determined to further human development formed the Advancements in Enhancements group: AiE. They operated in secret, fearing the fate of the scientists."

Mother hesitated, casting a quick glance at Ash before continuing. "We were some of the early members of AiE. We haven't been involved in a while but still have a couple of contacts there."

"What?" Lucas sputtered. "Why risk your lives for *that*?"

Lillian pierced her brother with a stare as Mother looked away. "Our reasons are our own."

Urban couldn't help but feel a sense of pride in her parents. They hadn't been involved in a scandal after all. Behind the façade of wealth and extravagant parties, they had risked their lives for a cause that mattered.

Everything she had known about her parents was slowly crumbling before her eyes. They cared about Naturals. Which meant they actually cared about *her*.

Father spoke up again, "Someone in our network exposed us. Many members suddenly found themselves facing 'scandals,' attacks, and in a few cases, even death. We are some of the fortunate few to recover."

"Yeah, who would have thought a couple of charity cases would have helped." Lucas snorted.

Urban felt a sudden rise of anger. Her brother was treating everything like it was an inconvenience. Her gaze went briefly to Trig and Ash. Their eyes were fixed on Lucas, their faces expressionless, though Urban noted a muscle twitch in Ash's neck.

"Your *sisters* were never a charity case." Mother's own eyes flashed. "We wanted a bigger family, and we also needed a way to get our sosh back. It just so happened those two things coincided."

"Lucky for them," Lucas muttered. "Our family would have been better off—"

"Enough." Mother's voice was low and dangerous.

Lucas pierced his parents with a stare. "Are you going to tell us the real reason Urban's here then? We know you and dad weren't planning to adopt her, so what happened?"

Urban flinched at his blunt words.

Father looked like he could strangle his son.

"It's true we applied to adopt only one Enhanced child," Mother said evenly. "But when Lillian arrived, Urban came with her. When we requested Urban's medical genomics record, we also found out she was a Natural. We tried to contact the orphanage to let them know there had been a mistake." Her voice was so quiet, Urban had to strain to hear her. "They insisted there wasn't. When we pulled the record to show them, it had all been modified to show the adoption of two Enhanced children."

"And you have no idea who tampered with those records?" Lillian spoke for the first time.

Mother shook her head. "We were already in a bad position with SAS and didn't want to attract additional attention to the fact we'd adopted a Natural. Eventually, we dropped the matter, and SAS left us alone."

"So, you think the Super that attacked us on the way here is a part of SAS?" Urban ventured to ask.

Father heaved a great sigh. "It's possible, but I don't see what could have triggered the sudden activity."

"Geez, let's think. What ever could it be?" Lucas scrunched up his face, then lifted a finger. "I know! How about the fact our little hero here," he gestured at Urban, "has managed to get her face plastered across the entire Asian Fed?"

Lillian nearly slapped the table. "Stop it, Lucas."

He only widened his eyes at her mockingly.

"We've considered it," Father said. "But that has nothing to do with SAS or AiE. The Games are just a sporting event. Nothing Urban did out there should threaten them or attract their attention."

Mother's voice was thoughtful. "Perhaps it is time we investigate further into Urban's birth origins."

Urban sat up straighter at this. "I thought you didn't know who my birth parents were."

"We don't. But perhaps finding out would aid in understanding why we are once more being targeted."

A knock on the door made them all jump.

"Yes?" Mother called out.

A maid opened the door and cautiously stepped in. "A hoverdrone has arrived for a Ms. Lee Urban."

Mother turned to Urban, jaw clenched. "Who did you tell about this meeting?"

"I promise, I didn't tell anyone I was coming here!"

But there had been someone who had enough clues to guess her location. The same person who had hacked her pings.

Qing Coral.

34

自爱

THE HOVERDRONE

"HAS IT BEEN SEARCHED?" MOTHER DEMANDED.

"Yes, ma'am," the maid said. "It appears to be a . . . box of . . . soup."

"Soup?" Father's bushy eyebrows rose in disbelief.

"Congee to be precise, sir."

Urban had a quick intake of breath.

"You're sure it's safe?" Mother asked.

The maid nodded.

"Then you may deposit it on the table and leave us."

As soon as the maid was gone, all eyes turned on Urban.

"I think I know who sent it." Urban fingered the sleeve of her XR suit. She quickly explained about Angel's warning and the discovery that Angel was actually her roommate.

"This Coral, or Angel, sounds dangerous. We should discard this"—Mother waved at the congee—"immediately."

Urban frowned. Something wasn't adding up. She thought back to every encounter she'd had with Coral. Her roommate had countless opportunities to hurt her if she had wanted. And yet, she never had. Urban was reminded of her last day at Gene-IQ, when Coral had sent her the encrypted message, then later in the bathroom stall at the party, and most recently, the message of warning which proved to be valid.

"No," Urban said slowly. "Coral has done nothing but warn me. I don't know who she is or how she knows things, but I think she's just trying to protect me."

There was a moment of silence.

"Why?" Father asked. "I cannot believe someone hacking into your system would have good intentions."

"I don't know . . . but I have a feeling this congee may have some answers." Urban picked up the container. It was warm like soup.

Everyone held a collective breath as Urban gingerly opened it. Whiffs of steam, and the aroma of rice filled the room, but otherwise, nothing happened.

Urban took the enclosed spoon and tasted a little. "It's just congee."

"Let me see," Lucas demanded. He, too, took a bite, then pushed the container away. "Bad congee, at that."

Urban took the rice soup back and studied it. "Hmm." She lifted the container up and examined its base. "Aha!" She removed a sheet of paper and held it triumphantly.

Urban opened the paper with shaking hands and studied the hastily scrawled note inside, instantly recognizing Coral's handwriting.

Urban—

Sorry for the secrecy, but all my avatar's activities and communications are being watched in QuanNao. So are yours.

I'm glad you're safe. I tried to discretely warn you about the attack by letting you know I was reading your pings. Obviously, my warning didn't work. This is the only way I could think to communicate. You probably have a lot of questions, and I want to try and help. You bet I can.

Are you familiar with the research around the final frontier being done in enhancements? Huge advancements and revelations have been made. It's rumored one of the scientists who went missing after the attacks and destruction of the research labs has cracked the code.

He was said to have created a hybrid child of sorts—one who could have multiple enhancements added at any age. He implanted an embryo with his research.

Recent intel affirms this and, in fact, suggests that embryo would now be eighteen years of age and somewhere in the Asian Federation. When you tried out for the Games, you inadvertently confirmed that rumor—though for the wrong reason.

As you know, Lillian and I were able to hack into the controls during your tryouts and change the mode from "entertainment" to "training." However, no one else knows that. Which means, to those searching for the hybrid, they saw your performance in the Games as confirmation that you are the hybrid. They saw Samson's reaction to you as endless challenges due to infinite enhancement possibilities in you.

Those who do not know you're actually a Natural are convinced of this. They believe your DNA is the key to allowing any enhancements to be programmed after birth.

This means you are now on the underground's most wanted list. For some of those groups, they'll take you dead or alive. That's why you were attacked in the motorcycle race and today. The Flyer you encountered today is a member of SAS and sent specifically to hunt you and kill you. There are others like him coming.

You must go into hiding.

I will try and keep an eye out for you where I can.

—Coral

P.S. Sorry for hacking and following you.

Her parents exchanged glances, and Father nodded slightly. Urban stared down at the congee, her mind whirring. Coral was supposedly trying to protect her. But was it true? Her father held out his hand for the paper, and she gave it to him.

Memories of the microneedle patch flashed before her as he read it out loud. Was this all connected somehow? Was it possible she actually was the one with the DNA they were all hunting for? Or could Coral be wrong?

She immediately discarded the idea. Lillian and Coral had switched modes in the Games. If she were actually the missing prodigy, Samson would have reacted differently.

Great, not only have I achieved fame, but I'm on the most-wanted list for something I'm not.

"Well, that explains a lot," Lucas muttered as Father returned the note to her.

"Angel knows you're a Natural then?" Mother's black eyes were full of worry and something more. Fear.

"Yes." Urban nodded.

"That still doesn't explain why she's been hacking and following you even before the Games."

"I . . . I . . . don't know what to make of that," Urban admitted. "She still has a lot of explaining to do, but I think she might be telling the truth. She already warned me several times and look where ignoring her warnings got me today."

"She's right." Father glanced at the note in Urban's hands. "We have no choice but to be extremely cautious. I think we have made wise plans."

Mother nodded in agreement. "You need to go into hiding. Now that the semester is nearly over, we're sending you to the one place SAS avoids—the Outskirts. We've already arranged it with Dr. Gong, Urban. You're exempt from finals."

Urban couldn't believe it. She didn't have to take finals. But that meant she didn't have time to pull her grades up. More important concerns crowded into her head. "Where exactly in the Outskirts will I go?"

"We've decided," Mother began slowly, "based on current

events, it is time to rejoin AiE."

There was a moment of silence.

"No." Lucas stood so suddenly his chair toppled backward with a crash. "You've already risked it once. Not again."

"Lucas," Father began wearily. "We have no choice. SAS is taking radical steps to eradicate Naturals and is targeting us now. With other potential organizations targeting Urban as well, we need a way to protect ourselves."

"And joining AiE will do that?" Lucas scoffed. "I thought that's why you left them in the first place. They couldn't protect you from SAS."

"We've been keeping tabs on them from a distance. They've grown significant in number and political influence."

"Not to mention, that was a different time," Mother added. "Ten years ago was too soon for the change we sought. People were inclined toward self-preservation and safety. There was still healing that needed to take place from the Genetic Revolution. There still is. But now, it's time for the next advancement in genetics. The tide is rising."

"It's true," Ash spoke for the first time. "I'd love enhancements after birth, and I know others who would too." Ash looked over at Urban, then to her parents. "If there's anything I can do to help, I'm ready."

"Thank you." Father inclined his head. "I'm sure there will be need of your assistance in gathering more AiE members within the university. We will reach out to our old contacts on campus to see who we can put you in touch with."

"Please," Lucas broke in abruptly. "Please don't risk our lives again. If SAS tanks our sosh, there won't be another charity case to save us."

Father pressed his lips together. "That is a risk we must accept."

Lucas set his cup down loudly, then strode to the window, his back to the table.

"So," Urban cut into the tension, "where am I going?"

"We've already reached out to some of the AiE leads. They recruit members, are in charge of communications, and lead research teams. They've agreed to take you, Trig, and Lillian in." Mother pressed a button for an attendant. "We've had your bags packed and brought here, along with a rental car. We'll be sending out five decoy cars, heading in different directions since it's evident you're being watched." She handed Urban a scrap of paper. "I don't want to send you the address virtually in case someone hacks into your pings again."

Urban read the paper, then blanched.

She was looking at the exact location of Chong Everest's family apartment.

Urban looked up quickly at her parents, but they were already talking about other necessary preparations. She tried to communicate silently with Lillian, but her sister only looked puzzled, uncertain what Urban was trying to say.

Still stunned, Urban tried to pay attention while her mother offered a few final instructions. Then both Father and Mother were saying good-bye.

The words doused Urban with reality. This was good-bye for . . . who knew how long.

Her mother's Bulgarian rose perfume was as overpowering as ever, but for the first time, it smelled sweet. Mother's thin fingers raked tenderly through Urban's silky hair.

With a gentle squeeze her mother pulled away and gazed at her. She saw tears shinning in her eyes.

"I hope you know everything I do is to protect you, daughter." Mother's choked whisper was tight with emotion.

Images of her mother forcing her to read gory stories about SAS torturing Naturals, berating her for low grades, or going over the rule book countless time flashed through Urban's mind. Was it really possible she had done it all out of love and not from selfish ambition or a desire to protect her own social standing?

Urban's heart leaped at the thought. Yet, a little doubt crept in. Mother and Father were always doting on Lucas, and they'd driven Urban to near slave labor when it came to studying and fitting in. But maybe, it really was for her own good.

"Come on, let's go," Lillian urged.

Urban looked over at Lucas. He pretended not to see her as he watched a school of silver fish swimming in harmony. Urban sighed.

With a last glance at her parents, she was pulled along by Lillian down the hallway and through the main lobby, where five identical Wasp G9s sat ready to go.

As Trig and Lillian climbed into the second to last car, Ash sidled up next to her. "Thanks for trusting me. Stay in touch and let me know how I can help."

Urban glanced up at him. Gratitude welled up in her chest. Ash was still a little pasty from his injuries, but he grinned widely, as if his sosh had jumped fifteen points. Her parents were right; she was lucky to have a friend like him. "Thank you for . . . saving my life." She barely managed to get the words out without her voice breaking.

"Let's just hope you don't need saving a third time or any time soon."

Urban cracked a smile. "Agreed."

His gray wings unfolded gracefully. He peered into the car. "Pleasure meeting you, Lillian. I do hope to see you again soon." His gaze stayed on her until Lillian blushed.

"Thank you." Lillian cast a confused look at Urban, who tried not to laugh.

Ash climbed into a different vehicle and left.

Urban watched him, a sense of loss at seeing him go. How many friends did she have who would risk their lives for her?

"I totally thought he had a crush on you, but . . . did he just hit on me?" Lillian asked as Urban joined them in the car.

"Totally." Urban's mouth quirked. "He has a thing for Inventors."

Lillian groaned.

"He's a good guy," Urban said.

Lillian didn't look convinced.

A low meow made Urban jump. Purple spots materialized in the seat next to her.

"Baozi!" Urban exclaimed and hugged her squirming cat.

"Mom thought you might want him to come with you," Lillian explained.

Urban was continuing to see her mother in a new light. She petted Baozi even as she turned her attention out the window. Her mind was swirling with all the new information.

"Urban." Lillian's voice broke into her thoughts. "I need to tell you something."

Urban looked at her, waiting.

Lillian hesitated. "Urban, Trig and I are current AiE members. Mom and Dad don't know, obviously."

Urban's mouth gaped. "How?"

"You know how I like to snoop," Lillian said with a quick smile. "I found our parents' old membership and used it to find the group and join. I met Trig there, and we've both been active members for the past few years. Trig has been watching you since your first day of school. I only pretended to hire him."

"But . . . why?"

"For you, of course." Lillian put a hand on Urban's arm. "When I read about what AiE was trying to accomplish, I knew I had to join. Remember at the orphanage how the other kids picked on you?"

Urban shuddered at the thought of the place. While she had only snippets of memories, she remembered the fear and despair. "I try not to think about it."

Lillian smiled sympathetically. "I've always been there to protect you, but I knew life would continue to be hard and unfair for you as a Natural. If AiE can find a way to cross the genetic barrier after birth, no one will have to endure what you have had to. I wanted a better world for us."

"So what do you do for them?" Urban's brain felt ready to explode.

"We're Protectors and Finders," Trig chimed in.

Urban squinted. "Meaning?"

"Trig and I protect at-risk Naturals from SAS. We also are constantly looking out for the genetic link Coral mentioned," Lillian explained.

"Have you made any progress?"

Lillian shook her head.

"Is it possible—" Urban stopped before getting the courage back up again. "Is it possible I'm the hybrid? I know Coral said it's not but . . . something isn't adding up."

Lillian and Trig shared a glance. Lillian looked at Urban a long moment. "There's a very small possibility," she said slowly.

The hairs on the back of Urban's neck rose.

"We need to do a lot more digging before that question can be answered, though."

I could be the hybrid. Her pulse quickened at the thought. What would that mean? Was that a good thing? Would she become a lab rat? Would she be forced to leave the Asian Federation? Where would she go?

Too many thoughts warred for her attention until the hint of a headache forced her to stop thinking about it. *It's a very small possibility,* she reminded herself.

As she looked back out the window, anxiousness bubbled up in her stomach at the thought of seeing Everest again. All too soon, the Wasp was nearing the edge of the Outskirts.

"You alright?" Lillian asked, eyeing Urban's pallid complexion.

Urban didn't answer as she swapped her colorful retina displays for ordinary translucent ones. What was there to say? She couldn't even get her own thoughts in line, much less form a coherent response. They strapped on masks as they prepared to enter the yellow zone. Soon, the car stopped.

"Baozi, invisible!" Urban ordered. Trig also disappeared, not wanting to alert the Naturals to an Enhanced in their midst.

The scent of body odor, rotting trash, and urine was overpowering. Urban and Lillian stood on a curb in the crowded streets with nothing but a few bags and an invisible cat and bodyguard.

Urban had only ever been on this street when she was with Everest. Her emotions formed a confusing tapestry of disconnected and tangled threads at being back without him.

Lillian ogled at their surroundings. Decrepit skyscrapers leaned in overhead, choking out the light. Hunched Naturals swarmed around them, wearing rusted and outdated headsets. A dog with matted and mangy hair chased after a rat.

"Wear your bag on the front and keep one hand on it at all times," Urban whispered to her. "And stop staring. Only Metropolis people do that. The last thing we need is to get mugged."

They picked their way around potholes and through masses of bodies. Urban weaved her way expertly through the crowds but at a slow pace, due to their injuries. She wasn't sure where Baozi had gone but judging by the occasional person who tripped on thin air or let out a yelp, she guessed he wasn't far off.

Soon, they stood in front of a vid cam at the entrance to a building with peeling paint. The facial-recognition software pinged Everest's house and then the door clicked open.

The smell of putrid trash greeted them as they made their way through the dark corridor and into the elevator.

All too soon, the elevator slowed to a stop at the 105th floor. Urban led the way to a low, dirty metal door, then stopped.

Lillian gave her a supportive nod.

Urban took a deep breath, straightened her shoulders, and knocked firmly.

35

A WORLD OF POSSIBILITIES

THE DOOR FLUNG OPEN.

Urban's memory of Mrs. Guo had been of a kind woman, who, despite being a Natural, had aged well. Now, the woman before her seemed haggard and worried. Her eyes widened at seeing Urban.

"Oh." Recovering quickly, she ushered them in, then shut the door behind them.

Urban and Lillian removed their masks. Trig materialized, and Mrs. Guo gasped.

"Sorry to frighten you, Mrs. Guo," he apologized. "I'm Urban's bodyguard, Trig. I didn't want anyone to see me arrive at your house."

Mrs. Guo gave his large translucent bat wings a once-over. Urban understood how uncomfortable she must be at having someone Enhanced in her house. She realized the kind woman must not know Lillian was also Enhanced.

Looking again at Urban, she seemed uncertain what to say. Apparently, Urban wasn't the only one surprised by this turn of events.

"Come this way," Mrs. Guo finally managed and led them toward the living room.

The house looked exactly as Urban remembered. The

maidbot offered them slippers, but this time there was no exchanging of gifts and pleasantries. The only sound was their plastic slippers sticking to the tile floor as they made their way to the parlor.

"Please sit." Mrs. Guo looked up briefly at Urban. "Everest's not home." She then looked quickly away.

Urban's stomach churned.

"Something to drink?" Mrs. Guo offered in an overly cheery tone.

"No," Urban said, then hastily added, "Thank you. You've helped enough already."

"No really, you must have something to drink. I'm sure you're thirsty from your journey." She turned to the maidbot. "Bring four cups of tea, some biscuits, and fruit."

Mrs. Guo faced them again. "I apologize, my husband is still at work."

They fell into a long silence.

The maidbot returned with steaming cups of green tea and snacks.

"Please, help yourself." Mrs. Guo gestured at the display of food. "I had no idea"–she held Urban's gaze–"you are a Lee."

Urban reached for an apple slice. "Nor did I know you were leading part of AiE in the Outskirts."

"Leading?" Mrs. Guo almost laughed. "Hardly. We're too old to be running around the streets at dark and avoiding the *Jingcha*. No, we do the boring administrative work these days."

Urban looked confused. "Then who's championing the effort in the Outskirts?"

"Isn't it obvious?" Mrs. Guo looked pointedly again at Urban. "Our son, Everest. He's one of five Captains in the Outskirts, reporting straight to the Premier of Operations," she said this with an air of pride.

Urban was too stunned to speak. Once more, her mind was a kaleidoscope of spinning details and memories.

She remembered how Everest had saved her the first time she'd met him. She had chalked his unnaturally good fighting skills up to Outskirt survival instinct. Then there was how he evaded certain questions of hers or the time he lied about what he was doing in the Outskirts. Even the way he smelled of smoke. Maybe he really did own a Magtouch M600.

She thought back to their last argument.

It all seemed so silly now. There were so many bigger things at stake.

And yet, he'd kept this from her all along.

A glass of tea flew off the table and crashed to the floor, jerking her back to the present.

Mrs. Guo shrieked.

"Oh! I'm so sorry." Urban turned in the direction of the mess. "Baozi, appear!"

With a reluctant swish of her giant tail, the cat appeared.

Mrs. Guo's hand flew to her chest.

"That's my cat." Urban's face reddened. "I apologize again. I am so sorry, but can he possibly stay? He actually keeps me calm."

Mrs. Guo recovered enough to nod her head. "Of course."

"Thank you. I appreciate your kindness. He's usually better behaved."

Lillian arched her eyebrows but didn't say anything.

After the maidbot cleaned up the mess, Mrs. Guo rose. "Trig you can sleep on the couch. You ladies can sleep in the other room."

She led the way with Urban and Lillian following. "Sorry it's so small. And there's only one bed . . ." Mrs. Guo seemed suddenly embarrassed. "We don't have another bed. I'm so sorry for the inconvenience."

"We can share a bed," Urban assured her quickly. "It's fine."

Relief flooded Mrs. Guo's face. She smiled and, for the first time, seemed to relax a little. She left the two girls alone.

Urban surveyed the room. A wave of emotions flooded her.

Though she'd never been here in person, she knew where she was. The huge sonic vibration basses, the poster of the TingBings, an assortment of microphones, the wall full of equipment for synthesizing music, the tiny desk littered with scrawlings of lyrics—all unmistakable.

"This is his room, isn't it?" Lillian asked quietly.

Urban nodded. Her eyes darted to the wall above his bed. The painting she'd given him wasn't there.

She sank onto the bed.

Her heart shredded within her chest. *Of course it isn't there. We're not together,* she told herself. But that didn't ease the pain.

Lillian made herself comfortable in a chair facing the window.

After a few agonizing moments trying to choke back tears, Urban turned to her sister. "Did you know Everest was in AiE too?"

Lillian took her time swiveling away from the window to face her. "I didn't. Though his name does sound familiar now that you mention it." She pursed her lips. "For security purposes, members are organized into small units and, for the most part, stay siloed. I've never met anyone from another unit."

Urban twisted a strand of hair in thought.

"Also, there's something I need to let you know." Lillian scratched at her neck. "The bracelet I gave you . . . it's a tracking device. That's how I found you when you raced and when you went to the hospital."

Urban looked down at her beaded bracelet.

"I'm really sorry," Lillian rushed to explain. "I just wanted to make sure you were safe."

Urban's eyes snapped up to her sister. "You've been babysitting me all semester?"

"Following you," Lillian corrected. "And only when you needed it. Which turned out to be more often than I thought." She gave a hesitant little laugh.

Urban fingered her bracelet. While it was more than annoying to have both her parents and sister tracking her, her face softened.

Lillian cared about her and was just trying to help. They'd talk later about boundaries. Urban shook her head. "You really take the protective big sister thing to the next level."

Lillian just smiled. "Sorry."

They fell back into silence for a while.

"I'm going to get some air on the roof," Urban said.

The rooftop looked different in the daylight. All its imperfections, its cracked walls, greasy cement, and littered surface exposed—a stark contrast to the warmth she'd experienced the night of Mooncake Festival.

She sat on the ground and leaned up against a graffitied wall. Her gaze shifted to the Outskirt's skyline. The building where she sat was one of the tallest, and she had line of sight all the way to the edges of the Outskirts. She inhaled the nonfiltered air. It smelled of cigarette smoke and mold.

The sound of feet shuffling caused her head to turn sharply.

"Hey." Everest stood a couple of meters away, watching her intensely. Her senses went into overdrive.

She took in his angular jaw, the curve of his lips, the glint in his eye, and his shock of wild black hair, standing on end—all of it as familiar as her sosh. Urban resisted the urge to run her hands through those silky strands. And yet, after the time and distance that had grown between them, he felt foreign.

His raven-black eyes didn't have their usual warmth. But neither did they have the emptiness she'd seen the last time they'd talked.

Hope rose in her chest, but just as quickly, pain and fear cut it off. She should keep her distance, play it safe. Everest had hurt her, and she wouldn't allow him to do it again.

"Can I sit?"

Urban nodded stiffly. She noticed he took care to leave adequate space between them as he joined her.

And yet, he was so close, Urban could hardly breathe. She stared at her hands until her breath steadied. "Why are you here?" she asked, voice hitching.

"Well, this is my house." There was a note of humor in Everest's tone, causing her to look up. Her heart fluttered as his eyes met hers.

"I heard you were attacked again. And I—" he paused. "I had to see for myself that you were okay."

"Well, I am." Her words came out forceful and clipped.

They fell into silence, looking out over the roof.

She wasn't sure how much time had passed when Everest spoke again. "It sounds like you could be staying—"

"Everest, why are you here?" Urban interrupted, turning blazing eyes on him.

Everest blinked in surprise.

"You've lied to me our entire relationship about what you're really doing. You broke up with me without warning. Then you never even checked on me when I almost died in the arena. You had to know about it." Urban's voice rose in pitch. "So why show up *now*?"

Everest gazed at her for a long moment. His eyes grew tender. "Because I care about you."

Urban said nothing as her pulse beat faster. Simultaneously, she reinforced the walls guarding her heart. She wanted his words to be true, but she couldn't believe them. "Oh really?" she huffed.

"Urban, I'm sorry for not telling you everything," he said softly. "I don't tell anyone what I really do. No one except my parents and the units I oversee know the truth. I had no idea your parents were also members."

She closed her eyes; the guardian walls were starting to crumble.

"I should have told you."

"Yeah. You should have." Urban turned on him. "I told you about being adopted, being a Natural, and going to uni. You should have told me."

There was a moment of silence in which Urban realized there were things she hadn't told Everest either. She was just as much to blame. The walls crumbled a little more.

"I raced," Urban blurted out.

Everest jerked up at her sudden confession.

Urban avoided his eyes. "I signed up for an Enhanced race. I never told you."

"So," he said with a quirk in his voice, "did you win?"

"If you consider totaling your motorcycle and coming in dead last a win, then yes, I did that." She peeked at him.

Everest was shaking his head. "I imagine there's more to the story than that." Then he studied her, his face growing serious again. "I just wanted to let you know that AiE is the real reason I'm never able to find time to work on my lyrics or singing. I really was trying to join you in the Metropolis. Commanding several units takes up all my spare time."

Urban picked at her sleeve.

"I wanted you to know the truth," Everest said.

"Well, now I know." Her attempt at humor sounded hollow.

Everest touched her arm. "Urban, I wanted you to know because . . . I'd like us to have another chance."

Urban looked up.

His expression brought a tidal wave of emotions as he continued, "There's a chance AiE will be sending me to command a larger cluster of units in the Metropolis. Maybe I can join you there after all and—"

"What?" Urban interrupted. "How? Your sosh is too low."

"Some of them seem to think I have natural leadership abilities." He seemed almost embarrassed by the mere admission. "They have many connections that would aid me. Of course, it could end up not happening. Who knows? The AiE strategy is constantly evolving."

He was watching, gauging her reaction closely. "But I was thinking maybe we could give us some time and . . . and a second chance."

Urban felt some of her anger melting away, but part of her pushed back. *Don't let him in. He could leave you again. He could rip your heart to shreds.*

Everest's eyes held hers. The intensity of his gaze sent heat through her amid the maelstrom of emotions. For that moment they were oblivious to everything around them.

She took a breath. "I'll consider it."

His face widened into his familiar grin. "I'll be here, awaiting your answer."

A gentle breeze blew a long tress of dark hair over Urban's face. Everest leaned in and gently tucked the loose strand behind her ear.

Urban's breath caught.

He stopped, as if realizing what he'd just done. A trace of crimson bloomed across his cheeks. "I'll . . . give you some space."

"I just received a message from my parents." Everest stopped and waited until he had Urban's attention. "They have a lead on your biological parents."

"Really?"

Everest nodded. "Your parents will be sending more info soon via a secure channel." He made to leave, then hesitated. "You joining us for dinner?"

"Should I?"

"Mom won't have it any other way. She's thrilled you're here."

Urban thought back to how uncomfortable Mrs. Guo seemed when they arrived. "She is?"

"She likes you. That and . . ." he rolled his eyes, "you're still her best shot at grandkids."

Everest laughed as Urban's eyes widened, and she sputtered.

For a second it was almost like old times. How she had missed him. Her gaze lingered on Everest's muscular arms. She remembered the sensation of being wrapped in their warmth and pulled against his sturdy chest. She'd felt safe there, both physically and emotionally. Her face flushed at the memory.

Everest, who was staring at her lips, let out a cough, and the moment ended. "See you in a bit."

Urban sat in silence after he'd left, pondering their conversation. Hope warmed her. It seemed too good to be true. She had hardly dared to let herself dream for fear of the fragile fantasy being shattered again.

When she looked back on their relationship and how it had evolved, she had a lot of regrets. *I was too self-centered and obsessed with my sosh to even notice his needs. I should have known he was up to something other than putting street rats in their place. If I had cared more, maybe I would have realized the reason he doesn't have time to worry about his sosh is because he's involved in something much more important. Maybe there's a path forward together yet.*

Urban still couldn't believe it all. Her parents were returning members of AiE, her sister and Trig were also members and had been keeping an eye on her the whole semester, and Everest was a Captain. Her Everest. Well, not her Everest anymore . . .

Was it worth trying again? Could she trust Everest with her heart? The last time he'd broken it without warning. She never wanted to experience that pain again.

But Everest was her closest friend and the person she wanted most to be with. The way he'd looked at her just a moment ago . . .

There are too many unknowns. What I do know, is I have time to figure out what I do now. We'll see if I can trust him again.

Everest's words came back to her: *"I'll be waiting."* They brought a calming wave over her. There was no rush. For now, all she needed was the next step. To find out what her parents had learned about her birth origins. To discover why she had memories of a microneedle patch.

She finally stood and made her way to the edge of the roof. Leaning against the cool cement wall, she peered at the busy life below. Hoverdrones zipped through the maze of buildings. Holographic signs lit up all around her as it grew dark.

Was the hybrid down there somewhere? Hiding? Was she the hybrid?

It's time to find answers. She went to join the others.
Before she left, Urban deactivated her retina display.
She had no thought of checking her sosh score.

ACKNOWLEDGMENTS

THERE'S A CHINESE SAYING 异想天开. TRANSLATED literally, it means *to indulge in a wild fantasy*. Which you, dear reader, have just done as you spent the last several hundred pages with me. Thank you! I'd love to hear what you thought on social media or via email!

Now, a few other *thank yous* are in order.

Thanks to my incredible beta readers! You all rock. Special thanks to Kathleen and Harrison for making me laugh so hard and for valuable feedback on several embarrassingly large plot holes. Thanks, Christian, for making the tech NOT sound like something out of the eighteen hundreds. Thanks to my BJJ instructor back in Beijing, who taught me more than I wanted to know about shrimping. Thanks, Nathan, for your tech wizardry. Daniela Liang and C.J. Milacci, thank you two for your incredible graphic design magic!

Thanks to the Enclave team! Thank you, Steve, for believing in my story. Thanks to Lisa for the fantastic edits. And to Sarah and Megan for the copyediting and proofreading. Thanks, Kirk, for your amazing cover design and allowing me to sneak in some Easter eggs. Thank you Trissina and Jamie for putting up with my endless questions and to Jamie for introducing me to Torchy's fried cookie dough. Or maybe I shouldn't thank you for that . . .

Thanks to my incredible friend and fellow author Nova McBee. You believed in me since high school, and I wouldn't be here without your faith in my stories. Your Calculated series is still one of my favorites! Thanks to my fabulous critique partners: Ellen

McGinty, Katie Wong, Becky Dean, Melissa Potker, Rebecca Alexandru, Hilary Bowen Magnuson, Jesse Chen, and Caleb Robinson. I cannot WAIT for the world to read your books!

Thanks to my mom for teaching me to read and write despite my adamant promises that I'd never need to know that particular skill set. Mom, I know you're far too kind to rub it in my face, but an "I told you so" is appropriate right about now. Thanks to the rest of my family for encouraging me and Dad, for all the times you read my stories out loud at family gatherings. As mortifying as some of those early books were, you all still believed in me, and I wouldn't be here otherwise.

Finally, thanks to my husband for allowing me to blast inspirational music throughout the house despite our vastly different tastes in tunes. Thanks for babysitting the *Xiao Baobao*, taking me to writing conferences while I was on crutches, and finding the most delicious Chinese food in Austin! I still dream about those Shanghai soup dumplings. Thanks for believing in me and supporting me every step of the way.

Most of all, thank you to the author of life.

The best stories come from you.

ABOUT THE AUTHOR

CANDACE IS A RECOVERING OVERACHIEVER who spends her time dreaming up stories typically involving tech, psychology, culture, and/or swords. She's a certified Krav Maga assistant instructor and loves writing action-packed martial art scenes. A third-culture kid, she considers Chengdu and Austin to be her homes. When she's not exploring new countries, she enjoys hiking in national parks, moving (again!), teaching her husband Mandarin, and keeping a baby human alive. She can be bribed with boba tea, fluffy puppies, and breakfast tacos.